errantry

strange

stories

errantry

strange

stories

elizabeth

hand

Small Beer Press
Easthampton, MA

Small Beer Press
150 Pleasant Street #306
Easthampton, MA 01027
www.smallbeerpress.com
www.weightlessbooks.com
info@smallbeerpress.com

Distributed to the trade by Consortium.

First Edition 1 2 3 4 5 6 7 8 9 0

Library of Congress Cataloging in Publication information on file.

ISBN: 9781618730305 (trade paper); 9781618730312 (ebook)

Text set in Centaur 12/14.4.
Printed on 50# Natures Natural 30% PCR Recycled Paper by C-M Books in Ann Arbor, MI.

Strange Stories

For Rafael Sa'adah,
Trusted guide in Bellona, and beyond
With all my love and thanks

The Maiden Flight
of McCauley's
Bellerophon

Being assigned to The Head for eight hours was the worst security shift you could pull at the museum. Even now, thirty years later, Robbie had dreams in which he wandered from the Early Flight gallery to Balloons & Airships to Cosmic Soup, where he once again found himself alone in the dark, staring into the bland gaze of the famous scientist as he intoned his endless lecture about the nature of the universe.

"Remember when we thought nothing could be worse than that?" Robbie stared wistfully into his empty glass, then signaled the waiter for another bourbon and Coke. Across the table, his old friend Emery sipped a beer.

"I liked The Head," said Emery. He cleared his throat and began to recite in the same portentous tone the famous scientist had employed. "Trillions and trillions of galaxies in which our own is but a mote of cosmic dust. It made you think."

"It made you think about killing yourself," said Robbie. "Do you want to know how many time I heard that?"

"A trillion?"

"Five thousand." The waiter handed Robbie a drink, his fourth. "Twenty-five times an hour, times eight hours a day, times five days a week, times five months."

"Five thousand, that's not so much. Especially when you think of all those trillions of galleries. I mean galaxies. Only five months? I thought you worked there longer."

"Just that summer. It only seemed like forever."

Emery knocked back his beer. "A long time ago, in a gallery far, far away," he intoned, not for the first time.

Thirty years before, the Museum of American Aviation and Aerospace had just opened. Robbie was nineteen that summer, a recent dropout from the University of Maryland, living in a group house in Mount Rainier. Employment opportunities were scarce; making $3.40 an hour as a security aide at the Smithsonian's newest museum seemed preferable to bagging groceries at Giant Food. Every morning he'd punch his time card in the guards' locker room and change into his uniform. Then he'd duck outside to smoke a joint before trudging downstairs for morning meeting and that day's assignments.

Most of the security guards were older than Robbie, with backgrounds in the military and an eye on future careers with the D.C. Police Department or FBI. Still, they tolerated him with mostly good-natured ribbing about his longish hair and bloodshot eyes. All except for Hedge, the security chief. He was an enormous man with a shaved head who sat, knitting, behind a bank of closed-circuit video monitors, observing tourists and guards with an expression of amused contempt.

"What are you making?" Robbie once asked. Hedge raised his hands to display an intricately patterned baby blanket. "Hey, that's cool. Where'd you learn to knit?"

"Prison." Hedge's eyes narrowed. "You stoned again, Opie? That's it. Gallery Seven. Relieve Jones."

Robbie's skin went cold, then hot with relief when he realized Hedge wasn't going to fire him. "Seven? Uh, yeah, sure, sure. For how long?"

"Forever," said Hedge.

"Oh, man, you got The Head." Jones clapped his hands gleefully when Robbie arrived. "Better watch your ass, kids'll throw shit at you," he said, and sauntered off.

Two projectors at opposite ends of the dark room beamed twin shafts of silvery light onto a head-shaped Styrofoam form. Robbie could never figure out if they'd filmed the famous scientist just once, or if they'd gone to the trouble to shoot him from two different angles.

However they'd done it, the sight of the disembodied Head was surprisingly effective: it looked like a hologram floating amid the hundreds of back-projected twinkly stars that covered the walls and ceiling. The creep factor was intensified by the stilted, slightly puzzled manner in which The Head blinked as it droned on, as though the famous scientist had just realized his body was gone, and was hoping no one else would notice. Once, when he was really stoned, Robbie swore that The Head deviated from its script.

"What'd it say?" asked Emery. At the time, he was working in the General Aviation Gallery, operating a flight simulator that tourists clambered into for three-minute rides.

"Something about peaches," said Robbie. "I couldn't understand, it sort of mumbled."

Every morning, Robbie stood outside the entrance to Cosmic Soup and watched as tourists streamed through the main entrance and into the Hall of Flight. Overhead, legendary aircraft hung from the ceiling. The 1903 *Wright Flyer* with its Orville mannequin; a Lilienthal glider; the Bell X-I in which Chuck Yeager broke the sound barrier. From a huge pit in the center of the Hall rose a Minuteman III ICBM, rust-colored stains still visible where a protester had tossed a bucket of pig's blood on it a few months earlier. Directly above the entrance to Robbie's gallery dangled the *Spirit of St. Louis.* The aides who worked upstairs in the planetarium amused themselves by shooting paperclips onto its wings.

Robbie winced at the memory. He gulped what was left of his bourbon and sighed. "That was a long time ago."

"Tempus fugit, baby. Thinking of which—" Emery dug into his pocket for a Blackberry. "Check this out. From Leonard."

Robbie rubbed his eyes blearily, then read.

From: l.scopes@MAAA.SI.edu
Subject: Tragic Illness
Date: April 6, 7:58:22 PM EDT
To: emeryubergeek@gmail.com

Dear Emery,

I just learned that our Maggie Blevin is very ill. I wrote
her at Christmas but never heard back. Fuad El-Hajj says
she was diagnosed with advanced breast cancer last fall.
Prognosis is not good. She is still in the Fayetteville area,
and I gather is in a hospice. I want to make a visit though
not sure how that will go over. I have something I want
to give her but need to talk to you about it.

L.

"Ahhh." Robbie sighed. "God, that's terrible."

"Yeah. I'm sorry. But I figured you'd want to know."

Robbie pinched the bridge of his nose. Four years earlier, his
wife, Anna, had died of breast cancer, leaving him adrift in a grief
so profound it was as though he'd been poisoned, as though his veins
had been pumped with the same chemicals that had failed to save her.
Anna had been an oncology nurse, a fact that at first afforded some
meager black humor, but in the end deprived them of even the faintest
of false hopes borne of denial or faith in alternative therapies.

There was no time for any of that. Zach, their son, had just
turned twelve. Between his own grief and Zach's subsequent acting-
out, Robbie got so depressed that he started pouring his first bourbon
and Coke before the boy left for school. Two years later, he got fired
from his job with the County Parks Commission.

He now worked in the shipping department at Small's, an off-
price store in a desolate shopping mall that resembled the ruins of
a regional airport. Robbie found it oddly consoling. It reminded
him of the museum. The same generic atriums and industrial carpeting; the same bleak sunlight filtered through clouded glass; the
same vacant-faced people trudging from Dollar Store to SunGlass
Hut, the way they'd wandered from the General Aviation Gallery to
Cosmic Soup.

"Poor Maggie." Robbie returned the Blackberry. "I haven't thought of her in years."

"I'm going to see Leonard."

"When? Maybe I'll go with you."

"Now." Emery shoved a twenty under his beer bottle and stood. "You're coming with me."

"What?"

"You can't drive—you're snackered. Get popped again, you lose your license."

"Popped? Who's getting popped? And I'm not snackered, I'm—" Robbie thought. "Snockered. You pronounced it wrong."

"Whatever." Emery grabbed Robbie's shoulder and pushed him to the door. "Let's go."

Emery drove an expensive hybrid that could get from Rockville to Utica, New York, on a single tank of gas. The vanity plate read MARVO and was flanked by bumper stickers with messages like GUNS DON'T KILL PEOPLE: TYPE 2 PHASERS KILL PEOPLE and FRAK OFF! as well as several slogans that Emery said were in Klingon.

Emery was the only person Robbie knew who was somewhat famous. Back in the early 1980s, he'd created a local-access cable TV show called Captain Marvo's Secret Spacetime, taped in his parents' basement and featuring Emery in an aluminum foil-costume behind the console of a cardboard spaceship. Captain Marvo watched video-taped episodes of low-budget 1950s science fiction serials with titles like PAYLOAD: MOONDUST while bantering with his co-pilot, a homemade puppet made by Leonard, named Mungbean.

The show was pretty funny if you were stoned. Captain Marvo became a cult hit, and then a real hit when a major network picked it up as a late-night offering. Emery quit his day job at the museum and rented studio time in Baltimore. He sold the rights after a few years, and was immediately replaced by a flashy actor in Lurex and a glittering robot sidekick. The show limped along for a season then died. Emery's fans claimed this was because their slacker hero had been sidelined.

But maybe it was just that people weren't as stoned as they used to be. These days the program had a surprising afterlife on the internet, where Robbie's son, Zach, watched it with his friends, and Emery did a brisk business selling memorabilia through his official Captain Marvo website.

It took them nearly an hour to get into D.C. and find a parking space near the Mall, by which time Robbie had sobered up enough to wish he'd stayed at the bar.

"Here." Emery gave him a sugarless breath mint, then plucked at the collar of Robbie's shirt, acid-green with SMALLS embroidered in purple. "Christ, Robbie, you're a freaking mess."

He reached into the backseat, retrieved a black T-shirt from his gym bag. "Here, put this on."

Robbie changed into it and stumbled out onto the sidewalk. It was mid-April but already steamy; the air shimmered above the pavement and smelled sweetly of apple blossom and coolant from innumerable air conditioners. Only as he approached the museum entrance and caught his reflection in a glass wall did Robbie see that his T-shirt was emblazoned with Emery's youthful face and foil helmet above the words O CAPTAIN MY CAPTAIN.

"You wear your own T-shirt?" he asked as he followed Emery through the door.

"Only at the gym. Nothing else was clean."

They waited at the security desk while a guard checked their IDs, called upstairs to Leonard's office, signed them in and took their pictures before finally issuing each a Visitor's Pass.

"You'll have to wait for Leonard to escort you upstairs," the guard said.

"Not like the old days, huh, Robbie?" Emery draped an arm around Robbie and steered him into the Hall of Flight. "Not a lot of retinal scanning on your watch."

The museum hadn't changed much. The same aircraft and space capsules gleamed overhead. Tourists clustered around the lucite pyramid that held slivers of moon rock. Sunburned guys sporting military haircuts and tattoos peered at a mockup of a F-15 flight deck. Everything had that old museum smell: soiled carpeting, machine oil, the wet-laundry odor wafting from steam tables in the public cafeteria.

But The Head was long gone. Robbie wondered if anyone even remembered the famous scientist, dead for many years. The General Aviation Gallery, where Emery and Leonard had operated the flight simulators and first met Maggie Blevin, was now devoted to Personal Flight, with models of jetpacks worn by alarmingly lifelike mannequins.

"Leonard designed those." Emery paused to stare at a child-sized figure who seemed to float above a solar-powered skateboard. "He could have gone to Hollywood."

"It's not too late."

Robbie and Emery turned to see their old colleague behind them.

"Leonard," said Emery.

The two men embraced. Leonard stepped back and tilted his head. "Robbie. I wasn't expecting you."

"Surprise," said Robbie. They shook hands awkwardly. "Good to see you, man."

Leonard forced a smile. "And you."

They headed toward the staff elevator. Back in the day, Leonard's hair had been long and luxuriantly blond. It fell unbound down the back of the dogshit-yellow uniform jacket, designed to evoke an airline pilot's, that he and Emery and the other General Aviation aides wore as they gave their spiel to tourists eager to yank on the controls of their Link Trainers. With his patrician good looks and stern gray eyes, Leonard was the only aide who actually resembled a real pilot.

Now he looked like a cross between Obi-Wan Kenobi and Willie Nelson. His hair was white, and hung in two braids that reached almost to his waist. Instead of the crappy polyester uniform, he wore a white linen tunic, a necklace of unpolished turquoise and coral, loose black trousers tucked into scuffed cowboy boots, and a skull earring the size of Robbie's thumb. On his collar gleamed the cheap knock-off pilot's wings that had once adorned his museum uniform jacket. Leonard had always taken his duties very seriously, especially after

Margaret Blevin arrived as the museum's first Curator of Proto-Flight. Robbie's refusal to do the same, even long after he'd left the museum himself, had resulted in considerable friction between them over the intervening years.

Robbie cleared his throat. "So, uh. What are you working on these days?" He wished he wasn't wearing Emery's idiotic T-shirt.

"I'll show you," said Leonard.

Upstairs, they headed for the old photo lab, now an imaging center filled with banks of computers, digital cameras, scanners.

"We still process film there," Leonard said as they walked down a corridor hung with production photos from *The Day the Earth Stood Still* and *Frau im Mond*. "Negatives, old motion picture stock—people still send us things."

"Any of it interesting?" asked Emery.

Leonard shrugged. "Sometimes. You never know what you might find. That's part of Maggie's legacy—we're always open to the possibility of discovering something new."

Robbie shut his eyes. Leonard's voice made his teeth ache. "Remember how she used to keep a bottle of Scotch in that side drawer, underneath her purse?" he said.

Leonard frowned, but Emery laughed. "Yeah! And it was good stuff, too."

"Maggie had a great deal of class," said Leonard in a somber tone.

You pompous asshole, thought Robbie.

Leonard punched a code into a door and opened it. "You might remember when this was a storage cupboard."

They stepped inside. Robbie did remember this place—he'd once had sex here with a General Aviation aide whose name he'd long forgotten. It had been a good-sized supply room then, with an odd, sweetish scent from the rolls of film stacked along the shelves.

Now it was a very crowded office. The shelves were crammed with books and curatorial reports dating back to 1981, and archival boxes holding God knows what—Leonard's original government job application, maybe. A coat had been tossed onto the floor in one corner. There was a large metal desk covered with bottles of nail polish, an ancient swivel chair that Robbie vaguely remembered having been deployed during his lunch-hour tryst.

Mostly, though, the room held Leonard's stuff: tiny cardboard dioramas, mockups of space capsules and dirigibles. It smelled overpoweringly of nail polish. It was also extremely cold.

"Man, you must freeze your ass off." Robbie rubbed his arms.

Emery picked up one of the little bottles. "You getting a manicurist's license?"

Leonard gestured at the desk. "I'm painting with nail polish now. You get some very unusual effects."

"I bet," said Robbie. "You're, like huffing nail polish." He peered at the shelves, impressed despite himself. "Jeez, Leonard. You made all these?"

"Damn right I did."

When Robbie first met Leonard, they were both lowly GS-1s. In those days, Leonard collected paper clips and rode an old Schwinn bicycle to work. He entertained tourists by making balloon animals. In his spare time, he created Mungbean, Captain Marvo's robot friend, out of a busted lamp and some spark plugs.

He also made strange ink drawings, hundreds of them. Montgolfier balloons with sinister faces; B-52s carrying payloads of soap bubbles; carictatures of the museum director and senior curators as greyhounds sniffing each others' nether quarters.

It was this last, drawn on a scrap of legal paper, which Margaret Blevin picked up on her first tour of the General Aviation Gallery. The sketch had fallen out of Leonard's jacket: he watched in horror as the museum's deputy director stooped to retrieve the crumpled page.

"Allow me," said the woman at the director's side. She was slight, forty-ish, with frizzy red hair and enormous hoop earrings, wearing an indian-print tunic over tight, sky-blue trousers and leather clogs. She snatched up the drawing, stuffed it in her pocket and continued her tour of the gallery. After the deputy director left, the woman walked to where Leonard stood beside his flight simulator, sweating in his polyester jacket as he supervised an overweight kid in a Chewbacca T-shirt. When the kid climbed down, the woman held up the crumpled sheet.

"Who did this?"

The other two aides—one was Emery—shook their heads.

"I did," said Leonard.

The woman crooked her finger. "Come with me."

"Am I fired?" asked Leonard as he followed her out of the gallery.

"Nope. I'm Maggie Blevin. We're shutting down those Link Trainers and making this into a new gallery. I'm in charge. I need someone to start cataloging stuff for me and maybe do some preliminary sketches. You want the job?"

"Yes," stammered Leonard. "I mean, sure."

"Great." She balled up the sketch and tossed it into a wastebasket. "Your talents were being wasted. That looks just like the director's butt."

"If he was a dog," said Leonard.

"He's a son of a bitch, and that's close enough," said Maggie. "Let's go see Personnel."

Leonard's current job description read Museum Effects Specialist, Grade 9, Step 10. For the last two decades, he'd created figurines and models for the museum's exhibits. Not fighter planes or commercial aircraft—there was an entire division of modelers who handled that.

Leonard's work was more rarefied, as evidenced by the dozens of flying machines perched wherever there was space in the tiny room. Rocket ships, bat-winged aerodromes, biplanes and triplanes and saucers, many of them striped and polka-dotted and glazed with, yes, nail polish in circus colors, so that they appeared to be made of ribbon candy.

His specialty was aircraft that had never actually flown; in many instances, aircraft that had never been intended to fly. Crypto-aviation, as some disgruntled curator dubbed it. He worked from plans and photographs, drawings and uncategorizable materials he'd found in the archives Maggie Blevin had been hired to organize. These were housed in a set of oak filing cabinets dating to the 1920s. Officially, the archive was known as the Pre-Langley Collection. But everyone in the museum, including Maggie Blevin, called it the Nut Files.

After Leonard's fateful promotion, Robbie and Emery would sometimes punch out for the day, go upstairs and stroll to his corner of the library. You could do that then—wander around workrooms and storage areas, the library and archives, without having to check in or get a special pass or security clearance. Robbie just went along for the ride, but Emery was fascinated by the things Leonard found in the Nut Files. Grainy black-and-white photos of purported UFOs; typescripts of encounters with deceased Russian cosmonauts in the Nevada desert; an account of a Raelian wedding ceremony attended by a glowing crimson orb. There was also a large carton donated by the widow of a legendary rocket scientist, which turned out to be filled with 1950s foot-fetish pornography, and 16-millimeter film footage of several Pioneers of Flight doing something unseemly with a spotted pig.

"Whatever happened to that pig movie?" asked Robbie as he admired a biplane with violet-striped ailerons.

"It's been deaccessioned," said Leonard.

He cleared the swivel chair and motioned for Emery to sit, then perched on the edge of his desk. Robbie looked in vain for another chair, finally settled on the floor beside a wastebasket filled with empty nail-polish bottles.

"So I have a plan," announced Leonard. He stared fixedly at Emery, as though they were alone in the room. "To help Maggie. Do you remember the *Bellerophon*?"

Emery frowned. "Vaguely. That old film loop of a plane crash?"

"*Presumed* crash. They never found any wreckage, everyone just assumes it crashed. But yes, that was the *Bellerophon*—it was the clip that played in our gallery. Maggie's gallery."

"Right—the movie that burned up!" broke in Robbie. "Yeah, I remember, the film got caught in a sprocket or something. Smoke detectors went off and they evacuated the whole museum. They got all on Maggie's case about it, they thought she installed it wrong."

"She didn't," Leonard said angrily. "One of the tech guys screwed up the installation—he told me a few years ago. He didn't vent it properly, the projector bulb overheated and the film caught on fire. He said he always felt bad she got canned."

"But they didn't fire her for that." Robbie gave Leonard a sideways look. "It was the UFO—"

Emery cut him off. "They were gunning for her," he said. "C'mon, Rob, everyone knew—all those old military guys running this place, they couldn't stand a woman getting in their way. Not if she wasn't Air Force or some shit. Took 'em a few years, that's all. Fucking assholes. I even got a letter-writing campaign going on the show. Didn't help."

"Nothing would have helped." Leonard sighed. "She was a visionary. She *is* a visionary," he added hastily. "Which is why I want to do this—"

He hopped from the desk, rooted around in a corner and pulled out a large cardboard box.

"Move," he ordered.

Robbie scrambled to his feet. Leonard began to remove things from the carton and set them carefully on his desk. Emery got up to make more room, angling himself beside Robbie. They watched as Leonard arranged piles of paper, curling 8x10s, faded blueprints and an old 35mm film viewer, along with several large manila envelopes closed with red string. Finally he knelt beside the box and very gingerly reached inside.

"I think the Lindbergh baby's in there," whispered Emery.

Leonard stood, cradling something in his hands, turned and placed it in the middle of the desk.

"Holy shit." Emery whistled. "Leonard, you've outdone yourself."

Robbie crouched so he could view it at eye level: a model of some sort of flying machine, though it seemed impossible that anyone, even Leonard or Maggie Blevin, could ever have dreamed it might fly. It had a zeppelin-shaped body, with a sharp nose like that of a Lockheed

Starfighter, slightly uptilted. Suspended beneath this was a basket filled with tiny gears and chains, and beneath that was a contraption with three wheels, like a velocipede, only the wheels were fitted with dozens of stiff flaps, each no bigger than a fingernail, and even tinier propellers.

And everywhere, there were wings, sprouting from every inch of the craft's body in an explosion of canvas and balsa and paper and gauze. Bird-shaped wings, bat-shaped wings; square wings like those of a box-kite, elevators and hollow cones of wire; long tubes that, when Robbie peered inside them, were filled with baffles and flaps. Ailerons and struts ran between them to form a dizzying grid, held together with fine gold thread and monofilament and what looked like human hair. Every bit of it was painted in brilliant shades of violet and emerald, scarlet and fuchsia and gold, and here and there shining objects were set into the glossy surface: minute shards of mirror or colored glass; a beetle carapace; flecks of mica.

Above it all, springing from the fuselage like the cap of an immense toadstool, was a feathery parasol made of curved bamboo and multicolored silk.

It was like gazing at the *Wright Flyer* through a kaleidoscope.

"That's incredible!" Robbie exclaimed. "How'd you do that?"

"Now we just have to see if it flies," said Leonard.

Robbie straightened. "How the hell can that thing fly?"

"The original flew." Leonard leaned against the wall. "My theory is, if we can replicate the same conditions—the *exact same* conditions—it will work."

"But." Robbie glanced at Emery. "The original didn't fly. It crashed. I mean, presumably."

Emery nodded. "Plus there was a guy in it. McCartney—"

"McCauley," said Leonard.

"Right, McCauley. And you know, Leonard, no one's gonna fit in that, right?" Emery shot him an alarmed look. "You're not thinking of making a full-scale model, are you? Because that would be completely insane."

"No." Leonard fingered the skull plug in his earlobe. "I'm going to make another film—I'm going to replicate the original, and I'm going to do it so perfectly that Maggie won't even realize it's *not* the original. I've got it all worked out." He looked at Emery. "I can shoot it on digital, if you'll lend me a camera. That way I can edit it on my laptop. And then I'm going to bring it down to Fayetteville so she can see it."

Robbie and Emery glanced at each other.

"Well, it's not completely insane," said Robbie.

"But Maggie knows the original was destroyed," said Emery. "I mean, I was there, I remember—she saw it. We all saw it. She has cancer, right? Not Alzheimer's or dementia or, I dunno, amnesia."

"Why don't you just Photoshop something?" asked Robbie. "You could tell her it was an homage. That way—"

Leonard's glare grew icy. "It is not an homage. I am going to Cowana Island, just like McCauley did, and I am going to recreate the maiden flight of the *Bellerophon*. I am going to film it, I am going to edit it. And when it's completed, I'm going to tell Maggie that I found a dupe in the archives. Her heart broke when that footage burned up. I'm going to give it back to her."

Robbie stared at his shoe, so Leonard wouldn't see his expression. After a moment he said, "When Anna was sick, I wanted to do that. Go back to this place by Mount Washington where we stayed before Zach was born. We had all these great photos of us canoeing there, it was so beautiful. But it was winter, and I said we should wait and go in the summer."

"I'm not waiting." Leonard sifted through the papers on his desk. "I have these—"

He opened a manila envelope and withdrew several glassine sleeves. He examined one, then handed it to Emery.

"This is what survived of the original footage, which in fact was *not* the original footage—the original was shot in 1901, on cellulose nitrate film. That's what Maggie and I found when we first started going through the Nut Files. Only of course nitrate stock is like a ticking time bomb. So the Photo Lab duped it onto safety film, which is what you're looking at."

Emery held the film to the light. Robbie stood beside him, squinting. Five frames, in shades of amber and tortoiseshell, with blurred images that might have been bushes or clouds or smoke damage, for all Robbie could see.

Emery asked, "How many frames do you have?"

"Total? Seventy-two."

Emery shook his head. "Not much, is it? What was it, fifteen seconds?"

"Seventeen seconds."

"Times twenty-four frames per second—so, out of about four hundred frames, that's all that's left."

"No. There was actually less than that, because it was silent film, which runs at more like eighteen frames per second, and they corrected the speed. So, about three hundred frames, which means we have about a quarter of the original stock." Leonard hesitated. He glanced up. "Lock that door, would you, Robbie?"

Robbie did, looked back to see Leonard crouched in the corner, moving aside his coat to reveal a metal strongbox. He prised the lid from the top.

The box was filled with water—Robbie *hoped* it was water. "Is that an aquarium?"

Leonard ignored him, tugged up his sleeves then dipped both hands below the surface. Very, very carefully he removed another metal box. He set it on the floor, grabbed his coat and meticulously dried the lid, then turned to Robbie.

"You know, maybe you should unlock the door. In case we need to get out fast."

"Jesus Christ, Leonard, what is it?" exclaimed Emery. "Snakes?"

"Nope." Leonard plucked something from the box, and Emery flinched as a serpentine ribbon unfurled in the air. "It's what's left of the original footage—the 1901 film."

"That's nitrate?" Emery stared at him, incredulous. "You *are* insane! How the hell'd you get it?"

"I clipped it before they destroyed the stock. I think it's okay—I take it out every day, so the gases don't build up. And it doesn't seem to interact with the nail-polish fumes. It's the part where you can actually see McCauley, where you get the best view of the plane. See?"

He dangled it in front of Emery, who backed toward the door. "Put it away, put it away!"

"Can I see?" asked Robbie.

Leonard gave him a measuring look, then nodded. "Hold it by this edge—"

It took a few seconds for Robbie's eyes to focus properly. "You're right," he said. "You can see him—you can see someone, anyway. And you can definitely tell it's an airplane."

He handed it back to Leonard, who fastidiously replaced it, first in its canister and then the water-filled safe.

"They could really pop you for that." Emery whistled in disbelief. "If that stuff blew? This whole place could go up in flames."

"You say that like it's a bad thing." Leonard draped his coat over the strongbox, then started to laugh. "Anyway, I'm done with it. I went into the Photo Lab one night and duped it myself. So I've got that copy at home. And this one—"

He inclined his head at the corner. "I'm going to take the nitrate home and give it a Viking funeral in the backyard. You can come if you want."

"Tonight?" asked Robbie.

"No. I've got to work late tonight, catch up on some stuff before I leave town."

Emery leaned against the door. "Where you going?"

"South Carolina. I told you. I'm going to Cowana Island, and..." Robbie caught a whiff of acetone as Leonard picked up the *Bellerophon*. "I am going to make this thing fly."

"He really is nuts. I mean, when was the last time he even saw Maggie?" Robbie asked as Emery drove him back to the mall. "I still don't know what really happened, except for the UFO stuff."

"She found out he was screwing around with someone else. It was a bad scene. She tried to get him fired; he went to Boynton and told him Maggie was diverting all this time and money to studying UFOs. Which unfortunately was true. They did an audit, she had some kind of nervous breakdown even before they could fire her."

"What a prick."

Emery sighed. "It was horrible. Leonard doesn't talk about it. I don't think he ever got over it. Over her."

"Yeah, but…" Robbie shook his head. "She must be, what, twenty years older than us? They never would have stayed together. If he feels so bad, he should just go see her. This other stuff is insane."

"I think maybe those fumes did something to him. Nitrocellulose, it's in nail polish, too. It might have done something to his brain."

"Is that possible?"

"It's a theory," said Emery broodingly.

Robbie's house was in a scruffy subdivision on the outskirts of Rockville. The place was small, a bungalow with masonite siding, cracked cinderblock foundation and the remains of a garden that Anna had planted. A green GMC pickup with expired registration was parked in the drive. Robbie peered into the cab. It was filled with empty Bud Light bottles.

Inside, Zach was hunched at a desk beside his friend Tyler, owner of the pickup. The two of them stared intently into a computer screen.

"What's up?" said Zach without looking away.

"Not much," said Robbie. "Eye contact."

Zach glanced up. He was slight, with Anna's thick blond curls reduced to a buzzcut that Robbie hated. Tyler was tall and gangly, with long black hair and wire-rimmed sunglasses. Both favored tie-dyed T-shirts and madras shorts that made them look as though they were perpetually on vacation.

Robbie went into the kitchen and got a beer. "You guys eat?"

"We got something on the way home."

Robbie drank his beer and watched them. The house had a smell that Emery once described as Failed Bachelor. Unwashed clothes, spilled beer, marijuana smoke. Robbie hadn't smoked in years, but Zach and Tyler had taken up the slack. Robbie used to yell at them but eventually gave up. If his own depressing example wasn't enough to straighten them out, what was?

After a minute, Zach looked up again. "Nice shirt, Dad."

"Thanks, son." Robbie sank into a beanbag chair. "Me and Emery dropped by the museum and saw Leonard."

"Leonard!" Tyler burst out laughing. "Leonard is so fucking sweet! He's, like, the craziest guy ever."

"All Dad's friends are crazy," said Zach.

"Yeah, but Emery, he's cool. Whereas that guy Leonard is just wack."

Robbie nodded somberly and finished his beer. "Leonard is indeed wack. He's making a movie."

"A real movie?" asked Zach.

"More like a home movie. Or, I dunno—he wants to reproduce another movie, one that was already made, do it all the same again. Shot by shot."

Tyler nodded. "Like *The Ring* and *Ringu*. What's the movie?"

"Seventeen seconds of a 1901 plane crash. The original footage was destroyed, so he's going to restage the whole thing."

"A plane crash?" Zach glanced at Tyler. "Can we watch?"

"Not a real crash—he's doing it with a model. I mean, I think he is."

"Did they even have planes then?" said Tyler.

"He should put it on YouTube," said Zach, and turned back to the computer.

"Okay, get out of there." Robbie rubbed his head wearily. "I need to go online."

The boys argued but gave up quickly. Tyler left. Zach grabbed his cell phone and slouched upstairs to his room. Robbie got another beer, sat at the computer and logged out of whatever they'd been playing, then typed in MCCAULEY BELLEROPHON.

Only a dozen results popped up. He scanned them, then clicked the Wikipedia entry for Ernesto McCauley.

> McCauley, Ernesto (18??–1901) American inventor whose eccentric aircraft, the *Bellerophon*, allegedly flew for seventeen seconds before it crashed during a 1901 test flight on Cowana Island, South Carolina, killing McCauley. In the 1980s, claims that this flight was successful and predated that of the Wright Brothers by two years were made by a Smithsonian expert, based upon archival film footage. The claims have since been disproved and the film record unfortunately lost in a fire. Curiously, no other record of either McCauley or his aircraft has ever been found.

Robbie took a long pull at his beer, then typed in MARGARET BLEVIN.

> Blevin, Margaret (1938–) Influential cultural historian whose groundbreaking work on early flight earned her the nickname "The Magnificent Blevin." During her tenure at the Smithsonian's Museum of American Aeronautics and Aerospace, Blevin redesigned the General Aviation Gallery to feature lesser-known pioneers of flight, including Charles Dellschau and Ernesto McCauley, as well as...

"'The Magnificent Blevin?'" Robbie snorted. He grabbed another beer and continued reading.

> But Blevin's most lasting impact upon the history of aviation was her 1986 bestseller *Wings for Humanity!*, in which she presents a dramatic and visionary account of the mystical aspects of flight, from Icarus to the Wright Brothers and beyond. Its central premise is that millennia ago a

benevolent race seeded the Earth, leaving isolated locations with the ability to engender huiman-powered flight. "We dream of flight because flight is our birthright," wrote Blevin, and since its publication *Wings for Humanity!* has never gone out of print.

"Leonard wrote this frigging thing!"

"What?" Zach came downstairs, yawning.

"This Wikipedia entry!" Robbie jabbed at the screen. "That book was never a bestseller—she snuck it into the museum gift shop and no one bought it. The only reason it's still in print is that she published it herself."

Zach read the entry over his father's shoulder. "It sounds cool."

Robbie shook his head adamantly. "She was completely nuts. Obsessed with all this New Age crap, aliens and crop circles. She thought that planes could only fly from certain places, and that's why all the early flights crashed. Not because there was something wrong with the aircraft design, but because they were taking off from the wrong spot."

"Then how come there's airports everywhere?"

"She never worked out that part."

"'We must embrace our galactic heritage, the spiritual dimension of human flight, lest we forever chain ourselves to earth,'" Zach read from the screen. "Was she in that plane crash?"

"No, she's still alive. That was just something she had a wild hair about. She thought the guy who invented that plane flew it a few years before the Wright Brothers made their flight, but she could never prove it."

"But it says there was a movie," said Zach. "So someone saw it happen."

"This is Wikipedia." Robbie stared at the screen in disgust. "You can say any fucking thing you want and people will believe it. Leonard wrote that entry, guarantee you. Probably she faked that whole film loop. That's what Leonard's planning to do now—replicate the footage then pass it off to Maggie as the real thing."

Zach collapsed into the beanbag chair. "Why?"

"Because he's crazy, too. He and Maggie had a thing together."

Zach grimaced. "Ugh."

"What, you think we were born old? We were your age, practically. And Maggie was about twenty years older—"

"A cougar!" Zach burst out laughing. "Why didn't she go for you?"

"Ha ha ha." Robbie pushed his empty beer bottle against the wall. "Women liked Leonard. Go figure. Even your Mom went out with him for a while. Before she and I got involved, I mean."

Zach's glassy eyes threatened to roll back in his head. "Stop."

"We thought it was pretty strange," admitted Robbie. "But Maggie was good-looking for an old hippie." He glanced at the Wikipedia entry and did the math. "I guess she's in her seventies now. Leonard's in touch with her. She has cancer. Breast cancer."

"I heard you," said Zach. He rolled out of the beanbag chair, flipped open his phone and began texting. "I'm going to bed."

Robbie sat and stared at the computer screen. After a while he shut it down. He shuffled into the kitchen and opened the cabinet where he kept a quart of Jim Beam, hidden behind bottles of vinegar and vegetable oil. He rinsed out the glass he'd used the night before, poured a jolt and downed it; then carried the bourbon with him to bed.

The next day after work, he was on his second drink at the bar when Emery showed up.

"Hey." Robbie gestured at the stool beside him. "Have a set."

"You okay to drive?"

"Sure." Robbie scowled. "What, you keeping an eye on me?"

"No. But I want you to see something. At my house. Leonard's coming over, we're going to meet there at six-thirty. I tried calling you but your phone's off."

"Oh. Right. Sorry." Robbie signaled the bartender for his tab. "Yeah, sure. What, is he gonna give us manicures?"

"Nope. I have an idea. I'll tell you when I get there, I'm going to Royal Delhi first to get some takeout. See you—"

Emery lived in a big townhouse condo that smelled of Moderately Successful Bachelor. The walls held framed photos of Captain Marvo and Mungbean alongside a lifesized painting of Leslie Nielsen as Commander J.J. Adams.

But there was also a climate-controlled basement filled with Captain Marvo merchandise and packing material, with another large room stacked with electronics equipment—sound system, video monitors and decks, shelves and files devoted to old Captain Marvo episodes and dupes of the Grade Z movies featured on the show.

This was where Robbie found Leonard, bent over a refurbished Steenbeck editing table.

"Robbie." Leonard waved, then returned to threading film onto a spindle. "Emery back with dinner?"

"Uh-uh." Robbie pulled a chair alongside him. "What are you doing?"

"Loading up that nitrate I showed you yesterday."

"It's not going to explode, is it?"

"No, Robbie, it's not going to explode." Leonard's mouth tightened. "Did Emery talk to you yet?"

"He just said something about a plan. So what's up?"

"I'll let him tell you."

Robbie flushed angrily, but before he could retort there was a knock behind them.

"Chow time, campers." Emery held up two steaming paper bags. "Can you leave that for a few minutes, Leonard?"

They ate on the couch in the next room. Emery talked about a pitch he'd made to revive Captain Marvo in cell phone format. "It'd be freaking perfect, if I could figure out a way to make any money from it."

Leonard said nothing. Robbie noted the cuffs of his white tunic were stained with flecks of orange pigment, as were his fingernails. He looked tired, his face lined and his eyes sunken.

"You getting enough sleep?" Emery asked.

Leonard smiled wanly. "Enough."

Finally the food was gone, and the beer. Emery clapped his hands on his knees, pushed aside the empty plates then leaned forward.

"Okay. So here's the plan. I rented a house on Cowana for a week, starting this Saturday. I mapped it online and it's about ten hours. If we leave right after you guys get off work on Friday and drive all night, we'll get there early Saturday morning. Leonard, you said you've got everything pretty much assembled, so all you need to do is pack it up. I've got everything else here. Be a tight fit in the Prius, though, so we'll have to take two cars. We'll bring everything we need with us, we'll have a week to shoot and edit or whatever, then on the way back we swing through Fayetteville and show the finished product to Maggie. What do you think?"

"That's not a lot of time," said Leonard. "But we could do it."

Emery turned to Robbie. "Is you car road-worthy? It's about twelve hundred miles round trip."

Robbie stared at him. "What the hell are you talking about?"

"The *Bellerophon*. Leonard's got storyboards and all kinds of drawings and still frames, enough to work from. The realtor's in Charleston, she said there wouldn't be many people this early in the season. Plus there was a hurricane a couple years ago, I gather the island got hammered and no one's had money to rebuild. So we'll have it all to ourselves, pretty much."

"Are you high?" Robbie laughed. "I can't just take off. I have a job."

"You get vacation time, right? You can take a week. It'll be great, man. The realtor says it's already in the eighties down there. Warm water, a beach—what more you want?"

"Uh, maybe a beach with people besides you and Leonard?" Robbie searched in vain for another beer. "I couldn't go anyway—next week's Zach's spring break."

"Yeah?" Emery shook his head. "So, you're going to be at the store all day, and he'll be home getting stoned. Bring him. We'll put him to work."

Leonard frowned, but Robbie looked thoughtful. "Yeah, you're right. I hadn't thought of that. I can't really leave him alone. I guess I'll think about it."

"Don't think, just do it. It's Wednesday, tell 'em you're taking off next week. They gonna fire you?"

"Maybe."

"I'm not babysitting some—" Leonard started.

Emery cut him off. "You got that nitrate loaded? Let's see it."

They filed into the workroom. Leonard sat at the Steenbeck. The others watched as he adjusted the film on its sprockets. He turned to Robbie, then indicated the black projection box in the center of the deck.

"Emery knows all this, so I'm just telling you. That's a quartz halogen lamp. I haven't turned it on yet, because if the frame was just sitting there it might incinerate the film, and us. But there's only about four seconds of footage, so we're going to take our chances and watch it, once. Maybe you remember it from the gallery?"

Robbie nodded. "Yeah, I saw it a bunch of times. Not as much as The Head, but enough."

"Good. Hit that light, would you, Emery? Everyone ready? Blink and you'll miss it."

Robbie craned his neck, staring at a blank white screen. There was a whir, the stutter of film running through a projector.

At the bottom of the frame the horizon lurched, bright flickers that might be an expanse of water. Then a blurred image, faded sepia and amber, etched with blotches and something resembling a beetle leg: the absurd contraption Robbie recognized as the original *Bellerophon*. Only it was moving—it was flying—its countless gears and propellers and wings spinning and whirring and flapping all at once, so it seemed the entire thing would vibrate into a thousand pieces. Beneath the fuselage, a dark figure perched precariously atop the velocipede, legs like black scissors slicing at the air. From the left corner of the frame leaped a flare of light, like a shooting star or burning firecracker tossed at the pedaling figure. The pilot listed to one side, and—

Nothing. The film ended as abruptly as it had begun. Leonard quickly reached to turn off the lamp, and immediately removed the film from the take-up drive.

Robbie felt his neck prickle—he'd forgotten how weird, uncanny even, the footage was.

"Jesus, that's some bizarre shit," said Emery.

"It doesn't even look real." Robbie watched as Leonard coiled the film and slid it in a canister. "I mean, the guy, he looks fake."

Emery nodded. "Yeah, I know. It looks like one of those old silents, *The Lost World* or something. But it's not. I used to watch it back when it ran a hundred times a day in our gallery, the way you used to watch The Head. And it's definitely real. At least the pilot, McCauley—that's a real guy. I got a big magnifier once and just stood there and watched it over and over again. He was breathing, I could see it. And the plane, it's real too, far as I could tell. The thing I can't figure is, who the hell shot that footage? And what was the angle?"

Robbie stared at the empty screen, then shut his eyes. He tried to recall the rest of the film from when it played in the General Aviation Gallery: the swift, jerky trajectory of that eerie little vehicle with its bizarre pilot, a man in a black suit and bowler hat; then the flash from the corner of the screen, and the man toppling from his perch into the white and empty air. The last thing you saw was a tiny hand at the bottom of the frame, then some blank leader, followed by the words THE MAIDEN FLIGHT OF MCCAULEY'S "BELLEROPHON" (1901). And the whole thing began again.

"It was like someone was in the air next to him," said Robbie. "Unless he only got six feet off the ground. I always assumed it was faked."

"It wasn't faked," said Leonard. "The cameraman was on the beach filming. It was a windy day, they were hoping that would help give the plane some lift but there must have been a sudden gust. When the *Bellerophon* went into the ocean, the cameraman dove in to save McCauley. They both drowned. They never found the bodies, or the wreckage. Only the camera with the film."

"Who found it?" asked Robbie.

"We don't know." Leonard sighed, his shoulders slumping. "We don't know anything. Not the name of the cameraman, nothing. When Maggie and I ran the original footage, the leader said 'Maiden Flight of McCauley's Bellerophon.' The can had the date and 'Cowana Island' written on it. So Maggie and I went down there to research it. A weird place. Hardly any people, and this was in the summer. There's a tiny historical society on the island, but we couldn't find anything about McCauley or the aircraft. No newspaper accounts, no gravestones. The only thing we did find was in a diary kept by the guy who delivered the mail back then. On May 13, 1901, he wrote that it was a very windy day and two men had drowned while attempting to launch a flying machine on the beach. Someone must have found the camera afterward. Somebody processed the film, and somehow it found its way to the museum."

Robbie followed Leonard into the next room. "What was that weird flash of light?"

"I don't know." Leonard stared out a glass door into the parking lot. "But it's not overexposure or lens flare or anything like that. It's something the cameraman actually filmed. Water, maybe—if it was a windy day, a big wave might have come up onto the beach or something."

"I always thought it was fire. Like a rocket or some kind of flare."

Leonard nodded. "That's what Maggie thought, too. The mailman—mostly all he wrote about was the weather. Which if you were relying on a horse-drawn cart makes sense. About two weeks before he mentioned the flying machine, he described something that sounds like a major meteor shower."

"And Maggie thought it was hit by a meteor?"

"No." Leonard sighed. "She thought it was something else. The weird thing is, a few years ago I checked online, and it turns out there was an unusual amount of meteor activity in 1901."

Robbie raised an eyebrow. "Meaning?"

Leonard said nothing. Finally he opened the door and walked outside. The others trailed after him.

They reached the edge of the parking lot, where cracked tarmac gave way to stony ground. Leonard glanced back, then stooped. He brushed away a few stray leaves and tufts of dead grass, set the film canister down and unscrewed the metal lid. He picked up one end of the coil of film, gently tugging until it trailed a few inches across the ground. Then he withdrew a lighter, flicked it and held the flame to the tail of film.

"What the—" began Robbie.

There was a dull *whoosh*, like the sound of a gas burner igniting. A plume of crimson and gold leaped from the canister, writhing in the air within a ball of black smoke. Leonard staggered to his feet, covering his head as he backed away.

"Leonard!" Emery grabbed him roughly, then turned and raced to the house.

Before Robbie could move, a strong chemical stink surrounded him. The flames shrank to a shining thread that lashed at the smoke then faded into flecks of ash. Robbie ducked his head, coughing. He grasped Leonard's arm and tried to drag him away, glanced up to see Emery running toward them with a fire extinguisher.

"Sorry," gasped Leonard. He made a slashing motion through the smoke, which dispersed. The flames were gone. Leonard's face was black with ash. Robbie touched his own cheek gingerly, looked at his fingers and saw they were coated with something dark and oily.

Emery halted, panting, and stared at the twisted remains of the film can. On the ground beside it, a glowing thread wormed toward a dead leaf, then expired in a gray wisp. Emery raised the fire extinguisher threateningly, set it down and stomped on the canister.

"Good thing you didn't do that in the museum," said Robbie. He let go of Leonard's arm.

"Don't think it didn't cross my mind," said Leonard, and walked back inside.

∞∞

They left Friday evening. Robbie got the week off, after giving his dubious boss a long story about a dying relative down south. Zach shouted and broke a lamp when informed he would be accompanying his father on a trip during his spring vacation.

"With Emery and *Leonard?* Are you fucking *insane?*"

Robbie was too exhausted to fight: he quickly offered to let Tyler come with them. Tyler, surprisingly, agreed, and even showed up on Friday afternoon to help load the car. Robbie made a pointed effort not to inspect the various backpacks and duffel bags the boys threw into the trunk of the battered Taurus. Alcohol, drugs, firearms: he no longer cared.

Instead he focused on the online weather report for Cowana Island. Eighty degrees and sunshine, photographs of blue water, white sand, a skein of pelicans skimming above the waves. Ten hours, that wasn't so bad. In another weak moment, he told Zach he could drive part of the way, so Robbie could sleep.

"What about me?" asked Tyler. "Can I drive?"

"Only if I never wake up," said Robbie.

Around six Emery pulled into the driveway, honking. The boys were already slumped in Robbie's Taurus, Zach in front with earbuds dangling around his face and a knit cap pulled down over his eyes, Tyler in the back, staring blankly as though they were already on I-95.

"You ready?" Emery rolled down his window. He wore a blue flannel shirt and a gimme cap that read STARFLEET ACADEMY. In the hybrid's passenger seat, Leonard perused a road atlas. He looked up and shot Robbie a smile.

"Hey, a road trip."

"Yeah." Robbie smiled back and patted the hybrid's roof. "See you."

It took almost two hours just to get beyond the gravitational pull of the Washington Beltway. Farms and forest had long ago disappeared beneath an endless grid of malls and housing developments, many of them vacant. Every time Robbie turned up the radio for a song he liked, the boys complained that they could hear it through their earphones.

Only as the sky darkened and Virginia gave way to North Carolina did the world take on a faint fairy glow, distant green and yellow lights reflecting the first stars and a shining cusp of moon. Sprawl gave way to pine forest. The boys had been asleep for hours, in that amazing, self-willed hibernation they summoned whenever in the presence of adults for more than fifteen minutes. Robbie put the radio on, low, searched until he caught the echo of a melody he knew, and then another. He thought of driving with Anna beside him, a restive Zach behind them in his car seat; the aimless trips they'd make until the toddler fell asleep and they could talk or, once, park in a vacant lot and make out.

How long had it been since he'd remembered that? Years, maybe. He fought against thinking of Anna; sometimes it felt as though he fought Anna herself, her hands pummeling him as he poured another drink or staggered up to bed.

Now, though, the darkness soothed him the way those long-ago drives had lulled Zach to sleep. He felt an ache lift from his breast, as though a splinter had been dislodged; blinked and in the rearview mirror glimpsed Anna's face, slightly turned from him as she gazed out at the passing sky.

He started, realized he'd begun to nod off. On the dashboard his fuel indicator glowed red. He called Emery, and at the next exit pulled off 95, the Prius behind him.

After a few minutes they found a gas station set back from the road in a pine grove, with an old-fashioned pump out front and yellow light streaming through a screen door. The boys blinked awake.

"Where are we?" asked Zach.

"No idea." Robbie got out of the car. "North Carolina."

It was like stepping into a twilight garden, or some hidden biosphere at the zoo. Warmth flowed around him, violet and rustling green, scented overpoweringly of honeysuckle and wet stone. He could hear rushing water, the stirring of wind in the leaves and countless small things—frogs peeping, insects he couldn't identify. A nightbird that made a burbling song. In the shadows behind the building, fireflies floated between kudzu-choked trees like tiny glowing fish.

For an instant he felt himself suspended in that enveloping darkness. The warm air moved through him, sweetly fragrant, pulsing with life he could neither see nor touch. He tasted something honeyed and faintly astringent in the back of his throat, and drew his breath in sharply.

"What?" demanded Zach.

"Nothing." Robbie shook his head and turned to the pump. "Just—isn't this great?"

He filled the tank. Zach and Tyler went in search of food, and Emery strolled over.

"How you holding up?"

"I'm good. Probably let Zach drive for a while so I can catch some Z's."

He moved the car, then went inside to pay. He found Leonard buying a pack of cigarettes as the boys headed out, laden with energy drinks and bags of chips. Robbie slid his credit card across the counter to a woman wearing a tank top that set off a tattoo that looked like the face of Marilyn Manson, or maybe it was Jesus.

"Do you have a restroom?"

The woman handed him a key. "Round back."

"Bathroom's here," Robbie yelled at the boys. "We're not stopping again."

They trailed him into a dank room with gray walls. A fluorescent light buzzed overhead. After Tyler left, Robbie and Zach stood side by side at the sink, trying to coax water from a rusted spigot to wash their hands.

"The hell with it," said Robbie. "Let's hit the road. You want to drive?"

"Dad." Zach pointed at the ceiling. "Dad, look."

Robbie glanced up. A screen bulged from a small window above the sink. Something had blown against the wire mesh, a leaf or scrap of paper.

But then the leaf moved, and he saw that it wasn't a leaf at all but a butterfly.

No, not a butterfly—a moth. The biggest he'd ever seen, bigger than his hand. Its fan-shaped upper wings opened, revealing vivid golden eyespots; its trailing lower wings formed two perfect arabesques, all a milky, luminous green.

"A luna moth," breathed Robbie. "I've never seen one."

Zach clambered onto the sink. "It wants to get out—"

"Hang on." Robbie boosted him, bracing himself so the boy's weight wouldn't yank the sink from the wall. "Be careful! Don't hurt it—"

The moth remained where it was. Robbie grunted—Zach weighed as much as he did—felt his legs trembling as the boy prised the screen from the wall then struggled to pull it free.

"It's stuck," he said. "I can't get it—"

The moth fluttered weakly. One wing-tip looked ragged, as though it had been singed.

"Tear it!" Robbie cried. "Just tear the screen."

Zach wedged his fingers beneath a corner of the window frame and yanked, hard enough that he fell. Robbie caught him as the screen tore away to dangle above the sink. The luna moth crawled onto the sill.

"Go!" Zach banged on the wall. "Go on, fly!"

Like a kite catching the wind, the moth lifted. Its trailing lower wings quivered and the eyespots seemed to blink, a pallid face gazing at them from the darkness. Then it was gone.

"That was cool." For an instant, Zach's arm draped across his father's shoulder, so fleetingly Robbie might have imagined it. "I'm going to the car."

When the boy was gone, Robbie tried to push the screen back into place. He returned the key and went to join Leonard, smoking a cigarette at the edge of the woods. Behind them a car horn blared.

"Come on!" shouted Zach. "I'm leaving!"

"Happy trails," said Leonard.

Robbie slept fitfully in back as Zach drove, the two boys arguing about music and a girl named Eileen. After an hour he took over again.

The night ground on. The boys fell back asleep. Robbie drank one of their Red Bulls and thought of the glimmering wonder that had been the luna moth. A thin rind of emerald appeared on the horizon, deepening to copper then gold as it overtook the sky. He began to see palmettos among the loblolly pines and pin oaks, and spiky plants he didn't recognize. When he opened the window, the air smelled of roses, and the sea.

"Hey." He poked Zach, breathing heavily in the seat beside him. "Hey, we're almost there."

He glanced at the directions, looked up to see the hybrid passing him and Emery gesturing at a sandy track that veered to the left. It was bounded by barbed wire fences and clumps of cactus thick with blossoms the color of lemon cream. The pines surrendered to palmettos and prehistoric-looking trees with gnarled roots that thrust up from pools where egrets and herons stabbed at frogs.

"Look," said Robbie.

Ahead of them the road narrowed to a path barely wide enough for a single vehicle, built up with shells and chunks of concrete. On one side stretched a blur of cypress and long-legged birds; on the other, an aquamarine estuary that gave way to the sea and rolling white dunes.

Robbie slowed the car to a crawl, humping across mounds of shells and doing his best to avoid sinkholes. After a quarter-mile, the makeshift causeway ended. An old metal gate lay in a twisted heap on the ground, covered by creeping vines. Above it a weathered sign clung to a cypress.

WELCOME TO COWANA ISLAND
NO DUNE BUGGIES

They drove past the ruins of a mobile home. Emery's car was out of sight. Robbie looked at his cell phone and saw there was no signal. In the back, Tyler stirred.

"Hey, Rob, where are we?"

"We're here. Wherever here is. The island."

"Sweet." Tyler leaned over the seat to jostle Zach awake. "Hey, get up."

Robbie peered through the overgrown greenery, looking for something resembling a beach house. He tried to remember which hurricane had pounded this part of the coast, and how long ago. Two years? Five?

The place looked as though it had been abandoned for decades. Fallen palmettos were everywhere, their leaves stiff and reddish-brown, like rusted blades. Some remained upright, their crowns lopped off. Acid-green lizards sunned themselves in driveways where ferns poked through the blacktop. The remains of carports and decks dangled above piles of timber and mold-blackened sheetrock. Now and then an intact house appeared within the jungle of flowering vines.

But no people, no cars except for an SUV crushed beneath a toppled utility pole. The only store was a modest grocery with a brick facade and shattered windows, through which the ghostly outlines of aisles and displays could still be glimpsed.

"It's like *28 Days Later*," said Zach, and shot a baleful look at his father.

Robbie shrugged. "Talk to the man from the Starfleet Academy."

He pulled down a rutted drive to where the hybrid sat beneath a thriving palmetto. Driftwood edged a path that led to an old wood-frame house raised on stiltlike pilings. Stands of blooming cactus surrounded it, and trees choked with honeysuckle. The patchy lawn was covered with hundreds of conch shells arranged in concentric circles and spirals. On the deck a tattered red whirligig spun in the breeze, and rope hammocks hung like flaccid cocoons.

"I'm sleeping there," said Tyler.

Leonard gazed at the house with an unreadable expression. Emery had already sprinted up the uneven steps to what Robbie assumed was the front door. When he reached the top, he bent to pick up a square of coconut matting, retrieved something from beneath it then straightened, grinning.

"Come on!" he shouted, turning to unlock the door; and the others raced to join him.

The house had linoleum floors, sifted with a fine layer of sand, and mismatched furniture—rattan chairs, couches covered with faded barkcloth cushions, a canvas seat that hung from the ceiling by a chain and groaned alarmingly whenever the boys sat in it. The sea breeze stirred dusty white curtains at the windows. Anoles skittered across the floor, and Tyler fled shouting from the outdoor shower, where he'd seen a black widow spider. The electricity worked, but there was no air-conditioning and no television; no internet.

"This is what you get for three hundred bucks in the off season," said Emery when Tyler complained.

"I don't get it." Robbie stood on the deck, staring across the empty road to where the dunes stretched, tufted with thorny greenery. "Even if there was a hurricane—this is practically oceanfront, all of it. Where is everybody?"

"Who can afford to build anything?" said Leonard. "Come on, I want to get my stuff inside before it heats up."

Leonard commandeered the master bedroom. He installed his laptop, Emery's camera equipment, piles of storyboards, the box that contained the miniature *Bellerophon*. This formidable array took up every inch of floor space, as well as the surface of a Ping-Pong table.

"Why is there a Ping-Pong table in the bedroom?" asked Robbie as he set down a tripod.

Emery shrugged. "You might ask, why is there not a Ping-Pong table in all bedrooms?"

"We're going to the beach," announced Zach.

Robbie kicked off his shoes and followed them, across the deserted road and down a path that wound through a miniature wilderness of cactus and bristly vines. He felt lightheaded from lack of sleep, and also from the beer he'd snagged from one of the cases Emery had brought. The sand was already hot; twice he had to stop and pluck sharp spurs from his bare feet. A horned toad darted across the path, and a skink with a blue tongue. His son's voice came to him, laughing, and the sound of waves on the shore.

Atop the last dune small yellow roses grew in a thick carpet, their soapy fragrance mingling with the salt breeze. Robbie bent to pluck a handful of petals and tossed them into the air.

"It's not a bad place to fly, is it?"

He turned and saw Emery, shirtless. He handed Robbie a bottle of Tecate with a slice of lime jammed in its neck, raised his own beer and took a sip.

"It's beautiful." Robbie squeezed the lime into his beer, then drank. "But that model. It won't fly."

"I know." Emery stared to where Zach and Tyler leaped in the shallow water, sending up rainbow spray as they splashed each other. "But it's a good excuse for a vacation, isn't it?"

"It is," replied Robbie, and slid down the dune to join the boys.

Over the next few days, they fell into an odd, almost sleepless rhythm, staying up till two or three a.m., drinking and talking. The adults pretended not to notice when the boys slipped a Tecate from the fridge, and ignored the incense-scented smoke that drifted from the deck after they stumbled off to bed. Everyone woke shortly after dawn, even the boys. Blinding sunlight slanted through the worn curtains. On the deck where Zach and Tyler huddled inside their hammocks, a treefrog made a sound like rusty hinges. No one slept enough, everyone drank too much.

For once it didn't matter. Robbie's hangovers dissolved as he waded into water warm as blood, then floated on his back and watched pelicans skim above him. Afterward he'd carry equipment from the house to the dunes, where Emery had created a shelter from old canvas deck chairs and bedsheets. The boys helped, the three of them lugging tripods and digital cameras, the box that contained Leonard's model of the *Bellerophon*, a cooler filled with beer and Red Bull.

That left Emery in charge of household duties. He'd found an ancient red wagon half-buried in the dunes, and used this to transport bags of tortilla chips and a cooler filled with Tecate and limes. There was no store on the island save the abandoned wreck they'd passed when they first arrived. No gas station, and the historical society building appeared to be long gone.

But while driving around, Emery discovered a roadside stand that sold homemade salsa in mason jars and sage-green eggs in recycled cardboard cartons. The drive beside it was blocked with a barbed-wire fence and a sign that said BEWARE OF TWO-HEADED DOG.

"You ever see it?" asked Tyler.

"Nope. I never saw anyone except an alligator." Emery opened a beer. "And it was big enough to eat a two-headed dog."

By Thursday morning, they'd carted everything from one end of the island to the other, waiting with increasing impatience as Leonard climbed up and down dunes and stared broodingly at the blue horizon.

"How will you know which is the right one?" asked Robbie.

Leonard shook his head. "I don't know. Maggie said she thought it would be around here—"

He swept his arm out, encompassing a high ridge of sand that crested above the beach like a frozen wave. Below, Tyler and Zach argued over whose turn it was to haul everything uphill again. Robbie shoved his sunglasses against his nose.

"This beach has probably been washed away a hundred times since McCauley was here. Maybe we should just choose a place at random. Pick the highest dune or something."

"Yeah, I know." Leonard sighed. "This is probably our best choice, here."

He stood and for a long time gazed at the sky. Finally he turned and walked down to join the boys.

"We'll do it here," he said brusquely, and headed back to the house.

Late that afternoon they made a bonfire on the beach. The day had ended gray and much cooler than it had been, the sun swallowed in a haze of bruise-tinged cloud. Robbie waded into the shallow water, feeling with his toes for conch shells. Beside the fire, Zach came across a shark's tooth the size of a guitar pick.

"That's probably a million years old," said Tyler enviously.

"Almost as old as Dad," said Zach.

Robbie flopped down beside Leonard. "It's so weird," he said, shaking sand from a conch. "There's a whole string of these islands, but I haven't seen a boat the whole time we've been here."

"Are you complaining?" said Leonard.

"No. Just, don't you think it's weird?"

"Maybe." Leonard tossed his cigarette into the fire.

"I want to stay." Zach rolled onto his back and watched as sparks flew among the first stars. "Dad? Why can't we just stay here?"

Robbie took a long pull from his beer. "I have to get back to work. And you guys have school."

"Fuck school," said Zach and Tyler.

"Listen." The boys fell silent as Leonard glared at them. "Tomorrow morning I want to set everything up. We'll shoot before the wind picks up too much. I'll have the rest of the day to edit. Then we pack and head to Fayetteville on Saturday. We'll find some cheap place to stay, and drive home on Sunday."

The boys groaned. Emery sighed. "Back to the salt mines. I gotta call that guy about the show."

"I want to have a few hours with Maggie." Leonard pulled at the silver skull in his ear. "I told the nurse I'd be there Saturday before noon."

"We'll have to leave pretty early," said Emery.

For a few minutes nobody spoke. Wind rattled brush in the dunes behind them. The bonfire leaped then subsided, and Zach fed it a knot of driftwood. An unseen bird gave a piping cry that was joined by another, then another, until their plaintive voices momentarily drowned out the soft rush of waves.

Robbie gazed into the darkening water. In his hand, the conch shell felt warm and silken as skin.

"Look, Dad," said Zach. "Bats."

Robbie leaned back to see black shapes dodging sparks above their heads.

"Nice," he said, his voice thick from drink.

"Well." Leonard stood and lit another cigarette. "I'm going to bed."

"Me too," said Zach.

Robbie watched with mild surprise as the boys clambered to their feet, yawning. Emery removed a beer from the cooler, handed it to Robbie.

"Keep an eye on the fire, compadre," he said, and followed the others.

Robbie turned to study the dying blaze. Ghostly runnels of green and blue ran along the driftwood branch. Salt, Leonard had explained to the boys, though Robbie wondered if that was true. How did Leonard know all this stuff? He frowned, picked up a handful of sand and tossed it at the feeble blaze, which promptly sank into sullen embers.

Robbie swore under his breath. He finished his beer, stood and walked unsteadily toward the water. The clouds obscured the moon, though there was a faint umber glow reflected in the distant waves. He stared at the horizon, searching in vain for some sign of life, lights from a cruise ship or plane; turned and gazed up and down the length of the beach.

Nothing. Even the bonfire had died. He stood on tiptoe and tried to peer past the high dune, to where the beach house stood within the grove of palmettos. Night swallowed everything,

He turned back to the waves licking at his bare feet. Something stung his face, blown sand or maybe a gnat. He waved to disperse it, then froze.

In the water, plumes of light coiled and unfolded, dazzling him. Deepest violet, a fiery emerald that stabbed his eyes; cobalt and a pure blaze of scarlet. He shook his head, edging backward; caught himself and looked around.

He was alone. He turned back, and the lights were still there, just below the surface, furling and unfurling to some secret rhythm.

Like a machine, he thought; some kind of underwater windfarm. A wavefarm?

But no, that was crazy. He rubbed his cheeks, trying to sober up. He'd seen something like this in Ocean City late one night—it was something alive, Leonard had explained, plankton or jellyfish, one of those things that glowed. They'd gotten high and raced into the Atlantic to watch pale-green streamers trail them as they body-surfed.

Now he took a deep breath and waded in, kicking at the waves, then halted to see if he'd churned up a luminous cloud.

Darkness lapped almost to his knees: there was no telltale glow where he'd stirred the water. But a few yards away, the lights continued to turn in upon themselves beneath the surface: scores of fist-sized nebulae, soundlesss and steady as his own pulse.

He stared until his head ached, trying to get a fix on them. The lights weren't diffuse, like phosphorescence. And they didn't float like jellyfish. They seemed to be rooted in place, near enough for him to touch.

Yet his eyes couldn't focus: the harder he tried, the more the lights seemed to shift, like an optical illusion or some dizzying computer game.

He stood there for five minutes, maybe longer. Nothing changed. He started to back away, slowly, finally turned and stumbled across the sand, stopping every few steps to glance over his shoulder. The lights were still there, though now he saw them only as a soft yellowish glow.

He ran the rest of the way to the house. There were no lights on, no music or laughter.

But he could smell cigarette smoke, and traced it to the deck where Leonard stood beside the rail.

"Leonard!" Robbie drew alongside him, then glanced around for the boys.

"They slept inside," said Leonard. "Too cold."

"Listen, you have to see something. On the beach—these lights. Not on the beach, in the water." He grabbed Leonard's arm. "Like— just come on."

Leonard shook him off angrily. "You're drunk."

"I'm not drunk! Or, okay, maybe I am, a little. But I'm not kidding. Look—"

He pointed past the sea of palmettos, past the dunes, toward the dark line of waves. The yellow glow was now spangled with silver. It spread across the water, narrowing as it faded toward the horizon, like a wavering path.

Leonard stared, then turned to Robbie in disbelief. "You idiot. It's the fucking moon."

Robbie looked up. And yes, there was the quarter-moon, a blaze of gold between gaps in the cloud.

"That's not it." He knew he sounded not just drunk but desperate. "It was *in* the water—"

"Bioluminescence." Leonard sighed and tossed his cigarette, then headed for the door. "Go to bed, Robbie."

Robbie started to yell after him, but caught himself and leaned against the rail. His head throbbed. Phantom blots of light swam across his vision. He felt dizzy, and on the verge of tears.

He closed his eyes; forced himself to breathe slowly, to channel the pulsing in his head into the memory of spectral whirlpools, a miniature galaxy blossoming beneath the water. After a minute he looked out again, but saw nothing save the blades of palmetto leaves etched against the moonlit sky.

He woke several hours later on the couch, feeling as though an ax were embedded in his forehead. Gray light washed across the floor. It was cold; he reached fruitlessly for a blanket, groaned and sat up.

Emery was in the open kitchen, washing something in the sink. He glanced at Robbie then hefted a coffee pot. "Ready for this?"

Robbie nodded, and Emery handed him a steaming mug. "What time is it?"

"Eight, a little after. The boys are with Leonard—they went out about an hour ago. It looks like rain, which kind of throws a monkey wrench into everything. Maybe it'll hold off long enough to get that thing off the ground."

Robbie sipped his coffee. "Seventeen seconds. He could just throw it into the air."

"Yeah, I thought of that too. So what happened to you last night?"

"Nothing. Too much Tecate."

"Leonard said you were raving drunk."

"Leonard sets the bar pretty low. I was—relaxed."

"Well, time to unrelax. I told him I'd get you up and we'd be at he beach by eight."

"I don't even know what I'm doing. Am I a cameraman?"

"Uh uh. That's me. You don't know how to work it, plus it's my camera. The boys are in charge of the windbreak and, I dunno, props. They hand things to Leonard."

"Things? What things?" Robbie scowled. "It's a fucking model airplane. It doesn't have a remote, does it? Because that would have been a *good* idea."

Emery picked up his camera bag. "Come on. You can carry the tripod, how's that? Maybe the boys will hand you things, and you can hand them to Leonard."

"I'll be there in a minute. Tell Leonard he can start without me."

After Emery left he finished his coffee and went into his room. He rummaged through his clothes until he found a bottle of Ibuprofen, downed six, then pulled on a hooded sweatshirt and sat on the edge of his bed, staring at the wall.

He'd obviously had some kind of blackout, the first since he'd been fired from the Parks Commission. Somewhere between his seventh beer and this morning's hangover was the blurred image of Crayola-colored pinwheels turning beneath dark water, his stumbling flight from the beach and Leonard's disgusted voice: *You idiot, it's the fucking moon.*

Robbie grimaced. He *had* seen something, he knew that.

But he could no longer recall it clearly, and what he could remember made no sense. It was like a movie he'd watched half-awake, or an accident he'd glimpsed from the corner of his eye in a moving car. Maybe it had been the moonlight, or some kind of fluorescent seaweed.

Or maybe he'd just been totally wasted.

Robbie sighed. He put on his sneakers, grabbed Emery's tripod and headed out.

A scattering of cold rain met him as he hit the beach. It was windy. The sea glinted gray and silver, like crumpled tinfoil. Clumps of seaweed covered the sand, and small round discs that resembled pieces of clouded glass: jellyfish, hundreds of them. Robbie prodded one with his foot, then continued down the shore.

The dune was on the north side of the island, where it rose steeply a good fifteen feet above the sand. Now, a few hours before low tide, the water was about thirty feet away. It was exactly the kind of place you might choose to launch a human-powered craft, if you knew little about aerodynamics. Robbie didn't know much, but he was fairly certain you needed to be higher to get any kind of lift.

Still, that would be for a full-sized craft. For a scale model you could hold in your two cupped hands, maybe it would be high enough. He saw Emery pacing along the water's edge, vidcam slung around his neck. The only sign of the others was a trail of footsteps leading to the dune. Robbie clambered up, using the tripod to keep from slipping on sand the color and texture of damp cornmeal. He was panting when he reached the top.

"Hey, Dad. Where were you?"

Robbie smiled weakly as Zach peered out from the windbreak. "I have a sinus infection."

Zach motioned him inside. "Come on, I can't leave this open."

Robbie set down the tripod, then crouched to enter the makeshift tent. Inside, bedsheet walls billowed in the wind, straining at an elaborate scaffold of broom handles, driftwood, the remains of wooden deck chairs. Tyler and Zach sat cross legged on a blanket and stared at their cell phones.

"You can get a strong signal here," said Tyler. "Nope, it's gone again."

Next to them, Leonard knelt beside a cardboard box. Instead of his customary white tunic, he wore one that was sky-blue, embroidered with yellow birds. He glanced at Robbie, his gray eyes cold and dismissive. "There's only room for three people in here."

"That's okay—I'm going out," said Zach, and crawled through the gap in the sheets. Tyler followed him. Robbie jammed his hands into his pockets and forced a smile.

"So," he said. "Did you see all those jellyfish?"

Leonard nodded without looking at him. Very carefully he removed the *Bellerophon* and set it on a neatly folded towel. He reached into the box again, and withdrew something else. A doll no bigger than his hand, dressed in black frockcoat and trousers, with a bowler hat so small that Robbie could have swallowed it.

"*Voila*," said Leonard.

"Jesus, Leonard." Robbie hesitated, then asked, "Can I look at it?"

To his surprise, Leonard nodded. Robbie picked it up. The little figure was so light he wondered if there was anything inside the tiny suit.

But as he turned it gently, he could feel slender joints under its clothing, a miniature torso. Tiny hands protruded from the sleeves, and it wore minute, highly polished shoes that appeared to be made of black leather. Under the frock coat was a waistcoat, with a watch-chain of gold thread that dangled from a nearly invisible pocket. From beneath the bowler hat peeked a fringe of red hair fine as milkweed down. The cameo-sized face that stared up at Robbie was Maggie Blevin's, painted in hairline strokes so that he could see every eyelash, every freckle on her rounded cheeks.

He looked at Leonard in amazement. "How did you do this?"

"It took a long time." He held out his hand, and Robbie returned the doll. "The hardest part was making sure the *Bellerophon* could carry her weight. And that she fit into the bicycle seat and could pedal it. You wouldn't think that would be difficult, but it was."

"It—it looks just like her." Robbie glanced at the doll again, then said, "I thought you wanted to make everything look like the original film. You know, with McCauley—I thought that was the point."

"The point is for it to fly."

"But—"

"You don't need to understand," said Leonard. "Maggie will."

He bent over the little aircraft, its multicolored wings and silken parasol bright as a toy carousel, and tenderly began to fit the doll-sized pilot into its seat.

Robbie shivered. He'd seen Leonard's handiwork before, mannequins so realistic that tourists constantly poked them to see if they were alive.

But those were life-sized, and they weren't designed to resemble someone he *knew*. The sight of Leonard holding a tiny Maggie Blevin tenderly, as though she were a captive bird, made Robbie feel light-headed and slightly sick. He turned toward the tent opening. "I'll see if I can help Emery set up."

Leonard's gaze remained fixed on the tiny figure. "I'll be right there," he said at last.

At the foot of the dune, the boys were trying to talk Emery into letting them use the camera.

"No way." He waved as Robbie scrambled down. "See, I'm not even letting your dad do it."

"That's because Dad would suck," Zach said as Emery grabbed Robbie and steered him toward the water. "Come on, just for a minute."

"Trouble with the crew?" asked Robbie.

"Nah. They're just getting bored."

"Did you see that doll?"

"The Incredible Shrinking Maggie?" Emery stopped to stare at the dune. "The thing about Leonard is, I can never figure out if he's brilliant or potentially dangerous. The fact that he'll be able to retire with a full government pension suggests he's normal. The Maggie voodoo doll, though…"

He shook his head and began to pace again. Robbie walked beside him, kicking at wet sand and staring curiously at the sky. The air smelled odd, of ozone or hot metal. But it felt too chilly for a thunderstorm, and the dark ridge that hung above the palmettos and live oaks looked more like encroaching fog than cumulus clouds.

"Well, at least the wind's from the right direction," said Robbie.

Emery nodded. "Yeah. I was starting to think we'd have to throw it from the roof."

A few minutes later, Leonard's voice rang out above the wind. "Okay, everyone over here."

They gathered at the base of the dune and stared up at him, his tunic an azure rent in the ominous sky. Between Leonard's feet was a cardboard box. He glanced at it and went on.

"I'm going to wait till the wind seems right, and then I'll yell '*Now!*' Emery, you'll just have to watch me and see where she goes, then do your best. Zach and Tyler—you guys fan out and be ready to catch her if she starts to fall. Catch her *gently*," he added.

"What about me?" called Robbie.

"You stay with Emery in case he needs backup."

"Backup?" Robbie frowned.

"You know," said Emery in a low voice. "In case I need help getting Leonard back to the rubber room."

The boys began to walk toward the water. Tyler had his cell phone out. He looked at Zach, who dug his phone from his pocket.

"Are they *texting* each other?" asked Emery in disbelief. "They're ten feet apart."

"Ready?" Leonard shouted.

"Ready," the boys yelled back.

Robbie turned to Emery. "What about you, Captain Marvo?"

Emery grinned and held up the camera. "I have never been readier."

Atop the dune, Leonard stooped to retrieve the *Bellerophon* from its box. As he straightened, its propellers began turning madly. Candy-striped rotators spun like pinwheels as he cradled it against his chest, his long white braids threatening to tangle with the parasol.

The wind gusted suddenly: Robbie's throat tightened as he watched the tiny black figure beneath the fuselage swing wildly back and forth, like an accelerated pendulum. Leonard slipped in the sand and fought to regain his balance.

"Uh-oh," said Emery.

The wind died, and Leonard righted himself. Even from the beach, Robbie could see how his face had gone white.

"Are you okay?" yelled Zach.

"I'm okay," Leonard yelled back.

He gave them a shaky smile, then stared intently at the horizon. After a minute his head tilted, as though listening to something. Abruptly he straightened and raised the *Bellerophon* in both hands. Behind him, palmettos thrashed as the wind gusted.

"*Now!*" he shouted.

Leonard opened his hands. As though it were a butterfly, the *Belllerophon* lifted into the air. Its feathery parasol billowed. Fan-shaped wings rose and fell; ailerons flapped and gears whirled like pinwheels. There was a sound like a train rushing through a tunnel, and Robbie stared open-mouthed as the *Bellerophon* skimmed the air above his head, its pilot pedaling furiously as it headed toward the sea.

Robbie gasped. The boys raced after it, yelling. Emery followed, camera clamped to his face and Robbie at his heels.

"This is fucking incredible!' Emery shouted. "Look at that thing go!"

They drew up a few yards from the water. The *Bellerophon* whirred past, barely an arm's-length above them. Robbie's eyes blurred as he stared after that brilliant whirl of color and motion, a child's dream of flight soaring just out of reach. Emery waded into the shallows with his camera. The boys followed, splashing and waving at the little plane. From the dune behind them echoed Leonard's voice.

"*Godspeed.*"

Robbie gazed silently at the horizon as the *Bellerophon* continued on, its pilot silhouetted black against the sky, wings opened like sails. Its sound grew fainter, a soft whirring that might have been a flock of birds. Soon it would be gone. Robbie stepped to the water's edge and craned his neck to keep it in sight.

Without warning a green flare erupted from the waves and streamed toward the little aircraft. Like a meteor shooting *upward*, emerald blossomed into a blinding radiance that engulfed the *Bellerophon*. For an instant Robbie saw the flying machine, a golden wheel spinning within a comet's heart.

Then the blazing light was gone, and with it the *Bellerophon*.

Robbie gazed, stunned, at the empty air. After an endless moment he became aware of something—someone—near him. He turned to see Emery stagger from the water, soaking wet, the camera held uselessly at his side.

"I dropped it," he gasped. "When that—whatever the fuck it was, when it came, I dropped the camera."

Robbie helped him onto the sand.

"I felt it." Emery shuddered, his hand tight around Robbie's arm. "Like a riptide. I thought I'd go under."

Robbie pulled away from him. "Zach?" he shouted, panicked. "Tyler, Zach, are you—"

Emery pointed at the water, and Robbie saw them, heron-stepping through the waves and whooping in triumph as they hurried back to shore.

"What happened?" Leonard ran up alongside Robbie and grabbed him. "Did you see that?"

Robbie nodded. Leonard turned to Emery, his eyes wild. "Did you get it? The *Bellerophon*? And that flare? Like the original film! The same thing, the exact same thing!"

Emery reached for Robbie's sweatshirt. "Give me that, I'll see if I can dry the camera."

Leonard stared blankly at Emery's soaked clothes, the water dripping from the vidcam.

"Oh no." He covered his face with his hands. "Oh no…"

"We got it!" Zach pushed between the grownups. "We got it, we got it!" Tyler ran up beside him, waving his cell phone. "Look!"

Everyone crowded together, the boys tilting their phones until the screens showed black.

"Okay," said Tyler. "Watch this."

Robbie shaded his eyes, squinting.

And there it was, a bright mote bobbing across a formless gray field, growing bigger and bigger until he could see it clearly—the whirl of wings and gears, the ballooning peacock-feather parasol and steadfast pilot on the velocipede; the swift silent flare that lashed from the water then disappeared in an eyeblink.

"Now watch mine," said Zach, and the same scene played again from a different angle. "Eighteen seconds."

"Mine says twenty," said Tyler. Robbie glanced uneasily at the water.

"Maybe we should head back to the house," he said.

Leonard seized Zach's shoulder. "Can you get me that? Both of you? Email it or something?"

"Sure. But we'll need to go where we can get a signal."

"I'll drive you," said Emery. "Let me get into some dry clothes."

He turned and trudged up the beach, the boys laughing and running behind him.

Leonard walked the last few steps to the water's edge, spray staining the tip of one cowboy boot. He stared at the horizon, his expression puzzled yet oddly expectant.

Robbie hesitated, then joined him. The sea appeared calm, green-glass waves rolling in long swells beneath parchment-colored sky. Through a gap in the clouds he could make out a glint of blue, like a noonday star. He gazed at it in silence, and after a minute asked, "Did you know that was going to happen?"

Leonard shook his head. "No. How could I?"

"Then—what was it?" Robbie looked at him helplessly. "Do you have any idea?"

Leonard said nothing. Finally he turned to Robbie. Unexpectedly, he smiled.

"I have no clue. But you saw it, right?" Robbie nodded. "And you saw her fly. The *Bellerophon*."

Leonard took another step, heedless of waves at his feet. "She flew." His voice was barely a whisper. "She really flew."

That night nobody slept. Emery drove Zach, Tyler and Leonard to a Dunkin Donuts where the boys got a cellphone signal and sent their movie footage to Leonard's laptop. Back at the house, he disappeared while the others sat on the deck and discussed, over and over again, what they had seen. The boys wanted to return to the beach, but Robbie refused to let them go. As a peace offering, he gave them each a beer. By the time Leonard emerged from his room with the laptop, it was after three a.m.

He set the computer on a table in the living room. "See what you think." When the others had assembled, he hit Play.

Blotched letters filled the screen: THE MAIDEN FLIGHT OF MCCAULEY'S BELLEROPHON. The familiar tipsy horizon appeared, sepia and amber, silvery flashes from the sea below. Robbie held his breath.

And there was the *Bellerophon* with its flickering wheels and wings propelled by a steadfast pilot, until the brilliant light struck from below and the clip abruptly ended, at exactly seventeen seconds. Nothing betrayed the figure as Maggie rather than McCauley; nothing seemed any different at all, no matter how many times Leonard played it back.

"So that's it," he said at last, and closed his laptop.

"Are you going to put it on YouTube?" asked Zach.

"No," he replied wearily. The boys exchanged a look, but for once remained silent.

"Well." Emery stood and stretched his arms, yawning. "Time to pack."

Two hours later they were on the road.

The hospice was a few miles outside town, a rambling old white house surrounded by neatly kept azaleas and rhododendrons. The boys were turned loose to wander the neighborhood. The others walked up to the veranda, Leonard carrying his laptop. He looked terrible, his gray eyes bloodshot and his face unshaved. Emery put an arm over his shoulder and Leonard nodded stiffly.

A nurse met them at the door, a trim blond woman in chinos and a yellow blouse.

"I told her you were coming," she said as she showed them into a sunlit room with wicker furniture and a low table covered with books and magazines. "She's the only one here now, though we expect someone tomorrow."

"How is she?" asked Leonard.

"She sleeps most of the time. And she's on morphine for the pain, so she's not very lucid. Her body's shutting down. But she's conscious."

"Has she had many visitors?" asked Emery.

"Not since she's been here. In the hospital a few neighbors dropped by. I gather there's no family. It's a shame." She shook her head sadly. "She's a lovely woman."

"Can I see her?" Leonard glanced at a closed door at the end of the bright room.

"Of course."

Robbie and Emery watched them go, then settled into the wicker chairs.

"God, this is depressing," said Emery.

"It's better than a hospital," said Robbie. "Anna was going to go into a hospice, but she died before she could."

Emery winced. "Sorry. Of course, I wasn't thinking."

"It's okay."

Robbie leaned back and shut his eyes. He saw Anna sitting on the grass with azaleas all around her, bees in the flowers and Zach laughing as he opened his hands to release a green moth that lit momentarily upon her head, then drifted into the sky.

"Robbie." He started awake. Emery sat beside him, shaking him gently. "Hey—I'm going in now. Go back to sleep if you want, I'll wake you when I come out."

Robbie looked around blearily. "Where's Leonard?"

"He went for a walk. He's pretty broken up. He wanted to be alone for a while."

"Sure, sure." Robbie rubbed his eyes. "I'll just wait."

When Emery was gone he stood and paced the room. After a few minutes he sighed and sank back into his chair, then idly flipped through the magazines and books on the table. *Tricycle*, *Newsweek*, the *Utne Reader*, some pamphlets on end-of-life issues, works by Viktor Frankl and Elizabeth Kubler-Ross.

And, underneath yesterday's newspaper, a familiar sky-blue dustjacket emblazoned with the garish image of a naked man and woman, hands linked as they floated above a vast abyss, surrounded by a glowing purple sphere. Beneath them the title appeared in embossed green letters.

Wings for Humanity!
The Next Step is OURS!
by Margaret S. Blevin, PhD

Robbie picked it up. On the back was a photograph of the younger Maggie in a white embroidered tunic, her hair a bright corona around her piquant face. She stood in the Hall of Flight beside a mockup of the Apollo Lunar Module, the *Wright Flyer* high above her head. She was laughing, her hands raised in welcome. He opened it to a random page.

> ...that time has come: With the dawn of the Golden Millennium we will welcome their return, meeting them at last as equals to share in the glory that is the birthright of our species.

He glanced at the frontispiece and title page, and then the dedication.

For Leonard, who never doubted

"Isn't that an amazing book?"

Robbie looked up to see the nurse smiling down at him.

"Uh, yeah," he said, and set it on the table.

"It's incredible she predicted so much stuff." The nurse shook her head. "Like the Hubble Telescope, and that caveman they found in the glacier, the guy with the lens? And those turbines that can make energy in the jet stream? I never even heard of that, but my husband said they're real. Everything she says, it's all so hopeful. You know?"

Robbie stared at her, then quickly nodded. Behind her the door opened. Emery stepped out.

"She's kind of drifting," he said.

"Morning's her good time. She usually fades around now." The nurse glanced at her watch, then at Robbie. "You go ahead. Don't be surprised if she nods off."

He stood. "Sure. Thanks."

The room was small, its walls painted a soft lavender-gray. The bed faced a large window overlooking a garden. Goldfinches and tiny green wrens darted between a bird feeder and a small pool lined with flat white stones. For a moment Robbie thought the bed was empty. Then he saw an emaciated figure had slipped down between the white sheets, dwarfed by pillows and a bolster.

"Maggie?"

The figure turned its head. Hairless, skin white as paper, mottled with bruises like spilled ink. Her lips and fingernails were violet; her face so pale and lined it was like gazing at a cracked egg. Only the eyes were recognizably Maggie's, huge, the deep slatey blue of an infant's. As she stared at him, she drew her wizened arms up, slowly, until her fingers grazed her shoulders. She reminded Robbie disturbingly of a praying mantis.

"I don't know if you remember me." He sat in a chair beside the bed. "I'm Robbie. I worked with Leonard. At the museum."

"He told me." Her voice was so soft he had to lean close to hear her. "I'm glad they got here. I expected them yesterday, when it was still snowing."

Robbie recalled Anna in her hospital bed, doped to the gills and talking to herself. "Sure," he said.

Maggie shot him a glance that might have held annoyance, then gazed past him into the garden. Her eyes widened as she struggled to lift her hand, fingers twitching. Robbie realized she was waving. He turned to stare out the window, but there was no one there. Maggie looked at him, then gestured at the door.

"You can go now," she said. "I have guests."

"Oh. Yeah, sorry."

He stood awkwardly, then leaned down to kiss the top of her head. Her skin was smooth and cold as metal. "'Bye, Maggie."

At the door he looked back, and saw her gazing with a rapt expression at the window, head cocked slightly and her hands open, as though to catch the sunlight.

Two days after they got home, Robbie received an email from Leonard.

Dear Robbie,

Maggie died this morning. The nurse said she became unconscious early yesterday, seemed to be in pain but at least it didn't last long. She had arranged to be cremated. No memorial service or anything like that. I will do something, probably not till the fall, and let you know.

Yours, Leonard

Robbie sighed. Already the week on Cowana seemed long ago and faintly dreamlike, like the memory of a childhood vacation. He wrote Leonard a note of condolence, then left for work.

Weeks passed. Zach and Tyler posted their clips of the *Bellerophon* online. Robbie met Emery for drinks ever week or two, and saw Leonard once, at Emery's Fourth of July barbecue. By the end of summer,

Tyler's footage had been viewed 347,623 times, and Zach's 347,401. Both provided a link to the Captain Marvo site, where Emery had a free download of the entire text of *Wings for Humanity!* There were now over a thousand Google hits for Margaret Blevin, and Emery added a *Bellerophon* T-shirt to his merchandise: organic cotton with a silk-screen image of the baroque aircraft and its bowler-hatted pilot.

Early in September, Leonard called Robbie.

"Can you meet me at the museum tomorrow, around eight-thirty? I'm having a memorial for Maggie, just you and me and Emery. After hours, I'll sign you in."

"Sure," said Robbie. "Can I bring something?"

"Just yourself. See you then."

He drove in with Emery. They walked across the twilit Mall, the museum a white cube that glowed against a sky swiftly darkening to indigo. Leonard waited for them by the side door. He wore an embroidered tunic, sky-blue, his white hair loose upon his shoulders, and held a cardboard box with a small printed label.

"Come on," he said. The museum had been closed since five, but a guard opened the door for them. "We don't have a lot of time."

Hedges sat at the security desk, bald and even more imposing than when Robbie last saw him, decades ago. He signed them in, eying Robbie curiously then grinning when he read his signature.

"I remember you—Opie, right?"

Robbie winced at the nickname, then nodded. Hedges handed Leonard a slip of paper. "Be quick."

"Thanks. I will."

They walked to the staff elevator, the empty museum eerie and blue-lit. High above them the silent aircraft seemed smaller than they had been in the past, battered and oddly toylike. Robbie noticed a crack in the Gemini VII space capsule, and strands of dust clinging to the *Wright Flyer.* When they reached the third floor, Leonard led them down the corridor, past the Photo Lab, past the staff cafeteria, past the library where the Nut Files used to be. Finally he stopped at a door near some open ductwork. He looked at the slip of paper

Hedges had given him, punched a series of numbers into the lock, opened it then reached in to switch on the light. Inside was a narrow room with a metal ladder fixed to one wall.

"Where are we going?" asked Robbie.

"The roof," said Leonard. "If we get caught, Hedges and I are screwed. Actually, we're all screwed. So we have to make this fast."

He tucked the cardboard box against his chest, then began to climb the ladder. Emery and Robbie followed him, to a small metal platform and another door. Leonard punched in another code and pushed it open. They stepped out into the night.

It was like being atop an ocean liner. The museum's roof was flat, nearly a block long. Hot air blasted from huge exhaust vents, and Leonard motioned the others to move away, toward the far end of the building.

The air was cooler here, a breeze that smelled sweet and rain-washed, despite the cloudless sky. Beneath them stretched the Mall, a vast green gameboard, with the other museums and monuments huge game pieces, ivory and onyx and glass. The spire of the Washington Monument rose in the distance, and beyond that the glittering reaches of Roslyn and Crystal City.

"I've never been here," said Robbie, stepping beside Leonard.

Emery shook his head. "Me neither."

"I have," said Leonard, and smiled. "Just once, with Maggie."

Above the Capitol's dome hung the full moon, so bright against the starless sky that Robbie could read what was printed on Leonard's box.

MARGARET BLEVIN.

"These are her ashes." Leonard set the box down and removed the top, revealing a ziplocked bag. He opened the bag, picked up the box again and stood. "She wanted me to scatter them here. I wanted both of you to be with me."

He dipped his hand into the bag and withdrew a clenched fist; held the box out to Emery, who nodded silently and did the same; then turned to Robbie.

"You too," he said.

Robbie hesitated, then put his hand into the box. What was inside felt gritty, more like sand than ash. When he looked up, he saw that Leonard had stepped forward, head thrown back so that he gazed at the moon. He drew his arm back, flung the ashes into the sky and stooped to grab more.

Emery glanced at Robbie, and the two of them opened their hands.

Robbie watched the ashes stream from between his fingers, like a flight of tiny moths. Then he turned and gathered more, the three of them tossing handful after handful into the sky.

When the box was finally empty Robbie straightened, breathing hard, and ran a hand across his eyes. He didn't know if it was some trick of the moonlight or the freshening wind, but everywhere around them, everywhere he looked, the air was filled with wings.

Near Zennor

He found the letters inside a round metal candy tin, at the bottom of a plastic storage box in the garage, alongside strings of outdoor Christmas lights and various oddments his wife had saved for the yard sale she'd never managed to organise in almost thirty years of marriage. She'd died suddenly, shockingly, of a brain aneurysm, while planting daffodil bulbs the previous September.

Now everything was going to Goodwill. The house in New Canaan had been listed with a Realtor; despite the terrible market, she'd reassured Jeffrey that it should sell relatively quickly, and for something close to his asking price.

"It's a beautiful house, Jeffrey," she said, "not that I'm surprised." Jeffrey was a noted architect: she glanced at him as she stepped carefully along a flagstone path in her Louboutin heels. "And these gardens are incredible."

"That was all Anthea." He paused beside a stone wall, surveying an emerald swathe of new grass, small exposed hillocks of black earth, piles of neatly raked leaves left by the crew he'd hired to do the work that Anthea had always done on her own. In the distance, birch trees glowed spectral white against a leaden February sky that gave a twilit cast to midday. "She always said that if I'd had to pay her for all this, I wouldn't have been able to afford her. She was right."

He signed off on the final sheaf of contracts and returned them to the Realtor. "You're in Brooklyn now?" she asked, turning back toward the house.

"Yes. Green Park. A colleague of mine is in Singapore for a few months, he's letting me stay there till I get my bearings."

"Well, good luck. I'll be in touch soon." She opened the door of her Prius and hesitated. "I know how hard this is for you. I lost my father two years ago. Nothing helps, really."

Jeffrey nodded. "Thanks. I know."

He'd spent the last five months cycling through wordless, image-less night terrors from which he awoke gasping; dreams in which Anthea lay beside him, breathing softly then smiling as he touched her face; nightmares in which the neuroelectrical storm that had killed her raged inside his own head, a flaring nova that engulfed the world around him and left him floating in an endless black space, the stars expiring one by one as he drifted past them.

He knew that grief had no target demographic, that all around him versions of this cosmic reshuffling took place every day. He and Anthea had their own shared experience years before, when they had lost their first and only daughter to sudden infant death syndrome. They were both in their late thirties at the time. They never tried to have another child, on their own or through adoption. It was as though some psychic house fire had consumed them both: it was a year before Jeffrey could enter the room that had been Julia's, and for months after her death neither he nor Anthea could bear to sit at the dining table and finish a meal together, or sleep in the same bed. The thought of being that close to another human being, of having one's hand or foot graze another's and wake however fleetingly to the realisation that this too could be lost—it left both of them with a terror that they had never been able to articulate, even to each other.

Now as then, he kept busy with work at his office in the city, and dutifully accepted invitations for lunch and dinner there and in New Canaan. Nights were a prolonged torment: he was haunted by the realisation that Anthea been extinguished, a spent match pinched between one's fingers. He thought of Houdini, arch-rationalist of another century, who desired proof of a spirit world he desperately wanted to believe in. Jeffrey believed in nothing, yet if there had been a drug to twist his neurons into some synaptic impersonation of faith, he would have taken it.

For the past month he'd devoted most of his time to packing up the house, donating Anthea's clothes to various charity shops, deciding what to store and what to sell, what to divvy up among nieces and nephews, Anthea's sister, a few close friends. Throughout he experienced grief as a sort of low-grade flu, a persistent, inescapable ache that suffused not just his thoughts but his bones and tendons: a throbbing in his temples, black sparks that distorted his vision; an acrid chemical taste in the back of his throat, as though he'd bitten into one of the pills his doctor had given him to help him sleep.

He watched as the Realtor drove off soundlessly, returned to the garage and transferred the plastic bin of Christmas lights into his own car, to drop off at a neighbour's the following weekend. He put the tin box with the letters on the seat beside him. As he pulled out of the driveway, it began to snow.

That night, he sat at the dining table in the Brooklyn loft and opened the candy tin. Inside were five letters, each bearing the same stamp: RETURN TO SENDER. At the bottom of the tin was a locket on a chain, cheap gold-coloured metal and chipped red enamel circled by tiny fake pearls. He opened it: it was empty. He examined it for an engraved inscription, initials, a name, but there was nothing. He set it aside and turned to the letters.

All were postmarked 1971—February, March, April, July, end of August—all addressed to the same person at the same address, carefully spelled out in Anthea's swooping, schoolgirl's hand.

> *Mr. Robert Bennington,*
> *Golovenna Farm,*
> *Padwithiel,*
> *Cornwall*

Love letters? He didn't recognise the name Robert Bennington. Anthea would have been thirteen in February; her birthday was in

May. He moved the envelopes across the table, as though performing a card trick. His heart pounded, which was ridiculous. He and Anthea had told each other about everything—three-ways at university, coke-fuelled orgies during the 1980s, affairs and flirtations throughout their marriage.

None of that mattered now; little of it had mattered then. Still, his hands shook as he opened the first envelope. A single sheet of onionskin was inside. He unfolded it gingerly and smoothed it on the table.

His wife's handwriting hadn't changed much in forty years. The same cramped cursive, each *i* so heavily dotted in black ink that the pen had almost poked through the thin paper. Anthea had been English, born and raised in North London. They'd met at the University of London, where they were both studying, and moved to New Canaan after they'd married. It was an area that Anthea had often said reminded her of the English countryside, though Jeffrey had never ventured outside London, other than a few excursions to Kent and Brighton. Where was Padwithiel?

21 February, 1971

Dear Mr. Bennington,

My name is Anthea Ryson . . .

And would a thirteen-year-old girl address her boyfriend as 'Mr.,' even forty years ago?

. . . I am thirteen years old and live in London. Last year my friend Evelyn let me read Still the Seasons *for the first time and since then I have read it two more times, also* Black Clouds Over Bragmoor *and* The Second Sun. *They are my favourite books! I keep looking for more but the library here doesn't have them. I have asked and they said I should try the shops but that is expensive. My teacher said that*

sometimes you come to schools and speak, I hope some day you'll come to Islington Day School. Are you writing more books about Tisha and the great Battle? I hope so, please write back! My address is 42 Highbury Fields, London NW1.

Very truly yours,
Anthea Ryson

Jeffrey set aside the letter and gazed at the remaining four envelopes. *What a prick,* he thought. He never even wrote her back. He turned to his laptop and googled Robert Bennington.

Robert Bennington (1932–), British author of a popular series of children's fantasy novels published during the 1960s known as The Sun Battles. *Bennington's books rode the literary tidal wave generated by J.R.R. Tolkien's work, but his commercial and critical standing were irrevocably shaken in the late 1990s, when he became the centre of a drawn-out court case involving charges of paedophilia and sexual assault, with accusations lodged against him by several girl fans, now adults. One of the alleged victims later changed her account, and the case was eventually dismissed amidst much controversy by child advocates and women's rights groups. Bennington's reputation never recovered: school libraries refused to keep his books on their shelves. All of his novels are now out of print, although digital editions (illegal) can be found, along with used copies of the four books in the* Battles *sequence . . .*

Jeffrey's neck prickled. The court case didn't ring a bell, but the books did. Anthea had thrust one upon him shortly after they first met.

"These were my *favourites.*" She rolled over in bed and pulled a yellowed paperback from a shelf crowded with textbooks and Penguin editions of the mystery novels she loved. "I must have read this twenty times."

"Twenty?" Jeffrey raised an eyebrow.

"Well, maybe seven. A *lot*. Did you ever read them?"

"I never even heard of them."

"You have to read it. Right now." She nudged him with her bare foot. "You can't leave here till you do."

"Who says I want to leave?" He tried to kiss her but she pushed him away.

"Uh-uh. Not till you read it. I'm serious!"

So he'd read it, staying up till 3:00 a.m., intermittently dozing off before waking with a start to pick up the book again.

"It gave me bad dreams," he said as grey morning light leaked through the narrow window of Anthea's flat. "I don't like it."

"I know." Anthea laughed. "That's what I liked about them— they always made me feel sort of sick."

Jeffrey shook his head adamantly. "I don't like it," he repeated.

Anthea frowned, finally shrugged, picked up the book and dropped it onto the floor. "Well, nobody's perfect," she said, and rolled on top of him.

A year or so later he did read *Still the Seasons*, when a virus kept him in bed for several days and Anthea was caught up with research at the British Library. The book unsettled him deeply. There were no monsters *per se*, no dragons or Nazgûl or witches. Just two sets of cousins, two boys and two girls, trapped in a portal between one of those grim post-war English cities, Manchester or Birmingham, and a magical land that wasn't really magical at all but even bleaker and more threatening than the council flats where the children lived.

Jeffrey remembered unseen hands tapping at a window, and one of the boys fighting off something invisible that crawled under the bedcovers and attacked in a flapping wave of sheets and blankets. Worst of all was the last chapter, which he read late one night and could never recall clearly, save for the vague, enveloping dread it engendered, something he had never encountered before or since.

Anthea had been right—the book had a weirdly visceral power, more like the effect of a low-budget, black-and-white horror movie than a children's fantasy novel. How many of those grown-up kids now knew their hero had been a paedophile?

Jeffrey spent a half-hour scanning articles on Bennington's trial, none of them very informative. It had happened over a decade ago; since then there'd been a few dozen blog posts, pretty equally divided between *Whatever happened to . . .?* and excoriations by women who themselves had been sexually abused, though not by Bennington.

He couldn't imagine that had happened to Anthea. She'd certainly never mentioned it, and she'd always been dismissive, even slightly callous, about friends who underwent counselling or psychotherapy for childhood traumas. As for the books themselves, he didn't recall seeing them when he'd sorted through their shelves to pack everything up. Probably they'd been donated to a library book sale years ago, if they'd even made the crossing from London.

He picked up the second envelope. It was postmarked 'March 18, 1971'. He opened it and withdrew a sheet of lined paper torn from a school notebook.

Dear Rob,

Well, we all got back on the train, Evelyn was in a lot of trouble for being out all night and of course we couldn't tell her aunt why, her mother said she can't talk to me on the phone but I see her at school anyway so it doesn't matter. I still can't believe it all happened. Evelyn's mother said she was going to call my mother and Moira's but so far she didn't. Thank you so much for talking to us. You signed Evelyn's book but you forgot to sign mine. Next time!!!

Yours sincerely your friend,
Anthea

Jeffrey felt a flash of cold through his chest. *Dear Rob, I still can't believe it all happened.* He quickly opened the remaining envelopes, read first one then the next and finally the last.

63

12 April 1971

Dear Rob,

Maybe I wrote down your address wrong because the last letter I sent was returned. But I asked Moira and she had the same address and she said her letter wasn't returned. Evelyn didn't write yet but says she will. It was such a really, really great time to see you! Thank you again for the books, I thanked you in the last letter but thank you again. I hope you'll write back this time, we still want to come again on holiday in July! I can't believe it was exactly one month ago we were there.

Your friend,
Anthea Ryson

July 20, 1971

Dear Rob,

Well I still haven't heard from you so I guess you're mad maybe or just forgot about me, ha ha. School is out now and I was wondering if you still wanted us to come and stay? Evelyn says we never could and her aunt would tell her mother but we could hitch-hike, also Evelyn's brother Martin has a caravan and he and his girlfriend are going to Wales for a festival and we thought they might give us a ride partway, he said maybe they would. Then we could hitch-hike the rest. The big news is Moira ran away from home and they called the POLICE. Evelyn said she went without us to see you and she's really mad. Moira's boyfriend Peter is mad too.

If she is there with you is it okay if I come too? I could come alone without Evelyn, her mother is a BITCH.

Please please write!
Anthea (Ryson)

Dear Rob,

I hate you. I wrote FIVE LETTERS including this one and I know it is the RIGHT address. I think Moira went to your house without us. FUCK YOU Tell her I hate her too and so does Evelyn. We never told anyone if she says we did she is a LIAR.

FUCK YOU FUCK YOU FUCK YOU

Where a signature should have been, the page was ripped and blotched with blue ink—Anthea had scribbled something so many times the pen tore through the lined paper. Unlike the other four, this sheet was badly crumpled, as though she'd thrown it away then retrieved it. Jeffrey glanced at the envelope. The postmark read 'August 28'. She'd gone back to school for the fall term, and presumably that had been the end of it.

Except, perhaps, for Moira, whoever she was. Evelyn would be Evelyn Thurlow, Anthea's closest friend from her school days in Islington. Jeffrey had met her several times while at university, and Evelyn had stayed with them for a weekend in the early 1990s, when she was attending a conference in Manhattan. She was a flight-test engineer for a British defence contractor, living outside Cheltenham; she and Anthea would have hour-long conversations on their birthdays, planning a dream vacation together to someplace warm—Greece or Turkey or the Caribbean.

Jeffrey had e-mailed her about Anthea's death, and they had spoken on the phone—Evelyn wanted to fly over for the funeral but was on deadline for a major government contract and couldn't take the time off.

"I so wish I could be there," she'd said, her voice breaking. "Everything's just so crazed at the moment. I hope you understand . . ."

"It's okay. She knew how much you loved her. She was always so happy to hear from you."

"I know." Evelyn choked. "I just wish—I just wish I'd been able to see her again."

Now he sat and stared at the five letters. The sight made him feel light-headed and slightly queasy: as though he'd opened his closet door and found himself at the edge of a precipice, gazing down some impossible distance to a world made tiny and unreal. Why had she never mentioned any of this? Had she hidden the letters for all these years, or simply forgotten she had them? He knew it wasn't rational; knew his response derived from his compulsive sense of order, what Anthea had always called his architect's left brain.

"Jeffrey would never even try to put a square peg into a round hole," she'd said once at a dinner party. "He'd just design a new hole to fit it."

He could think of no place he could fit the five letters written to Robert Bennington. After a few minutes, he replaced each in its proper envelope and stacked them atop each other. Then he turned back to his laptop, and wrote an e-mail to Evelyn.

He arrived in Cheltenham two weeks later. Evelyn picked him up at the train station early Monday afternoon. He'd told her he was in London on business, spent the preceding weekend at a hotel in Bloomsbury and wandered the city, walking past the building where he and Anthea had lived right after university, before they moved to the U.S.

It was a relief to board the train and stare out the window at an unfamiliar landscape, suburbs giving way to farms and the gently rolling outskirts of the Cotswolds.

Evelyn's husband, Chris, worked for one of the high-tech corporations in Cheltenham; their house was a rambling, expensively renovated cottage twenty minutes from the congested city centre.

"Anthea would have loved these gardens," Jeffrey said, surveying swathes of narcissus already in bloom, alongside yellow primroses and a carpet of bluebells beneath an ancient beech. "Everything at home is still brown. We had snow a few weeks ago."

"It must be very hard, giving up the house." Evelyn poured him a glass of Medoc and sat across from him in the slate-floored sunroom.

"Not as hard as staying would have been." Jeffrey raised his glass. "To old friends and old times."

"To Anthea," said Evelyn.

They talked into the evening, polishing off the Medoc and start-ing on a second bottle long before Chris arrived home from work. Evelyn was florid and heavy-set, her unruly raven hair long as ever and braided into a single plait, thick and grey-streaked. She'd met her con-tract deadline just days ago, and her dark eyes still looked hollowed from lack of sleep. Chris prepared dinner, lamb with fresh mint and new peas; their children were both off at university, so Jeffrey and Chris and Evelyn lingered over the table until almost midnight.

"Leave the dishes," Chris said, rising. "I'll get them in the morn-ing." He bent to kiss the top of his wife's head, then nodded at Jeffrey. "Good to see you, Jeffrey."

"Come on." Evelyn grabbed a bottle of Armagnac and headed for the sunroom. "Get those glasses, Jeffrey. I'm not going in till noon. Project's done, and the mice will play."

Jeffrey followed her, settling onto the worn sofa and placing two glasses on the side table. Evelyn filled both, flopped into an armchair and smiled. "It *is* good to see you."

"And you."

He sipped his Armagnac. For several minutes they sat in silence, staring out the window at the garden, narcissus and primroses faint gleams in the darkness. Jeffrey finished his glass, poured another, and asked, "Do you remember someone named Robert Bennington?"

Evelyn cradled her glass against her chest. She gazed at Jeffrey for a long moment before answering. "The writer? Yes. I read his books when I was a girl. Both of us did—me and Anthea."

"But—you knew him. You met him, when you were thirteen. On vacation or something."

Evelyn turned, her profile silhouetted against the window. "We did," she said at last, and turned back to him. "Why are you asking?"

"I found some letters that Anthea wrote to him. Back in 1971, after you and her and a girl named Moira saw him in Cornwall. Did you know he was a paedophile? He was arrested about fifteen years ago."

"Yes, I read about that. It was a big scandal." Evelyn finished her Armagnac and set her glass on the table. "Well, a medium-sized scandal. I don't think many people even remembered who he was by then. He was a cult writer, really. The books were rather dark for children's books."

She hesitated. "Anthea wasn't molested by him, if that's what you're asking about. None of us were. He invited us to tea—we invited ourselves, actually, he was very nice and let us come in and gave us Nutella sandwiches and tangerines."

"Three little teenyboppers show up at his door, I bet he was very nice," said Jeffrey. "What about Moira? What happened to her?"

"I don't know." Evelyn sighed. "No one ever knew. She ran away from home that summer. We never heard from her again."

"Did they question him? Was he even taken into custody?"

"Of course they did!" Evelyn said, exasperated. "I mean, I don't know for sure, but I'm certain they did. Moira had a difficult home life, her parents were Irish and the father drank. And a lot of kids ran away back then, you know that—all us little hippies. What did the letters say, Jeffrey?"

He removed then from his pocket and handed them to her. "You can read them. He never did—they all came back to Anthea. Where's Padwithiel?"

"Near Zennor. My aunt and uncle lived there, we went and stayed with them during our school holidays one spring." She sorted through the envelopes, pulled out one and opened it, unfolding the letter with care. "February twenty-first. This was right before we knew we'd be going there for the holidays. It was my idea. I remember when she wrote this—she got the address somehow, and that's how we realised he lived near my uncle's farm. Padwithiel."

She leaned into the lamp and read the first letter, set it down and continued to read each of the others. When she was finished, she placed the last one on the table, sank back into her chair and gazed at Jeffrey.

"She never told you about what happened."

"You just said that nothing happened."

"I don't mean with Robert. She called me every year on the anniversary. March 12." She looked away. "Next week, that is. I never told Chris. It wasn't a secret, we just—well, I'll just tell you.

"We went to school together, the three of us, and after Anthea sent that letter to Robert Bennington, she and I cooked up the idea of going to see him. Moira never read his books—she wasn't much of a reader. But she heard us talking about his books all the time, and we'd all play these games where we'd be the ones who fought the Sun Battles. She just did whatever we told her to, though for some reason she always wanted prisoners to be boiled in oil. She must've seen it in a movie.

"Even though we were older now, we still wanted to believe that magic could happen like in those books—probably we wanted to believe it even more. And all that New Agey, hippie stuff, Tarot cards and Biba and 'Ride a White Swan'—it all just seemed like it could be real. My aunt and uncle had a farm near Zennor, my mother asked if we three could stay there for the holidays and Aunt Becca said that would be fine. My cousins are older, and they were already off at university. So we took the train and Aunt Becca got us in Penzance.

"They were turning one of the outbuildings into a pottery studio for her, and that's where we stayed. There was no electricity yet, but we had a kerosene heater and we could stay up as late as we wanted. I think we got maybe five hours sleep the whole time we were there." She laughed. "We'd be up all night, but then Uncle Ray would start in with the tractors at dawn. We'd end up going into the house and napping in one of my cousin's beds for half the afternoon whenever we could. We were very grumpy houseguests.

"It rained the first few days we were there, just pissing down. Finally one morning we got up and the sun was shining. It was cold, but we didn't care—we were just so happy we could get outside for a while. At first we just walked along the road, but it was so muddy from all the rain that we ended up heading across the moor. Technically it's not really open moorland—there are old stone walls criss-crossing everything, ancient field systems. Some of them are thousands of years old, and farmers still keep them up and use them. These had not been kept up. The land was completely overgrown, though you could still see the walls and climb them. Which is what we did.

"We weren't that far from the house—we could still see it, and I'm pretty sure we were still on my uncle's land. We found a place where the walls were higher than elsewhere, more like proper hedgerows. There was no break in the wall like there usually is, no gate or old entryway. So we found a spot that was relatively untangled and we all climbed up and then jumped to the other side. The walls were completely overgrown with blackthorn and all these viney things. It was like Sleeping Beauty's castle—the thorns hurt like shit. I remember I was wearing new boots and they got ruined, just scratched everywhere. And Moira tore her jacket and we knew she'd catch grief for that. But we thought there must be something wonderful on the other side— that was the game we were playing, that we'd find some amazing place. Do you know *The Secret Garden*? We thought it might be like that. At least I did."

"And was it?"

Evelyn shook her head. "It wasn't a garden. It was just this big overgrown field. Dead grass and stones. But it was rather beautiful in a bleak way. Ant laughed and started yelling 'Heathcliff, Heathcliff!' And it was warmer—the walls were high enough to keep out the wind, and there were some trees that had grown up on top of the walls as well. They weren't in leaf yet, but they formed a bit of a windbreak.

"We ended up staying there all day. Completely lost track of the time. I thought only an hour had gone by, but Ant had a watch, at one point she said it was past three and I was shocked—I mean, really shocked. It was like we'd gone to sleep and woken up, only we weren't asleep at all."

"What were you doing?"

Evelyn shrugged. "Playing. The sort of let's-pretend game we always did when we were younger and hadn't done for a while. Moira had a boyfriend, Ant and I really *wanted* boyfriends—mostly that's what we talked about whenever we got together. But for some reason, that day Ant said 'Let's do Sun Battles,' and we all agreed. So that's what we did. Now of course I can see why—I've seen it with my own kids when they were that age, you're on the cusp of everything, and you just want to hold on to being young for as long as you can.

"I don't remember much of what we did that day, except how strange it all felt. As though something was about to happen. I felt like that a lot, it was all tied in with being a teenager; but this was different. It was like being high, or tripping, only none of us had ever done any drugs at that stage. And we were stone-cold sober. Really all we did was wander around the moor and clamber up and down the walls and hedgerows and among the trees, pretending we were in Gearnzath. That was the world in *The Sun Battles*—like Narnia, only much scarier. We were mostly just wandering around and making things up, until Ant told us it was after three o'clock.

"I think it was her idea that we should do some kind of ritual. I know it wouldn't have been Moira's, and I don't think it was mine. But I knew there was going to be a full moon that night—I'd heard my uncle mention it—and so we decided that we would each sacrifice a sacred thing, and then retrieved them all before moonrise. We turned our pockets inside-out looking for what we could use. I had a comb, so that was mine—just a red plastic thing, I think it cost ten pence. Ant had a locket on a chain from Woolworths, cheap but the locket part opened.

"And Moira had a pencil. It said RAVENWOOD on the side, so we called the field Ravenwood. We climbed up on the wall and stood facing the sun, and made up some sort of chant. I don't remember what we said. Then we tossed our things onto the moor. None of us threw them far, and Ant barely tossed hers—she didn't want to lose the locket. I didn't care about the comb, but it was so light it just fell a few yards from where we stood. Same with the pencil. We all marked where they fell—I remember mine very clearly, it came down right on top of this big flat stone.

"Then we left. It was getting late, and cold, and we were all starving—we'd had nothing to eat since breakfast. We went back to the house and hung out in the barn for a while, and then we had dinner. We didn't talk much. Moira hid her jacket so they couldn't see she'd torn it, and I took my boots off so no one would see how I'd got them all mauled by the thorns. I remember my aunt wondering if we were up to something, and my uncle saying what the hell could we possibly be up to in Zennor? After dinner we sat in the living room and waited for the sun to go down, and when we saw the moon start to rise above the hills, we went back outside.

"It was bright enough that we could find our way without a torch—a flashlight. I think that must have been one of the rules, that we had to retrieve our things by moonlight. It was cold out, and none of us had dressed very warmly, so we ran. It didn't take long. We climbed back over the wall and then down onto the field, at the exact spot where we'd thrown our things.

"They weren't there. I knew exactly where the rock was where my comb had landed—the rock was there, but not the comb. Ant's locket had landed only a few feet past it, and it wasn't there either. And Moira's pencil was gone, too."

"The wind could have moved them," said Jeffrey. "Or an animal."

"Maybe the wind," said Evelyn. "Though the whole reason we'd stayed there all day was that there was no wind—it was protected, and warm."

"Maybe a bird took it? Don't some birds like shiny things?"

"What would a bird do with a pencil? Or a plastic comb?"

Jeffrey made a face. "Probably you just didn't see where they fell. You thought you did, in daylight, but everything looks different at night. Especially in moonlight."

"I knew where they were." Evelyn shook her head and reached for the bottle of Armagnac. "Especially my comb. I have that engineer's eye, I can look at things and keep a very precise picture in my mind. The comb wasn't where it should have been. And there was no reason for it to be gone, unless . . ."

"Unless some other kids had seen you and found everything after you left," said Jeffrey.

"No." Evelyn sipped her drink. "We started looking. The moon was coming up—it rose above the hill, and it was very bright. Because it was so cold there was hoarfrost on the grass, and ice in places where the rain had frozen. So all that reflected the moonlight. Everything glittered. It was beautiful, but it was no longer fun—it was scary. None of us was even talking; we just split up and crisscrossed the field, looking for our things.

"And then Moira said, 'There's someone there,' and pointed. I thought it was someone on the track that led back to the farmhouse—it's not a proper road, just a rutted path that runs alongside one edge of that old field system. I looked up and yes, there were three people there—three torches, anyway. Flashlights. You couldn't see who was carrying them, but they were walking slowly along the path. I thought maybe it was my uncle and two of the men who worked with him, coming to tell us it was time to go home. They were walking from the wrong direction, across the moor, but I thought maybe they'd gone out to work on something. So I ran to the left edge of the field and climbed up on the wall."

She stopped, glancing out the window at the black garden, and finally turned back. "I could see the three lights from there," she said. "But the angle was all wrong. They weren't on the road at all—they were in the next field, up above Ravenwood. And they weren't flashlights. They were high up in the air, like this—"

She set down her glass and got to her feet, a bit unsteadily, extended both her arms and mimed holding something in her hands. "Like someone was carrying a pole eight or ten feet high, and there was a light on top of it. Not a flame. Like a ball of light . . ."

She cupped her hands around an invisible globe the size of a soccer ball. "Like that. White light, sort of foggy. The lights bobbed as they were walking."

"Did you see who it was?"

"No. We couldn't see anything. And, this is the part that I can't explain—it just felt bad. Like, horrible. Terrifying."

"You thought you'd summoned up whatever it was you'd been playing at." Jeffrey nodded sympathetically and finished his drink. "It was just marsh gas, Ev. You know that. Will-o'-the-wisp, or whatever you call it here. They must get it all the time out there in the country. Or fog. Or someone just out walking in the moonlight."

Evelyn settled back into her armchair. "It wasn't," she said. "I've seen marsh gas. There was no fog. The moon was so bright you could see every single rock in that field. Whatever it was, we all saw it. And you couldn't hear anything—there were no voices, no footsteps, nothing. They were just there, moving closer to us—slowly," she repeated, and moved her hand up and down, as though calming a cranky child. "That was the creepiest thing, how slowly they just kept coming."

"Why didn't you just run?"

"Because we couldn't. You know how kids will all know about something horrible, but they'll never tell a grown-up? It was like that. We knew we had to find our things before we could go.

"I found my comb first. It was way over—maybe twenty feet from where I'd seen it fall. I grabbed it and began to run across the turf, looking for the locket and Moira's pencil. The whole time the moon was rising, and that was horrible too—it was a beautiful clear night, no clouds at all. And the moon was so beautiful, but it just terrified me. I can't explain it."

Jeffrey smiled wryly. "Yeah? How about this: three thirteen-year-old girls in the dark under a full moon, with a very active imagination?"

"Hush. A few minutes later Moira yelled: she'd found her pencil. She turned and started running back toward the wall, I screamed after her that she had to help us find the locket. She wouldn't come back. She didn't go over the wall without us, but she wouldn't help. I ran over to Ant but she yelled at me to keep searching where I was. I did, I even started heading for the far end of the field, toward the other wall—where the lights were.

"They were very close now, close to the far wall, I mean. You could see how high up they were, taller than a person. I could hear Moira crying, I looked back and suddenly I saw Ant dive to the ground. She screamed 'I found it!' and I could see the chain shining in her hand.

"And we just turned and hightailed it. I've never run so fast in my life. I grabbed Ant's arm, by the time we got to the wall Moira was already on top and jumping down the other side. I fell and Ant had to help me up, Moira grabbed her and we ran all the way back to the farm and locked the door when we got inside.

"We looked out the window and the lights were still there. They were there for hours. My uncle had a border collie, we cracked the door to see if she'd hear something and bark but she didn't. She wouldn't go outside—we tried to get her to look and she wouldn't budge."

"Did you tell your aunt and uncle?"

Evelyn shook her head. "No. We stayed in the house that night, in my cousin's room. It overlooked the moor, so we could watch the lights. After about two hours they began to move back the way they'd come—slowly, it was about another hour before they were gone completely. We went out next morning to see if there was anything there—we took the dog to protect us."

"And?"

"There was nothing. The grass was all beat down, as though someone had been walking over it, but probably that was just us."

She fell silent. "Well," Jeffrey said after a long moment. "It's certainly a good story."

"It's a true story. Here, wait."

She stood and went into the other room, and Jeffrey heard her go upstairs. He crossed to the window and stared out into the night, the dark garden occluded by shadow and runnels of mist, blueish in the dim light cast from the solarium.

"Look. I still have it."

He turned to see Evelyn holding a small round tin. She withdrew a small object and stared at it, placed it back inside and handed him the tin. "My comb. There's some pictures here too."

"That tin." He stared at the lid, blue enamel with the words ST. AUSTELL SWEETS: FUDGE FROM REAL CORNISH CREAM stamped in gold above the silhouette of what looked like a lighthouse beacon. "It's just like the one I found, with Anthea's letters in it."

Evelyn nodded. "That's right. Becca gave one to each of us the day we arrived. The fudge was supposed to last the entire two weeks, and I think we ate it all that first night."

He opened the tin and gazed at a bright-red plastic comb sitting atop several snapshots; dug into his pocket and pulled out Anthea's locket.

"There it is," said Evelyn wonderingly. She took the locket and dangled it in front of her, clicked it open and shut then returned it to Jeffrey. "She never had anything in it that I knew. Here, look at these."

She took back the tin. He sat, waiting as she sorted through the snapshots then passed him six small black-and-white photos, each time-stamped OCTOBER 1971.

"That was my camera. A Brownie." Evelyn sank back into the armchair. "I didn't finish shooting the roll till we went back to school."

There were two girls in most of the photos. One was Anthea, apple-cheeked, her face still rounded with puppy fat and her brown hair longer than he'd ever seen it; eyebrows unplucked, wearing baggy bell-bottom jeans and a white peasant shirt. The other girl was taller, sturdy but long-limbed, with long straight blonde hair and a broad smooth forehead, elongated eyes and a wide mouth bared in a grin.

"That's Moira," said Evelyn.

"She's beautiful."

"She was. We were the ugly ducklings, Ant and me. Fortunately I was taking most of the photos, so you don't see me except in the ones Aunt Becca took."

"You were adorable." Jeffrey flipped to a photo of all three girls laughing and feeding each other something with their hands, Evelyn still in braces, her hair cut in a severe black bob. "You were all adorable. She's just—"

He scrutinised a photo of Moira by herself, slightly out of focus so all you saw was a blurred wave of blonde hair and her smile, a flash of narrowed eyes. "She's beautiful. Photogenic."

Evelyn laughed. "Is that what you call it? No, Moira was very pretty, all the boys liked her. But she was a tomboy like us. Ant was the one who was boy-crazy. Me and Moira, not so much."

"What about when you saw Robert Bennington? When was that?"

"The next day. Nothing happened—I mean, he was very nice, but there was nothing strange like that night. Nothing *untoward*," she added, lips pursed. "My aunt knew who he was—she didn't know him except to say hello to at the post office, and she'd never read his books. But she knew he was the children's writer, and she knew which house was supposed to be his. We told her we were going to see him, she told us to be polite and not be a nuisance and not stay long.

"So we were polite and not nuisances, and we stayed for two hours. Maybe three. We trekked over to his house, and that took almost an hour. A big old stone house. There was a standing stone and an old barrow nearby, it looked like a hayrick. A fogou. He was very proud that there was a fogou on his land—like a cave, but man-made. He said it was three thousand years old. He took us out to see it, and then we walked back to his house and he made us Nutella sandwiches and tangerines and Orange Squash. We just walked up to his door and knocked—*I* knocked, Ant was too nervous and Moira was just embarrassed. Ant and I had our copies of *The Second Sun*, and he was very sweet and invited us in and said he'd sign them before we left."

"Oh, sure—'Come up and see my fogou, girls'."

"No—he wanted us to see it because it gave him an idea for his book. It was like a portal, he said. He wasn't a dirty old man, Jeffrey! He wasn't even that old—maybe forty? He had long hair, longish, anyway—to his shoulders—and he had cool clothes, an embroidered shirt and corduroy flares. And pointy-toed boots—blue boot, bright sky-blue, very pointy toes. That was the only thing about him I thought was odd. I wondered how his toes fit into them—if he had long pointy toes to go along with the shoes." She laughed. "Really, he was very charming, talked to us about the books but wouldn't reveal any secrets—he said there would be another in the series but it never appeared. He signed our books—well, he signed mine, Moira didn't have one and for some reason he forgot Ant's. And eventually we left."

"Did you tell him about the lights?"

"We did. He said he'd heard of things like that happening before. That part of Cornwall is ancient, there are all kinds of stone circles and menhirs, cromlechs, things like that."

"What's a cromlech?"

"You know—a dolmen." At Jeffrey's frown she picked up several of the snapshots and arranged them on the side table, a simple house of cards: three photos supporting a fourth laid atop them. "Like that. It's a kind of prehistoric grave, made of big flat stones. Stonehenge, only small. The fogou was a bit like that. They're all over West Penwith—that's where Zennor is. Alaister Crowley lived there, and D.H. Lawrence and his wife. That was years before Robert's time, but he said there were always stories about odd things happening. I don't know what kind of things—it was always pretty boring when I visited as a girl, except for that one time."

Jeffrey made a face. "He was out there with a flashlight, Ev, leading you girls on."

"He didn't even know we were there!" protested Evelyn, so vehemently that the makeshift house of photos collapsed. "He looked genuinely startled when we knocked on his door—I was afraid he'd yell at us to leave. Or, I don't know, have us arrested. He said that field had a name. It was a funny word, Cornish. It meant something, though of course I don't remember what."

She stopped and leaned toward Jeffrey. "Why do you care about this, Jeffrey? *Did* Anthea say something?"

"No. I just found those letters, and . . ."

He lay his hands atop his knees, turned to stare past Evelyn into the darkness, so that she wouldn't see his eyes welling. "I just wanted to know. And I can't ask her."

Evelyn sighed. "Well, there's nothing to know, except what I told you. We went back once more—we took torches this time, and walking sticks and the dog. We stayed out till 3:00 a.m. Nothing happened except we caught hell from my aunt and uncle because they heard the dog barking and looked in the barn and we were gone.

"And that was the end of it. I still have the book he signed for me. Ant must have kept her copy—she was always mad he didn't sign it."

"I don't know. Maybe. I couldn't find it. Your friend Moira, you're not in touch with her?"

Evelyn shook her head. "I told you, she disappeared—she ran away that summer. There were problems at home, the father was a drunk and maybe the mother, too. We never went over there—it wasn't a welcoming place. She had an older sister but I never knew her. Look, if you're thinking Robert Bennington killed her, that's ridiculous. I'm sure her name came up during the trial, if anything had happened we would have heard about it. An investigation."

"Did you tell them about Moira?"

"Of course not. Look, Jeffrey—I think you should forget about all that. It's nothing to do with you, and it was all a long time ago. Ant never cared about it—I told her about the trial, I'd read about it in *The Guardian*, but she was even less curious about it than I was. I don't even know if Robert Bennington is still alive. He'd be an old man now."

She leaned over to take his hand. "I can see you're tired, Jeffrey. This has all been so awful for you, you must be totally exhausted. Do you want to just stay here for a few days? Or come back after your meeting in London?"

"No—I mean, probably not. Probably I need to get back to Brooklyn. I have some projects I backburnered, I need to get to them in the next few weeks. I'm sorry, Ev."

He rubbed his eyes and stood. "I didn't mean to hammer you about this stuff. You're right—I'm just beat. All this—" He sorted the snapshots into a small stack, and asked, "Could I have one of these? It doesn't matter which one."

"Of course. Whichever, take your pick."

He chose a photo of the three girls, Moira and Evelyn doubled over laughing as Anthea stared at them, smiling and slightly puzzled.

"Thank you, Ev," he said. He replaced each of Anthea's letters into its envelope, slid the photo into the last one, then stared at the sheaf in his hand, as though wondering how it got there. "It's just, I dunno. Meaningless, I guess; but I want it to mean something. I want *something* to mean something."

"Anthea meant something." Evelyn stood and put her arms around him. "Your life together meant something. And your life now means something."

"I know." He kissed the top of her head. "I keep telling myself that."

Evelyn dropped him off at the station next morning. He felt guilty, lying that he had meetings back in London, but he sensed both her relief and regret that he was leaving.

"I'm sorry about last night," he said as Evelyn turned into the parking lot. "I feel like the Bad Fairy at the christening, bringing up all that stuff."

"No, it was interesting." Evelyn squinted into the sun. "I hadn't thought about any of that for awhile. Not since Ant called me last March."

Jeffrey hesitated, then asked, "What do you think happened? I mean, you're the one with the advanced degree in structural engineering."

Evelyn laughed. "Yeah. And see where it's got me. I have no idea, Jeffrey. If you ask me, logically, what do I think? Well, I think it's just one of those things that we'll never know what happened. Maybe two different dimensions overlapped—in superstring theory, something like that is theoretically possible, a sort of duality."

She shook her head. "I know it's crazy. Probably it's just one of those things that don't make any sense and never will. Like how did Bush stay in office for so long?"

"That I could explain." Jeffrey smiled. "But it's depressing and would take too long. Thanks again, Ev."

They hopped out of the car and hugged on the curb. "You should come back soon," said Ev, wiping her eyes. "This is stupid, that it took so long for us all to get together again."

"I know. I will—soon, I promise. And you and Chris, come to New York. Once I have a place, it would be great."

He watched her drive off, waving as she turned back onto the main road; went into the station and walked to a ticket window.

"Can I get to Penzance from here?"

"What time?"

"Now."

The station agent looked at her computer. "There's a train in about half-an-hour. Change trains in Plymouth, arrive at Penzance a little before four."

He bought a first-class, one-way ticket to Penzance, found a seat in the waiting area, took out his phone and looked online for a place to stay near Zennor. There wasn't much—a few farmhouses designed for summer rentals, all still closed for the winter. An inn that had in recent years been turned into a popular gastropub was open; but even now, the first week of March, they were fully booked. Finally he came upon a B&B called Cliff Cottage. There were only two rooms, and the official opening date was not until the following weekend, but he called anyway.

"A room?" The woman who answered sounded tired but friendly. "We're not really ready yet, we've been doing some renovations and—"

"All I need is a bed," Jeffrey broke in. He took a deep breath. "The truth is, my wife died recently. I just need some time to be away from the rest of the world and . . ."

His voice trailed off. He felt a pang of self-loathing, playing the pity card; listened to a long silence on the line before the woman said, "Oh, dear, I'm so sorry. Well, yes, if you don't mind that we're really not up and running. The grout's not even dry yet in the new bath. Do you have a good head for heights?"

"Heights?"

"Yes. Vertigo? Some people have a very hard time with the driveway. There's a two night minimum for a stay."

Jeffrey assured her he'd never had any issues with vertigo. He gave her his credit card info, rang off and called to reserve a car in Penzance.

He slept most of the way to Plymouth, exhausted and faintly hungover. The train from Plymouth to Penzance was nearly empty. He bought a beer and a sandwich in the buffet car, and went to his seat. He'd bought a novel in London at Waterstones, but instead of reading gazed out at a landscape that was a dream of books he'd read as a child—granite farmhouses, woolly-coated ponies in stone paddocks; fields improbably green against lowering grey sky, graphite clouds broken by blades of golden sun, a rainbow that pierced a thunderhead then faded as though erased by some unseen hand. Ringnecked pheasants, a running fox. More fields planted with something that shone a startling goldfinch-yellow. A silvery coastline hemmed by arches of russet stone. Children wrestling in the middle of an empty road. A woman walking with head bowed against the wind, hands extended before her like a diviner.

Abandoned mineshafts and slagheaps; ruins glimpsed in an eye-flash before the train dove into a tunnel; black birds wheeling above a dun-coloured tor surrounded by scorched heath.

And, again and again, groves of gnarled oaks that underscored the absence of great forests in a landscape that had been scoured of trees thousands of years ago. It was beautiful yet also slightly disturbing, like watching an underpopulated, narratively fractured silent movie that played across the train window.

The trees were what most unsettled Jeffrey: the thought that men had so thoroughly occupied this countryside for so long that they had flensed it of everything—rocks, trees, shrubs all put to some human use so that only the abraded land remained. He felt relieved when the train at last reached Penzance, with the beachfront promenade to one side, glassy waves breaking on the sand and the dark towers of St. Michael's Mount suspended between aquamarine water and pearly sky.

He grabbed his bag and walked through the station, outside to where people waited on the curb with luggage or headed to the parking lot. The clouds had lifted: a chill steady wind blew from off the water, bringing the smell of salt and sea wrack. He shivered and pulled on his wool overcoat, looking around for the vehicle from the rental car company that was supposed to meet him.

He finally spotted it, a small white sedan parked along the sidewalk. A man in a dark blazer leaned against the car, smoking and talking to a teenage boy with dreadlocks and rainbow-knit cap and a woman with matted dark-blonde hair.

"You my ride?" Jeffrey said, smiling.

The man took a drag from his cigarette and passed it to the woman. She was older than Jeffrey had first thought, in her early thirties, face seamed and sun-weathered and her eyes bloodshot. She wore tight flared jeans and a fuzzy sky-blue sweater beneath a stained Arsenal windbreaker.

"Spare anything?" she said as he stopped alongside the car. She reeked of sweat and marijuana smoke.

"Go on now, Erthy," the man said, scowling. He turned to Jeffrey. "Mr. Kearin?"

"That's me," said Jeffrey.

"Gotta 'nother rollie, Evan?" the woman prodded.

"Come on, Erthy," said the rainbow-hatted boy. He spun and began walking toward the station. "Peace, Evan."

"I apologise for that," Evan said as he opened the passenger door for Jeffrey. "I know the boy, his family's neighbours of my sister's."

"Bit old for him, isn't she?" Jeffrey glanced to where the two huddled against the station wall, smoke welling from their cupped hands.

"Yeah, Erthy's a tough nut. She used to sleep rough by the St. Erth train station. Only this last winter she's taken up in Penzance. Every summer we get the smackhead hippies here, there's always some poor souls who stay and take up on the street. Not that you want to hear about that," he added, laughing as he swung into the driver's seat. "On vacation?"

Jeffrey nodded. "Just a few days."

"Staying here in Penzance?"

"Cardu. Near Zennor."

"Might see some sun, but probably not till the weekend."

He ended up with the same small white sedan. "Only one we have, this last minute," Evan said, tapping at the computer in the rental office. "But it's better really for driving out there in the countryside. Roads are extremely narrow. Have you driven around here before? No? I would strongly recommend the extra damages policy . . ."

It had been decades since Jeffrey had been behind the wheel of a car in the U.K. He began to sweat as soon as he left the rental car lot, eyes darting between the map Evan had given him and the GPS on his iPhone. In minutes the busy roundabout was behind him; the car crept up a narrow, winding hillside, with high stone walls to either side that swiftly gave way to hedgerows bordering open farmland. A brilliant yellow field proved to be planted with daffodils, their constricted yellow throats not yet in bloom. After several more minutes, he came to a crossroads.

Almost immediately he got lost. The distances between villages and roads were deceptive: what appeared on the map to be a mile or more instead contracted into a few hundred yards, or else expanded into a series of zigzags and switchbacks that appeared to point him back toward Penzance. The GPS directions made no sense, advising him to turn directly into stone walls or gated driveways or fields where cows grazed on young spring grass. The roads were only wide enough for one car to pass, with tiny turnouts every fifty feet or so where one could pull over, but the high hedgerows and labyrinthine turns made it difficult to spot oncoming vehicles.

His destination, a village called Cardu, was roughly seven miles from Penzance; after half an hour, the odometer registered that he'd gone fifteen miles, and he had no idea where he was. There was no cell phone reception. The sun dangled a hand's span above the western horizon, staining ragged stone outcroppings and a bleak expanse of moor an ominous reddish-bronze, and throwing the black fretwork of stone walls into stark relief. He finally parked in one of the narrow turnouts, sat for a few minutes staring into the sullen blood-red eye of the sun, and at last got out.

The hedgerows offered little protection from the harsh wind that raked across the moor. Jeffrey pulled at the collar of his wool coat, turning his back to the wind, and noticed a small sign that read PUBLIC FOOTPATH. He walked over and saw a narrow gap in the hedgerow, three steps formed of wide flat stones. He took the three in one long stride and found himself at the edge of an overgrown field, similar to what Evelyn had described in her account of the lights near Zennor. An ancient-looking stone wall bounded the far edge of the field, with a wider gap that opened to the next field and what looked like another sign. He squinted, but couldn't make out what it read, and began to pick his way across the turf.

It was treacherous going—the countless hummocks hid deep holes, and more than once he barely kept himself from wrenching his ankle. The air smelled strongly of raw earth and cow manure. As the sun dipped lower, a wedge of shadow was driven between him and the swiftly darkening sky, making it still more difficult to see his way. But after a few minutes he reached the far wall, and bent to read the sign beside the gap into the next field.

CAS CIRCLE

He glanced back, saw a glint of white where the rental car was parked, straightened and walked on.

There was a footpath here. Hardly a path, really; just a trail where turf and bracken had been flattened by the passage of not-many feet. He followed it, stopping when he came to a large upright stone that came up his waist. He looked to one side then the other and saw more stones, forming a group more ovoid than circular, perhaps thirty feet in diameter. He ran his hand across the first stone—rough granite, ridged with lichen and friable bits of moss that crumbled at his touch.

The reek of manure was fainter here: he could smell something fresh and sweet, like rain, and when he looked down saw a silvery gleam at the base of the rock. He crouched and dipped his fingers into a tiny pool, no bigger than his shoe. The water was icy cold, and even after he withdrew his hand, the surface trembled.

A spring. He dipped his cupped palm into it and sniffed warily, expecting a foetid whiff of cow muck.

But the water smelled clean, of rock and rain. Without thinking he drew his hand to his mouth and sipped, immediately flicked his fingers to send glinting droplets into the night.

That was stupid, he thought, hastily wiping his hand on his trousers. *Now I'll get dysentery. Or whatever one gets from cows.*

He stood there for another minute, then turned and retraced his steps to the rental car. He saw a pair of headlights approaching and flagged down a white delivery van.

"I'm lost," he said, and showed the driver the map that Evan had given him.

"Not too lost." The driver perused the map, then gave him directions. "Once you see the inn you're almost there."

Jeffrey thanked him, got back into the car and started to drive. In ten minutes he reached the inn, a rambling stucco structure with a half-dozen cars out front. There was no sign identifying Cardu, and no indication that there was anything more to the village than the inn and a deeply rutted road flanked by a handful of granite cottages in varying states of disrepair. He eased the rental car by the mottled grey buildings, to where what passed for a road ended; bore right and headed down a cobblestoned, hairpin drive that zigzagged along the cliff edge.

He could hear but could not see the ocean, waves crashing against rocks hundreds of feet below. Now and then he got a skin-crawling glimpse of immense cliffs like congealed flames—ruddy stone, apricot-yellow gorse, lurid flares of orange lichen all burned to ash as afterglow faded from the western sky.

He wrenched his gaze back to the narrow strip of road immediately in front of him. Gorse and brambles tore at the doors; once he bottomed out, then nosed the car across a water-filled gulley that widened into a stream that cascaded down the cliff to the sea below.

"Holy fucking Christ," he said, and kept the car in first gear. In another five minutes he was safely parked beside the cottage, alongside a small sedan.

"We thought maybe you weren't coming," someone called as Jeffrey stepped shakily out onto a cobblestone drive. Straggly rose-bushes grew between a row of granite slabs that resembled headstones. These were presumably to keep cars from veering down an incline that led to a ruined outbuilding, a few faint stars already framed in its gaping windows. "Some people, they start down here and just give up and turn back."

Jeffrey looked around, finally spotted a slight man in his early sixties standing in the doorway of a grey stone cottage tucked into the lee of the cliff. "Oh, hi. No, I made it."

Jeffrey ducked back into the car, grabbed his bag and headed for the cottage.

"Harry," the man said, and held the door for him.

"Jeffrey. I spoke to your wife this afternoon."

The man's brow furrowed. "Wife?" He was a head shorter than Jeffrey, clean-shaven, with a sun-weathered face and sleek grey-flecked dark brown hair to his shoulders. A ropey old cable knit sweater hung from his lank frame.

"Well, someone. A woman."

"Oh. That was Thomsa. My sister." The man nodded, as though this confusion had never occurred before. "We're still trying to get unpacked. We don't really open till this weekend, but . . ."

He held the door so Jeffrey could pass inside. "Thomsa told me of your loss. My condolences."

Inside was a small room with slate floors and plastered walls, sparely furnished with a plain deal table and four chairs intricately carved with Celtic knots; a sideboard holding books and maps and artfully mismatched crockery; large gas cooking stove and a side table covered with notepads and pens, unopened bills, and a laptop. A modern cast-iron woodstove had been fitted into a wide, old-fashioned hearth. The stove radiated warmth and an acrid, not unpleasant scent, redolent of coal smoke and burning sage. Peat, Jeffrey realised with surprise. There was a closed door on the other side of the room, and from behind this came the sound of a television. Harry looked at Jeffrey, cocking an eyebrow.

"It's beautiful," said Jeffrey.

Harry nodded. "I'll take you to your room," he said.

Jeffrey followed him up a narrow stair beneath the eaves, into a short hallway flanked by two doors. "Your room's here. Bath's down there, you'll have it all to yourself. What time would you like breakfast?"

"Seven, maybe?"

"How about seven-thirty?"

Jeffrey smiled wanly. "Sure."

The room was small, white plaster walls and a window seat overlooking the sea, a big bed heaped with a white duvet and myriad pillows, corner wardrobe carved with the same Celtic knots as the chairs below. No TV or radio or telephone, not even a clock. Jeffrey unpacked his bag and checked his phone for service: none.

He closed the wardrobe, looked in his backpack and swore. He'd left his book on the train. He ran a hand through his hair, stepped to the window-seat and stared out.

It was too dark now to see much, though light from windows on the floor below illuminated a small, winding patch of garden, bound at the cliffside by a stone wall. Beyond that there was only rock and, far below, the sea. Waves thundered against the unseen shore, a muted roar like a jet turbine. He could feel the house around him shake.

And not just the house, he thought; it felt as though the ground and everything around him trembled without ceasing. He paced to the other window, overlooking the drive, and stared at his rental car and the sedan beside it through a freize of branches, a tree so contorted by wind and salt that its limbs only grew in one direction. He turned off the room's single light, waited for his eyes to adjust; stared back out through one window, and then the other.

For as far as he could see, there was only night. Ghostly light seeped from a room downstairs onto the sliver of lawn. Starlight touched on the endless sweep of moor, like another sea unrolling from the line of cliffs brooding above black waves and distant headlands. There was no sign of human habitation: no distant lights, no street-lamps, no cars, no ships or lighthouse beacons: nothing.

He sank onto the window seat, dread knotting his chest. He had never seen anything like this—even hiking in the Mojave Desert with Anthea ten years earlier, there had been a scattering of lights sifted across the horizon and satellites moving slowly through the constellations. He grabbed his phone, fighting a cold black solitary horror. There was still no reception.

He put the phone aside and stared at a framed sepia-tinted photograph on the wall: a three-masted schooner wrecked on the rocks beneath a cliff he suspected was the same one where the cottage stood. Why was he even here? He felt as he had once in college, waking in a strange room after a night of heavy drinking, surrounded by people he didn't know in a squalid flat used as a shooting gallery. The same sense that he'd been engaged in some kind of psychic somnambulism, walking perilously close to a precipice.

Here, of course he actually *was* perched on the edge of a precipice. He stood and went into the hall, switching on the light; walked into the bathroom and turned on all the lights there as well.

It was almost as large as his bedroom, cheerfully appointed with yellow and blue towels piled atop a wooden chair, a massive porcelain tub, hand-woven yellow rugs and a fistful of daffodils in a cobalt glass vase on a wide windowsill. He moved the towels and sat on the chair for a few minutes, then crossed to pick up the vase and drew it to his face.

The daffodils smelled sweetly, of overturned earth warming in the sunlight. Anthea had loved daffodils, planting a hundred new bulbs every autumn; daffodils and jonquil and narcissus and crocuses, all the harbingers of spring. He inhaled again, deeply, and replaced the flowers on the sill. He left a light on beside the sink, returned to his room and went to bed.

⁊ᖯᏻ

He woke before seven. Thin sunlight filtered through the white curtains he'd drawn the night before, and for several minutes he lay in bed, listening to the rhythmic boom of surf on the rocks. He finally got up, pulled aside the curtain and looked out.

A line of clouds hung above the western horizon, but over the headland the sky was pale blue, shot with gold where the sun rose above the moor. Hundreds of feet below Jeffrey's bedroom, aquamarine swells crashed against the base of the cliffs and swirled around ragged granite pinnacles that rose from the sea, surrounded by clouds of white seabirds. There was a crescent of white sand, and a black cavern-mouth gouged into one of the cliffs where a vortex rose and subsided with the waves.

The memory of last night's horror faded: sunlight and wheeling birds, the vast expanse of air and sea and all but treeless moor made him feel exhilarated. For the first time since Anthea's death, he had a premonition not of dread but of the sort of exultation he felt as a teenager, waking in his boyhood room in early spring.

He dressed and shaved—there was no shower, only that dinghy-sized tub, so he'd forgo bathing till later. He waited until he was certain he heard movement in the kitchen, and went downstairs.

"Good morning." A woman who might have been Harry's twin leaned against the slate sink. Slender, small-boned, with straight dark hair held back with two combs from a narrow face, brown-eyed and weathered as her brother's. "I'm Thomsa."

He shook her hand, glanced around for signs of coffee then peered out the window. "This is an amazing place."

"Yes, it is," Thomsa said evenly. She spooned coffee into a glass cafetière, picked up a steaming kettle and poured hot water over the grounds. "Coffee, right? I have tea if you prefer. Would you like eggs? Some people have all sorts of food allergies. Vegans, how do you feed them?" She stared at him in consternation, turned back to the sink, glancing at a bowl of eggs. "How many?"

The cottage was silent, save for the drone of a television behind the closed door and the thunder of waves beating against the cliffs.

Jeffrey sat at a table set for one, poured himself coffee and stared out to where the moor rose behind them. "Does the sound of the ocean ever bother you?" he asked.

Thomsa laughed. "No. We've been here thirty-five years, we're used to that. But we're building a house in Greece, in Hydra, that's where we just returned from. There's a church in the village and every afternoon the bells ring, I don't know why. At first I thought, isn't that lovely, church bells! Now I'm sick of them and just wish they'd just shut up."

She set a plate of fried eggs and thick-cut bacon in front of him, along with slabs of toasted brown bread and glass bowls of preserves, picked up a mug and settled at the table. "So are you here on holiday?"

"Mmm, yes." Jeffrey nodded, his mouth full. "My wife died last fall. I just needed to get away for a bit."

"Yes, of course. I'm very sorry."

"She visited here once when she was a girl—not here, but at a farm nearby, in Zennor. I don't know the last name of the family, but the woman was named Becca."

"Becca? Mmm, no, I don't think so. Maybe Harry will know."

"This would have been 1971."

"Ah—no, we didn't move here till '75. Summer, us and all the other hippie types from back then." She sipped her tea. "No tourists around this time of year. Usually we don't open till the second week in March. But we don't have anyone scheduled yet, so." She shrugged, pushing back a wisp of dark hair. "It's quiet this time of year. No German tour buses. Do you paint?"

"Paint?" Jeffrey blinked. "No. I'm an architect, so I draw, but mostly just for work. I sketch sometimes."

"We get a lot of artists. There's the Tate in St. Ives, if you like modern architecture. And of course there are all the prehistoric ruins—standing stones, and Zennor Quoit. There are all sorts of legends about them, fairy tales. People disappearing. They're very interesting if you don't mind the walk.

"Are there places to eat?"

"The inn here, though you might want to stop in and make a booking. There's the pub in Zennor, and St. Ives of course, though it can be hard to park. And Penzance."

Jeffrey winced. "Not sure I want to get back on the road again immediately."

"Yes, the drive here's a bit tricky, isn't it? But Zennor's only two miles, if you don't mind walking—lots of people do, we get hikers from all over on the coastal footpath. And Harry might be going out later, he could drop you off in Zennor if you like."

"Thanks. Not sure what I'll do yet. But thank you."

He ate his breakfast, making small talk with Thomsa and nodding at Harry when he emerged and darted through the kitchen, raising a hand as he slipped outside. Minutes later, Jeffrey glimpsed him pushing a wheelbarrow full of gardening equipment.

"I think the rain's supposed to hold off," Thomsa said, staring out the window. "I hope so. We want to finish that wall. Would you like me to make more coffee?"

"If you don't mind."

Jeffrey dabbed a crust into the blackcurrant preserves. He wanted to ask if Thomsa or her brother knew Robert Bennington, but was afraid he might be stirring up memories of some local scandal, or that he'd be taken for a journalist or some other busybody. He finished the toast, thanked Thomsa when she poured him more coffee, then reached for one of the brochures on the sideboard.

"So does this show where those ruins are?"

"Yes. You'll want the ordnance map. Here—"

She cleared the dishes, gathered a map and unfolded it. She tapped the outline of a tiny cove between two spurs of land. "We're here."

She traced one of the spurs, lifted her head to stare out the window to a grey-green spine of rock stretching directly to the south. "That's Gurnard's Head. And there's Zennor Head—"

She turned and pointed in the opposite direction, to a looming promontory a few miles distant, and looked back down at the map. "You can see where everything's marked."

Jeffrey squinted to make out words printed in a tiny, Gothic font. TUMULI, STANDING STONE, HUT CIRCLE, CAIRN. "Is there a fogou around here?"

"A fogou?" She frowned slightly. "Yes, there is—out toward Zennor, across the moor. It's a bit of a walk."

"Could you give me directions? Just sort of point the way? I might try and find it—give me something to do."

Thomsa stepped to the window. "The coastal path is there—see? If you follow it up to the ridge, you'll see a trail veer off. There's an old road there, the farmers use it sometimes. All those old fields run alongside it. The fogou's on the Golovenna Farm, I don't know how many fields back that is. It would be faster if you drove toward Zennor then hiked over the moor, but you could probably do it from here. You'll have to find an opening in the stone walls or climb over—do you have hiking shoes?" She looked dubiously at his sneakers. "Well, they'll probably be all right."

"I'll give it a shot. Can I take that map?"

"Yes, of course. It's not the best map—the Ordnance Survey has a more detailed one, I think."

He thanked her and downed the rest of his coffee, went upstairs and pulled a heavy woollen sweater over his flannel shirt, grabbed his cell phone and returned downstairs. He retrieved the map and stuck it in his coat pocket, said goodbye to Thomsa rinsing dishes in the sink, and walked outside.

The air was warmer, almost balmy despite a stiff wind that had torn the line of clouds into grey shreds. Harry knelt beside a stone wall, poking at the ground with a small spade. Jeffrey paused to watch him, then turned to survey clusters of daffodils and jonquils, scores of them scattered across the terraced slopes among rocks and apple trees. The flowers were not yet in bloom, but he could glimpse sunlit yellow and orange and saffron petals swelling within the green buds atop each slender stalk.

"Going out?" Harry called.

"Yes." Jeffrey stooped to brush his fingers across one of the flowers. "My wife loved daffodils. She must have planted thousands of them."

Harry nodded. "Should open in the next few days. If we get some sun."

Jeffrey waved farewell and turned to walk up the drive.

In a few minutes, the cottage was lost to sight. The cobblestones briefly gave way to cracked concrete, then a deep rut that marked a makeshift path that led uphill, toward the half-dozen buildings that made up the village. He stayed on the driveway, and after another hundred feet reached a spot where a narrow footpath meandered off to the left, marked by a sign. This would be the path that Thomsa had pointed out.

He shaded his eyes and looked back. He could just make out Cliff Cottage, its windows a flare of gold in the sun. He stepped onto the trail, walking with care across loose stones and channels where water raced downhill, fed by the early spring rains. To one side, the land sheared away to cliffs and crashing waves; he could see where the coastal path wound along the headland, fading into the emerald crown of Zennor Head. Above him, the ground rose steeply, overgrown with coiled ferns, newly sprung grass, thickets of gorse in brilliant sun-yellow bloom where bees and tiny orange butterflies fed. At the top of the incline, he could see the dark rim of a line of stone walls. He stayed on the footpath until it began to bear toward the cliffs, then looked for a place where he could break away and make for the ancient fields. He saw what looked like a path left by some kind of animal and scrambled up, dodging gorse, his sneakers sliding on loose scree, until he reached the top of the headland.

The wind here was so strong he nearly lost his balance as he hopped down into a grassy lane. The lane ran parallel to a long ridge of stone walls perhaps four feet high, braided with strands of rusted barbed wire. On the other side, endless intersections of yet more walls divided the moor into a dizzyingly ragged patchwork: jade-green, beryl, creamy yellow; ochre and golden amber. Here and there, twisted trees grew within sheltered corners, or rose from atop the walls themselves, gnarled branches scraping at the sky. High overhead, a bird arrowed toward the sea, and its plaintive cry rose above the roar of wind in his ears.

He pulled out the map, struggling to open it in the wind, finally gave up and shoved it back into his pocket. He tried to count back four fields, but it was hopeless—he couldn't make out where one field ended and another began.

And he had no idea what field to start with. He walked alongside the lane, away from the cottage and the village of Cardu, hoping he might find a gate or opening. He finally settled on a spot where the barbed wire had become engulfed by a protective thatch of dead vegetation. He clambered over the rocks, clutching desperately at dried leaves as the wall gave way beneath his feet and nearly falling onto a lethal-looking knot of barbed wire. Gasping, he reached the top of the wall, flailed as wind buffeted him then crouched until he could catch his breath.

The top of the wall was covered with vines, grey and leafless, as thick as his fingers and unpleasantly reminiscent of veins and arteries. This serpentine mass seemed to hold the stones together, though when he tried to step down the other side, the rocks once again gave way and he fell into a patch of whip-like vines studded with thorns the length of his thumbnail. Cursing, he extricated himself, his chinos torn and hands gouged and bloody, and staggered into the field.

Here at least there was some protection from the wind. The field sloped slightly uphill, to the next wall. There was so sign of a gate or breach. He shoved his hands into his pockets and strode through knee-high grass, pale green and starred with minute yellow flowers. He reached the wall and walked alongside it. In one corner several large rocks had fallen. He hoisted himself up until he could see into the next field. It was no different from the one he'd just traversed, save for a single massive evergreen in its centre.

Other than the tree, the field seemed devoid of any vegetation larger than a tussock. He tried to peer into the field beyond, and the ones after that, but the countryside dissolved into a glitter of green and topaz beneath the morning sun, with a few stone pinnacles stark against the horizon where moor gave way to sky.

He turned and walked back, head down against the wind; climbed into the first field and crossed it, searching until he spied what looked like a safe place to gain access to the lane once more. Another tangle of blackthorn snagged him as he jumped down and landed hard, grimacing as a thorn tore at his neck. He glared at the wall, then headed back to the cottage, picking thorns from his overcoat and jeans.

He was starving by the time he arrived at the cottage, also filthy. It had grown too warm for his coat; he slung it over his shoulder, wiping sweat from his cheeks. Thomsa was outside, removing a shovel from the trunk of the sedan.

"Oh, hello! You're back quickly!"

He stopped, grateful for the wind on his overheated face. "Quickly?"

"I thought you'd be off till lunchtime. A few hours, anyway?"

"I thought it *was* lunchtime." He looked at his watch and frowned. "That can't be right. It's not even ten."

Thomsa nodded, setting the shovel beside the car. "I thought maybe you forgot something." She glanced at him, startled. "Oh my. You're bleeding—did you fall?"

He shook his head. "No, well, yes," he said sheepishly. "I tried to find that fogou. Didn't get very far. Are you sure it's just ten? I thought I was out there for hours—I figured it must be noon, at least. What time did I leave?"

"Half-past nine, I think."

He started to argue, instead shrugged. "I might try again. You said there's a better map from the Ordnance Survey? Something with more details?"

"Yes. You could probably get it in Penzance—call the bookstore there if you like, phone book's on the table."

He found the phone book in the kitchen and rang the bookshop. They had a copy of the Ordnance map and would hold it for him. He rummaged on the table for a brochure with a map of Penzance, went upstairs to spend a few minutes washing up from his trek, and hurried outside. Thomsa and Harry were lugging stones across the grass to repair the wall. Jeffrey waved, ducked into the rental car and crept back up the drive toward Cardu.

In broad daylight it still took almost ten minutes. He glanced out to where the coastal footpath wound across the top of the cliffs, could barely discern a darker trail leading to the old field systems, and, beyond that, the erratic cross-stitch of stone walls fading into the eastern sky. Even if he'd only gone as far as the second field, it seemed impossible that he could have hiked all the way there and back to the cottage in half-an-hour.

The drive to Penzance took less time than that; barely long enough for Jeffrey to reflect how unusual it was for him to act like this, impulsively, without a plan. Everything an architect did was according to plan. Out on the moor and gorse-grown cliffs, the strangeness of the immense, dour landscape had temporarily banished the near-constant presence of his dead wife. Now, in the confines of the cramped rental car, images of other vehicles and other trips returned, all with Anthea beside him. He pushed them away, tried to focus on the fact that here at last was a place where he'd managed to escape her; and remembered that was not true at all.

Anthea had been here, too. Not the Anthea he had loved but her mayfly self, the girl he'd never known; the Anthea who'd contained an entire secret world he'd never known existed. It seemed absurd, but he desperately wished she had confided in him about her visit to Bennington's house, and the strange night that had preceded it. Evelyn's talk of superstring theory was silly—he found himself sympathising with Moira, content to let someone else read the creepy books and tell her what to do. He believed in none of it, of course. Yet it didn't matter what he believed, but whether Anthea had, and why.

Penzance was surprisingly crowded for a weekday morning in early March. He circled the town's winding streets twice before he found a parking space, several blocks from the bookstore. He walked past shops and restaurants featuring variations on themes involving pirates, fish, pixies, sailing ships. As he passed a tattoo parlour, he glanced into the adjoining alley and saw the same rainbow-hatted boy from the train station, holding a skateboard and standing with several other teenagers who were passing around a joint. The boy looked up, saw Jeffrey and smiled. Jeffrey lifted his hand and smiled back. The boy called out to him, his words garbled by the wind, put down his skateboard and did a headstand alongside it. Jeffrey laughed and kept going.

There was only one other customer in the shop when he arrived, a man in a business suit talking to two women behind the register.

"Can I help you?" The older of the two women smiled. She had close-cropped red hair and fashionable eyeglasses, and set aside an iPad as Jeffrey approached.

"I called about an Ordnance map?"

"Yes. It's right here."

She handed it to him, and he unfolded it enough to see that it showed the same area of West Penwith as the other map, enlarged and far more detailed.

The woman with the glasses cocked her head. "Shall I ring that up?"

Jeffrey closed the map and set it onto the counter. "Sure, in a minute. I'm going to look around a bit first."

She returned to chatting. Jeffrey wandered the shop. It was small but crowded with neatly stacked shelves and tables, racks of maps and postcards, with an extensive section of books about Cornwall—guidebooks, tributes to Daphne du Maurier and Barbara Hepworth, DVDs of *The Pirates of Penzance* and *Rebecca*, histories of the mines and glossy photo volumes about surfing Newquay. He spent a few minutes flipping through one of these, and continued to the back of the store. There was an entire wall of children's books, picture books near the floor, chapter books for older children arranged alphabetically above them. He scanned the Bs, and looked aside as the younger woman approached, carrying an armful of calendars.

"Are you looking for something in particular?"

He glanced back at the shelves. "Do you have anything by Robert Bennington?"

The young woman set the calendars down, ran a hand along the shelf housing the Bs; frowned and looked back to the counter. "Rose, do we have anything by Robert Bennington? It rings a bell but I don't see anything here. Children's writer, is he?" she added, turning to Jeffrey.

"Yes. *The Sun Battles*, I think that's one of them."

The other customer nodded goodbye as Rose joined the others in the back.

"Robert Bennington?" She halted, straightening a stack of coffee-table books, tapped her lower lip then quickly nodded. "Oh yes! The fantasy writer. We did have his books—he's fallen out of favour." She cast a knowing look at the younger clerk. "He was the child molester."

"Oh, right." The younger woman made a face. "I don't think his books are even in print now, are they?"

"I don't think so," said Rose. "I'll check. We could order something for you, if they are."

"That's okay—I'm only here for a few days."

Jeffrey followed her to the counter and waited as she searched online.

"No, nothing's available." Rose shook her head. "Sad bit of business, wasn't it? I heard something recently, he had a stroke I think. He might even have died, I can't recall now who told me. He must be quite elderly, if he's still alive."

"He lived around here, didn't he?" said Jeffrey.

"Out near Zennor, I think. He bought the old Golovenna Farm, years ago. We used to sell quite a lot of his books—he was very popular. Like the *Harry Potter* books now. Well, not that popular." She smiled. "But he did very well. He came in here once or twice, it must be twenty years at least. A very handsome man. Theatrical. He wore a long scarf, like Doctor Who. I'm sure you could find used copies online, or there's a second-hand bookstore just round the corner—they might well have something."

"That's all right. But thank you for checking."

He paid for the map and went back out onto the sidewalk. It was getting on to noon. He wandered the streets for several minutes looking for a place to eat, settled on a small, airy Italian restaurant where he had grilled sardines and spaghetti and a glass of wine. Not very Cornish, perhaps, but he promised himself to check on the pub in Zennor later.

The Ordnance map was too large and unwieldy to open at his little table, so he stared out the window, watching tourists and women with small children in tow as they popped in and out of the shops across the street. The rainbow-hatted boy and his cronies loped by, skateboards in hand. Dropouts or burnouts, Jeffrey thought; the local constabulary must spend half its time chasing them from place to place. He finished his wine and ordered a cup of coffee, gulped it down, paid the check, and left.

A few high white clouds scudded high overhead, borne on a steady wind that sent up flurries of grit and petals blown from ornamental cherry trees. Here in the heart of Penzance, the midday sun was almost hot: Jeffrey hooked his coat over his shoulder and ambled back to his car. He paused to glance at postcards and souvenirs in a shop window, but could think of no one to send a card to. Evelyn? She'd rather have something from Zennor, another reason to visit the pub.

He turned the corner, had almost reached the tattoo parlour when a plaintive cry rang out.

"*Have you seen him?*"

Jeffrey halted. In the same alley where he'd glimpsed the boys earlier, a forlorn figure sat on the broken asphalt, twitchy fingers toying with an unlit cigarette. Erthy, the thirtyish woman who'd been at the station the day before. As Jeffrey hesitated she lifted her head, swiped a fringe of dirty hair from her eyes and stumbled to her feet. His heart sank as she hurried toward him, but before he could flee she was already in his face, her breath warm and beery. "Gotta light?"

"No, sorry," he said, and began to step away.

"Wait—you're London, right?"

"No, I'm just visiting."

"No—I saw you."

He paused, thrown off-balance by a ridiculous jolt of unease. Her eyes were bloodshot, the irises a peculiar marbled blue like flawed bottle-glass, and there was a vivid crimson splotch in one eye, as though a capillary had burst. It made it seem as though she looked at him sideways, even though she was staring at him straight on.

"You're on the London train!" She nodded in excitement. "I need to get back."

"I'm sorry." He spun and walked off as quickly as he could without breaking into a run. Behind him he heard footsteps, and again the same wrenching cry.

"Have you seen him?"

He did run then, as the woman screamed expletives and a shower of gravel pelted his back.

He reached his rental car, his heart pounding. He looked over his shoulder, jumped inside and locked the doors before pulling out into the street. As he drove off, he caught a flash in the rear-view mirror of the woman sidling in the other direction, unlit cigarette still twitching between her fingers.

When he arrived back at the cottage, he found Thomsa and Harry sitting at the kitchen table, surrounded by the remains of lunch, sandwich crusts and apple cores.

"Oh, hello." Thomsa looked up, smiling, and patted the chair beside her. "Did you go to The Tinners for lunch?"

"Penzance." Jeffrey sat and dropped his map onto the table. "I think I'll head out again, then maybe have dinner at the pub."

"He wants to see the fogou," said Thomsa. "He went earlier but couldn't find it. There is a fogou, isn't there, Harry? Out by Zennor Hill?"

Jeffrey hesitated, then said, "A friend of mine told me about it—she and my wife saw it when they were girls."

"Yes," said Harry after a moment. "Where the children's writer lived. Some sort of ruins there, anyway."

Jeffrey kept his tone casual. "A writer?"

"I believe so," said Thomsa. "We didn't know him. Someone who stayed here once went looking for him, but he wasn't home—this was years ago. The old Golovenna Farm."

Jeffrey pointed to the seemingly random network of lines that covered the map, like crazing on a piece of old pottery. "What's all this mean?"

Harry pulled his chair closer and traced the boundaries of Cardu with a dirt-stained finger. "Those are the field systems—the stone walls."

"You're kidding." Jeffrey laughed. "That must've driven someone nuts, getting all that down."

"Oh, it's all GPS and satellite photos now," said Thomsa. "I'm sorry I didn't have this map earlier, before you went for your walk."

"It'll be on this survey." Harry angled the map so the sunlight illuminated the area surrounding Cardu. "This is our cove, here . . ."

They pored over the ordnance survey. Jeffrey pointed at markers for hut circles and cairns, standing stones and tumuli, all within a hand's-span of Cardu, as Harry continued to shake his head.

"It's this one, I think," Harry said at last, and glanced at his sister. He scored a square half-inch of the page with a blackened fingernail, minute Gothic letters trapped within the web of field systems.

CHAMBERED CAIRN

"That looks right," said Thomsa. "But it's a ways off the road. I'm not certain where the house is—the woman who went looking for it said she roamed the moor for hours before she came on it."

Jeffrey ran his finger along the line marking the main road. "It looks like I can drive to here. If there's a place to park, I can just hike in. It doesn't look that far. As long as I don't get towed."

"You shouldn't get towed," said Thomsa. "All that land's part of Golovenna, and no one's there. He never farmed it, just let it all go back to the moor. You'd only be a mile or so from Zennor if you left your car. They have musicians on Thursday nights, some of the locals come in and play after dinner."

Jeffrey refolded the map. When he looked up, Harry was gone. Thomsa handed him an apple.

"Watch for the bogs," she said. "Marsh grass, it looks sturdy but when you put your foot down it gives way and you can sink under. Like quicksand. They found a girl's body ten years back. Horses and sheep, too." Jeffrey grimaced and she laughed. "You'll be all right— just stay on the footpaths."

He thanked her, went upstairs to exchange his overcoat for a windbreaker, and returned to his car. The clouds were gone: the sun shone high in a sky the summer blue of gentians. He felt the same surge of exultation he'd experienced that morning, the sea-fresh wind tangling the stems of daffodils and iris, white gulls crying overhead. He kept the window down as he drove up the twisting way to Cardu, and the honeyed scent of gorse filled the car.

The road to Zennor coiled between hedgerows misted green with new growth and emerald fields where brown-and-white cattle grazed. In the distance a single tractor moved so slowly across a black furrow that Jeffrey could track its progress only by the skein of crows that followed it, the birds dipping then rising like a black thread drawn through blue cloth.

Twice he pulled over to consult the map. His phone didn't work here—he couldn't even get the time, let alone directions. The car's clock read 14:21. He saw no other roads, only deeply rutted tracks protected by stiles, some metal, most of weathered wood. He tried counting stone walls to determine which marked the fields Harry had said belonged to Golovenna Farm, and stopped a third time before deciding the map was all but useless. He drove another hundred feet, until he found a swathe of gravel between two tumbledown stone walls, a rusted gate sagging between them. Beyond it stretched an overgrown field bisected by a stone-strewn path.

He was less than a mile from Zennor. He folded the map and jammed it into his windbreaker pocket along with the apple, and stepped out of the car.

The dark height before him would be Zennor Hill. Golovenna Farm was somewhere between there and where he stood. He turned slowly, scanning everything around him to fix it in his memory: the winding road, intermittently visible between walls and hedgerows; the ridge of cliffs falling down to the sea, book-ended by the dark bulk of Gurnards Head in the southwest and Zennor Head to the northeast. On the horizon were scattered outcroppings that might have been tors or ruins or even buildings. He locked the car, checked that he had his phone, climbed over the metal gate and began to walk.

The afternoon sun beat down fiercely. He wished he'd brought a hat, or sunglasses. He crossed the first field in a few minutes, and was relieved to find a break in the next wall, an opening formed by a pair of tall, broad stones. The path narrowed here, but was still clearly discernible where it bore straight in front of him, an arrow of new green grass flashing through ankle-high turf overgrown with daisies and fronds of young bracken.

The ground felt springy beneath his feet. He remembered Thomsa's warning about the bogs, and glanced around for something he might use as a walking stick. There were no trees in sight, only wicked-looking thickets of blackthorn clustered along the perimeter of the field.

He found another gap in the next wall, guarded like the first by two broad stones nearly as tall as he was. He clambered onto the wall, fighting to open his map in the brisk wind, and examined the survey, trying to find some affinity between the fields around him and the crazed pattern on the page. At last he shoved the map back into his pocket, set his back to the wind and shaded his eyes with his hand.

It was hard to see—he was staring due west, into the sun—but he thought he glimpsed a black bulge some three or four fields off, a dark blister within the haze of green and yellow. It might be a ruin, or just as likely a farm or outbuildings. He clambered down into the next field, crushing dead bracken and shoots of heather; picked his way through a breach where stones had fallen and hurried until he reached yet another wall.

There were the remnants of a gate here, a rusted latch and iron pins protruding from the granite. Jeffrey crouched beside the wall to catch his breath. After a few minutes he scrambled to his feet and walked through the gap, letting one hand rest for an instant upon the stone. Despite the hot afternoon sun it felt cold beneath his palm, more like metal than granite. He glanced aside to make sure he hadn't touched a bit of rusted hardware, but saw only a boulder seamed with moss.

The fields he'd already passed through had seemed rank and overgrown, as though claimed by the wilderness decades ago. Yet there was no mistaking what stretched before him as anything but open moor. Clumps of gorse sprang everywhere, starbursts of yellow blossom shadowing pale-green ferns and tufts of dogtooth violets. He walked cautiously—he couldn't see the earth underfoot for all the new growth—but the ground felt solid beneath mats of dead bracken that gave off a spicy October scent. He was so intent on watching his step that he nearly walked into a standing stone.

He sucked his breath in sharply and stumbled backward. For a fraction of a second he'd perceived a figure there, but it was only a stone, twice his height and leaning at a forty-five degree angle, so that it pointed toward the sea. He circled it, then ran his hand across its granite flank, sun-warmed and furred with lichen and dried moss. He kicked at the thatch of ferns and ivy that surrounded its base, stooped and dug his hand through the vegetation, until his fingers dug into raw earth.

He withdrew his hand and backed away, staring at the ancient monument, at once minatory and banal. He could recall no indication of a standing stone between Cardu and Zennor, and when he checked the map he saw nothing there.

But something else loomed up from the moor a short distance away—a house. He headed toward it, slowing his steps in case someone saw him, so that they might have time to come outside.

No one appeared. After five minutes he stood in a rutted drive beside a long, one-storey building of grey stone similar to those he'd passed on the main road; slate-roofed, with deep small windows and a wizened tree beside the door, its branches rattling in the wind. A worn hand-lettered sign hung beneath the low eaves: GOLOVENNA FARM.

Jeffrey looked around. He saw no car, only a large plastic trash bin that had blown over. He rapped at the door, waited then knocked again, calling out a greeting. When no one answered he tried the knob, but the door was locked.

He stepped away to peer in through the window. There were no curtains. Inside looked dark and empty, no furniture or signs that someone lived here, or indeed if anyone had for years. He walked round the house, stopping to look inside each window and half-heartedly trying to open them, without success. When he'd completed this circuit, he wandered over to the trash bin and looked inside. It too was empty.

He righted it, then stood and surveyed the land around him. The rutted path joined a narrow, rock-strewn drive that led off into the moor to the west. He saw what looked like another structure not far from where the two tracks joined, a collapsed building of some sort.

He headed towards it. A flock of little birds flittered from a gorse bush, making a sweet high-pitched song as they soared past him, close enough that he could see their rosy breasts and hear their wings beat against the wind. They settled on the ruined building, twittering companionably as he approached, then took flight once more.

It wasn't a building but a mound. Roughly rectangular but with rounded corners, maybe twenty feet long and half again as wide; as tall as he was, and so overgrown with ferns and blackthorn that he might have mistaken it for a hillock. He kicked through brambles and clinging thorns until he reached one end, where the mound's curve had been sheared off.

Erosion, he thought at first; then realised that he was gazing into an entryway. He glanced behind him before drawing closer, until he stood knee-deep in dried bracken and whip-like blackthorn.

In front of him was a simple doorway of upright stones, man-high, with a larger stone laid across the tops to form a lintel. Three more stones were set into the ground as steps, descending to a passage choked with young ferns and ivy mottled black and green as malachite.

Jeffrey ducked his head beneath the lintel and peered down into the tunnel. He could see nothing but vague outlines of more stones and straggling vines. He reached to thump the ceiling to see if anything moved.

Nothing did. He checked his phone—still no signal—turned to stare up into the sky. He'd left the car around 2:30, and he couldn't have been walking for more than an hour. Say it was four o'clock, to be safe. He still had a good hour and a half to get back to the road before dark.

He took out the apple Thomsa had given him and ate it, dropped the core beside the top step; zipped his windbreaker and descended into the passage.

He couldn't see how long it was, but he counted thirty paces, pausing every few steps to look back at the entrance, before the light faded enough that he needed to use his cell phone for illumination. The walls glittered faintly where broken crystals were embedded in the granite, and there was a moist, earthy smell, like a damp cellar. He could stand upright with his arms outstretched, his fingertips grazing the walls to either side. The vegetation disappeared after the first ten paces, except for moss, and after a few more steps there was nothing beneath his feet but bare earth. The walls were of stone, dirt packed between them and hardened by the centuries so that it was almost indistinguishable from the granite.

He kept going, glancing back as the entryway diminished to a bright mouth, then a glowing eye, and finally a hole no larger than that left by a finger thrust through a piece of black cloth.

A few steps more and even that was gone. He stopped, his breath coming faster, then walked another five paces, the glow from his cell phone a blue moth flickering in his hand. Once again he stopped to look back.

He could see nothing behind him. He shut off the cell phone's light, experimentally moved his hand swiftly up and down before his face; closed his eyes then opened them. There was no difference.

His mouth went dry. He turned his phone on, took a few more steps deeper into the passage before halting again. The phone's periwinkle glow was insubstantial as a breath of vapour: he could see neither the ground beneath him nor the walls to either side. He raised his arms and extended them, expecting to feel cold stone beneath his fingertips.

The walls were gone. He stepped backward, counting five paces, and again extended his arms. Still nothing. He dropped his hands and began to walk forward, counting each step—five, six, seven, ten, thirteen—stopped and slowly turned in a circle, holding the phone at arm's-length as he strove to discern some feature in the encroaching darkness. The pallid blue gleam flared then went out.

He swore furiously, fighting panic. He turned the phone on and off, to no avail; finally shoved it into his pocket and stood, trying to calm himself.

It was impossible that he could be lost. The mound above him wasn't that large, and even if the fogou's passage continued for some distance underground, he would eventually reach the end, at which point he could turn around and painstakingly wend his way back out again. He tried to recall something he'd read once, about navigating the maze at Hampton Court—always keep your hand on the left-hand side of the hedge. All he had to do was locate a wall, and walk back into daylight.

He was fairly certain that he was still facing the same way as when he had first entered. He turned, so that he was now facing where the doorway should be, and walked, counting aloud as he did. When he reached one hundred he stopped.

There was no way he had walked more than a hundred paces into the tunnel. Somehow, he had gotten turned around. He wiped his face, slick and chill with sweat, and breathed deeply, trying to slow his racing heart. He heard nothing, saw nothing save that impenetrable darkness. Everything he had ever read about getting lost advised staying put and waiting for help; but that involved being lost above ground, where someone would eventually find you. At some point Thomsa and Harry would notice he hadn't returned, but that might not be till morning.

And who knew how long it might be before they located him? The thought of spending another twelve hours or more here, motionless, unable to see or hear, or touch anything save the ground beneath his feet, filled Jeffrey with such overwhelming horror that he felt dizzy.

And that was worst of all: if he fell, would he even touch the ground? He crouched, felt an absurd wash of relief as he pressed his palms against the floor. He straightened, took another deep breath and began to walk.

He tried counting his steps, as a means to keep track of time, but before long a preternatural stillness came over him, a sense that he was no longer awake but dreaming. He pinched the back of his hand, hard enough that he gasped. Yet still the feeling remained, that he'd somehow fallen into a recurring dream, the horror deadened somewhat by a strange familiarity. As though he'd stepped into an icy pool, he stopped, shivering, and realised the source of his apprehension.

It had been in the last chapter of Robert Bennington's book, *Still the Seasons*; the chapter that he'd never been able to recall clearly. Even now it was like remembering something that had happened *to* him, not something he'd read: the last of the novel's four children passing through a portal between one world and another, surrounded by utter darkness and the growing realisation that with each step the world around her was disintegrating and that she herself was disintegrating as well, until the book ended with her isolated consciousness fragmented into incalculable motes within an endless, starless void.

The terror of that memory jarred him. He jammed his hands into his pockets and felt his cell phone and the map, his car keys, some change. He walked more quickly, gazing straight ahead, focused on finding the spark within the passage that would resolve into the entrance.

After some time his heart jumped—it was there, so small he might have imagined it, a wink of light faint as a clouded star.

But when he ran a few paces he realised it was his mind playing tricks on him. A phantom light floated in the air, like the luminous blobs behind one's knuckled eyelids. He blinked and rubbed his eyes: the light remained.

"Hello?" he called, hesitating. There was no reply.

He started to walk, but slowly, calling out several times into the silence. The light gradually grew brighter. A few more minutes and a second light appeared, and then a third. They cast no glow upon the tunnel, nor shadows: he could see neither walls nor ceiling, nor any sign of those who carried the lights. All three seemed suspended in the air, perhaps ten feet above the floor, and all bobbed slowly up and down, as though each was borne upon a pole.

Jeffrey froze. The lights were closer now, perhaps thirty feet from where he stood.

"Who is it?" he whispered.

He heard the slightest of sounds, a susurrus as of escaping air. With a cry he turned and fled, his footsteps echoing through the passage. He heard no sounds of pursuit, but when he looked back, the lights were still there, moving slowly toward him. With a gasp he ran harder, his chest aching, until one foot skidded on something and he fell. As he scrambled back up, his hand touched a flat smooth object; he grabbed it and without thinking jammed it into his pocket, and raced on down the tunnel.

And now, impossibly, in the vast darkness before him he saw a jot of light that might have been reflected from a spider's eye. He kept going. Whenever he glanced back, he saw the trio of lights behind him.

They seemed to be more distant now. And there was no doubt that the light in front of him spilled from the fogou's entrance—he could see the outlines of the doorway, and the dim glister of quartz and mica in the walls to either side. With a gasp he reached the steps, stumbled up them and back out into the blinding light of afternoon. He stopped, coughing and covering his eyes until he could see, then staggered back across first one field and then the next, hoisting himself over rocks heedless of blackthorns tearing his palms and clothing, until at last he reached the final overgrown tract of heather and bracken, and saw the white roof of his rental car shining in the sun.

He ran up to it, jammed the key into the lock and with a gasp fell into the driver's seat. He locked the doors, flinching as another car drove past, and finally looked out the window.

To one side was the gate he'd scaled, with field after field beyond; to the other side the silhouettes of Gurnard's Head and its sister promontory. Beyond the fields, the sun hung well above the lowering mass of Zennor Hill. The car's clock read 15:23.

He shook his head in disbelief: it was impossible he'd been gone for scarcely an hour. He reached for his cell phone and felt something in the pocket beside it—the object he'd skidded on inside the fogou.

He pulled it out. A blue metal disc, slightly flattened where he'd stepped on it, with gold-stamped words above a beacon.

ST. AUSTELL SWEETS: FUDGE FROM REAL CORNISH CREAM

He turned it over in his hands and ran a finger across the raised lettering.

Becca gave one to each of us the day we arrived. The fudge was supposed to last the entire two weeks, and I think we ate it all that first night.

The same kind of candy tin where Evelyn had kept her comb and Anthea her locket and chain. He stared at it, the tin bright and enamel glossy-blue as though it had been painted yesterday. Anyone could have a candy tin, especially one from a local company that catered to tourists.

After a minute he set it down, took out his wallet and removed the photo Evelyn had given him: Evelyn and Moira doubled-up with laughter as Anthea stared at them, slightly puzzled, a half-smile on her face as though trying to determine if they were laughing at her.

He gazed at the photo for a long time, returned it to his wallet, then slid the candy lid back into his pocket. He still had no service on his phone.

He drove very slowly back to Cardu, nauseated from sunstroke and his terror at being underground. He knew he'd never been seriously lost—a backwards glance as he fled the mound reassured him that it hadn't been large enough for that.

Yet he was profoundly unnerved by his reaction to the darkness, the way his sight had betrayed him and his imagination reflexively dredged up the images from Evelyn's story. He was purged of any desire to remain another night at the cottage, or even in England, and considered checking to see if there was an evening train back to London.

But by the time he edged the car down the long drive to the cottage, his disquiet had ebbed somewhat. Thomsa and Harry's car was gone. A stretch of wall had been newly repaired, and many more daffodils and narcissus had opened, their sweet fragrance following him as he trudged to the front door.

Inside he found a plate with a loaf of freshly baked bread and some local blue cheese, beside it several pamphlets with a yellow Sticky note.

Jeffrey—

Gone to see a play in Penzance. Please turn off lights downstairs. I found these books today and thought you might be interested in them.

Thomsa

He glanced at the pamphlets—another map, a flyer about a music night at the pub in Zennor, a small paperback with a green cover—crossed to the refrigerator and foraged until he found two bottles of ale. Probably not proper B&B etiquette, but he'd apologise in the morning.

He grabbed the plate and book and went upstairs to his room. He kicked off his shoes, groaning with exhaustion, removed his torn windbreaker and regarded himself in the mirror, his face scratched and flecked with bits of greenery.

"What a mess," he murmured, and collapsed onto the bed.

He downed one of the bottles of ale and most of the bread and cheese. Outside, light leaked from a sky deepening to ultramarine. He heard the boom and sigh of waves, and for a long while he reclined in the window seat and stared out at the cliffs, watching as shadows slipped down them like black paint. At last he stood and got some clean clothes from his bag. He hooked a finger around the remaining bottle of ale, picked up the book Thomsa had left for him, and retired to the bathroom.

The immense tub took ages to fill, but there seemed to be unlimited hot water. He put all the lights on and undressed, sank into the tub and gave himself over to the mindless luxury of hot water and steam and the scent of daffodils on the windowsill.

Finally he turned the water off. He reached for the bottle he'd set on the floor and opened it, dried his hands and picked up the book. A worn paperback, its creased cover showing a sweep of green hills topped by a massive tor, with a glimpse of sea in the distance.

OLD TALES FOR NEW DAYS
BY ROBERT BENNINGTON

Jeffrey whistled softly, took a long swallow of ale and opened the book. It was not a novel but a collection of stories, published in 1970—Cornish folktales, according to a brief preface, 'told anew for today's generation'. He scanned the table of contents—'Pisky-Led', 'Tregeagle and the Devil', 'Jack the Giant Killer'—then sat up quickly in the tub, spilling water as he gazed at a title underlined with red ink: 'Cherry of Zennor'. He flipped through the pages until he found it.

> Sixteen-year-old Cherry was the prettiest girl in Zennor, not that she knew it. One day while walking on the moor she met a young man as handsome as she was lovely.
>
> "Will you come with me?" he asked, and held out a beautiful lace handkerchief to entice her. "I'm a widower with an infant son who needs tending. I'll pay you better wages than any man or woman earns from here to

Kenidjack Castle, and give you dresses that will be the envy of every girl at Morvah Fair."

Now, Cherry had never had a penny in her pocket in her entire young life, so she let the young man take her arm and lead her across the moor . . .

There were no echoes here of *The Sun Battles*, no vertiginous terrors of darkness and the abyss; just a folk tale that reminded Jeffrey a bit of 'Rip Van Winkle', with Cherry caring for the young son and, as the weeks passed, falling in love with the mysterious man.

Each day she put ointment on the boy's eyes, warned by his father never to let a drop fall upon her own. Until of course one day she couldn't resist doing so, and saw an entire host of gorgeously dressed men and women moving through the house around her, including her mysterious employer and a beautiful woman who was obviously his wife. Betrayed and terrified, Cherry fled; her lover caught up with her on the moor and pressed some coins into her hand.

"You must go now and forget what you have seen," he said sadly, and touched the corner of her eye. When she returned home she found her parents dead and gone, along with everyone she knew, and her cottage a ruin open to the sky. Some say it is still a good idea to avoid the moors near Zennor.

Jeffrey closed the book and dropped it on the floor beside the tub. When he at last headed back down the corridor, he heard voices from the kitchen, and Thomsa's voice raised in laughter. He didn't go downstairs; only returned to his room and locked the door behind him.

He left early the next morning, after sharing breakfast with Thomsa at the kitchen table.

"Harry's had to go to St. Ives to pick up some tools he had repaired." She poured Jeffrey more coffee and pushed the cream across the table toward him. "Did you have a nice ramble yesterday and go to the Tinners?"

Jeffrey smiled but said nothing. He was halfway up the winding driveway back to Cardu before he realised he'd forgotten to mention the two bottles of ale.

He returned the rental car then got a ride to the station from Evan, the same man who'd picked him up two days earlier.

"Have a good time in Zennor?"

"Very nice," said Jeffrey.

"Quiet this time of year." Evan pulled the car to the curb. "Looks like your train's here already."

Jeffrey got out, slung his bag over his shoulder and started for the station entrance. His heart sank when he saw two figures arguing on the sidewalk a few yards away, one a policeman.

"Come on now, Erthy," he said, glancing as Jeffrey drew closer. "You know better than this."

"Fuck you!" she shouted, and kicked at him. "Not my fucking name!"

"That's it."

The policeman grabbed her wrist and bent his head to speak into a walkie-talkie. Jeffrey began to hurry past. The woman screamed after him, shaking her clenched fist. Her eye with its bloody starburst glowed crimson in the morning sun.

"London!" Her voice rose desperately as she fought to pull away from the cop. "London, please, take me—"

Jeffrey shook his head. As he did, the woman raised her fist and flung something at him. He gasped as it stung his cheek, clapping a hand to his face as the policeman shouted and began to drag the woman away from the station.

"London! *London!*"

As her shrieks echoed across the plaza, Jeffrey stared at a speck of blood on his finger. Then he stooped to pick up what she'd thrown at him: a yellow pencil worn with toothmarks, its graphite tip blunted but the tiny, embossed black letters still clearly readable above the ferrule.

RAVENWOOD.

Hungerford Bridge

I hadn't heard from Miles for several months when he wrote to ask if I wanted to get together for lunch. Of course I did, and several days later I met him at a noisy, cheerful restaurant at South Bank. It was early February, London still somewhat dazed by the heavy snowfall that had recently paralyzed the city. The Thames seemed a river of lead; a black skim of ice made the sidewalks treacherous—I'd seen another man fall as I'd walked from Waterloo Station—and I wished I'd worn something warmer than the old wool greatcoat I'd had since college.

But once settled into the seat across from Miles, all that fell away.

"You're looking well, Robbie," he said, smiling.

"You too."

He smiled again, his pale eyes still locked with mine, and I felt that familiar frisson: caught between chagrin and joy that I'd been summoned. We'd met decades earlier at Cambridge; if I hadn't been a Texan, with the faint gloss of exoticism conferred by my accent and Justin boots, I doubt if he would have bothered with me at all.

But he did. Being chosen as a friend by Miles carried something of the unease of being hypnotized: Even now, I felt as I imagine a starling would, staring into the seed-black eyes of a krait. It wasn't just his beauty, still remarkable enough to turn heads in the restaurant, or his attire, though these would have been enough. Miles looked and dressed as though he'd stepped from a Beardsley drawing, wearing bespoke Edwardian suits and vintage Clark shoes he found at charity shops. He still wore his graying hair longish, artfully swept back from a delicate face to showcase a mustache that, on special occasions, would be waxed and curled so precisely it resembled a tiny pair of spectacles perched above his upper lip.

On anyone else this would have looked twee. Actually, on Miles it looked twee; but his friends forgave him everything, even his drunken recitations from *Peter Pan*, in which he'd played the lead as a boy.

I knew my place in the Neverland hierarchy: I was Smee, sentimental and loyal, slightly ridiculous. I doubt that, even as an infant, Miles had ever been ridiculous. His demeanor was at once aloof and good-natured, as though he'd wandered into the wrong party but was too well mannered to embarrass his host or the other guests by bringing this fact to their attention. His mother was a notorious groupie who was living out her twilight years in Exeter; his father could have been any one of a number of major or minor rock stars whose luxurious hair and petulant mouth Miles had inherited. Back at Cambridge, he'd scattered offhand anecdotes the way other students scattered cigarette ash. His great-aunt had been Diana Mitford's best friend; as a child, Miles had tea with Mitford, and upon the aunt's death he inherited a sterling lemon squeezer engraved with the initials AH. Once, camping with a friend on Dartmoor, he'd found a dead stag slung over the branches of a tree, the footprints of an enormous cat in the boggy earth beneath. A German head of state had fellated him in a public men's room in Marrakech. He'd been Jeanne Moreau's lover when he was thirteen, and had his first play produced at the Donmar Warehouse two years later.

That sort of thing. Now he gazed at me, and unexpectedly laughed in delight.

"Robbie! It really is so good to see you."

When the waiter arrived, Miles asked for a Malbec that was not on the wine list, but which appeared and was opened with a flourish several minutes later.

"We'll pour, thanks." Miles gently shooed the waiter off. "Here—" He filled my glass, then his own. "To happy endings."

Over lunch we gossiped about old friends. Kevin Bailey had lost everything in the crash and was rumored to be living under an assumed name in Portugal. Missy Severence had some work done with a plastic surgeon Miles knew, and looked fabulous. Khalil Devan's third wife was expecting twins.

"And you've been OK?" Miles refilled my glass. "You really look great, Robbie. And happy—you even look relatively happy."

I shrugged. "I *am* happy. Happy enough, anyway. I mean, it doesn't take much. I've still got a job, at any rate. And my rent hasn't gone up."

"Mmm."

For a minute Miles stared at me thoughtfully. I was used to these silences, which usually preceded an account of recent disturbances among some subset of sexual specialists in a town I'd never heard of.

Now, however, Miles just tapped his lower lip. Finally he tilted his head, nodded, and gave me a sharp look.

"Come on," he said. He removed a sheaf of notes from his wallet and shoved them under the empty wine bottle, pulled on his fawn-colored overcoat and wide-brimmed hat as he headed for the door.

"Let's get out of here."

We walked across Hungerford Bridge in the intermittent rain, skirting puddles and pockets of slush. Below us the Thames reflected empty, parchment-colored sky. When I looked back across the water, the buildings on the opposite bank seemed etched upon a vast blank scroll, a barge's wake providing a single ink stroke. Gulls wheeled and screamed. The air smelled of petrol, and snow. Beside me Miles walked slowly, heedless of damp staining the tips of his oxblood shoes.

"I think I'm going away," he said at last.

"Away? Where?"

"I don't know. Australia, maybe. Or Tierra del Fuego. Someplace warm."

"Tierra del Fuego's not warm."

He laughed. "That settles it then. Australia!"

We'd reached the other side of the bridge. Miles stopped, staring down past a dank alley. On the far side of the alley, a wedge of green gleamed between grimy buildings and cars rushing past the Thames, the intricate warren of doors and tunnels that led into Embankment tube station. I always noted this bit of park as I rushed to or from work: a verdant mirage suspended between Victoria Embankment and the roil of central London, like a shard of stained-glass window that had survived the bombing of its cathedral. Depending on the season, the sidewalk leading into it might be rain washed or sifted with autumn leaves beneath a huge ivy-covered plane tree.

Now the swatch of green glowed, lamplike, in the cold drizzle.

"Let's go down there," said Miles. "I want to show you something."

We wound our way through the pedestrian tunnel and downstairs into the street. A flower stall stood outside the subway entrance, banks of Asian lilies and creamy roses, bundled green wands of daffodils that had yet to bloom. It smelled like a garden after rain, or a wedding. A black-clad girl moved slowly among her wares, rearranging delphiniums and setting up placards with prices scrawled in red marker. Miles tipped his hat to her as we passed. She smiled, and the sweet scents of damp earth and freesia trailed us into the park.

"You know, I've never been here." I drew alongside Miles. "All these years I've just seen it from up there—"

I pointed to where the bridge's span had disappeared behind a crosshatch of brick and peeling billboards. "I don't even know what it's called."

"Victoria Embankment Park." Miles stopped and looked around, like a fox testing the air. "I haven't been here in a while myself." For a few minutes we walked in silence. The park was much larger than I'd thought. There was an ornate water gate to one side, relic of a Tudor mansion now long gone. Several maintenance men smoked and laughed outside a brick utility building. A few other people strolled along the sidewalk, hunched against the frigid rain. Businessmen, a young woman walking a small dog. Tall rhododendrons clustered alongside the path, leaves glossy as carven jade, and box trees that smelled mysteriously of my childhood.

"This was all the tidal shore of the Thames." Miles gestured at the river. "They filled it in around 1851, thus Embankment. I always wonder what they'd find if they dug it up again."

We continued on. Signs warned us from the grass, close cropped as a golf green. A large statue of Robert Burns stared at us impassively, and I wondered if this was what Miles wanted me to see.

But we walked past Burns, past the immense plane trees shedding bark like a lizard's skin, past an outdoor café open despite the weather, and some wildly incongruous-looking palms with long spear-shaped leaves. Perhaps a hundred feet away, Cleopatra's Needle rose above the traffic, guarded by two patient sphinxes.

"Here. This is as good a spot as any."

Miles walked to a bench and sat. I settled next to him, tugging my collar against the cold. "I should've worn a hat."

He didn't even glance at me. His eyes were fixed on a small, curved patch of garden on the other side of the path, two steps away. Forlorn cowslips with limp stems and papery leaves had been recently planted at the garden's edge. The wind carried the cold scent of overturned earth, and a fainter, sweeter fragrance: lilies of the valley, though I saw none in bloom. Here too the grass was close cropped, though there were several small depressions where the roots of a great plane tree thrust through the dirt. Moles, I thought, or maybe the marks of older plantings. Behind it all ran a crumbling brick wall about six feet in height, topped by the knotty, intertwined branches of an espaliered tree growing on the other side. This, along with the ancient plane tree, made our bench feel part of a tiny enclave. The sounds of traffic grew muffled. People passing us on the main path just a few yards off seemed to lower their voices.

"It's lovely," I murmured.

"Hush," said Miles.

He continued to gaze fiercely at the green sward across from us. I leaned back against the bench and tried to get comfortable. The brick wall provided some shelter from the rain, but I still shivered. After a few minutes Miles moved so that he pressed against my side, and I sighed in thanks, grateful for the warmth.

We sat there for a long time. Over an hour, I noted when I glanced at my watch, though Miles frowned so vehemently I didn't check again. Now and then I'd glance at him from the corner of my eye. He still stared resolutely at the patch of garden, his expression remote as Cleopatra's sphinxes.

Another hour might have passed. The wind shifted. The rain stopped, and it felt warmer; the light slanting through the linden branches grew tinged with violet.

Beside me, Miles abruptly drew a deeper breath as his body tensed. His face grew rigid, his eyes widened, and his mouth parted. I must have moved as well—he hissed warningly, and my gaze flashed back to the swath of green.

At the base of the plane tree something moved. A falling leaf, I thought, or a ribbon of peeling bark trapped between the tangled roots.

Then it gave an odd, sudden hop, and I thought it was some sort of wren, or even a large frog, or perhaps a child's toy.

The something scurried across the turf and stopped. For the first time I saw it clearly: a creature the size of my balled fist, a hedgehog surely—pointed snout, upraised spines, a tiny out-thrust arrow of a tail, legs invisible beneath its rounded torso.

But it was green—a brilliant, jewel-like green, like the carapace of a scarab beetle. Its spikes weren't spikes at all but tiny overlapping scales, or maybe feathers shot through with iridescent mauve and amethyst as it moved. Its eyes were the rich damson of a pansy's inner petals, and as it nosed at the grass I saw that its snout ended in a beak like an echidna's, the same deep purple as its eyes. I gasped, and felt Miles stiffen as the creature froze and raised its head slightly. A moment later it looked down and once more began poking at the grass.

My heart raced. I shut my eyes, fighting to calm myself but also to determine if this was a dream or some weird drunken flashback inspired by Miles.

But when I looked again the creature was still there, scurrying obliviously between tree roots and cowslips. Its beaklike snout poked into the soft black earth, occasionally emerged with a writhing worm or beetle impaled upon it. Once, the wind stirred a dead leaf: startled, the creature halted. Its scales rose to form a stiff, brilliantly colored armor, a farthingale glimmering every shade of violet and green.

Vermilion claws protruded from beneath its body; a bright droplet appeared at the end of the pointed beak as it made an ominous, low humming sound, like a swarm of bees.

A minute crept by, and when no predator appeared, the scales flattened, the shining claws withdrew, and the creature scurried as before. Sometimes it came to the very edge of the garden plot, where upright paving stones formed an embankment. I would hold my breath then, terrified that I'd frighten it, but the creature only thrust its beak fruitlessly between the cracks, and finally turned back.

In all that time I neither heard nor saw another person save Miles, silent as a statue beside me—I was so focused upon the creature's solitary hunt that I might have been bludgeoned or robbed, and never known it.

Gradually the afternoon wore away; gradually the world about us took on a lavender cast that deepened, from hyacinth to heliotrope to the leaden, enveloping gloom of London's winter twilight. Without warning, the creature lifted its head from where it had been feeding, turned, scurried back toward the plane tree, and disappeared into one of the holes there. I blinked and held my breath again, willing it to reappear.

It never did. After a minute Miles leaned back against the bench and stretched. He looked at me and smiled, yet his eyes were sad. More than sad: he appeared heartbroken.

"What the *hell* was that?" I demanded. Two teenagers walking side by side and texting on their mobiles glanced at me and laughed.

"The emerald foliot," Miles replied.

"What the hell is the emerald foliot?"

He shrugged. "What you saw—that's it. Don't get pissy with me; it's all I know."

He jumped to his feet and bounced up and down on his heels.

"Jesus, I'm frozen. Let's get out of here. I'll walk you back across the bridge."

My leg was asleep, so it was a moment before I could run to catch up with him.

"For fuck's sake, Miles, you have to tell me what that was—what that was all about."

"I told you all I know." He shoved his hands into his pockets, shivering now himself. "God, it's cold. It's called the emerald foliot—"

"Who calls it the emerald foliot?"

"Well, me. And the person who showed me. And now you."

"But who showed you? Are there more? I mean, it should be in a museum or a zoo or—Christ, I don't know! Something. Are they studying it? Why doesn't anyone know about it?"

Miles stopped beneath the overhang at the entrance to the tube station. He leaned against the wall, out of the wind, and a short distance from the throngs hurrying home from work. "Nobody knows because nobody knows, Robbie. You know, and I know, and the person who told me knows. And I guess if he—or she—is still alive, the person who told him knows.

"But that's it—that's all. In the whole entire world, we're the only ones."

His eyes glittered—with excitement, but also tears. He wiped them away, unashamed, and smiled. "I wanted you to know, Robbie. I wanted you to be the next one."

I rubbed my forehead, in impatience and disbelief, swore loudly, then aligned myself against the wall at his side. I was trying desperately to keep my temper.

"Next one what?" I said at last.

"The next one who knows. That's how it works—someone shows you, just like I showed you. But then—"

His voice broke, and he went on. "But then the other person, the first person—we never go there again. We never see it again. Ever."

"You mean it only comes out once a year or something?"

He shook his head sadly. "No. It comes out all the time—I mean, I assume it does, but who knows? I've only seen it twice. The first time was when someone showed me. And now, the second time, the last time—with you."

"But." I took a deep breath, fumbled instinctively in my pocket for a cigarette, though I'd quit years ago.

"Here." Miles withdrew a leather cigarette case, opened it, and offered one to me, took one for himself, then lit both.

I inhaled deeply, waited before speaking again. "OK. So you showed it to me, and someone showed it to you—who? When?"

"I can't tell you. But a long time ago—right after college, I guess."

"Why can't you tell me?"

"I just can't." Miles stared at the pavement. "It's not allowed."

"Who doesn't allow it?"

"I don't know. It's just not done. And you—"

He lifted his head to gaze at me, his eyes burning. "You can't tell anyone either, Robbie. Ever. Not until it's your turn, and you show someone else."

"And then it's over? I never see it again?"

He nodded. "That's right. You never see it again."

I felt a surge of impatience, and despair. "Just twice, in my whole life?"

He smiled. "That's more than most people get. More than anyone gets, except us."

"And whoever showed you, and whoever showed her. Or him."

Miles finished his cigarette, dropped it, and ground it fastidiously beneath the tip of one oxblood shoe. I did the same, and together we began to walk back upstairs.

"So how long has this been going on?" We stepped onto Hungerford Bridge, and I stopped to look down at the fractal view of the park, no longer green but yellowish from the glow of crime lights. "A hundred years? Thousands?"

"I don't know. Maybe. I mean, the park wasn't always there, but something was, before they made the embankment. The river. Enormous houses. But I think it's gone on longer than that."

"And no one else knows?"

"No one else knows." He gazed at the park, then glanced over his shoulder at people rushing across the bridge. Someone bumped me, muttered, "Sorry," and trudged on. "Unless everyone does, and they're all very good at keeping a secret."

He laughed, and we started walking again. "Why did you decide to tell me?"

"I don't know. I've known you so long. You seem like someone who'd appreciate it. And also, you can keep a secret. Like you never told about Brian and that dog in Sussex."

I winced at the memory. "Is there a set time when you tell the next person? Or do you just make up your mind and do it?"

"You can tell whoever you want, whenever you want. Some people do right away—the next day, or a week later. But I think most people wait—that's what I was told, anyway. Though you don't want to wait too long—I mean, you don't want to wait till you're so ancient and infirm you forget about it or die before you tell the next one."

I must have looked stricken, because he laughed again and put his arm around me. "No, I'm fine, Robbie, I swear! I just, you know, decided it was time for a change of scenery. Warmer climes, adventures. A new career in a new town."

We'd reached the far side of the bridge.

"I'll leave you here." Miles glanced at his mobile, read a message, and smiled slightly before glancing at me again. "I'm not falling off the end of the earth, Robbie! I'll be in touch. Till then—"

He raised a finger and touched it to my lips. "Not a word," he murmured, then kissed my cheek in farewell, spun on his heel, and began striding back across the bridge.

I watched him go, his fawn-colored greatcoat and wide-brimmed hat, until night swallowed him. For a few minutes I stood there, gazing past the bridge's span to the dark river below, the image of a gemlike creature flickering across my vision and Miles's kiss still warm upon my cheek.

Then I turned, head down, as a blast of wind blew up from the underground station, and hurried to catch my train.

The Far Shore

In dreams he fell: from planes, trees, roofs, cliffs, bridges. Whatever awaited him below, the impact was the same. His right leg buckled and a bolt of pain flared from ankle to knee, so that even after decades he woke with his old injury throbbing, bathed in sweat and hands outstretched to restore his balance. The pain subsided as the hours passed. Still, he no longer stood in the studio while his students practiced their moves, épaulement croisé, balloté, rise, ciseaux, but sat in a plain, straight-backed wooden chair, marking time with an elegant silver-topped cane.

When he received notice that he was to be replaced by someone younger, he reacted with the same calm he always displayed, the classical dancer's legacy of stoicism serving him now as it had for the last three decades.

"I hope you understand." The ballet master's face creased. "You know I don't want to do this. If something opens up, we'll find a place for you."

Philip inclined his head. "Of course."

That night he called Emma, his oldest friend.

"Oh, Philip, that's terrible!"

He shrugged, gazing out the window of his tiny studio apartment at the glass edifice that had been erected across the street. "Well, I was lucky they kept me as long as they did."

"What will you do?"

"I have no fucking idea."

She laughed, and he felt better. They spoke for a good hour, gossip mostly about dancers he knew and Emma had never heard of.

Then, "Why don't you come stay here at the camp while we're gone?" she suggested. "Not for the winter—a few weeks, or a month, however long you want. We'll have Joe Moody close up when you leave."

"Just like *The Shining*," said Philip. "What a great idea."

"It won't be like that in early November. Well, okay, it might snow. But then you just call Joe and he'll come plow you out. I think it would be good for you, Philip," she added. "I mean, being alone here might be better than feeling alone there. I think you just need to get away from the city for a few weeks. See if you can clear your head of all this. You know?"

He knew.

"Sure, what the hell." He heard Emma's sigh of relief.

He called a few friends to say good-bye, arranged for someone to watch his place, and several days later left in his rent-a-wreck. It was after midnight when he reached the camp. He missed the turnoff twice, its sign so overgrown with lichen and old-man's-beard that he'd mistaken it for a dead tree limb in the dark.

CAMP TUONELA

EST. 1908

An hour earlier, the highway had dwindled to a track guarded by ghostly armies of oak and tamaracks. All the landmarks he'd loved as a boy had disappeared. Where was the ancient ice cream stand shaped like an Abenaki longhouse? And Lambert's Gun Emporium? Where was the general store where he and Emma had made forbidden trips to buy fresh doughnuts, inevitably betrayed by the smells of lard and burnt sugar that clung to them when they returned to their cabin?

"Christ, Philip, those are long gone," said Emma when she greeted him in front of the lodge. "The general store burned down in the eighties. Chimney fire. Bob Lambert sold his place, he died a while back. I don't remember what happened to the teepee."

They'd met at Tuonela decades ago, bonding over a shared love of *The Red Shoes* and cheesy Mexican horror movies. They passed most of their childhood summers there, first as campers, then counselors-in-training, before Philip defected to a dance camp in New York State, and finally to the School of American Ballet. Emma eventually parlayed her love for the place into an actual romance, marrying Sam, a fellow counselor, at a lakeside ceremony twenty-odd years before. Philip had been her best man. He stood beside the pastor of the old Finnish Church who performed the ceremony, surprised to learn that the name *Tuonela* was Finnish, not Abenaki in origin, though no one seemed to know what the word meant. Shortly afterward, Emma and Sam bought the camp, and raised their two daughters there.

But the last few years had been tough.

"Parents want high-tech camps now," she told Philip as they carried his bags inside. "Wi-fi, all that. We don't even have a cell tower around here. This year our enrollment dropped to about half what it was last year. We could barely make payroll. So we figured this was a good time to do what all real Mainers do in the winter."

"Which is...?"

She laughed. "Go to Florida."

Their girls were in college now, so Emma and Sam would be housesitting for friends in Key West, a midlife second honeymoon. Philip hadn't visited Tuonela, or anyplace else, in ages. He'd spent his entire adult life in the New York City Ballet, first as an apprentice, then a member of the corps de ballet, and finally as an instructor. He'd been like the other boys, at once necessary and interchangeable: a rat in *The Nutcracker*; one of the debauched revelers in *The Prodigal Son*; a huntsman in Balanchine's one-act *Swan Lake*. He'd passed hours watching Edward Villella and Jacques d'Amboise with mingled admiration and wonder, but—almost unheard of for a dancer—with very little envy. He knew how fortunate he was to pace the same darkened hallways as they had, sleepwalking into class before nine a.m., then burning through rehearsal and performance, often not departing the cavernous theater until almost midnight.

But he also knew he would never be a soloist, or even a fine second-rank dancer. He dreamed of the lead in *Square Dance*. He'd have happily settled for a side part in *Concerto Baroco.* Instead, there'd been a dozen years as a dancing rat.

"You're a foot soldier," a former lover told him once. "A foot soldier of the arts. Canon fodder!" he added with a laugh. "Get it?"

Philip wryly admitted that he did.

Not that it mattered to him; not much, anyway. He adored being part of the corps, its discipline and competitive fellowship, the perverse haven of a routine that often felt like a calculus of pain. He loved the fleeting nature of dance itself—of all the arts the one that left almost no permanent mark upon the world, even as it casually disfigured its adherents with deformed feet, eating disorders, careers like mayflies. Most of all, he loved those moments during a performance when he could feel himself suspended within an ephemeral web of music and movement, gravity momentarily defeated by the ingrained memory of muscle and bone.

It all ended suddenly. When he was twenty-eight ("that's ninety in dance years," he told Emma) Philip shattered his metatarsal during a rehearsal. His foot turned in as he landed from a jump; he hit the floor, crying out in anguish as his leg twisted beneath him. The other dancers rushed over with icepacks and pillows, and arranged transport to NYU Hospital. He spent weeks in a haze of painkillers, his leg in a cast. Months of physical rehab followed, but ever after he walked with a slight limp.

Still, he'd always been popular within the corps, and the ballet masters and rehearsal teachers liked him. At twenty-nine he found himself teaching the company. His former colleagues were now living eidolons of youth, beauty, health, joy, desire flitting past him in the studio, lovely and remote as figures from a medieval allegory. What he felt then was less envy than a terrible, physical ache, as for a lover who'd died. He could still be transported by watching a good performance, the smells of adrenaline and sweat that seeped backstage.

But his ecstatic dreams of flight became recurring nightmares of falling.

✀

Sam had already driven down to the Keys. Emma's flight left on Sunday, which gave her most of the weekend to show Philip how to work the composting toilet, emergency generator, kerosene lamps, hand pump, outboard motor, woodstove. Philip knew the camp's layout as though it were the musculature of a familiar body: the old Adirondack-style lodge overlooking the lake; the campers' log cabins tucked into the surrounding forest, moss-covered roofs and bark exteriors nearly invisible among birch groves and bracken. In the middle of summer, filled with damp children and smelling of sunblock and balsam, it was heartstoppingly lovely.

Now, with only him and Emma kicking through drifts of brown leaves, it all seemed cheerless and slightly sinister. Two miles of gravel road separated the camp from the blue highway that led to an intersection with a convenience store that sold gas, lottery tickets, beer, and not much else. The nearest town was twenty miles away.

"What happens if I cut my hand off with a chainsaw?" Philip asked.

"Well, you'll be better off treating yourself than calling 911. It could take them an hour to get here. That's if the roads are clear."

They spent one morning on a nostalgic circuit of the old camp road, Philip replacing his silver-topped cane with the sturdy walking stick Emma gave him. They were back at the lodge by lunchtime. A stone's throw from its front steps stretched Lake Tuonela, a cerulean crescent that could, in seconds, turn into frigid, steel-colored chop powerful enough to swamp a Boston Whaler. This time of year there were few boaters on the water: an occasional canoe or kayak, hunters making a foray from a hunting camp. The opposite shore was a nature preserve, or maybe it belonged to a private landowner—Philip had never gotten the details straight. He dimly recalled some ghost story told around the campfire, about early Finnish settlers who claimed the far shore was haunted or cursed.

More likely it was just wildly unsuitable for farming. Philip only knew it formed some kind of no-man's-land. In all his years visiting Lake Tuonela, he'd never set foot there.

Not that he was tempted to. A mile of icy water lay between the camp and the far shore, and his bad foot kept him from anything resembling a strenuous hike.

"Whenever you go outside, make sure you wear an orange jacket. Even if you're just walking out to the car," Emma warned him as they headed back inside. "Waterfowl season now, then deer season. The camp is posted, but we still hear gunshots way too close. Here—"

She pointed to a half-dozen blaze-orange vests hanging beside the door. "Take your pick. You can have your pick of bedrooms, too." she added. "If you get bored, move to a different room. Like the Mad Tea Party. Just strip the bed and fold the sheets on top, we'll deal with laundry when we come back in March."

He chose his usual room on the main floor, with French doors that opened on to the porch overlooking the lake, though he wondered vaguely why he didn't simply camp in the living room. The lodge had been built over a century ago with hand-hewn logs and slate floor, a flagstone fireplace so massive Philip could have slept inside it. The place had most of the original furnishings, along with the original windows and concomitant lack of insulation, which meant one was warm only within a six-foot radius of the woodstove or fireplace.

Sunday morning Emma gave him final instructions regarding frozen pipes, power outages, wildlife safety. "If you meet a moose, run. If you meet a bear, don't."

"What about a mountain lion?"

"Hit him with a rock."

And that was it. In the afternoon he drove Emma to Bangor to catch her flight. It was very late when he returned, the night sky overcast. He had to use a flashlight to find his way along the leaf-covered path. Branches scraped against each other, the wind rustled in dead burdock. He could hear but not see the water a few yards off, waves slapping softly against the shore, and the distant murmur of wild geese disturbed by the sound of the car.

He slept that night with the outside light on, an extravagance Emma would have deplored.

The camp was less remote than he'd feared. Or, rather, he could choose how isolated he wanted to be. He had to drive thirty minutes to a grocery store, but its shelves held mostly familiar products. If he wanted company, there was a bean supper every Saturday at the Finnish Church, though Emma had advised him to get there early, before they sold out of plates. There was no wireless or DSL at Tuonela; dial-up took so long that Philip soon gave up using it more than once or twice a week. Instead he devoted himself to reading, hauling in firewood, and wandering the trails around the lake.

As a boy, he'd been able to find his way in the dark from his cabin to the main road. Now he was pleased to discover that he could, at least, follow the same woodland paths in daylight, even those trails that had been neglected for the last ten or fifteen years. Stripling oaks and beeches now towered above him; grassy clearings had become dense, unrecognizable thickets of alder and black willow.

Still, some combination of luck and instinct and sense memory guided him: he rarely got lost, and never for long.

He liked to walk in the very early morning, shortly before sunrise when mist hid the world from him, the only sound a faint dripping from branches and dead leaves. After a few days, he began to experience the same strange dislocation he'd experienced when dancing: that eerie sense of being absent from his body even as he occupied it more fully than at other times. The smell of woodstove followed him from the lodge; field mice rustled in the underbrush. As the fog burned off, trees and boulders slowly materialized. Scarlet-crowned oaks atop gray ledges; white slashes of birch; winterberry peppered with bright red fruit. Gold and crimson leaves formed intricate scrollwork upon the lake's surface, and ducks and geese fed in the shallows.

That was why he went out early, before the sound of shotguns startled them into a frenzy of beating wings. The lake was a flyway for migrating waterfowl. The loons were long gone, but others had taken their place. Goldeneye and teal, pintails and ringnecks; easily spooked wood ducks that whistled plaintively as they fled; hooded mergansers with gaudy crests and wings so vividly striped they looked airbrushed. There were always noisy flotillas of Canada geese, and sometimes a solitary swan that he only glimpsed if he went out while it was still almost dark.

Even as a boy, Philip loved swans. Part of it was their association with ballet; mostly it was just how otherworldly they looked. Some mornings he set his alarm for four a.m., hoping to see the one that now and then emerged from the mist near the far shore like an apparition: silent, moving with uncanny slowness across the dark water. Alone among the other birds, it never took flight at the sound of guns, only continued its languid passage, until it was lost among thick stands of alder and cattails.

He'd been at the camp for two weeks before dawn broke cold and clear, the first cloudless day since he arrived. Vapor streamed across glassy blue water to disappear as the sun rose above the firs. Philip finished his coffee, then walked along the edge of the lake, skirting gulleys where rain had cut deep channels into the bank. A small flock of green-winged teal swam close to shore, the mask above their eyes shining emerald in the sun. It was now early November, and until today the weather had been unseasonably warm. Hundreds, even thousands, of migrating waterfowl had lingered much longer than he'd expected.

Though what did he know about birds? He only recognized those species he'd identified as a boy, or that Emma had pointed out to him over the years. Most stayed on the far side of the lake, though they must have fed elsewhere—at twilight the air rang with their piping cries and the thunderous echo of wings as they flew overhead, heading for the distant line of black firs that shadowed the desolate waters where they slept each night. The sound of their passage, the sight of all those madly beating wings against the evening sky, filled him with the same wild joy he'd felt waiting backstage when the first bars of *A Midsummer Night's Dream* or *Le Baiser de Fée* insinuated themselves in the dim theater. He seldom saw birds in flight during his early morning walks—a group of six or eight, perhaps, but never the endless ranks that rippled across the evening sky like waves buffeting an unseen shore.

Now, he saw only the teal bobbing across the bright water. Above him ravens flew from tree to tree, croaking loudly at his approach. He tipped his head back to watch them, slowing his pace so he wouldn't trip. Something soft yielded beneath his foot, as though he'd stepped on thick moss. He glanced down, and with a shout stumbled backward.

On the ground a body lay curled upon its side. Naked, thin arms drawn protectively about its head. A man.

No, not a man—a boy. Seventeen or eighteen and emaciated, his skin dead-white save for bruised shadows at his groin, the deep hollow of his throat. One shoulder was spattered with blood and dirt. Lank black hair was plastered across his face. A tiny black beetle crawled into a fringe of black hair.

Philip stared at him, light-headed. He took a deep breath, leaned on his walking stick, and reached to touch the corpse, gingerly, on the chest.

The boy moaned. Philip recoiled, watched as a pink tinge spread across the boy's broad cheekbones and hairless chest. The bluish skin in the cleft of his throat tightened then relaxed. He was alive.

Philip tore off his orange vest and covered him. He ran his hands across the boy's neck and wrists and breast, searching for a pulse, broken bones, bleeding. Except for that wounded shoulder, he could see or feel nothing wrong.

He sank back onto his heels, fighting panic. He couldn't leave him here while he ran back to the lodge—the boy looked near dead already.

And what if he'd been attacked? What if his attackers returned?

Philip ran a hand across his forehead. "Okay. Okay, listen. I'm going to help you. I'm just going to try and lift you up—"

Gently as he could, he grasped the boy's uninjured shoulder. The boy moaned again, louder this time. His eyes opened, pupils so dilated the irises showed no color. He gazed at Philip, then hissed, struggling to escape.

"Hey." Philip's panic grew. What if the boy died, now, at his side? He stared into those huge black eyes, willing him to be calm. "Hold on, let me help you. Here, put your weight on me...."

He took the boy's hand, felt sticklike fingers vibrating beneath his own. An odd, spasmodic quivering, as though bones, not muscles or skin, responded to his touch. Abruptly the hand grew slack. Philip looked down, terrified that the boy had died.

But the boy only nodded, his strange black eyes unblinking, and let Philip help him to his feet.

They walked to the lodge. The boy moved awkwardly, the vest draped across his shoulders, and flinched at Philip's touch.

"Does it hurt?" asked Philip anxiously.

The boy said nothing. He was taller than Philip, so thin and frail his bones might have been wrapped in paper, not skin. He stepped tentatively among stones and fallen branches, muddy water puddling up around his bare feet. As they approached the lodge his eyes widened and he hissed again, from pain or alarm.

"Lie here," Philip commanded once they were inside. He eased the boy onto the couch facing the woodstove, then hurried to get blankets. "You'll warm up in a minute."

He returned with the blankets. The boy sat, staring fixedly at the window. He was trembling.

"You must be frozen," Philip exclaimed. The boy remained silent.

Before, Philip been struck by the leaden pallor of his skin. Now he saw that the hair on his arms and legs was also white—not sun-bleached but silvery, a bizarre contrast to the oil-black hair that fell to his shoulders, the dark hair at his groin. His eyebrows were black as well, arched above those staring eyes.

"What's your name?" asked Philip.

The boy continued to gaze at the window. After a moment he looked away. "What has happened?"

"You tell me." Philip crossed the room to pick up the phone. "I'm going to call 911. It might take them a while to get here, so—"

"No!"

"Listen to me. You're in shock. You need help—"

"I'm not hurt."

"It doesn't look that way to me. Did you—has someone been hurting you?"

The boy gave a sharp laugh, displaying small, very white teeth. "I'm not hurt." He had an oddly inflected voice, a faint childlike sibilance. "I'm cold."

"Oh." Philip winced. "Right, I'm sorry. I'll get you some clothes."

He put down the phone, went to his room, and rummaged through the bureau, returning a few minutes later with a pair of faded corduroy trousers, a new flannel shirt. "Here."

The boy took them, and Philip retreated to the kitchen. He picked up the phone again, replaced it, and swore under his breath.

He was stalling, he knew that—he should call 911. He didn't know anything about this kid. Was he drunk? On drugs? The dilated pupils suggested he was, also the muted hostility in his voice. Not to mention Philip had found him stark naked by the lake in thirty-degree weather.

But who to call? 911? Police? His parents? What if he'd run away for a good reason? Would Philip truly be saving him if he rang for help? Or would this be one of those awful things you read about, where a well-meaning outsider wreaks havoc by getting involved in small-town life?

Maybe he'd just been out all night with his girlfriend, or boyfriend. Or maybe he'd been kidnapped and left for dead....

Philip angled himself so he could peer into the living room, and watched as the boy shoved aside the blankets. The bright hairs on his arms caught the sunlight and shone as though washed with rain. He pulled on the corduroy trousers, fumbled with the zipper until he got it halfway up, leaving the fly unbuttoned, then stood and clumsily put on the flannel shirt. It was too big; the pants too short, exposing knobby ankles and those long white feet.

He's beautiful, thought Philip, and his face grew hot. Clothed, the boy seemed less exotic; also younger. Philip felt a stab of desire and guilt. He stepped away from the door, counted to sixty, then loudly cleared his throat before walking into the living room.

"They fit?"

The boy stood beside the woodstove, turning his hands back and forth. After a moment he looked at Philip. The swollen black pupils made his angular face seem ominous, skull-like.

"I'm thirsty," he said.

"I'm sorry—of course. I'll be right back—"

Philip went into the kitchen, waited as the pipes rumbled and shook, and finally produced a thin stream of water. He filled a glass and returned.

"Here...."

Cold air rushed through the open front door, sending a flurry of dead leaves across the slate.

"God damn it." Philip set the glass down. "Hey—hey, come back!"

But the boy was gone.

Philip walked along the driveway, then retraced his steps to the water's edge. He considered taking the car to search on the main road, but decided that would be a waste of time. He trudged back to the lodge, his annoyance shading into relief and a vague, shameful disappointment.

The boy had been a diversion: from solitude, boredom, the unending threnody of Philip's own thoughts. He was already imagining himself a hero, calling 911, saving the kid from—well, whatever.

Now he felt stupid, and uneasy.

What had he been thinking, bringing a stranger inside? It was clear Philip lived alone. The boy might return to rob the place, enlist his friends to break into the cabins, lay waste to the entire camp....

He slammed the front door behind him. Angrily he grabbed the old Hudson Bay blankets and folded them, then picked up the discarded vest from beside the woodstove.

The boy had made off with his clothes, too. The pants were old, but Philip had just bought the shirt for this trip. He glared at the vest and crossed the room to hang it with the other coats. As he reached for the hook, something pricked his hand. He glanced down to see a droplet of blood welling from the fleshy part of his palm. He wiped it on his sleeve, then inspected the vest.

A twig or thorn must have gotten caught in it, or maybe a stray fish hook. He found nothing, until he turned the collar and saw a pale spur protruding from the fabric. He pinched it between his fingers and tugged it free.

It was a white feather, maybe an inch long. The tiny quill had poked through the cloth, sharp as a pin. He examined it curiously, placed it in the center of his palm, and blew.

For an instant it hung suspended in a shaft of light, like a feather trapped in amber; then drifted to the floor. It should have been easy to see, white against dark stone in the early morning sun. Philip searched for several minutes, but never found it.

The rest of that day he felt restless and guilt-wracked. He should have done something about the boy, but what? His remorse was complicated by a growing anxiety. The boy was sick, or injured, or crazy. He'd freeze out there alone in the woods.

And, too, there was the unwanted twinge of longing Philip experienced whenever he thought of him. He'd spent years keeping his own desires in check—he had no choice, with those endless ranks of beautiful creatures that surrounded him in the studio, constant reminders of his own fallibility, the inevitable decay of his limited gifts. The boy seemed a weird rebuke to all that, appearing out of nowhere to remind Philip of what it was like, not to be young, but to be in thrall to youth.

He distracted himself by splitting wood for kindling. As the afternoon wore on, skeins of geese passed overhead, not Canada geese but a species he didn't recognize, black with white wings and slate-colored necks and heads. They circled above the lodge, making a wild, high-pitched keening; then arrowed downward, so close that he could see the indigo gleam of their bills and their startlingly bright, almost baleful, golden eyes. Philip watched as they flew past, not once but three times, as though searching for a place to land.

They never did. His presence spooked them, even when he stood motionless for their final transit. They swept into the sky and across the lake, their fretful cries echoing long after they were out of sight.

Late that afternoon the wind picked up. Dead leaves rattled in oaks and beech as a cold gale blasted from the north, accompanied by an ominous ridge of cloud the color of basalt. Ice skimmed the gray water closest to shore. Another phalanx of the strange birds wheeled above the lodge, veering toward the woodpile, then soaring back into the darkening sky. Philip was relieved when a flock of quite ordinary Canada geese honked noisily overhead, followed by a ragged group of pintails. Four ravens landed in the oak beside the woodpile and hopped from branch to branch. They cocked their heads toward him, but remained silent.

That unnerved Philip more than anything else. He leaned on the ax handle and stared back, then yelled at them. The ravens stared down with yellow eyes. One clacked its bill, but they made no sign of leaving. He picked up a piece of wood and lobbed it at the tree. The birds flapped their wings and retreated to a higher branch, where they sat in a row and continued to stare at him. Philip picked up the walking stick, brandished it in a feeble show of force, then gave up. He dragged a tarp from the storage shed, covered the woodpile, and painstakingly carried in several armfuls of logs. The ravens remained on the oak tree, heads lowered so they resembled a line of somber, black-clad jurors observing him. When he had brought the last load of wood inside he closed the door, then crossed to the window to gaze out. The birds hopped sideways to huddle together, and in unison turned their heads to stare at the house.

Philip stepped back from the window, his neck and arms prickling. The ravens did not move. When it grew full dark he took a flashlight and shone it through the window.

They were there still, watching him.

He forced himself to move about the room, hoping that routine would eventually drive them from his thoughts. He turned on the radio and listened to the local news. A meteorologist predicted steady high winds all night and a chance of snow. Philip stoked the woodstove and made sure that matches and candles were near to hand. He ate early, lentil soup he'd made several days ago, then settled on the couch beside the stove and tried to read. Once he went to check if the ravens were still outside, and saw to his relief that they were finally gone.

The lodge had always seemed inviolable, with its log walls and beams, stone floor and fireplace. But tonight the windows shuddered as though someone pounded at them. The candles Philip lit for atmosphere guttered, and even in the center of the room, beside the woodstove, he could feel a draft where wind nosed through chinks in the walls and windowpanes. Occasionally the old stove huffed loudly, gray smoke billowing from its seams. Philip would cough and curse and readjust the damper, poking the coals in a vain attempt to create an illusion of heat. Between the cold and smoke and ceaseless clamor of the wind, he found it difficult and finally impossible to concentrate on his book.

"I give up," he announced to the empty room. He blew out the candles, stuffed another log into the woodstove, and stalked off to bed.

It was barely eight o'clock. Back in the city he might be starting to think about dinner. Here, he felt exhausted. No lights shone beyond the windows of his room. The reflection from the bedside lamp seemed insubstantial as a candle flame; the darkness outside a solid mass, huge and inescapable, that pressed against the panes. His room sat beneath the eaves, where the wind didn't roar but crooned, a sound like mourning doves. The electric space heater Emma had left for him buzzed alarmingly, so he switched it off and heaped the cast-iron bedstead with Hudson Bay blankets. These smelled comfortingly of cedar, and were so warm he almost forgot the room was chill enough that he could see his breath.

Within minutes he was asleep, and dreaming.

Or perhaps not. Because as he slept, he heard the sound of wings overhead, yet knew these were not wings but wind buffeting glass. The frigid air that bit his face wasn't a dream, either. He shivered and burrowed deeper beneath the blankets, so that only his nose and cheek were exposed.

When a hand like ice was laid against his cheek, he knew that, too, was no dream.

With a shout he rolled away from the edge of the bed, thrashing against the heavy blankets as he sat up. The darkness was impenetrable: even the faint outlines of window and furniture had vanished. Everything had vanished, save a shape beside the bed. It loomed above him, darker than the surrounding room, so dark that Philip's eyes were drawn to it as if it had been a flame.

The hand touched him a second time, lingering upon his cheek. "I'm cold," someone whispered.

Philip lunged for the lamp on his nightstand. Light flooded the room, and for a moment he thought he must be dreaming—nothing extraordinary could withstand a one-hundred-watt bulb.

Then he saw the boy. He still wore Philip's clothes, the flannel shirt unbuttoned, corduroy pants clumped with burdock and specks of leaf mold. He hugged his arms to his chest and stared with huge black eyes at Philip.

"What the hell are you doing?" shouted Philip.

"I'm cold," the boy repeated.

Philip stumbled to his feet. He wore only an old T-shirt and flannel boxers, and yes, the room was cold—the door onto the porch was open. He yanked a blanket around him, tossed another at the boy.

"Put that on," he snapped.

The boy stared at the blanket, then pulled it over his shoulders. Philip edged warily around the bed to close the door, and turned.

The boy didn't look dangerous, but he was obviously in distress. Mentally ill, probably. And bigger than Philip, too. He cursed himself again for not calling the police earlier.

"What's your name?" he asked.

The boy grimaced, baring those small white teeth.

"Suru," he said.

"Suru?"

The boy hesitated, then nodded.

"Well, Suru, we need to call your parents." Philip fought to keep his voice calm. "I'm Philip. What's your phone number?"

Suru said nothing. He stared at his own hand, lifted then lowered one arm, the blanket suspended beneath like a crimson bat's wing.

"Come on," pleaded Philip. "Either you give me your parents' number or I'll have to call the police."

Without warning the boy drew up beside him. His fingers closed around Philip's hand, a sheath of ice. Again he whispered, "I'm cold."

The blanket dropped to the floor as he pressed himself against Philip's chest. Philip tried to pull away, but the boy moved with him, his expression calm even as he thrust Philip back into the room. Philip shoved him, angry, then frightened, as he struck desperately at the boy's arms and chest.

It was like grasping handfuls of something soft and gelid, fine dry snow or down that shifted beneath his fingers. Emaciated as he was, the boy was frighteningly strong. Philip cried out as the boy forced him onto the bed. He gazed up into Suru's eyes, no longer black but glaucous, a bright spark within each like a tiny shimmering seed.

Then the boy's skeletal arms were around him, holding him gently, hesitantly. He cocked his head, as though he listened for a sound other than Philip's ragged breathing, then slowly lowered his cheek until it rested against Philip's.

"You're warm," said Suru, marveling.

Philip tensed for an assault or whispered threat; a kiss; flight.

But the boy only nestled against him. A minute passed, and Philip extended his hand cautiously, touching Suru's shoulder where the flannel shirt gaped open.

"Oh my God," he exclaimed.

It wasn't dirt flecked across the boy's shoulder, as he'd first thought, but a number of small black holes. Philip brushed one with a finger, dislodging something that fell to the floor with a loud *ping*.

Buckshot.

"Someone shot you?" he said, incredulous. "Good lord, you need to see a doctor—"

"No!"

"Don't be crazy—it'll get infected. Doesn't it hurt?"

Suru shook his head. Philip started to scramble from the bed, stopped when the boy cried out.

"No. Please. It does not hurt. Only see—"

Suru gazed out at the snow eddying around the windows and French door, then turned to Philip.

"I lost the way," he said. "When I fell. I returned but it was gone."

Philip frowned. "The way?"

"From Tuonela. I fell, and you found me. I tried to go back. The way is gone."

He clutched his head and began to sob, anguished.

"No—stop, please, really, it's okay!" said Philip. "I'll get you back. Just wait a minute and—"

Suru looked at him. His eyes were huge, still that pale gray-green; but they held no tears. "Will you come with me?"

"Go with you?"

"Yes."

Philip glanced outside. He must be out of his mind, to even think of getting into the car with a stranger in the middle of the night. Though god only knew what kind of people were lurking out there in the woods, if Philip let the boy go off alone.

"All right," he said at last. "I'll go with you. But—well, you know where you're going, right?"

Suru pointed at the window. "There," he said. "Tuonela."

"Right." Philip made a face. "But not from this side, right? You came from over there, by the nature preserve, or whatever it is? I don't know those roads at all. You'll have to tell me where to go. I really think we should just call someone."

But the boy was already walking toward the door.

"Wait!" Philip grabbed him. "Let's get you some proper clothes, okay? Stay here. And don't go outside again. Don't go anywhere, or I swear to god I'll call the cops."

He waited until Suru settled back onto the bed, then went to dig around in a closet for shoes and a coat. The snow seemed to demand something more substantial than a blaze-orange vest. He retrieved his own heavy barn coat, after a few minutes located a worn parka for Suru.

Shoes were more difficult. Philip had an old, well-broken-in pair of gumshoes, but when he presented Suru with a similar pair he'd found in Sam's office, the boy flatly refused to wear them. He dismissed a second pair as well. Only when Philip threatened to remain at the lodge did Suru consent to a pair of high yellow fishing boots, unlined and smelling of mildew.

But no amount of coercion would get him to wear socks. He still hadn't buttoned his flannel shirt, either, or his fly.

"You better finish getting dressed," said Philip. Suru stared at him blankly. "Oh, for God's sake...."

He stooped to button the boy's shirt. The silvery hairs on Suru's arms stiffened, though when Philip's hand brushed against them they felt soft as fur or down. The boy sat compliantly, watching him, and Philip felt a stir of arousal. He finished with the shirt and glanced at the boy's trousers.

The zipper had come undone. Philip hesitated, then zipped it, fumbling with the fly button. He felt the boy's cock stir beneath the fabric, looked up to see Suru staring at him. Philip flushed and stood.

"Come on." He walked from the room. "I'll start the car."

Outside, snow fine as sand stung his face. He started the car and sat inside without turning on the headlights, staring at tossing trees, the black chasm where the lake stretched. When he finally headed back, Suru met him on the steps. Philip was relieved to see he still wore the boots and parka.

"You all set?"

Suru gave a small nod. Philip went inside to check the woodstove, grabbing two orange watchcaps and his walking stick as he returned. He shoved one hat onto his head, tossed the other to Suru, and gestured at the car. "Your chariot awaits."

Suru crouched to peer into one headlight, then pointed at the lake, past the spit of land where Philip had found him. "There."

"We still have to drive. I've got a map in the car, we can figure it out."

Suru shook his head. "That is not the way."

"You said you didn't know the way!"

"I said the way is *gone*."

"And?" Philip's voice rose dangerously. "Has it come back?"

Suru gazed at the sky. Above the lake the clouds parted, a rent just big enough to reveal a moon near full. Beneath it a broken lane of silver stretched across the water, fading then reappearing to ignite a stand of white birch along the shore.

"There!" exclaimed Suru, and headed for the trees.

Philip swore and hurried to turn off the car. When he stumbled back into the snow, Suru was nowhere to be seen. Neither was his walking stick. He kicked at the snow, trying to see where it had fallen, and at last gave up.

"Suru!" he yelled.

A faint voice echoed back from the trees. Philip walked as quickly as he could, praying he wouldn't fall. At the edge of the woods he halted.

All around him, the ground seemed to erupt into silvery waves. The air glittered and spun with falling snow, incandescent in the moonlight; the black lake appeared endless. A desert of obsidian, or some awful, bottomless canyon, as though the world had suddenly sheared away at Philip's feet.

He turned, shielding his eyes against the snow, but he could no longer see the lodge. The wind carried a voice to him.

"*Here!*"

A bright shape bobbed in the distance: Suru, waving excitedly. Philip headed toward him, his feet sliding across the slick ground.

In a few minutes he reached the alder thicket crowding the bank. Here it became less treacherous to move, if no easier—he had to grab handfuls of whiplike alder branches and pull himself between them. Too late he realized he hadn't worn gloves, but soon his fingers grew so numb he no longer felt where the branches slashed them. Suru's voice came again, inches from where Philip struggled to free himself from a tangle of snow-covered vines. Fingers stronger than his own closed around his hand, and the boy pulled him through.

"See?" cried Suru with a note of triumph.

Philip blinked. The snow fell more heavily here, though a spinney of young birches served as a small windbreak. Beside him, Suru stared out across the black lake, to where moonlight touched the far shore. Spruce and fir glittered as with hoarfrost. Between that shore and where they stood, moonlight traced a thin, shining crescent along the water's edge, marking a narrow path.

"The way to Tuonela," said Suru.

Philip shoved his hands into his pockets, shivering. "I thought this was all Tuonela. It's a big lake."

Suru shook his head. "This is not Tuonela. I could not find the way, until you found me."

"Good thing I did. You would have stayed there till spring. You might have died."

"No. I would not have died."

Another sound cut through the steady rush of wind, staccato and higher pitched. Philip cupped his hands around his eyes and stared up through the whirling snow.

A vast, cloudlike shape flowed across the sky, heading toward the opposite shore. As it drew nearer, Philip saw it was not a cloud, but an immense flock of birds—geese with black necks and long white wings. They moved as a school of fish does in deep water, as though they formed a single huge creature that soared high above the trees, blotting out the moon so that only faint shafts of light showed through. He felt again the horror that had gripped him earlier, when a black chasm seemed to yawn at his feet.

For days he had watched them in flight—flock upon flock of mergansers and pintails and teal, endless battalions of geese—yet, until now, he had never registered which horizon they'd been striving toward.

All this time, they should have been flying south.

But they were flying *north*.

Suru gave a low cry and darted forward, stumbling on a snow-covered rock. There were stones everywhere, frozen black waves that slashed Philip's hand like razors when he bent to help Suru to his feet. The boy trembled, and pointed at the lake.

The moonlit path had been extinguished, save for a glimmering thread that wound between trees and underbrush, more the memory of moonlight than the real thing. Philip rubbed his eyes—the lashes felt glued together by snow—then looked over his shoulder.

"We have to go back." His chest ached with cold; it hurt to speak. "We'll freeze, we're not dressed for this."

"No. I cannot return there. You must come with me."

He gazed down at Philip, unblinking. His sunken eyes seemed part of the surrounding darkness, a skull disinterred by the storm.

Yet the boy's words held no command, but a plea. The wind whipped his black hair around his face, as in one smooth motion he shrugged the parka from his shoulders. The flannel shirt billowed about his exposed chest, then was torn from him. He lowered his head until his lips grazed Philip's forehead, a kiss that burned like molten iron.

"Come with me."

He embraced Philip, and the silvery hairs lengthened into tendrils that coiled around his shoulders. The boy's mouth pressed against his, as icy thorns pricked Philip's chest, blossomed into something soft yet fluid that enveloped him from throat to knees. As in his nightmares he fell.

Yet instead of striking granite and frozen earth, he hung suspended between ground and sky, neither falling nor flying but somehow held aloft. As when he had been airborne above the stage, muscles straining as he traced a *grand jeté en avant*, a leap into the darkness he had never completed in waking life without tumbling to the floor. The dream of flight consumed him: he was part of it, as each individual bird formed part of the vast shadow that wheeled above them in the snow-filled sky. He cried out, overcome with a joy close to pain; felt the boy's embrace tighten and knew it was not arms that bore him but great wings and feathers like flashing blades. Philip clung to him, his terror flaring into desire as the wings beat furiously against the snow, Suru's legs tightening around his until with a cry Philip came, and fell back onto the frozen ground.

He rolled onto his side, struggled to pull himself upright and raised his arm, afraid to see what stood before him. White wings and arched neck and those glittering onyx eyes; a bill parted to reveal a tongue like an ebony serpent.

White wings blurred into a vortex of snow. The long neck coiled back upon itself. Only the eyes glowed as before, black and fathomless within that skull-like face.

Philip stumbled to his feet. Freezing wind tore at his clothes, yet it no longer overwhelmed him as it had just minutes before.

"Who are you?" he whispered.

"The Guardian of Tuonela," replied Suru.

Philip shuddered. He was delirious, that was why the cold didn't bother him—that, or he'd already succumbed to hypothermia, the waking dream that claimed people before they froze to death.

"The guardian of Tuonela?" he repeated stupidly. "But not *this* Tuonela."

"No. That is just a name. Tuonela is there." Suru pointed to the far shore, invisible behind snow and the storm of birds. "I have never left it unguarded. Until now."

"But—why?"

"I wished to see the other shore. But I had never fallen, or imagined that I could." He lifted his head to stare at the wheeling birds. "They cannot return until I do. And it will be a terrible thing if they do not return."

"They're migrating, that's all." Philip's voice cracked. "Birds fly south in autumn, the storm confused them—"

"They are not birds. I must go back." Suru extended his hand. "Come with me."

"I—I can't. I'll freeze—I'll die."

"You will not die with me. But—"

The boy gestured in the direction of the lodge. A gust of wind stirred the trees, and for the first time Philip could see the glow of yellow windows in the frigid night.

"If you wish to return there," said Suru, "you must travel alone."

The boy fell silent. After a moment he went on in a low voice. "I do not want to leave you here, alone. You saved me from exile. In exchange I have given you a gift."

One finger reached to touch Philip's forehead, and again icy flame blazed beneath Philip's skin.

"You're insane," said Philip. "Or I am."

He pulled away, then drove his fingernails into his palm, trying to wake himself; stamped his bad foot upon the frozen ground, a motion that should have sent him reeling.

But just as he no longer felt cold, he could no longer feel pain. The boy's touch had drawn that from him, as well.

You saved me. In exchange I have given you a gift. . . .

The wind died. Night once more claimed the glowing windows. Philip stared at the darkness that hid the lodge, that hid everything and everyone he had ever known.

Life did not work like this, love did not work like this. Philip knew that. Only stories did, where wonder trumped despair and desire overcame death. The fairy's kiss, the sacrificial faun; enchanted swans and shoes that sliced like blades, like ice. That was why he had become a dancer, not just to dream of fellowship and flight, but to partake, however fleetingly, in something close to ecstasy—and how long since he had experienced that?

Even if he hadn't lost his mind—even if this was somehow real, some crazed dream-bargain he'd made with his unconscious—he couldn't imagine leaving it all behind. How could he leave Emma and their shared childhood? Or the young dancers he'd taught and promised to see when he returned to the city; the city itself, and the little world that nested inside it, with its hierarchy of striving men and women, ballet masters and earnest intructors who might never take the stage again but still couldn't bring themselves to abandon it completely.

If something opens up, you know we'll find a place for you.

"This gift." Philip glanced at Suru. "If I go back, will it—will I still have it?"

The boy nodded, and Philip flexed his leg tentatively.

He could go back. Even if he couldn't return to his old position, he could look for other work, a smaller company, some private school in the suburbs.

Or he could stay here until he found something. Emma would love it, and Sam. He could see spring for the first time at Tuonela. Wild geese and swallows returning from their winter migration; a solitary swan plying blue water, dark ripples in its wake.

He took a deep breath and turned to where Suru stood, waiting. "I'll go with you."

Suru took his hand and drew him to his side, then led him, slowly, along the water's edge. Before them the thread of moonlight wove between stones and ice-skimmed pools, frozen cattails and snow-covered spruce and birch. Birds filled the sky, not just waterfowl but owls and ravens, gulls and hawks, great crested herons and tiny kinglets and scissor-winged swallows that soared and skimmed above the lake but never touched its surface.

Pinwheels of snow spun in their wake, extinguished by the black waters of Tuonela. With every step that Suru took, more birds appeared. The air became a living whirlwind, wings and shrill chatter, whistles and croaks; over it all a solitary, heartrending song like a mockingbird's, that ended in a convulsive throb of grief or joy.

Philip didn't know how long they walked. Hours, perhaps. The moon never seemed to move from where it shone above the far shore. Snow blew across the moonlit path, but no more fell from the sky. The birds no longer sang, though Philip still felt the rush of untold wings. He was neither tired nor chilled; whenever his hand brushed Suru's, cold fire flashed through his veins.

The snow grew very deep, so powdery it was like swimming through drifts of cloud. Overhead, evergreen branches made a pattern like frost crystals against the stars. The trees grew taller, and Philip now saw that each had been slashed as with an ax, two deep grooves that formed a V. Suru touched one, withdrew a white finger glistening with sap and fragrant as balsam.

"These mark the border," he said. "We are within Tuonela now."

They walked on. Gradually, the distant shore came into view. A long rock-strewn beach and towering pines, stands of birch larger than any Philip had ever seen. Behind the beach rose a sheer black cliff hundreds of feet tall, dappled silver where moonlight touched fissures and ragged outcroppings.

Suru halted. He stared at the desolate trees and that impassable wall of stone, the onyx waves lapping at the beach. Above the cliff countless birds circled restlessly. The great pines bowed beneath the wind of their flight.

"We are nearly there," said Suru.

He turned to Philip and smiled. The flesh melted from his face. Sparks flickered within empty eye sockets; his mouth opened onto a darkness deeper than the sky. He was neither boy nor swan but bone and flame.

Yet he was not terrible, and he bowed as he took Philip's hand, indicating where a deep ravine split the ground a short distance from where they stood. A stream rushed through the channel, tumbling over rocks and bubbles of ice, before plunging in a shining waterfall that spilled into the lake. A fallen birch tree spanned the cleft. Ribbons of mottled bark peeled from its trunk, and there were jagged spurs where branches had broken or rotted away.

"I will cross before you," he said. "Wait until I have reached the other side. Do not look down."

Philip shook his head. "I can't."

His tongue seemed to freeze against the roof of his mouth as he stared into the ravine, those knife-edged rocks and roaring cataract. At its center a whirlpool spun, a dreadful mouth gaping at the moon overhead.

Suru lifted a fleshless hand. "You must. All things make this crossing." He pointed to where the birds wheeled against the sky.

"That is their road. This is mine. No living thing has ever taken it with me. That is my second gift to you."

Before Philip could reply, Suru turned. His arms stretched upward, all bones and light as he crouched, then leapt above the chasm. For an instant his skull merged with the moon, and a face gazed pityingly down upon the man who remained on the shore.

Then moonlight splintered the cage of bone. Feathers unfurled in a glory of wings that rose and fell, slowly at first, then more and more swiftly, until the night sky fell back before them and light touched the clifftops. The great pines kindled red and gold as thousands upon thousands of birds dove toward the surface of the lake and landed, the cliffs ringing with their cries.

"*Come!*"

Philip looked up to see the great swan hovering above the far shore, its eyes no longer black but blazing argent. The terrifying joy he'd felt earlier returned. For a second he closed his eyes, trying to summon every memory of the world behind him.

Then he walked to the tree, lifted one foot, and carefully stepped onto it.

Icy spume lashed his face as dread jolted him along with bitter cold. He looked up, terrified, but was blinded by needles of ice; shaded his eyes and took a second, lurching step.

Beneath him the great birch trembled like a live thing. Philip gasped, then edged forward. He could no longer see the other shore; could see nothing but a glittering arc of frozen spray as he inched across the fallen tree. When he was halfway across, he glanced down.

At the edge of the waterfall a figure knelt, her skin white as birch, her head bowed so he could only see a cascade of long black hair tangled in the whirlpool. As Philip watched she grasped her hair with both hands and began to drag it back through the frigid water, as though it were a net, then hoisted it upon the frozen shore, so that he saw what she had captured: countless men and women, infants and children, their eyes wide and staring and hands plucking uselessly at the net that had ensnared them.

With a cry Philip stumbled and nearly fell. The woman looked up, her eyes empty sockets in a barren skull, mouth bared in a rictus of hunger and rage. Philip righted himself, then lurched toward the other bank.

Something coiled around his ankle, taut as a wire. He gave a muffled shout, looked up to see the great swan still hovering above the shore. The bank was yet a few yards off. Another strand of black hair snaked toward him, writhing as it sought to loop around his wrist.

"*Jump!*" cried Suru.

Philip raised his arms, felt his balance shift from shoulders to calves to the balls of his feet. Faint chiming sounded in his ears: cracking ice, the ballet mistress's bell when he was a boy; the tree beneath him splintering. Pain sheared his foot as he arched forward; and jumped.

His face burned, his eyes. The chiming became a roar. Around him all was flame but it was not the air that was ablaze but Philip himself. His skin peeled away in petals of black and gold, embers blown like snow.

But it was not snow but wings: Suru's and his own, beating against the air. Far below, the black waters erupted as wave after wave of birds rose to greet them, geese and hawks and swallows, cranes and swifts and tanagers, gulls with the eyes of women and child-faced doves: all swallowed by the sunrise as they mounted the sky above the cliffs, and two swans like falling stars disappeared into the horizon.

It was several days before Joe Moody checked on the camp. The storm had brought down power lines, but he assumed that Emma's friend would be fine, what with the generator and four cords of firewood.

He found the lodge deserted, and Philip's rental car buried under the snow. There were no footprints leading to or from the lodge; no sign of forced entry or violence. Emma and her husband were notified in Key West and returned, heartsick, to aid the warden service and police in the search. Divers searched the frigid waters of Lake Tuonela, but no body was ever found.

Only Emma ever noticed afterward, year after year, that a pair of swans appeared each spring—silent, inseparable—to make their slow passage across dark water before vanishing in the mist.

Winter's Wife

Winter's real name was Roderick Gale Winter. But everyone in Paswegas County, not just me and people who knew him personally, called him Winter. He lived in an old school bus down the road from my house, and my mother always tells how when she first moved here he scared the crap out of her. It wasn't even him that scared her, she hadn't even met him yet; just the fact that there was this creepy-looking old school bus stuck in the middle of the woods, with smoke coming out of a chimney and these huge piles of split logs around and trucks and cranes and heavy equipment, and in the summer all kinds of chain saws and stuff, and in the fall deer and dead coyotes hanging from this big pole that my mother said looked like a gallows, and blood on the snow, and once a gigantic dead pig's head with tusks, which my mother said was scarier even than the coyotes. Which, when you think of it, does sound pretty bad, so you can't blame her for being freaked out. It's funny now because she and Winter are best friends, though that doesn't mean so much as it does other places, like Chicago, where my mother moved here from, because I think everyone in Shaker Harbor thinks Winter is their friend.

The school bus, when you get inside it, is sweet.

Winter's family has been in Shaker Harbor for six generations, and even before that they lived somewhere else in Maine.

"I have Passamaquoddy blood," Winter says. "If I moved somewhere else, I'd melt."

He didn't look like a Native American, though, and my mother said if he did have Indian blood it had probably been diluted by now. Winter was really tall and skinny, not sick skinny but bony and muscular, stooped from having to duck through the door of the school bus all those years. He always wore a gimme cap that said WINTER TREE SERVICE, and I can remember how shocked I was once when I saw him at Town Meeting without his hat, and he had almost no hair. He'd hunt and butcher his own deer, but he wouldn't eat it— he said he'd grown up dirt-poor in a cabin that didn't even have a wooden floor, just pounded earth, and his family would eat anything they could hunt, including snake and skunk and snapping turtle. So he'd give all his venison away, and when people hired him to butcher their livestock and gave him meat, he'd give that away, too.

That was how my mother met him, that first winter fifteen years ago when she was living here alone, pregnant with me. There was a big storm going on, and she looked out the window and saw this tall guy stomping through the snow carrying a big paper bag.

"You a vegetarian?" he said, when she opened the door. "Everyone says there's a lady from away living here who's going to have a baby and she's a vegetarian. But you don't look like one to me."

My mother said no, she wasn't a vegetarian, she was a registered certified massage therapist.

"Whatever the hell that is," said Winter. "You going to let me in? Jesus Q. Murphy, is that your woodstove?"

See, my mother had gotten pregnant by a sperm donor. She had it all planned out, how she was going to move way up north and have a baby and raise it—him, me—by herself and live off the land and be a massage thera-pist and hang crystals in the windows and there would be this good energy and everything was going to be perfect. And it would have been, if she had moved to, like, Huntington Beach or even Boston, someplace like that, where it would be warmer and there would be good skate parks, instead of a place where you have to drive two hours to a skate park and it snows from November till the end of May. And in the spring you can't even skate on the roads here because they're all dirt roads and so full of potholes you could live in one. But the snowboarding is good, especially since Winter let us put a jump right behind his place.

But this part is all before any snowboarding, because it was all before me, though not much before. My mother was living in this tiny two-room camp with no indoor plumbing and no running water, with an ancient woodstove, what they call a parlor stove, which looked nice but didn't put out any heat and caused a chimney fire. Which was how Winter heard about her, because the volunteer fire department came and afterwards all anyone was talking about at the Shaker Harbor Variety Store was how this crazy lady from away had bought Martin Weed's old run-down camp and now she was going to have a baby and freeze to death or burn the camp down—probably both—which probably would have been okay with them except no one liked to think about the baby getting frozen or burned up.

So Winter came by and gave my mother the venison and looked at her woodpile and told her she was burning green wood, which builds up creosote, which was why she had the chimney fire, and he asked her who sold her the wood, so she told him. And the next day the guy who sold her the wood came by and dumped off three cords of seasoned wood and drove off without saying a word, and the day after that two other guys came by with a brand-new woodstove, which was ugly but very efficient and had a sheath around it so a baby wouldn't get burned if he touched it. And the day after *that,* Winter came by to make sure the stove was hooked up right, and he went to all the cabin's windows with sheets of plastic and a hair dryer and covered them so the cold wouldn't get in, and then he showed my mother where there was a spring in the woods that she could go to and fill water jugs rather than buy them at the grocery store. He also gave her a chamber pot so she wouldn't have to use the outhouse, and told her he knew of someone who had a composting toilet they'd sell to her cheap.

All of which might make you think that when I say "Winter's wife" I'm referring to my mom. But I'm not. Winter's wife is someone else.

Still, when I was growing up, Winter was always at our house. And I was at his place, when I got older. Winter chops down trees, what they call wood lot management—he cuts trees for people, but in a good way, so the forest can grow back and be healthy. Then he'd split the wood so the people could burn it for firewood. He had a portable sawmill—one of the scary things Mom had seen in his yard—and he also mills wood so people can build houses with the lumber. He's an auctioneer, and he can play the banjo and one of those washboard things like you see in old movies. He showed me how to jump-start a car with just a wire coat hanger, also how to carve wood and build a tree house and frame a window. When my mother had our little addition put on with a bathroom in it, Winter did a lot of the carpentry, and he taught me how to do that, too.

He's also a dowser, a water witch. That's someone who can tell where water is underground, just by walking around in the woods holding a stick in front of him. You'd think this was more of that crazy woo-woo stuff my mother is into, which is what I thought whenever I heard about it.

But then one day me and my friend Cody went out to watch Winter do it. We were hanging out around Winter's place, clearing brush. He let us use the hill behind the school bus for snowboarding, and that's where we'd built that sweet jump, and Winter had saved a bunch of scrap wood so that when spring came we could build a half-pipe for skating, too.

But now it was spring, and since we didn't have any money really to pay Winter for it, he put us to work clearing brush. Cody is my age, almost fourteen. So we're hacking at this brush and swatting blackflies, and I could tell that at any minute Cody was going to say he had to go do homework, which was a lie because we didn't have any, when Winter shows up in his pickup, leans out the window, and yells at us.

"You guys wanna quit goofing off and come watch someone do some real work?"

So then me and Cody had an argument about who was going to ride shotgun with Winter, and then we had another argument about who was going to ride in the truck bed, which is actually more fun. And then we took so long arguing that Winter yelled at us and made us both ride in the back.

So we got to the place where Winter was going to work. This field that had been a dairy farm, but the farm wasn't doing too good and the guy who owned it had to sell it off. Ms. Whitton, a high school teacher, was going to put a little modular house on it. There'd been a bad drought a few years earlier, and a lot of wells ran dry. Ms. Whitton didn't have a lot of money to spend on digging around for a well, so she hired Winter to find the right spot.

"Justin!" Winter yelled at me as he hopped out of the truck. "Grab me that hacksaw there—"

I gave him the saw, then me and Cody went and goofed around some more while Winter walked around the edge of the field, poking at brush and scrawny trees. After a few minutes he took the hacksaw to a spindly sapling.

"Got it!" Winter yelled, and stumbled back into the field. "If we're going to find water here, we better find a willow first."

It was early spring, and there really weren't any leaves out yet, so what he had was more like a pussy willow, with furry gray buds and green showing where he'd sawn the branch off. Winter stripped the buds from it until he had a forked stick. He held the two ends like he was holding handlebars and began to walk around the field.

It was weird. Cause at first, me and Cody were laughing—we didn't mean to, we couldn't help it. It just looked funny, Winter walking back and forth with his arms out holding that stick. He kind of looked like Frankenstein. Even Ms. Whitton was smiling.

But then it was like everything got very still. Not quiet—you could hear the wind blowing in the trees, and hear birds in the woods, and someone running a chain saw far off—but still, like all of a sudden you were in a movie and you knew something was about to happen. The sun was warm, I could smell dirt and cow manure and meadowsweet. Cody started slapping blackflies and swearing. I felt dizzy, not bad dizzy, but like you do when the school bus drives fast over a high bump and you go up on your seat. A few feet away Winter continued walking in a very straight line, the willow stick held out right in front of him.

And all of a sudden the stick began to bend. I don't mean that Winter's arms bent down holding it: I mean the stick itself, the point that stuck straight out, bent down like it was made of rubber and someone had grabbed it and yanked it towards the ground. Only it wasn't made of rubber, it was stiff wood, and there was no one there— but it still bent, pointing at a mossy spot between clumps of dirt.

"Holy crap," I said.

Cody shut up and looked. So did Ms. Whitton.

"Oh my God," she said.

Winter stopped, angling the stick back and forth like he was fighting with it. Then it lunged down, and he yelled "Whoa!" and opened his hands and dropped it. Me and Cody ran over.

"This is it," said Winter. He pulled a spool of pink surveyor's tape from his pocket and broke off a length. I stared warily at the willow stick, half expecting it to wiggle up like a snake, but it didn't move. After a moment I picked it up.

"How'd you do that?" demanded Cody.

"I didn't do it," said Winter evenly. He took the stick from my hand, snapped off the forked part, and tossed it; tied the surveyor's tape to what remained and stuck it in the ground. "Wood does that. Wood talks to you, if you listen."

"No lie," I said. "Can you show me how to do that sometime?"

"Sure," said Winter. "Can't today, got a towing job. But someday."

He and Ms. Whitton started talking about money and who had the best rates for drilling. The next time my mom drove past that field, the drill rig was there hammering at the ground right where Winter's stick had pointed, and the next time I ran into Ms. Whitton in the hall at school she told me the well was already dug and all geared up to pump a hundred gallons a minute, once she got her foundation dug and her house moved in.

Not long after that, Winter announced he was going to Reykjavik.

It was after school one day, and Winter had dropped by to shoot the breeze.

"What's Reykjavik?" I asked.

"It's in Iceland," said my mother. She cracked the window open and sat at the kitchen table opposite Winter and me. "Why on earth are you going to Reykjavik?"

"To pick up my wife," said Winter.

"Your wife?" My eyes widened. "You're married?"

"Nope. That's why I'm going to Iceland to pick her up. I met her online, and we're going to get married."

My mother looked shocked. "In *Iceland!*"

Winter shrugged. "Hey, with a name like mine, where else you gonna find a wife?"

So he went to Iceland. I thought he'd be gone for a month, at least, but a week later the phone rang and my mom answered and it was Winter, saying he was back safe and yes, he'd brought his wife with him.

"That's incredible," said Mom. She put the phone down and shook her head. "He was there for four days, got married, and now they're back. I can't believe it."

A few days later they dropped by so Winter could introduce us to her. It was getting near the end of the school year, and me and Cody were outside throwing stuff at my tree house, using the open window as a target. Sticks, a Frisbee, a broken yo-yo. Stuff like that.

"Why are you trying to break the house?" a woman asked.

I turned. Winter stood there grinning, hands in the pockets of his jeans, his gimme cap pushed back so the bill pointed almost straight up. Beside him stood a woman who barely came up to his shoulder. She was so slight that for a second I thought she was another kid, maybe one of the girls from school who'd ridden her bike over or hopped a ride in Winter's truck. But she didn't have a kid's body, and she sure didn't have a kid's eyes.

"Justin." Winter squared his shoulders and his voice took on a mock-formal tone. "I'd like you to meet my wife. Vala, this is Justin."

"Justin." The way she said my name made my neck prickle. It was like she was turning the word around in her mouth; like she was tasting it. "*Gleour mig ao kynnast per.* That's Icelandic for 'I am glad to meet you.'"

She didn't really have an accent, although her voice sounded more English than American. And she definitely didn't look like anyone I'd ever seen in Maine, even though she was dressed pretty normal. Black jeans, a black T-shirt. Some kind of weird-looking bright blue shoes with thick rubber soles, which I guess is what people wear in Iceland; also a bright blue windbreaker. She had long, straight black hair done in two ponytails—one reason she looked like a kid—kind of slanted eyes and a small mouth and the palest skin I've ever seen.

It was the eyes that really creeped me out. They were long and narrow and very very dark, so dark you couldn't even see the pupil. And they weren't brown but blue, so deep a blue they were almost black. I'd never seen eyes that color before, and I didn't really like seeing them now. They were cold—not mean or angry, just somehow *cold*; or maybe it was that they made me feel cold, looking at them.

And even though she looked young, because she was skinny and her hair didn't have any gray in it and her face wasn't wrinkled, it was like she was somehow pretending to be young. Like when someone pretends to like kids, and you know they don't, really. Though I didn't get the feeling Vala didn't like kids. She seemed more puzzled, like maybe we looked as strange to her as she did to me.

"You haven't told me why you are trying to break the house," she said.

I shrugged. "Uh, we're not. We're just trying to get things through that window."

Cody glanced at Vala, then began searching for more rocks to throw.

Vala stared at him coolly. "Your friend is very rude."

She looked him up and down, then walked over to the tree house. It was built in the crotch of a big old maple tree, and it was so solid you could live in it, if you wanted to, only it didn't have a roof.

"What tree is this?" she asked, and looked at Winter.

"Red maple," he said.

"Red maple," she murmured. She ran her hand along the trunk, stroking it, like it was a cat. "Red maple..."

She turned and stared at me. "You made this house? By yourself?"

"No." She waited, like it was rude of me not to say more. So I walked over to her and stood awkwardly, staring up at the bottom of the tree house. "Winter helped me. I mean, your husband—Mr. Winter."

"Mr. Winter." Unexpectedly she began to laugh. A funny laugh, like a little kid's, and after a moment I laughed, too. "So I am Mrs. Winter? But who should be Winter's proper wife—Spring, maybe?"

She made a face when she said this, like she knew how dumb it sounded; then reached to take my hand. She drew me closer to her, until we both stood beside the tree. I felt embarrassed—maybe this was how they did things in Iceland, but not here in Maine—but I was flattered, too. Because the way she looked at me, sideways from the corner of her eyes, and the way she smiled, not like I was a kid but another grown-up . . . it was like she knew a secret, and she acted like I knew it, too.

Which of course I didn't. But it was kind of cool that she thought so. She let go of my hand and rested hers against the tree again, rubbing a patch of lichen.

"There are no trees in Iceland," she said. "Did you know that? No trees. Long long ago they cut them all down to build houses or ships, or to burn. And so we have no trees, only rocks and little bushes that come to here—"

She indicated her knee, then tapped the tree trunk. "And like this—lichen, and moss. We have a joke, do you know it?"

She took a breath, then said, "What do you do if you get lost in a forest in Iceland?"

"I shook my head. "I dunno."

"Stand up."

It took me a moment to figure that out. Then I laughed, and Vala smiled at me. Again she looked like she was waiting for me to say something. I wanted to be polite, but all I could think was how weird it must be, to come from a place where there were no trees to a place like Maine, where there's trees everywhere.

So I said, "Uh, do you miss your family?"

She gave me a funny look. "My family? They are happy to live with the rocks back in Iceland. I am tired of rocks."

A shadow fell across her face. She glanced up as Winter put his hands on her shoulders. "Your mother home, Justin?" he asked. "We're on our way into town, just wanted to say a quick hello and introduce the new wife—"

I nodded and pointed back to the house. As Winter turned to go, Vala gave me another sharp look.

"He tells me many good things about you. You and he are what we would call *feogar*—like a father and his son, Winter says. So I will be your godmother."

She pointed a finger at me, then slowly drew it to my face until she touched my chin. I gasped: her touch was so cold it burned.

"There," she murmured. "Now I will always know you."

And she followed Winter inside. When they were gone, Cody came up beside me.

"Was that freaky or what?" he said. He stared at the house. "She looks like that weird singer, Boink."

"You mean Bjork, you idiot."

"Whatever. Where is Iceland, anyway?"

"I have no clue."

"Me neither." Cody pointed at my chin. "Hey, you're bleeding, dude."

I frowned, then gingerly touched the spot where Vala had pressed her finger. It wasn't bleeding; but when I looked at it later that night I saw a red spot, shaped like a fingerprint. Not a scab or blister or scar but a spot like a birthmark, deep red like blood. Over the next few days it faded, and finally disappeared; but I can still feel it there sometimes even now, a sort of dull ache that gets worse when it's cold outside, or snowing.

That same month, Thomas Tierney returned to Paswegas County. He was probably the most famous person in this whole state, after

Stephen King, but everyone up here loves Stephen King and I never heard anyone say anything good about Thomas Tierney except after he disappeared; and then the only thing people said was good riddance to bad rubbish. Even my mom, who gets mad if you say something bad about anyone, even if they hit you first, never liked Thomas Tierney.

"He's one of those people who thinks they can buy anything. And if he can't buy it, he ruins it for everyone else."

Though the truth was there wasn't much that he wasn't able to buy, especially in Paswegas. People here don't have a lot of money. They had more after Tierney's telemarketing company moved into the state and put up its telephone centers everywhere, even one not too far from Shaker Harbor, which is pretty much the end of nowhere. Then people who used to work as fishermen or farmers or teachers or nurses, but who couldn't make a living at it anymore, started working for International Corporate Enterprises. ICE didn't pay a lot, but I guess it paid okay, if you didn't mind sitting in a tiny cubicle and calling strangers on the phone when they were in the middle of dinner and annoying them so they swore at you or just hung up.

Once when she heard me and Cody ranking on people who worked at ICE, my mom took us aside and told us we had to be careful what we said, because even if we hated the company, it gave people jobs, and that was nothing to sneeze at. Of course a lot of those people who worked for ICE ended up not being able to afford to live here anymore, because Tierney gave all his friends from away the expensive jobs; and then they bought land here, which used to be cheap, and built these big fancy houses. So now normal people can't afford to live here, unless they were lucky enough to already own a house or land, like my mom and Winter.

But then Tierney got caught doing something bad, sneaking money from his company or something, and ICE got bought by a bigger company, and they shut down all their operations in Maine, and all the people who worked there got thrown out of work and a lot of them who did own their own houses or land got them taken away because they couldn't afford to pay their bills anymore. Then people *really* hated Thomas Tierney; but it didn't do any good, because he never even got in trouble for what he did. I mean he didn't go to jail or anything, and he didn't lose his money or his house down in Kennebunkport or his yacht or his private airplane.

As a matter of fact, the opposite happened: he bought the land next to Winter's. Winter dropped by the day he found out about it.

"That sumbitch bought old Lonnie Packard's farm!" he yelled.

Me and Cody looked at each other and sort of smirked, but we didn't say anything. I could tell Cody wanted to laugh, like I did— who the hell actually says "sumbitch?"—but at the same time it was scary, because we'd never seen Winter get mad before.

"I can't blame Lonnie," Winter went on, shifting from one foot to the other and tugging at his cap. "He had to sell his lobster boat last year 'cause he couldn't pay his taxes, and then he had that accident and couldn't pay the hospital. And it's a salt farm right there on the ocean, so he never got much out of it except the view."

Cody asked, "Why didn't he sell it to you?"

Winter whacked his palm against the wall. "That's what I said! I told Lonnie long time ago, ever he wanted to sell that land, I'd take it. But yesterday he told me, 'Winter, your pockets just ain't that deep.' I said, 'Well, Lonnie, how deep is deep?' And he pointed out there at the Atlantic Ocean, and said, 'You see that? You go out to the Grand Banks and find the deepest part, and I'm telling you it ain't deep as Thomas Tierney's pockets.'"

So that was that. Tell you the truth, I didn't give much thought to it. Where we snowboarded in the woods was safely on Winter's property, I knew that; besides which, it was late spring now, and me and Cody were busy working on that half-pipe behind Winter's house and, once it was done, skating on it.

Sometimes Winter's wife would come out and watch us. Winter had made her a bench from a hunk of oak, laid slats across it, and carved her name on the seat, VALA, with carved leaves and vines coming out of the letters. The bench was set up on a little rise, so that you could look out across the tops of the trees and just catch a glimpse of the ocean, silver-blue above the green. Vala was so tiny she looked like another kid sitting there, watching us and laughing when we fell, though never in a mean way. Her laugh was like her eyes: there was a kind of coldness to it, but it wasn't nasty, more like she had never seen anyone fall before and every time it happened (which was a lot) it was a surprise to her. Even though it was warmer now, she always wore that same blue windbreaker, and over it a sweatshirt that I recognized as one of Winter's, so big it was like a saggy dress. It could get wicked hot out there at the edge of the woods, but I never saw her take that sweatshirt off.

"Aren't you hot?" I asked her once. She'd brought some water for us and some cookies she'd made, gingersnaps that were thin and brittle as ice and so spicy they made your eyes sting.

"Hot?" She shook her head. "I never get warm. Except with Winter." She smiled then, one of her spooky smiles that always made me nervous.

"I tell him it's the only time winter is ever warm, when he is lying beside me."

I felt my face turn red. On my chin, the spot where she had touched me throbbed as though someone had shoved a burning cigarette against my skin. Vala's smile grew wider, her eyes, too. She began to laugh.

"You're still a boy." For a moment she sounded almost like my mother. "Good boys, you and your friend. You will grow up to be good men. Not like this man Tierney, who thinks he can own the sea by buying salt. There is nothing more dangerous than a man who thinks he has power." She lifted her head to gaze into the trees, then turned to stare at me. "Except for one thing."

But she didn't say what that was.

I had always heard a lot about Thomas Tierney, and even though I had never seen him, there were signs of him everywhere around Shaker Harbor. The addition to the library; the addition to the school; the big old disused mill—renamed the ICE Mill—that he bought and filled with a thousand tiny cubicles, each with its own computer and its own telephone. The ICE Mill employed so many people that some of them drove two hours each way to work—there weren't enough people around Shaker Harbor to fill it.

But now it was empty, with big FOR SALE signs on it. Winter said it would stay empty, too, because no one in Paswegas County could afford to buy it.

"And no one outside of Paswegas County would *want* to buy it," he added. "Watch that doesn't drip—"

I was helping Winter varnish a crib he'd made, of wood milled from an elm tree that had died of the blight. He wouldn't say who it was for, even when I asked him outright, but I assumed it was a present for Vala. She didn't look pregnant, and I was still a little fuzzy about the precise details of what exactly might make her pregnant, in spite of some stuff me and Cody checked out online one night. But there didn't seem much point in making a trip to Iceland to get a wife if you weren't going to have kids. That's what Cody's dad said, anyway, and he should know since Cody has five brothers and twin sisters.

"I think they should make the mill into an indoor skate park," I said, touching up part of the crib I'd missed. "That would be sweet."

We were working outside, so I wouldn't inhale varnish fumes, in the shadow of a tower of split logs that Winter sold as firewood. I had to be careful that sawdust didn't get onto the newly varnished crib, or bugs.

Winter laughed. "Not much money in skate parks."

"I'd pay."

"That's my point." Winter shoved his cap back from his forehead. "Ready to break for lunch?"

Usually Winter made us sandwiches, Swiss cheese and tomato and horseradish sauce. Sometimes Vala would make us lunch, and then I'd lie and say I wasn't hungry or had already eaten, since the sandwiches she made mostly had fish in them—not tuna fish, either—and were on these tiny little pieces of bread that tasted like cardboard.

But today Winter said we'd go into town and get something from Shelley's Place, the hot dog stand down by the harbor. It was warm out, mid-August; school would start soon. I'd spent the summer hanging out with Cody and some of our friends, until the last few weeks, when Cody had gone off to Bible camp.

That's when Winter put me to work. Because along with the crib, Winter had started building a house—a real house, not an addition to the school bus. I helped him clear away brush, then helped build the forms for the foundation to be poured into. Once the concrete cured, we began framing the structure. Sometimes Vala helped, until Winter yelled at her to stop, anyway. Then she'd go off to tend the little garden she'd planted at the edge of the woods.

Now I didn't know where Vala was. So I put aside the can of varnish and hopped into Winter's pickup, and we drove into town. Most of the summer people had already left, but there were still a few sailboats in the harbor, including one gigantic yacht, the *Ice Queen*, a three-masted schooner that belonged to Thomas Tierney. According to Winter she had a crew of ten, not just a captain and mate and deckhands but a cook and housekeeper, all for Tierney; as well as a red-and-white-striped mainsail, not that you'd ever have any trouble telling her apart from any of the other boats around here.

When he saw the *Ice Queen*, Winter scowled. But there was no other sign of Tierney, not that I could see. A few summer holdovers stood in line in front of Shelley's little food stand, trying to act like they fit in with the locals, even though the only other people were contractors working on job sites.

And Lonnie Packard. He was at the very front of the line, paying for a hot dog with onions and sauerkraut wrapped in a paper towel. It was the first time I'd seen Lonnie since I'd heard about him selling his farm to Thomas Tierney, and from the look on Winter's face, it was the first time he'd seen him, too. His mouth was twisted like he wasn't sure if he was going to smile or spit something out, but then Lonnie turned and nodded at him.

"Winter," he said. He pronounced it "Wintah" in this exaggerated way he had, like he was making fun of his own strong accent. "How's it hanging?"

Winter poked at the bill of his cap and gave his head a small shake. "Not bad." He looked at Lonnie's hot dog, then flashed me a sideways grin. "Now *that* looks like lunch. Right, Justin?"

So that's how I knew Winter wasn't going to stay pissed about Lonnie selling his farm, which was kind of a relief.

But Lonnie didn't look relieved. He looked uncomfortable, although Lonnie usually looked uncomfortable. He was a big rough-faced guy, not as tall as Winter but definitely plus-sized, with a bushy brown beard and baggy jeans tucked into high rubber fisherman's boots, which kind of surprised me since I knew he'd had to sell his boat. Then I remembered all the money he must have gotten from Thomas Tierney; enough to buy another boat, probably. Enough to buy anything he wanted.

"Gotta run," said Lonnie. "Got you an assistant there, eh, Winter?"

"Justin does good work," said Winter, and moved up to the window to place our order. For a moment Lonnie stared at him like he was going to say something else, but Winter was already talking to Shelley.

Instead, Lonnie glanced at me again. It was a funny look, not like he was going to speak to me, more like he was trying to figure something out. Lonnie's not stupid, either. He puts on that heavy accent and acts like he's never been south of Bangor, but my mother said he actually has a law degree and fishes just because he likes it better than being a lawyer, which I think I would, too. I waited to see if he was going to talk to me, but instead he turned and walked quickly to where a brand-new SUV was parked in one of the spots reserved for fishermen, got inside, and drove off. I watched him go, then angled up beside Winter to get my food.

Shelley gave me a quick smile and went back to talking to Winter. "See you're putting a house up by your place," she said, and handed him a paper towel with two hot dogs on it, a container of fried clams for Winter, and two bottles of Moxie. Winter nodded but didn't say anything, just passed her some money.

"Regular housing boom going on down there," Shelley added, then looked past us to the next customer. "Can I help you?"

We drove back to Winter's place and ate, sitting outside on a couple of lawn chairs and listening to woodpeckers in the pine grove. The air smelled nice, like sawdust and varnish and fried clams. When I was almost done, Vala stepped out of the school bus and walked over to me.

"Ertu buinn?" she said teasingly. "Are you finished? And you didn't save any for me?"

I looked uncertainly at Winter, still chewing.

"Mmm-mm," he said, flapping his hand at me. "None for her! Nothing unhealthy!"

"Hmph." Vala tossed her head, black ponytails flying. "Like I'd eat that—it's nothing but grease."

She watched disapprovingly as the last fried clam disappeared into Winter's mouth, then looked at me. "Come here, Justin. I want to show you something."

"Hey!" Winter called in mock alarm as Vala beckoned me towards the edge of the woods. "He's on the clock!"

"Now he's off," retorted Vala, and stuck her tongue out. "Come on."

Vala was strange. Sometimes she acted like my mother, grumpy about me forgetting to take my shoes off when I went into the school bus, or if me and Cody made too much noise. Other times, like now, she acted more like a girl my own age, teasing and unpredictable.

The way she looked changed, too. I don't mean her clothes— she pretty much wore the same thing all the time—but the way that sometimes she would look old, like my mom does, and other times she'd look the same age as me and my friends. Which creeped me out, especially if it was one of those times when she was acting young, too.

Fortunately, just then she was acting young but looking older, like someone who would be married to Winter. For one thing, she was wearing his clothes, a pair of jeans way too big for her and cuffed up so much you couldn't even see her shoes, and that baggy sweatshirt, despite it being so hot.

"I said *come,"* she repeated, and whacked me on the shoulder.

I stood hastily and followed her, wondering if everyone in Iceland was like this, or if it was just Vala.

Under the trees everything was green and gold and warm; not hot like out in the full sun, but not cool, either. It made me sweat, and my sweat and the dim light made the mosquitoes come out, lots of them, though they never seemed to bother Vala, and after a few minutes I ignored them and (mostly) forgot about them. The ground was soft and smelled like worms, a good smell that made me think of fishing, and now and then we'd go by a kind of tree that smelled so good I'd stop for a second, a tree that Winter calls Balm of Gilead, because its buds smell like incense.

Winter owned a lot of land, more than a hundred acres. Some of it he cut for firewood or lumber, but not this part. This part he left wild, because it joined up with Lonnie's land—Thomas Tierney's land, now—and because it was old-growth forest. People think that all the woods in Maine are wild and old, but most of it isn't much older than what you'd find someplace like New Jersey—the trees were cut hundreds or maybe a thousand years ago by the Passamaquoddy or other Indians, and when those trees grew back they were cut by Vikings, and when those trees grew back they were cut by the English and the French and everyone else, all the way up till now.

So there's actually not a lot of true virgin forest, even if the trees look ancient, like what you see in a movie when they want you to think it's someplace totally wild, when it's really, like, trees that are maybe forty or fifty years old. Baby trees.

But these trees weren't like that. These were old trees—wolf trees, some of them, the kind of trees that Winter usually cuts down. A wolf tree is a big crooked tree with a huge canopy that hogs all the light and soil and crowds out the other trees. Wolf trees are junk trees, because they're crooked and spread out so much they're not much good for lumber, and they overwhelm other, smaller trees and keep them from growing up tall and straight so they can be harvested.

When I was little I'd go with Winter into the woods to watch him work, and I was always afraid of the wolf trees. Not because there was anything scary about them—they looked like ordinary trees, only big.

But I thought wolves lived in them. When I said that to Winter once, he laughed.

"I thought that too, when I was your age." He was oiling his chain saw, getting ready to limb a wolf tree, a red oak. Red oaks smell terrible when you cut them, the raw wood stinks—they smell like dog crap. "Want to know the real reason they call them that?"

I nodded, breathing through my mouth.

"It's because a thousand years ago, in England and around there, they'd hang outlaws from a tree like this. Wolf's-head trees, they called them, because the outlaws were like wolves, preying on weaker people."

Where the wolf trees grew here, they had shaded out most other trees. Now and then I saw an old apple tree overgrown with wild grape vines, remnants of Lonnie's family farm. Because even though this was old-growth forest, birds and animals don't know that. They eat fruit from the farm then poop out the seeds—that's how you get apple trees and stuff like that in the middle of the woods.

I was getting hot and tired of walking. Vala hadn't said anything since we started, hadn't even looked back at me, and I wondered if she'd forgotten I was even there. My mother said pregnancy makes women spacey, more than usual even. I was trying to think of an excuse to turn back, when she stopped.

"Here," she said.

We'd reached a hollow on the hillside above the farm. I could just make out the farmhouse and barn and outbuildings, some apple trees and the overgrown field that led down to the ocean. There was no real beach there, just lots of big granite rocks, also a long metal dock that I didn't remember having seen before.

It was still a pretty spot, tucked into the woods. A few yards from the farmhouse, more trees marched down to a cliff above the rocky beach. Small trees, all twisted from the wind: except for three huge white pines, each a hundred feet tall.

Winter called these the King's Pines, and they were gigantic.

"These trees are ancient," he'd told me, pointing up at one. "See anything up there?"

I squinted. I knew bald eagles nested near the ocean, but I didn't see anything that looked like a nest. I shook my head.

Winter put his hand on my shoulder. "There, on the trunk—see where the bark's been notched?"

I saw it then, three marks of an axe in the shape of an arrow.

"That's the King's Mark," said Winter. "Probably dating back to about 1690. That means these were the King's Trees, to be used for masts in the King's naval fleet. Over three hundred years ago, this was a big tree. And it was probably at least three hundred years old then."

Now, with Vala, I could see the King's Pines jutting out above the other trees, like the masts of a schooner rising from a green sea. I figured that's what Vala was going to show me, and so I got ready to be polite and act like I already didn't know about them.

Instead she touched my arm and pointed just a few feet away, towards a clearing where trees had grown around part of the pasture.

"Whoa," I whispered.

In the middle of the clearing was a bush. A big bush, a quince, its long thin branches covered with green leaves and small red flowers—brilliant red, the color of Valentines, and so bright after the dim woods that I had to blink.

And then, after blinking, I thought something had gone wrong with my eyes; because the bush seemed to be *moving*. Not moving in the wind—there wasn't any wind—but moving like it was breaking apart then coming back together again, the leaves lifting away from the branches and flickering into the air, going from dark green to shining green like metallic paint, and here and there a flash of red like a flower had spun off, too.

But what was even more bizarre was that the bush made a noise. It was *buzzing*, not like bees but like a chain saw or weed whacker, a high-pitched sound that got louder, then softer, then louder again. I rubbed my eyes and squinted into the overgrown field, thinking maybe Thomas Tierney had hired someone to clean up, and that's what I was hearing.

There was no one there, just tall grass and apple trees and rocks, and beyond that the cliff and open sea.

"Do you see what they are?"

Vala's voice was so close to my ear that I jumped, then felt my skin prickle with goose bumps at her breath, cold as though a freezer door had opened. I shook my head and she touched my sleeve, her hand cold through the cloth, and led me into the clearing, until the bush rose above us like a red cloud.

"See?" she murmured.

The bush was full of hummingbirds—hundreds of them, darting in and out as though the bush were a city, and the spaces between the leaves streets and alleys. Some hovered above the flowers to feed, though most flew almost too fast to see. Some sat on the branches, perfectly still, and that was the weirdest thing of all, like seeing a raindrop hanging in the air.

But they didn't stay still; just perched long enough that I could get a look at one, its green green wings and the spot of red on its throat, so deep a red it was like someone had crushed its tiny body by holding it too hard. I thought maybe I could hold it, too, or touch it, anyway.

So I tried. I stood with my palm open and held my breath and didn't move. Hummingbirds whizzed around like I was part of the quince, but they didn't land on me.

I glanced at Vala. She was doing the same thing I was, this amazed smile on her face, holding both arms out in front of her so she reminded me of Winter when he was dowsing. The hummingbirds buzzed around her, too, but didn't stop. Maybe if one of us had been wearing red. Hummingbirds like red.

Vala wasn't wearing red, just Winter's grubby old gray sweatshirt and jeans. But she looked strange standing there, eerie even, and for a second I had this weird feeling that I wasn't seeing Vala at all, that she had disappeared, and I was standing next to a big gray rock.

The feeling was so strong that it creeped me out. I opened my mouth, I was going to suggest that we head back to Winter's house, when a hummingbird flickered right in front of Vala's face. Right in front of Vala's *eye.*

"Hey!" I yelled; and at the same instant Vala shouted, a deep grunting noise that had a word in it, but not an English word. Her hand flashed in front of her face, there was a greenish blur, and the bird was gone.

"Are you okay?" I said. I thought the hummingbird's sharp beak had stabbed her eye. "Did it——?"

Vala brought her hands to her face and gasped, blinking quickly. "I'm sorry! It frightened me—so close, I was surprised——"

Her hands dropped. She gazed at the ground by her feet. "Oh no."

Near the toe of one rubber shoe, the hummingbird lay motionless, like a tiny bright green leaf.

"Oh, I am sorry, Justin!" cried Vala. "I only wanted you to see the tree with all the birds. But it scared me——"

I crouched to look at the dead hummingbird. Vala gazed back into the woods.

"We should go," she said. She sounded unhappy, even nervous. "Winter will think we got lost and get mad at me for taking you away. You need to work," she added, and gave me a tight smile. "Come on."

She walked away. I stayed where I was. After a moment I picked up a stick and tentatively prodded at the dead bird. It didn't move.

It was on its back, and it looked sadder that way. I wanted to turn it over. I poked it again, harder.

It still didn't budge.

Cody doesn't mind touching dead things. I do. But the hummingbird was so small, only as long as my finger. And it was beautiful, with its black beak and the red spot at its throat and those tiny feathers, more like scales. So I picked it up.

"Holy crap," I whispered.

It was heavy. Not heavy like maybe a bigger bird would have been, a sparrow or chickadee, but *heavy,* like a rock. Not even a rock—it reminded me of one of those weights you see hanging from an old clock, those metal things shaped like pinecones or acorns, but when you touch them they feel heavy as a bowling ball, only much smaller.

The hummingbird was like that—so little I could cradle it in my cupped palm, and already cold. I guessed that rigor mortis had set in, the way it does when you hang a deer. Very gently I touched the bird's wing. I even tried to wiggle it, but the wing didn't move.

So I turned the bird in my cupped palm onto its stomach. Its tiny legs were folded up like a fly's, its eyes dull. Its body didn't feel soft, like feathers. It felt hard, solid as granite; and cold.

But it looked exactly like a live hummingbird, emerald green where the sun hit it, beak slightly curved; a band of white under the red throat. I ran my finger along its beak, then swore.

"What the frig?"

A bright red bead welled up where the dead bird's beak had punctured my skin, sharp as a nail.

I sucked my finger, quickly looked to make sure Vala hadn't seen me. I could just make her out in the distance, moving through the trees. I felt in my pocket till I found a wadded-up Kleenex, wrapped the hummingbird in it, and very carefully put it into my pocket. Then I hurried after Vala.

We walked back in silence. Only when the skeletal frame of the new house showed brightly through the trees did Vala turn to me.

"You saw the bird?" she asked.

I looked at her uneasily. I was afraid to lie, but even more afraid of what she might do if she knew what was in my pocket.

Before I could reply, she reached to touch the spot on my chin. I felt a flash of aching cold as she stared at me, her dark eyes somber but not unkind.

"I did not mean to hurt it," she said quietly. "I have never seen a bird like that one, not so close. I was scared. Not scared—startled. My reaction was too fast," she went on, and her voice was sad. Then she smiled and glanced down at my jeans pocket.

"You took it," she said.

I turned away, and Vala laughed. In front of the house, Winter looked up from a pile of two-by-sixes.

"Get your butt over here, Justin!" he yelled. "Woman, don't you go distracting him!"

Vala stuck her tongue out again, then turned back to me. "He knows," she said matter-of-factly. "But maybe you don't tell your friend? Or your mother."

And she walked over to kiss Winter's sunburned cheek.

I muttered, "Yeah, sure," then crossed to where I'd left the varnish. Vala stood beside her husband and sighed as she stared at the cloudless sky and the green canopy of trees stretching down to the bay. A few boats under sail moved slowly across the blue water. One was a three-masted schooner with a red-striped mainsail: Thomas Tierney's yacht.

"So, Vala," said Winter. He winked at his wife. "You tell Justin your news yet?"

She smiled. "Not yet." She pulled up the sweatshirt so I could see her stomach sticking out. "Here—"

She beckoned me over, took my hand, and placed it on her stomach. Despite the heat, her hand was icy cold. So was her stomach; but I felt a sudden heat beneath my palm, and then a series of small thumps from inside her belly. I looked at her in surprise.

"It's the baby!"

"*Eg veit,*" she said, and laughed. "I know."

"Now don't go scaring him off, talking about babies," said Winter. He put his arm around his wife. "I need him to help me finish this damn house before it snows."

I went back to varnishing. The truth is, I was glad to have something to do, so I wouldn't think about what had happened. When I got home that evening I put the hummingbird in a drawer, wrapped in an old T-shirt. For a while I'd look at it every night, after my mother came in to give me a kiss; but after a week or so I almost forgot it was there.

80C3

A few days later Cody got back from Bible camp. It was September now. Labor Day had come and gone, and most of the summer people. School started up. Me and Cody were in eighth grade; we were pretty sick of being with the same people since kindergarten, but it was okay. Some days we skated over at Winter's place after school. It was getting crowded there, with the piles of split firewood and all the stacks of lumber for the new house, and sometimes Winter yelled at us for getting in the way.

But mostly everything was like it usually was, except that Vala was getting more pregnant and everyone was starting to think about winter coming down.

You might not believe that people really worry about snow all the time, but here they do. My mother had already gotten her firewood from Winter back in August, and so had most of his other regular customers. Day by day, the big stacks of split wood dwindled, as Winter hauled them off for delivery.

And day by day the new house got bigger, so that soon it looked less like a kid's drawing of a stick house and more like a fairy-tale cottage come to life, with a steep roof and lots of windows, some of them square and some of them round, like portholes, and scallop-shaped shingles stained the color of cranberries. I helped with that part, and inside, too, which was great.

Because inside—inside was amazing. Winter did incredible things with wood, everyone knew that. But until then, I had only seen the things he made for money, like furniture, or things he made to be useful, like the cabinets he'd done for my mother.

Now I saw what Winter had done for himself and Vala. And if the outside of the little house looked like a fairy tale, the inside looked like something from a dream.

Winter usually carved from pine, which is a very soft wood. But he'd used oak for the beams, and covered them with faces—wind-faces with their mouths open to blow, foxes and wolves grinning from the corners, dragons and people I didn't recognize but who Vala said were spirits from Iceland.

"*Huldufolk,*" she said when I asked about them. "The hidden people."

But they weren't hidden here. They were carved on the main beam that went across the living room ceiling, and on the oak posts in each corner, peeking out from carved leaves and vines and branches that made the posts look almost like real trees. There were *huldufolk* carved into the cupboards, and on benches and cabinets and bookshelves, and even on the headboard that Winter had made from a single slab of chestnut, so highly polished with beeswax that the entire bedroom smelled like honey.

So even though the house looked small from the outside, when you got inside you could get lost, wandering around and looking at all the wonderful carved things. Not just carved so the wood resembled something new, but so that you could see what was *inside* the wood, knots and whorls turned to eyes and mouths, the grain sanded and stained till it felt soft, the way skin might feel if it grew strong enough to support walls and ceilings and joists, while still managing to remain, somehow, skin, and alive.

It was the most amazing house I've ever seen. And maybe the most amazing thing wasn't that it made me want to live in it, but that after spending hours working on it, I began to feel that the house lived in *me*, the way the baby lived inside Vala.

Only, of course, I could never tell anyone that, especially Cody. He would think I'd gone nuts from inhaling varnish fumes—even though I wore a dust mask, like Vala wore a fancy ventilating mask that made her look like Darth Vader.

She was working inside, too, building a stone fireplace. She found rocks in the woods and brought them up in a wheelbarrow. Big rocks, too, I was amazed she could lift them.

"Don't tell Winter," she whispered to me when I found her once, hefting a huge chunk of granite from the edge of the woods. "He'll just worry, and yell at me. And then *I* will yell at *you*," she added, and narrowed her spooky blue-black eyes.

Once the rocks were all piled inside she took forever, deciding which one would go where in the fireplace. When I made a joke about it she frowned.

"You do not want to make rocks angry, Justin." She wasn't kidding, either. She looked pissed off. "Because rocks have a very, very long memory."

It was early morning, just after seven on a Saturday. My mom had dropped me off at Winter's place on her way to see a client. It was a beautiful day, Indian summer, the leaves just starting to turn. I could see two sailboats on the water, heading south for the winter. I would rather have been skating with Cody, but Winter was anxious to get the inside of his house finished before it got too cold, so I said I'd come over and help trim up some windows.

Winter was outside. Vala, after yelling at me about the rocks, had gone up to the bedroom to get something. I yawned, wishing I'd brought my iPod, when upstairs Vala screamed.

I froze. It was a terrifying sound, not high-pitched like a woman's voice but deep and booming. And it went on and on, without her taking a breath. I started for the steps as Winter raced in. He knocked me aside and took the stairs two at a time.

"*Vala!*"

I ran upstairs after him, through the empty hall and into the bedroom. Vala stood in front of the window, clutching her face as she gazed outside. Winter grabbed her shoulders.

"Is it the baby?" he cried. He tried to pull her towards him, but she shook her head, then pushed him away so violently that he crashed against the wall.

"What is it?" I ran to the window. Vala fell silent as I looked out across the yellowing canopy of leaves.

"Oh no." I stared in disbelief at the cliff above the Bay. "The King's Pines—"

I rubbed my eyes, hardly aware of Winter pushing me aside so he could stare out.

"*No!*" he roared.

One of the three great trees was gone—the biggest one, the one that stood nearest to the cliff edge. A blue gap showed where it had been, a chunk of sky that made me feel sick and dizzy. It was like lifting my own hand to find a finger missing. My chin throbbed and I turned so the others wouldn't see me crying.

Winter pounded the windowsill. His face was dead white, his eyes so red they looked like they'd been smeared with paint. That frightened me more than anything, until I looked up and saw Vala.

She had backed against the wall—an unfinished wall, just gray Sheetrock, blotched where the seams had been coated with putty. Her face had paled, too; but it wasn't white.

It was gray. Not a living gray, like hair or fur, but a dull, mottled color, the gray of dead bark or granite.

And not just her face but her hands and arms: everything I could see of her that had been skin, now seemed cold and dead as the heap of fireplace rocks downstairs. Her clothes drooped as though tossed on a boulder, her hair stiffened like strands of reindeer moss. Even her eyes dulled to black smears, save for a pinpoint of light in each, as though a drop of water had been caught in the hollow of a stone.

"Vala." Winter came up beside me. His voice shook, but it was low and calm, as though he were trying to keep a frightened dog from bolting. "Vala, it's all right—"

He reached to stroke the slab of gray stone wedged against the wall, reindeer moss tangling between his fingers, then let his hand drop to move across a rounded outcropping.

"Think of the baby," he whispered. "Think of the girl . . ."

The threads of reindeer moss trembled, the twin droplets welled and spilled from granite to the floor; and it was Vala there and not a stone at all, Vala falling into her husband's arms and weeping uncontrollably.

"It's *not* all right—it's *not* all right—"

He held her, stroking her head as I finally got the nerve up to speak.

"Was it—was it a storm?"

"A storm?" Abruptly Winter pulled away from Vala. His face darkened to the color of mahogany. "No, it's not a storm—"

He reached for the window and yanked it open. From the direction of the cliff came the familiar drone of a chain saw.

"It's Tierney!" shouted Winter. He turned and raced into the hall. Vala ran after him, and I ran after her.

"No—you stay here!" Winter stopped at the top of the stairs. "Justin, you wait right here with her—"

"No," I said. I glanced nervously at Vala, but to my surprise she nodded.

"No," she said. "I'm going, and Justin, too."

Winter sucked his breath through his teeth.

"Suit yourself," he said curtly. "But I'm not waiting for you. And listen—you stay with her, Justin, you understand me?"

"I will," I said, but he was already gone.

Vala and I looked at each other. Her eyes were paler than I remembered, the same dull gray as the Sheetrock; but as I stared at her they grew darker, as though someone had dropped blue ink into a glass of water.

"Come," she said. She touched my shoulder, then headed out the door after her husband. I followed.

All I wanted to do was run and catch up with Winter. I could have, too—over the summer I'd gotten taller, and I was now a few inches bigger than Vala.

But I remembered the way Winter had said *You stay with her, Justin, you understand me?* And the way he'd looked, as though I were a stranger, and he'd knock me over, or worse, if I disobeyed him. It scared me and made me feel sick, almost as sick as seeing the King's Pine chopped down; but I had no time to think about that now. I could still hear the chain saw buzzing from down the hill, a terrible sound, like when you hear a truck brake but you know it's not going to stop in time. I walked as fast as I dared, Vala just a few steps behind me. When I heard her breathing hard I'd stop and try to keep sight of Winter far ahead of us.

But after a few minutes I gave up on that. He was out of sight, and I could only hope he'd get down to the cliff and stop whoever was doing the cutting, before another tree fell.

"Listen," said Vala, and grabbed my sleeve. I thought the chain saw was still running, but then I realized it was just an echo. Because the air grew silent, and Vala had somehow sensed it before I did. I looked at her and she stared back at me, her eyes huge and round and sky-blue, a color I'd never seen them.

"There is still time," she whispered. She made a strange deep noise in the back of her throat, a growl but not an animal growl; more like the sound of thunder, or rocks falling. "Hurry—"

We crashed through the woods, no longer bothering to stay on the path. We passed the quince bush shimmering through its green haze of feeding hummingbirds. Vala didn't pause, but I slowed down to look back, then stopped.

A vehicle was parked by the farmhouse, the same new SUV I'd seen that day down at Shelley's hot dog stand: Lonnie Packard's truck. As I stared, a burly figure came hurrying through the field, the familiar orange silhouette of a chain saw tucked under his arm. He jumped into the SUV, gunned the engine, and drove off.

I swore under my breath.

"Justin!" Vala's anxious voice came from somewhere in the woods. "Come on!"

I found her at the head of the trail near the cliff. Through a broken wall of scrawny, wind-twisted trees I could just make out the two remaining pines, and the bright yellow gash that was the stump of the one that had fallen. The sharp scent of pine resin and sawdust hung in the air, and the smell of exhaust fumes from the chain saw.

But there was no other sign of Lonnie, obviously, or of anyone else.

"Look," said Vala in a hoarse whisper. She clutched me and pulled me towards her, her touch so cold it was like I'd been shot up with Novocain. My entire arm went numb. "There! The boat—"

She pointed down to the boulder-strewn beach where the dock thrust into the bay. At the end of the dock bobbed a small motorboat, a Boston Whaler. Farther out, the hulking form of the *Ice Queen* rose above the gray water, sails furled.

She was at anchor. Several small forms moved across the deck. I squinted, trying to see if I recognized any of them. A frigid spasm shot through my ribs as Vala nudged me, indicating the rocks below.

"Is that him?" she hissed. "This man Tierney?"

I saw Winter loping across the beach towards the dock, jumping from one boulder to the next. On the shore, right next to the end of the dock, stood two men. One was tall, wearing an orange life vest and a blaze-orange watch cap and high rubber boots. The other was shorter, white-haired, slightly heavyset, wearing sunglasses and a red-and-white windbreaker, striped like the *Ice Queen's* sails.

"That's him," I said.

Vala fixed her intense sky-blue gaze on me. "You're sure?"

"Yeah. I've seen his picture in the newspaper. And online."

She stood at the top of the trail and stared down. An angry voice rose from the rocks—Winter's—then another voice joined in, calmer, and a third, calm at first, then laughing. I heard Winter curse, words I couldn't believe he knew. The third man, Tierney, laughed even harder.

I glanced at Vala, still staring at what was below us. One of her hands grasped the branch of a birch tree beside the path. She seemed to be thinking; almost she might have been daydreaming, she looked so peaceful, like somehow she'd forgotten where she was and what was happening. Finally, she shook her head. Without looking back at me, she snapped the branch from the tree, dropped it, and started down the trail towards the beach.

I started after her, then hesitated.

The branch lay across the narrow path at my feet. Where Vala had touched them, the leaves had shriveled and faded, from yellow-green to the dull gray of lichen, and the white birch bark had blackened into tight, charred-looking curls.

I tried to lift the branch. It was too heavy to move.

"It's *my* land now." Thomas Tierney's voice echoed from the cliff face. "So I suggest you get the hell off it!"

I looked down to see Vala's small form at the bottom of the trail, hopping lightly from one boulder to the next as she headed for the dock. I scrambled down the path after her.

But I couldn't go as fast. For some reason, maybe because first Winter, then Vala had raced down before me, rocks had tumbled across the narrow trail. Not big rocks, but enough of them that I had to pick my way carefully to keep from falling.

Not only that: in spots a white slick of frost covered the ground, so that my feet slipped, and once I almost fell and cracked my head. I stopped for a minute, panting. As I caught my breath, I looked away from the beach, to where the cliff plunged into a deep crevice in the granite.

There, caught in the gigantic crack so that it looked as though it had grown up from the rocks, was the fallen pine. It tilted over the water, black in the shadow of the cliff, its great branches still green and strong-looking, the smell of pine sap overpowering the smell of the sea. In its uppermost branches something moved, then lifted from the tree and flew out above the bay—a bald eagle, still mottled brown and black with its young plumage.

I couldn't help it. I began to cry. Because no matter how strong and alive the tree looked, I knew it was dead. Nothing would bring it back again. It had been green when no one lived here but the Passamaquoddy, it had seen sailors come from far across the sea, and tourists in boats from Paswegas Harbor, and maybe it had even seen the *Ice Queen* earlier that morning with her red-and-white-striped mainsail and Thomas Tierney on the deck, watching as Lonnie Packard took a chain saw to its great trunk, and the tree finally fell, a crash that I hadn't heard.

But Vala had.

You stay with her, Justin, you understand me?

I took a deep breath and wiped my eyes, checked to make sure I could still see Vala on the rocks below, then continued my climb down. When I finally reached the bottom, I still had to be careful—there were tidal pools everywhere between the granite boulders, some of them skimmed with ice and all of them greasy with kelp and sea lettuce. I hurried as fast as I could towards the dock.

"*You don't own those trees.*" Winter's voice rang out so loudly that my ears hurt. "Those are the King's Pines—no man owns them."

"Well, I own this land," retorted Tierney. "And if that doesn't make me the goddamn king, I don't know what does."

I clambered over the last stretch of rocks and ran up alongside Vala. Winter stood a few yards away from us, towering above Thomas Tierney. The other man stood uneasily at the edge of the dock. I recognized him—Al Alford, who used to work as first mate on one of the daysailers in Paswegas Harbor. Now, I guessed, he worked for Tierney.

"King?" Vala repeated. *"Hann er klikkapor."* She looked at me from the corner of her eyes. "He's nuts."

Maybe it was her saying that, or maybe it was me being pissed at myself for crying. But I took a step out towards Tierney and shouted at him.

"It's against the law to cut those trees! It's against the law to do any cutting here without a permit!"

Tierney turned to stare at me. For the first time he looked taken aback, maybe even embarrassed or ashamed. Not by what he'd done, I knew that; but because someone else—a kid—knew he'd done it.

"Who's this?" His voice took on that fake-nice tone adults use when they're caught doing something, like smoking or drinking or fighting with their wives. "This your son, Winter?"

"No," I said.

"Yes," said Vala, and under her breath said the word she'd used when I first met her: *feogar.*

But Winter didn't say anything, and Tierney had already turned away.

"Against the law?" He pulled at the front of his red-and-white windbreaker, then shrugged. "I'll pay the fine. No one goes to jail for cutting down trees."

Tierney smiled then, as though he was thinking of a joke no one else would ever get, and added, "Not me, anyway."

He looked at Al Alford and nodded. Al quickly turned and walked—ran, practically—to where the Boston Whaler rocked against the metal railing at the end of the dock. Tierney followed him, but slowly, pausing once to stare back up the hillside—not at the King's

Pines but at the farmhouse, its windows glinting in the sun where they faced the cliff. Then he walked to where Alford waited by the little motorboat, his hand out to help Tierney climb inside.

I looked at Winter. His face had gone slack, except for his mouth: he looked as though he were biting down on something hard.

"He's going to cut the other ones, too," he said. He didn't sound disbelieving or sad or even angry; more like he was saying something everyone knew was true, like *It'll snow soon* or *Tomorrow's Sunday*. "He'll pay the twenty-thousand-dollar fine, just like he did down in Kennebunkport. He'll wait and do it in the middle of the night when I'm not here. And the trees will be gone."

"No, he will not," said Vala. Her voice was nearly as calm as Winter's. There was a subdued roar as the motorboat's engine turned over, and the Boston Whaler shot away from the dock, towards the *Ice Queen*.

"No," Vala said again, and she stooped and picked up a rock. A small gray rock, just big enough to fit inside her fist, one side of it encrusted with barnacles. She straightened and stared at the ocean, her eyes no longer sky-blue but the pure deep gray of a stone that's been worn smooth by the sea, with no pupil in them; and shining like water in the sun.

"*Skammastu pei, Thomas Tierney. Farthu til fjandanns!*" she cried, and threw the rock towards the water. "*Farthu! Ldttu peog hverfa!*"

I watched it fly through the air, then fall, hitting the beach a long way from the waterline with a small thud. I started to look at Vala, and stopped.

From the water came a grinding sound, a deafening noise like thunder; only this was louder than a thunderclap and didn't last so long, just a fraction of a second. I turned and shaded my eyes, staring out to where the Boston Whaler arrowed towards Tierney's yacht. A sudden gust of wind stung my eyes with spray; I blinked, then blinked again in amazement.

A few feet from the motorboat a black spike of stone shadowed the water. Not a big rock—it might have been a dolphin's fin, or a shark's, but it wasn't moving.

And it hadn't been there just seconds before. It had never been there, I knew that. I heard a muffled shout, then the frantic whine of the motorboat's engine being revved too fast—and too late.

With a sickening crunch, the Boston Whaler ran onto the rock. Winter yelled in dismay as Alford's orange-clad figure was thrown into the water. For a second Thomas Tierney remained upright, his arms flailing as he tried to grab at Alford. Then, as though a trapdoor had opened beneath him, he dropped through the bottom of the boat and disappeared.

Winter raced towards the water. I ran after him.

"Stay with Vala!" Winter grabbed my arm. Alford's orange life vest gleamed from on top of the rock where he clung. On board the *Ice Queen*, someone yelled through a megaphone, and I could see another craft, a little inflated Zodiac, drop into the gray water. Winter shook me fiercely. "Justin! I said, *stay with her*—"

He looked back towards the beach. So did I.

Vala was nowhere to be seen. Winter dropped my arm, but before he could say anything there was a motion among the rocks.

And there was Vala, coming into sight like gathering fog. Even from this distance I could see how her eyes glittered, blue-black like a winter sky; and I could tell she was smiling.

The crew of the *Ice Queen* rescued Alford quickly, long before the Coast Guard arrived. Winter and I stayed on the beach for several hours, while the search-and-rescue crews arrived and the Navy Falcons flew by overhead, in case Tierney came swimming to shore, or in case his body washed up.

But it never did. That spar of rock had ripped a huge hole in the Boston Whaler, a bigger hole even than you'd think; but no one blamed Alford. All you had to do was take a look at the charts and see that there had never been a rock there, ever. Though it's there now, I can tell you that. I see it every day when I look out from the windows at Winter's house.

I never asked Vala about what happened. Winter had a grim expression when we finally went back to his place late that afternoon. Thomas Tierney was a multimillionaire, remember, and even I knew there would be an investigation and interviews and TV people.

But everyone on board the *Ice Queen* had witnessed what happened, and so had Al Alford; and while they'd all seen Winter arguing with Tierney, there'd been no exchange of blows, not even any pushing, and no threats on Winter's part—Alford testified to that. The King's Pine was gone, but two remained; and a bunch of people from the Audubon Society and the Sierra Club and places like that immediately filed a lawsuit against Tierney's estate, to have all the property on the old Packard Farm turned into a nature preserve.

Which I thought was good, but it still won't bring the other tree back.

One day after school, a few weeks after the boat sank, I was helping to put the finishing touches on Winter's house. Just about everything was done, except for the fireplace—there were still piles of rocks everywhere and plastic buckets full of mortar and flat stones for the hearth.

"Justin." Vala appeared behind me so suddenly I jumped. "Will you come with me, please?"

I stood and nodded. She looked really pregnant now, and serious. But happy, too. In the next room we could hear Winter working with a sander. Vala looked at me and smiled, put a finger to her lips then touched her finger to my chin. This time, it didn't ache with cold.

"Come," she said.

Outside it was cold and gray, the middle of October, but already most of the trees were bare, their leaves torn away by a storm a few nights earlier. We headed for the woods behind the house, past the quince bush, its branches stripped of leaves and all the hummingbirds long gone to warmer places. Vala wore her same bright blue rubber shoes and Winter's rolled-up jeans.

But even his big sweatshirt was too small now to cover her belly, so my mother had knit her a nice big sweater and given her a warm plaid coat that made Vala look even more like a kid, except for her eyes and that way she would look at me sometimes and smile, as though we both knew a secret. I followed her to where the path snaked down to the beach and tried not to glance over at the base of the cliff. The King's Pine had finally fallen and wedged between the crack in the huge rocks there, so that now seaweed was tangled in its dead branches, and all the rocks were covered with yellow pine needles.

"Winter has to go into town for a few hours," Vala said, as though answering a question. "I need you to help me with something."

We reached the bottom of the path and picked our way across the rocks until we reached the edge of the shore. A few gulls flew overhead, screaming, and the wind blew hard against my face and bare hands. I'd followed Vala outside without my coat. When I looked down, I saw that my fingers were bright red. But I didn't feel cold at all.

"Here," murmured Vala.

She walked, slowly, to where a gray rock protruded from the gravel beach. It was roughly the shape and size of an arm.

Then I drew up beside Vala and saw that it really *was* an arm—part of one, anyway, made of smooth gray stone, like marble only darker, but with no hand and broken just above the elbow. Vala stood and looked at it, her lips pursed; then stooped to pick it up.

"Will you carry this, please?" she said.

I didn't say anything, just held out my arms, as though she were going to fill them with firewood. When she set the stone down I flinched—not because it was heavy, though it was, but because it looked exactly like a real arm. I could even see where the veins had been, in the crook of the elbow, and the wrinkled skin where the arm had bent.

"Justin," Vala said. I looked up to see her blue-black eyes fixed on me. "Come on. It will get dark soon."

I followed her as she walked slowly along the beach, like someone looking for sea glass or sand dollars. Every few feet she would stop and pick something up—a hand, a foot, a long piece of stone that was most of a leg—then turn and set it carefully into my arms.

When I couldn't carry any more, she picked up one last small rock—a clenched fist—and made her way slowly back to the trail.

We made several more trips that day, and for several days after that.

Each time, we would return to the house and Vala would fit the stones into the unfinished fireplace, covering them with other rocks so that no one could see them. Or if you did see one, you'd think maybe it was just part of a broken statue, or a rock that happened to *look* like a foot, or a shoulder blade, or the cracked round back of a head.

I couldn't bring myself to ask Vala about it. But I remembered how the Boston Whaler had looked when the Coast Guard dragged it onshore, with a small ragged gash in its bow, and a much, much bigger hole in the bottom, as though something huge and heavy had crashed through it. Like a meteor, maybe. Or a really big rock, or like if someone had dropped a granite statue of a man into the boat.

Not that anyone had seen that happen. I told myself that maybe it really was a statue—maybe a statue had fallen off a ship or been pushed off a cliff or something.

But then one day we went down to the beach, the last day actually, and Vala made me wade into the shallow water. She pointed at something just below the surface, something round and white, like a deflated soccer ball.

Only it wasn't a soccer ball. It was Thomas Tierney's head: the front of it, anyway, the one part Vala hadn't already found and built into the fireplace.

His face.

I pulled it from the water and stared at it. A green scum of algae covered his eyes, which were wide and staring. His mouth was open so you could see where his tongue had been before it broke off, leaving a jagged edge in the hole of his screaming mouth.

"*Loksins,*" said Vala. She took it from me easily, even though it was so heavy I could barely hold it. "At last …"

She turned and walked back up to the house.

☙◦❧

That was three months ago. Winter's house is finished now, and Winter lives in it, along with Winter's wife.

And their baby. The fireplace is done, and you can hardly see where there is a round broken stone at the very top, which if you squint and look at it in just the right light, like at night when only the fire is going, looks kind of like a face. Winter is happier than I've ever seen him, and my mom and I go over a lot, to visit him and Vala and the baby, who is just a few weeks old now and so cute you wouldn't believe it, and tiny, so tiny I was afraid to hold her at first but Vala says not to worry—I may be like her big brother now, but someday, when the baby grows up, she will be the one to always watch out for me. They named her Gerda, which means Protector; and for a baby she is incredibly strong.

Cruel Up North

She left him in the hotel asleep, curled in bed with his fist against his mouth, face taut as though something bit at him. Cigarette ash on the carpet, laptop's eye pulsing green then fading into darkness. Outside on the sidewalk, shards of broken glass. The night before the streets had chimed with the sound of bottles shattering, laughter, men shouting. Women stumbled along the curb, boys pissed on storefronts.

This morning, nothing. The broken glass was gone. There were few cars, no other people. The sky was gray and rainlashed, clouds whipped by wind so strong it tore the beret from her head. She stumbled into the street to retrieve it then stood, gazing at a rent in the sky that glowed brighter than the sea glimpsed a few blocks to the north, between blocks of apartments and construction equipment. Overhead a phalanx of swans hung nearly motionless, beaten by the gale. With a sound like creaking doors they swooped down. She saw their legs, blackened twigs caught in a flurry of white and downy grey, before as one they veered towards the ocean.

She headed east, to the outskirts of the city.

The streets were narrow, cobblestone; the low buildings a jumble of Art Deco, modernist boxes, brick spidered with graffiti in a language she couldn't decipher. In the windows of posh clothing designers, rows of faceless mannequins in hooded black woolens, ramrod straight, shoulders squared as though facing the firing squad. No dogs, no cats. The air had no scent, not the sulfurous stink of the hotel shower, not even diesel exhaust. Now and then she caught the hot reek of burning grease from a shuttered restaurant. There were no trees. As she approached the central intersection the gale picked up and rain raced through the street, a nearly horizontal band that filled the gutters to overflowing. She darted up three steps to stand beneath an awning, watched as the cobbles disappeared beneath water that gleamed like mercury then ebbed as the rain moved on.

In another half hour she reached the city's edge. Beyond the highway, a broad manmade declivity held a stadium, scattered concrete outbuildings, a cluster of leafless trees. She stood for a few minutes, watching SUVs barrel past; then crossed the street and started back to the hotel.

She had gone only a few blocks when the wind carried to her a sweet, musky smell, like incense. She halted, turned her face toward the sea and saw set back from a row of houses a tangle of overgrown hedges, their formless bulk broken by a dozen or so trees. Frowning, she tugged at the collar of her pea coat, then walked towards them. In the distance she could see the frozen lava fields that ringed the city, an endless waste of ragged black like shattered tarmac, crusted with lichen and pallid moss. Here, sidewalk and cobblestones gave way to sodden turf ringed by skeletal bushes thick with plastic bags, crumpled newsprint; spotted, diseased-looking leaves that rattled in the wind.

Yet despite the coming winter, the trees—birches—had shafts of pliant green growth at their tips. It was these she had smelled, and as she drew nearer, their scent grew so strong she could taste it at the back of her throat, as though she'd inhaled pollen. She coughed, wiping her eyes, looked down and saw something in a tufted yellow patch at the base of one tree. A dead bird, a bit larger than her hand and lying on its side, head bent toward its breast so it formed a pied comma, roan and beryl-green. She crouched to look at it more closely.

Her tongue cleaved to the roof of her mouth, the taste of pollen froze into copper, saltwater. She picked up a twig and tentatively poked the small form, instinctively recoiled though its sole motion was in response to her prodding. Its skin jeweled with scales that gleamed palest green in the light, tiny withered arms folded like a bat's wings against the russet hollow where its chest had been eaten away by insects or rodents. Its face sunken, eyes tightly shut and jaws parted to bare a ridge of minute teeth and a black tongue coiled like a millipede.

When she stroked it, strands of long reddish hair caught between her fingers. Long afterward, her hand smelled at once sweet and faintly sour, like rotting apples. Where she touched it, her finger blistered then scarred. It never properly healed.

Summerteeth

The rolltop desk in this cabin belonged to your parents, you told me last night. Earlier in the evening you pointed to a top shelf in the lodge kitchen, three blown-glass bottles shaped like little birds, red, piss-yellow, the deep brownish violet of kelp on the ledges outside.

"Those glass things were my grandmother's. They were always in her house in Stony Brook. Now they're here. It's so weird, this stuff. All this stuff."

I would have said, It follows you. I was there; I am here now. One of the things that followed you.

This morning you interviewed me in your cabin, your computer set up on another desk, a big microphone on a stand. You sat in the chair before the computer and adjusted the mike, singing snatches of an old Bill Withers song, whispering, clicking your tongue, snapping your fingers.

"Don't look at this." You pointed at the monitor. Fizzy spikes rose and fell as you spoke. "It can be distracting. Seeing your voice."

You're interviewing all the visitors to the island. One by one all last week, today, after I leave. The Marriage Project. They go to your cabin and you ask them Have you ever been married? What does love mean to you? The sound bites are beautiful, spliced into swooping piano cadences, your guitar. Back on the mainland flames erupt, lines of peoples snake outside airports. Here on the island, there is music, wind in the trees, the persistent thump of the windmill that gives us power, rising from the island's highest point, a giant with one great eye. From your computer the sound of a woman laughing—*we're all doomed*—your brother's voice soft with alcohol. Your cigarette smoke in the cabin around me. Prayer flags strung from the ceiling, tiny red lights. A piano, every year the piano tuner stays on the island for a week in exchange for keeping it in tune. Your Gibson guitar. Bottles of your medication silhouetted against the window, sunlight glinting from the plastic vials like a tiny cityscape. A city I visit. You live there.

Neither of us lives here. Nothing can be sustained. Sex, drugs, art, electricity, even the trees. It's over.

Yesterday morning you showed me a letter, written to you by the poet who left the day before I arrived. Almost twenty years younger than me; you showed me her poems as well. Hard-edged, hard for me to read.

"This letter she wrote to me. It reminded me of your letters."

You handed it to me. The letter typed, an inky scrawl across the envelope. *The boy in the tree.* My name for you since we were seventeen. She has read all my books, she was explaining them to you, explaining what it means. The boy in the tree, a Dionysian figure, the consort of the goddess, a symbol of the eternal return.

Blah blah blah, I thought.

Then panic. My letters to you were written thirty-two years ago. She wasn't born yet.

Yesterday we walked along the ledges above the sea. Immense granite boulders split in two; we jumped between them, that horrifying jolt when I saw the long black mouth opening and knew how quickly it could happen.

"I feel like it's checking in on me regularly now," you said. Matter-of-fact, as always. You lit another cigarette. Your voice dropped. "Every month or so it taps me on the shoulder. 'Hey, just checking. Just checking in. Another month.'"

I felt sick, with nothing to steady myself against. If you. If we fell. Eventually they would find us, or the tide would. No radio here, no TV; one computer tied in to a router. Sometimes I hear a burst of static and words bleat from the radio on Billy's boat.

Everything is falling.

"We'll go up that way," you said, and pointed. A green spill of moss and lichen, cat firs. We clambered up the last long expanse of granite and into the woods, and returned to your cabin.

There are eleven people here. Writers, poets, painters. One performer: you. Your brother, who owns the island. A cook. The caretaker, Billy, who lives in Ellisport. Every year someone disappears; one person, maybe two. Usually they show up again in their hometowns, weeks or months later.

But sometimes people never come back. A few years ago, the body of one woman, a poet, was found in the woods near her home in Montana. Bones, hair, teeth; no clothing or jewelry. Her front teeth had been worn away to nubs. The first two joints of all her fingers were gone. There was no other sign of trauma. The official cause of death was exposure.

I arrived in Ellisport early in the morning. Billy came to get me in the boat.

"That all you got?" He looked at my one bag. "Some of these people, they bring everything. Cases of wine. One lady, she had two white Persian cats. She didn't last long."

"Cats?"

He nodded and peered at the boat's nav screen. Outlines of rocks, Ellisport's coastline. The island. "Traps, they don't show up," he said as the boat eased away from the dock. In the dark water, hundreds of bobbing lobster buoys, neon orange and green and blue and red. "That lady with the cats, she just showed up at the dock on the island yesterday morning, told me to bring her back. Never said anything, just left."

"Maybe the cats didn't like it."

Billy laughed. "The cats were gone. She was freaking crazy about it, too."

"Gone? Like they got lost?"

He shrugged. "Maybe. Well, no. Something got them."

"Like an animal?"

"Something. No animals on the island. I mean, birds. Sometimes a moose might swim over, that happened once." He squinted to where the sun shone through the morning fog. Jagged rocks and huge clumps of drifting kelp. Rising from the fog a gray-green cloud, your brother's island. "Nope. Something got 'em, though."

You were waiting at the dock when we arrived.

I could not stop trembling. We kissed in the clearing by the island sawmill. We had kissed the week before that at my house on the mainland, two bottles of wine, a joint. I hadn't been stoned in twenty years. A stash I'd saved for all that time, for when I might need it. Medicinal; now.

The full moon rose above the lake, yellow. Liquid, everything falling away into your mouth. Salt, smoke, your tongue sour with nicotine. Lying on your bed last night you said, "This is a great blowjob—this is the most beautiful blowjob. Much better than the other night."

"I was drunk then," I said.

I kissed you last week for the first time in twenty-six years. Your smell was the same. Your eyes, I always write of them as green, leafgreen, sap-green, beryl.

But they're not green. They're blue, turquoise, the most astonishing aquamarine. Liquid. Everything else about you is burning away. When I licked the blood from your cock I tasted ash. Your skin like the leaden bloom that covers the tiny fir seedlings in the forest; I touch it and it disappears, until I draw my hand before my face and smell you. Rotting wood. Rain and the sea. Blue not green. That glow from the mainland. Everything is burning away.

୭ଓଷ

"I had an ominous voice mail from my dentist." You lit another cigarette. We were sitting by the picnic table outside your brother's house on the windward side of the island, the only place where a cell phone can pick up a signal. All day long people drift there and back again, walking in slow circles, talking to ghosts on the mainland. "He said, Angus, call me right away. We have to talk about your X-rays."

You laughed. I felt my heart skip. "Are you going to call?"

"Nah. When I go home. I don't want to hear any of that shit here. Work. Someone else quit this morning. Everyone's leaving."

You shook your head and laughed again. "What, do I have teeth cancer? I'm not afraid of dying."

I stared out at the water, a lobster boat heading towards Ellisport. "Lots of people have fake teeth," you said. We walked back to your cabin.

After breakfast this morning I brought two of my books over to the lodge and left them on a table in the reading room. My other books are there, all the stories I wrote about you. We are on an island, surrounded by the reach and the open Atlantic. I am surrounded only by you.

What we took: cellphones, computers, paper, pens, paints, canvas, guitars, a harmonica, wine, scotch, beer, vodka, marijuana, amphetamines, cold medicine, sleeping pills, cigarettes, volumes of poetry, warm clothes, iPods, two white Persian cats. What we left: wives, husbands, children, cars, houses, air-conditioning, TVs, radios, pets, houseplants, offices. Everyone keeps talking about those cats.

Everyone here is working on something, feverishly. You are doing The Marriage Project. You interviewed me and I spoke of my brief marriage. How inconsequential it is. All those interviews, all those people telling you about their first marriage. All those chopped-off voices.

Yesterday I saw a letter on your desk dated months ago, when the mail still came on time. Little Buddhas lined up on top of your computer. Taped to the wall above the piano, pictures of your children. The two grown girls; the three children by your second wife. I sat on the chair in front of the mike and removed my glasses. Not for vanity, but because if I saw you clearly I would not be able to speak. The air inside the cabin was close, pine resin and cigarette smoke, marijuana, Shambala incense. Your sweat. The tang the medication leaves on your skin; bitter. You wore jeans, leather moccasins, a tie-dyed T-shirt. I shivered uncontrollably and asked if I could wear something of yours, so that my voice wouldn't break up for my trembling. You gave me a brown zipped sweatshirt with yellow stripes, a fake heraldic sigil. The kind of thing someone might wear in high school. Did you wear something like this, a jacket, a sweater?

I can't remember.

There is a painter here named Annie. You're obsessed with her.

"Annie, she's a feral artist," you told me. We were in the lodge kitchen. The cook was chopping parsley for dinner at the long wooden countertop. Bottles of wine on the long mahogany table Billy made, your iPod on the counter. The Beach Boys, Outkast, "Hey Ya." Happy music. The cook was dancing. "She gets up every day before the sun comes up and goes out to her rock and just stays there all day, waiting."

"For what?"

"Who the fuck knows. The right moment. The final curtain. She stays there all day, she only comes back here at dinnertime to eat. She doesn't talk much. She paints, just this one spot. Her rock. She's been coming here for three years now. I don't know when she sleeps, she works all night and goes out again at 4 a.m."

Annie.

That night I met her at dinner. Tall, rawboned, long straight straw-colored hair. Slightly rough skin, wide-set gray eyes. She wore stained khakis, a blue sweater, ancient hip waders. Big hands, the nails chewed down to nothing. She spoke very softly, her gaze flickering around the room the whole time.

"So you just go out there and work?" I asked. We were drinking red wine, moving slowly around the perimeter of the room. Annie kept her head down, her hair obscuring her face. Now and then she'd look aside, furtively, then gaze at me head-on for a moment before turning.

"Yes." Her voice soft, without affect yet musical. A swallow's voice. "On the far side of the island. By the rocks. Those trees there." She held her wineglass in one hand and kept the other hand in her pocket. "That tree. Yes."

"And you just...wait?"

She looked up. Her eyes flared. "Yes."

Her expression never changed; only those eyes. As though something moved inside her skull, cutting off the light. "Yes," she murmured again, and walked away.

"You know what I started to think about?"

You stared out at the edge of the woods, cat fir and moss-covered boulders, birch trees. Sea urchin shells broken on the rocks. "A woman having sex with a dog. Like a wolf or something. If she tries to get away, it rips her throat out."

I laughed. "I would never say something like that."

"Yeah. A really big dog."

Each cabin contains a single bed—a cot, really—so narrow it can barely hold one person, let alone two. At night I lie beside you as you sleep, your head turned from me, your arms curled up in front of your face, your fingers curled. Like one of those bodies at Pompeii. On the windowsills burn candles in small glasses. The smell of smoke on everything. My own skin; my mouth. Everything burns.

You asked me, "Have you noticed how you can smell things here?" We sat on the cabin steps, sheltered beneath cat firs, and watched rain spatter the rocky beach below us. "Things you never notice back there, you can smell them here. I can, anyway. Like I can smell my brother when he's way down the path. And Annie—I went down to her place yesterday and I knew she wasn't there, because I couldn't smell her."

"Can you smell me?"

You stared out at the water graying beneath the storm. "No. You smell like me."

"The light," I said. "That's what's different for me. The light everywhere, it's so bright but I can look right at it. I can stare at the sun. Have you noticed that?"

"No. I mean, a little, maybe. I guess it's being on an island—the water everywhere, and the sky. It must all reflect off the rocks."

"I guess." I blinked and it hurt. Even with my glasses on, the dark lenses—my eyes ached. I turned and looked at you. "Hold still, there's something caught…"

You grimaced as I touched your tooth. "A piece of fluff," I said, and scraped it onto my finger. "There."

I stared at the tiny matted wad on my fingertip. At first I thought it was feathers, or a frayed bit of cloth. But when I held it up to the light I saw it was a minute clump of hair, silky, silvery-white.

"That's weird," I said, and flicked it into the rain.

That evening before dinner I stood on the porch at the lodge and stared out to sea. The wind so strong I wondered about the windmill, that sound like an airplane preparing for takeoff, steady thump and drone. When the wind dies, the windmill stops turning. Power fluctuates, the lights flicker and fail then shine once more. A vast black wedge of cloud loomed above the reach and sent spurs of lightning across the water. Each bolt seared my eyes, my nails left little half-moons in my arms but I didn't look away.

"You should be careful." Annie came up beside me, wrapped in a brown sweatshirt with yellow stripes. She pulled the hood up, her hands invisible inside the sleeves. "It will hurt you."

"Lightning? From way out there?" I laughed, but turned so she wouldn't see my face. Your shirt. "I think I'm okay here."

"Not lightning." She crouched beside me. The hood spilled over her forehead so that it was difficult to discern her features, anything but her eyes. "Oh, poor thing—"

She reached for a citronella candle in a large, netted glass holder. A brown leaf the size of my hand protruded from the opening. Annie tilted the glass towards her, wincing, then stroked the edge of the leaf.

"Polyphemous," she said.

It wasn't a leaf, but the remains of a moth, forewing and hindwing, each longer than my finger. The color of browned butter, edged with pale-orange, with a small eyespot on the forewing and a larger eyespot on the hindwing. The spots were the same vivid sea-blue as your eyes but ringed with black, as though the eye had been kohled. Within a sheath of yellow wax I could glimpse its body, like a furred thumb, its long feathered antenna and the other wing, charred, ragged.

"It's beautiful," I said. "That's so sad."

She lifted her finger, brown scales on the tip like soot. "The eyes, when it opens its wings suddenly they look like an owl's eyes."

She set down the candle and pressed her hands together, palm to palm, then spread them. "See? That's how it scares off whatever tries to eat it."

"What're you looking at?"

You came up the steps, stopped beside Annie and glanced down at the candle.

"It's a moth," I said.

"A Polyphemous moth," said Annie.

You stared at it then laughed. "What a way to go, huh?"

You lit another cigarette. I held out my hand and you gave me the lighter. I flicked it and stared at the flame, brought it so close to my face that I felt a hot pulse between my eyes, you and Annie blurred into lightning.

"Hey," you said. "Watch it."

"She keeps doing that," said Annie.

⁖⁗

"Listen to this."

We were in your cabin. Another night, late. We'd left everyone else by the bonfire. A meteor shower was expected, someone said; maybe tonight, maybe tomorrow. No one could remember when. You sat in front of the computer and stared at your files, lines and graphs, adjusted the volume then leaned back. "Listen."

Crickets. Outside faint laughter and voices from the fire, wind, but no insects. The crickets were inside with us.

"You're recording crickets?" I asked.

"No." Your brow furrowed. "I don't know what the fuck happened. These are the files—"

You tapped the monitor, columns of data with initials beneath them, words and numerals. "Those are my edits. But something got screwed up. I played them back this afternoon and this is all I get."

A steady line moved across the screen as crickets sang. You stood abruptly. "Come on, let's go look for Annie. I want to see if I can find her in the dark."

We walked into the woods. Behind us the sound of crickets faded into your cabin. The dull orange glow from the bonfire disappeared behind the trees. It was cool, autumn weather not August. Wind brisk with salt and the scent of rugosa roses in bloom along the beach. Sky filled with stars, so many stars; a lake that holds a burning city.

Annie's rock was on the far side of the island and faced the open sea, a narrow spur of granite like a pointing finger. A fissure split its center, water pooled there and the pinpoint reflection of stars. You took my hand so I wouldn't fall. Twisted birches grew between the rocks, their leaves black with salt. Even in the dark I could see them.

But we couldn't see Annie. You called her name, quietly at first, then louder. At our feet waves lapped at the rocks; behind us, in the ferns, crickets. I heard bats ricochet and whine above our heads. You kissed me and we fucked on the rocks, my hands and knees soaked and bloodied. Your nails broke my skin, everything hurt so much that lights flashed behind my eyelids. I blinked and the lights were still there, streaking down the sky, a soundless eruption of green and crimson.

The voices by the distant bonfire softened into insect song.

The wind died, the windmill, the sound of a falling plane silenced. You held me and we were completely still. Neither of us came. In the trees above us the muted flutter of wings and two round eyes, green not blue; a soft flurry as it lifted from the branch and something soft fell and caught between my teeth.

"That was an owl," you whispered. "I think it was Annie."

You laughed. As we walked back to the beach we heard a low wailing from the other side of the island, one voice then another, and a third. Coyotes. Everyone was gone. The bonfire had burned to embers. You gave me your lighter and I started the fire again, fed it birch bark and twigs and red oak logs until the flames rose. In the sky above the sea things fell and burned. I watched as you walked along the beach, the red tip of your cigarette as you danced and swayed and sang. In the darkness something swooped above your head.

You should be careful, she whispered.

I held my hands in the flames until they glowed.

The Return of the Fire Witch

Insensibility, melancholia, hebetude; ordinary mental tumult and more elaborate physical vexations (boils, a variety of thrip that caused the skin of an unfaithful lover to erupt in a spectacular rash, the color of violet mallows)—Saloona Morn cultivated these in her parterre in the shadow of Cobalt Mountain. A lifetime of breathing the dusky, spore-rich air of her hillside had inoculated her against the most common human frailties and a thousand others. It was twelve years since she had felt the slightest stirring of ennui or regret, two decades since she had suffered from despondency or alarm. Timidity and childish insouciance she had never known. There were some, like her nearest neighbor, the fire witch Paytim Noringal, who claimed she had never been a child; but Paytim Noringal was wrong.

Likewise, Saloona had been inoculated against rashness, optimistic buoyancy, and those minor but troubling disinclinations that can mar one's sleep—fear of traveling beyond alpen climes, the unease that accompanied the hours-long twilight marking the months of autumn. Despair had been effaced from Saloona's heart, and its impish cousin, desire. If one gazed into her calm, ice-colored eyes, one might think she was happy. But happiness had not stitched a single line upon her smooth face.

Imperturbability was an easy emotion to design and grow, and was surprisingly popular with her clients. So it was, perhaps, that she had inhaled great quantities of the spores of impenetrability, because that was the sole quality that she could be seen to possess. Apart, of course, from her beauty, which was noted if not legendary.

This morning, she was attempting to coax an air of distinction from a row of Splendid Blewits, mushrooms that resembled so many ink-stained thumbs. The blewits were saprophytes, their favored hosts carnivorous Deodands that Saloona enticed by bathing in the nearby river. She disabled the Deodands with a handful of dried spores from the Amethyst Deceiver, then dragged them up the hillside to her cottage. There she split each glistening, eel-black chest with an ax and sowed them with spores while their hearts still pumped. Over the course of seven or eight days, the sky-blue sacs would slowly deflate as the Splendid Blewits appeared, releasing their musty scent of woodlice and turmeric.

After a week, she could harvest the spores. These became part of an intricate though commonplace formula usually commissioned by men with aristocratic aspirations—in this instance, a dull optimate of middle years who sought to impress his much younger lover, a squireen who favored ocelex pantolons that did not flatter him.

It was no concern of hers if her clients were vain or foolish, or merely jaded by a terminal ennui that colored their judgment, much as the sun's sanguine rays stained the sky. Still, she needed to eat. And the optimate would pay well for his false magnificence. So: arrogance and feigned modesty; a dash of servility to offset the stench of self-love...a few grains from the Splendid Blewits, and the physic would be complete.

But something was wrong.

Yesterday evening, she had unrolled nets of raw linen fine as froghair, arranging the filmy cloth beneath those indigo thumbs to catch the spores they released at nightfall. Morning should have displayed delicate spore-paintings, the blewits' gills traced upon the nets in powdery lines, pollen-yellow, slate-blue.

Instead, the gauze bore but a single bruised smear of violet and citron. Saloona bent her head to inspect it, holding back her long marigold hair so that it wouldn't touch the cloth.

"You needn't bother."

She glanced aside to see a Twk-woman astride a luna moth, hovering near her head. "And why is that?" Saloona asked.

The Twk-woman tugged at the moth's antennae. It fluttered down and settled on one of the dwarf conifers that kept the fungus garden in shade.

"Give me salt," she said.

Saloona reached into her pharmacopoeia bag and handed the Twk-woman a salt pod, waiting as she lashed it to the moth's thorax. The Twk-woman straightened, adjusted her cap, then struck a pose like that of Paeolina II in his most well-known execution portrait.

"Paytim Noringal came here at moonfall and shook your spore-net. I watched unobserved. The resulting cloud gave me a coughing fit, but my leman swears I appear more distinguished than this time yestermorn."

Saloona cocked her head. "Why would Paytim do that?"

"More I cannot say." The luna moth rose into the air and drifted off, its bright wings lost amid the ripple of jade and emerald trees crowding the hillside. Saloona rolled up the spore-net and set it with those to be laundered. She was neither perturbed nor angered by Paytim's action, nor curious.

Still, she had to eat.

She had promised the optimate his physic two days hence. If she captured another Deodand this evening, it would be a week before the spores were ripe. She secured the spore-nets against rain or intruders, then walked to the paddock beside her cottage and beckoned her prism ship.

"I would see Paytim Noringal," she said.

A moment where only dappled sunlight fell through the softly waving fronds of cat-firs and spruce. Then the autumn air shimmered as with heat. There was a stinging scent of ozone and scorched metal, and the prism ship hovered before her, translucent petals unfolding so that she could spring inside.

"Paytim Noringal is a harlot and a thief," said the prism ship in a peevish tone.

"She now appears to have become a vandal as well." Saloona settled into the couch, mindful that her pharmacopoeia pouch was not crushed. "Perhaps she will have prepared lunch. It's not too early, is it?"

"Paytim Noringal will poison you in your sleep." The ship lifted into the air, until it floated above the hillside like a rainbow bubble.

"If you're hungry, there are salmon near the second waterfall, and the quince-apples are ripe."

Saloona stared down at her little farmstead, a pied checkerboard of fungi, cerulean and mauve and creamy yellow, russet and lavender and a dozen hues that Saloona had invented, for which there was no name. "Paytim is a very fine cook," she said absently. "I hope she will have blancmange. Or that locust jelly. Do you think she will?"

"I have no opinion on the subject."

The ship banked sharply. Saloona laid a hand upon its controls and made a soothing sound. "There, you don't need to worry. I have the Ubiquitous Antidote. It was a twenty-seven-year locust jelly. It was generous of her to send me some of it."

"She means you harm."

Saloona yawned, covering her mouth with a small freckled hand. "I will sleep, ship. Rouse me when we approach her enclosure."

The glorious spruce and granite-clad heights of Cobalt Mountain fell away, unseen by Saloona Morn and unremarked by the prism ship, which had little use for what humans call beauty.

The fire witch's villa nestled in a small valley near the caves of Gonder. The structure had seen better days. It had been commissioned as a sera-glio by the Crimson Court lutist Hayland Strife, whose unrestrained dalliances caused three of his aggrieved lovers (one of them Paytim Noringal) to first seduce then subject him to the torment known as Red Dip. When, after seventeen days, the lutist expired, the fire witch prepared a celebratory feast for her fellow torturers, using skewers of oleander for the satay. All died convulsing before daybreak. In the decades since then, the seraglio had been damaged by earthquakes, windstorms, and, once, an ill-conceived attack by Air General Sha's notorious Crystal Squadron.

And, of course, Paytim's own mantic enterprises had left the gray marble walls and sinuous columns blackened with soot, and the famous tapestries singed and smoke-damaged beyond repair. She paced now before the ruins of the arras known as *The Pursuit of the Vinx*, heedless of the geckos and yellow-snouted lemurs that clambered across the backdrop to one of her more notable love affairs.

Paytim disdained magic to enhance her charms, though she had for many decades employed the Nostrum of Prodigious Regeneration to retain the dew of youth. She remained a remarked beauty. Like her neighbor, she was flame-haired, though Paytim's braid was brazen tigerlily to Saloona's pale margiold, and Paytim's eyes were green. Her skin was the bluish-white of weak milk and bore numerous scars where she had been burned while conjuring, repairing the *bouche a feu*, or carelessly removing a pot from the oven. The scars were a mark of pride rather than shame; also a warning against overconfidence, in particular when dealing with souffles, or basilisks.

Today, her thoughts wandered along their customary paths: concocting a receipt for the season's bountiful quince-apple harvest; estimating when her young basilisk might be successfully mated; brooding upon various old wounds and offenses. She paused in her pacing, withdrew a shining vial like a ruby teardrop from the pocket of her trousers, and, with a frown, gazed into it.

A dark shape, so deep a red that it was almost black, coiled and uncoiled within the vial. At intervals, the shape cohered into the image of a gysart in scarlet and saffron motley, which would extend its arms—in joy or anguish, she could not say—then, in a voice pitched like a bat's, exhort her.

"*Paytim Noringal, Incendiary and Recusant! Your exile has been revoked, following the abrupt and unfortunate death of Her Majesty Paeolina the Twenty-Eighth. His Majety Paeolina the Twenty-Ninth hereby requests your attendance at the after-ball following his coronation. Regrets only to be tendered by . . .*"

Here the harlequin doubled over in a spasm and began once more to writhe.

Paytim's frown smoothed into a small smile: for anyone who knew her, a far more alarming sight. She crossed the chamber to a low table, pressed a button that caused a cylindrical steel cage to rise from the floor. The young basilisk slept inside. Minute jets of flame flickered around its nostrils as it exhaled, also a faint sulfurous stink.

The vial bore a summons, not a request. Paytim's exile had been voluntary, although, in fact, she loathed all of the Paeolinas, going back to their progenitor, a court dancer who claimed to have invented the gavot.

His new Majesty, Paeolina XXIX, was indulging a customarily vulgar display of power. When Paytim had been at court, she had noted the lascivious glances he directed her way. The looks had been easy to ignore at the time—the present Paeolina had been little more than a spindle-necked boy. Now his attentions would be more difficult to deflect.

Despite this knowledge, she had already decided to attend the coronation's after-ball. She had not traveled beyond the mountains in some time. Also, she had recently made a discovery, an arcane and unusual spell which she hoped to implement, although its success was dependent upon Paytim receiving some assistance.

Not, however, from the monad gysart. She lifted her hand and gazed impassively into the vial, then nudged the steel cage with her foot. The basilisk stirred. It made a soft croaking sound, opened its mouth in a yawn that displayed a fiery tongue and molten throat.

"Inform His Majesty that I will be delighted to attend," announced Paytim. "May I bring a guest?"

The mote ceased its wriggling to regard her with bright pinprick eyes. Flashes of silver phosphorescence overtook the whorls of crimson and jet. The gysart shuddered, then nodded.

"In that case," said Paytim, "Please inform His Majesty that I will be accompanied by Saloona Morn."

"*Your reply has been registered with the equerry of invitations. You are welcome to bring one guest. Further instructions will be—*"

Paytim's eyes narrowed. With one long finger, she flicked open a slot in the lid of the basilisk cage. Its inhabitant scrambled to its feet and stretched out its neck expectantly, as she held the ruby vial above the opening. A nearly inaudible shriek stirred the chamber, startling the geckos so that they skittered back behind the tapestry as the vial dropped into the basilisk's mouth, and, with a burst of acrid steam, disappeared.

From the air, Paytim's villa resembled a toy that had been kicked to bits by a petulant child. Ivy and snowmoss covered heaps of hand-painted tiles fallen from the roof. The entire east wing had collapsed, burying solarium and manta pool. The collection of musical scrolls Hayland Strife had painstakingly assembled when not dandling some fawn-eyed courtesan was ash, destroyed when lightning struck the library tower. Its skeletal remains rose above the north wing like a blackened scaffold. Spiderwebs choked the famed boxwood maze, and the orchards of pomegranate trees and senna grew wild and blackly tangled. Saloona spied a thrasher's nest atop a quince-apple, the white bones of some unfortunate snagged in its branches like a broken kite.

Only the kitchen-wing was intact. Smoke streamed from its five chimneys, and the windows gleamed. Troilers wheeled through the herb and root-vegetable gardens, harvesting choi and sweet basil and yams. Saloona gazed down, her mouth filling with saliva.

"Poison," hissed the prism ship. "Ergot, chokecherry, baneberry, tansy!"

"Fah." Saloona waved a hand, signaling that they should descend. "Remain in the garden and do not antagonize her. I smell braised pumpkin."

Other, less attractive odors assailed her as she approached the dilapidated household, scents associated with the fire witch's metier: sulphur, burnt cloth, scorched hair, gunpowder; the odd sweetish reek of basilisks, reminiscent of barbecued peaches and fish. Paytim stood at the entrance to the kitchen wing, her wild hair barely restrained by a shimmering web of black garnets, her trousers flecked with pumpkin seeds and soot.

"Mother's sister's favored child." Paytim used the familiar, if archaic, salutation favored by the fourth caste of witches. "Will you

215

join me for luncheon? Port-steeped pumpkin, larks-tongues in aspic, I just picked some fresh cheeps. And I saved some of the locust jelly. I remember how much you liked it."

Saloona dipped her head. "Just a bite. And only if we share it."

"Of course." Paytim smiled, revealing the carven placebit she'd made of the lutist's finger-bone and implanted in her right eye-tooth. "Please, come in."

Over lunch, they made polite conversation. Saloona inquired after the newest litter of basilisks and feigned dismay to learn that only one had survived. Paytim wondered innocently if the prism ship had been confiscated during the most recent wave of enforced vehicular inspections.

When the dishes were cleared and the last of the locust jelly spooned from a shared bowl, Paytim poured two jiggers of amber whiskey. She removed a pair of red-hot pokers from the kitchen athanor, plunged one into each jigger, then dropped the spent pokers into the sink. She handed a steaming whiskey to Saloona, and, without hesitation, downed her own.

Saloona stared at her unsteady reflection in the simmering liquid. When it cooled, she took a sip.

"What a remarkable cook you are," she said. "This is utterly delectable. And the aspic of larks-tongue was sublime. Why did you shake my sporenets last moonfall?"

Paytim smiled unconvincingly. "I long for company. I wished to invite you for luncheon, and feared you would refuse an invitation."

Saloona thought on this. "Probably I would have," she conceded. "But your invitation has cost me a week's worth of spores I need for a client's physic. I can't afford to—"

"Your cantrap is a childish game," exclaimed Paytim. She could forestall her habitual impatience for an hour, no more. "I have discovered a charm of immense power, which Gesta Restille would have slain her own infant to possess! Eight sorcerers and twice that many witches died in their efforts to retrieve this spell. Do not think you can thwart me, Saloona Morn!"

"I have but this instant learned of your spell." Saloona set her unfinished tumbler of whiskey back upon the table. "I am unlikely to thwart you."

"Then you agree to assist me?"

Saloona raised a marigold-colored eyebrow. "I am a humble farmer of psychoactive fungus, not a fire witch. I can't be of any use to you."

"It's not an incendiary spell. It's far more lethal."

Saloona's lips pursed oh so slightly. "I have taken a vow not to cause death by intent."

"Any death would not appear intentional."

"I have taken a vow," repeated Saloona.

"I am without transport and require the use of your prism ship."

"No one but myself may use my ship."

"The aspic you just devoured was made with tingling spurge and an infusion of castorbean. I took a mithradatic dose two days ago."

Outside, the prism ship made a keening sound. Saloona began to unloosen the ribbons of her pharmacopoeia bag. "I have the Ubiquitous Antidote…"

"There is no antidote. Save this—" Paytim opened her hand. In the palm quivered what appeared to be a drop of water.

"That could be rainwater," said Saloona. "I think you are lying."

"I am not. You will imbibe the last of your panacea and still die convulsively."

The ship's lament grew so loud that the dishes in the sink began to rattle. Saloona sighed. "Oh, very well." She extended her tongue to Paytim's outstretched hand, felt a drop like freezing hail upon its tip, and then a pulse of heat. She grimaced. "What is the spell?"

Paytim bade her accompany her to the ruins of the library tower.

"I found it here," the fire witch said, her voice hushed with excitement. "I have not removed it, lest someone arrive unexpectedly and sense my discovery. Clans have fought and died over this periapt. My great-great-great-grandame sawed the windpipe from a bel canto singer who was rumored to have possession of it."

"In his throat?"

Paytim stood on tiptoe to avoid a puddle of green muck. "None knew where the spell might reside. Throats were slashed, golden thulcimers melted down, kettledrums covered with the skin of youths and maidens. Hayland Strife swore his father strangled his mother while she slept, then restrung his lute with her hair. All for naught—all for this."

She stopped at the foot of a crumbling stair that curved up and up into the skeletal remnants of the library tower. Swiftly, almost girlishly, she grasped Saloona's hand and led her up the rickety steps. Around them, the structure shuddered and swayed, its exposed struts of hornbeam and maskala tusk all that remained of the tower walls.

Cold wind tangled Saloona's hair. It carried the smells of fermenting quince-apple and moldering paper, scents overpowered by the stink of smoke and ozone as they approached the topmost level, which shook as though they stood atop a storm-tossed tree. They stepped out into a small platform, inefficiently protected by makeshift panels of oiled silk.

The fire witch dropped Saloona's hand, and, with care, crossed the unwieldy space. A single wall had miraculously survived that long-ago lightning strike, festooned now with cobwebs. Bowed and mildewed, it held row upon row of small round holes, so that it resembled an oversized martinhouse.

"Hayland kept his musical scrolls here," explained Paytim Noringal. "I use them to start the cookstove sometimes. It was purest chance, or mischance, that I found it."

She stepped lightly among the desiccated scrolls scattered across the uneven floor. Some had unspooled so that their singed notations could still be read. Others were little more than skeins of dust and vellum. More scrolls were wedged into the wall's pigeonholes, along with miniature assemblages of circuitry and glass, a theramin wand, coils of lutestrings and ivory lute-keys, stacks of crystal discs, a broken gamelan.

When Paytim reached the wall, she hesitated. A crimson flush spread across her cheeks; a bead of blood welled where she bit her lower lip. She drew a quick breath, then thrust her hand into one of the holes. Saloona was reminded of a time years before, when she had spent an idle afternoon with a lover, catching fileels in the shallows of the Gaspar Reef. The young man had reached into a crevice, intending to grasp a wriggling fileel. Instead, he had inadvertently antagonized a luray. Or so she assumed, as a cloud of blood and pulverized bone bloomed around the crevice and she quickly swam back to their waiting caravel.

No luray appeared now, of course, though there was an instant where an inky blackness spread across Paytim's arm like a thrasher's bite. With a gasp, the fire witch snatched her hand back. The stain was gone, or perhaps had never been.

But her fingers were closed tightly around a shining silver rod, slender as a bastinado and half again as long as her hand. It was inscribed with a luminous equation, numerals unrecognizable to Saloona, and which even the fire witch seemed to regard with profound unease.

Saloona asked, "Is that the charm which Gesta Restille so desired?"

The fire witch nodded. "Yes. The Seventeenth Iteration of Blase's 'Azoic *Notturno*,' known by some as the Black Peal."

Her lips had barely uttered that final word when a frigid gale tore through the flimsy walls, shredding silken panels and making shrapnel of scrolls and shattered instruments. At the same moment, a strange sound clove the air, a sound which Saloona sensed in her bones as much as her ears: a deep and plangent *twang*, as though an immense theorbo, too tightly strung, had been plucked.

"Quickly!" gasped Paytim Noringal, and lunged for the spiral stairs.

Saloona ducked to avoid being decapitated by a brazen gong, then followed her. With each step, the stairs buckled and fell away behind them. What remained of the tower walls crumbled into ivory and sawdust. A steady hail of blasted scrolls and blackened silk fell upon their heads, until, at last, they reached the ground and dashed from the tower seconds before it collapsed.

Scarcely had they raced into the corridor before it, too, began to fall away. Marble columns and tiled floor disintegrated as though a vast invisible grinding wheel bore down upon the fortress. Saloona dashed through a narrow door that opened onto the kitchen garden. Paytim Noringal stumbled after her, still brandishing the glowing silver rod.

"Wisdom suggests you should divest yourself of that," Saloona shouted above the din of crashing stone and brick. She ran to where the prism ship hovered, a rainbow teardrop whose petals expanded at her approach.

"Calamity!" exclaimed the ship. Saloona touched it gently, settling into her seat; but the ship continued to express alarm, especially when Paytim Noringal hauled herself in beside Saloona.

"My poor basilisk." The fire witch gazed at the ruins of her home. A single tear glistened at the corner of her eye, before expiring in a minute puff of steam.

"Perhaps it escaped," said Saloona as the prism ship floated upward. In truth, her greatest regret was for the loss of Paytim's kitchen, in particular the last remaining globe of locust jelly. "It may well follow us."

She glanced at the silver rod Paytim grasped. The lustre of its glowing numerals had diminished, but now and then a bright ripple flashed across its surface. The sight made Saloona shiver. She seemed to hear an echo of that strange, plangent tone, and once she flinched, as though someone had struck a gong beside her ear. She wished that she had heeded the wanings of her prism ship, and remained at home among her mushrooms.

Now, no matter the imminent danger to herself, Saloona was bound by ancient laws of hospitality. It would be gauche to refuse an offer of refuge to the fire witch; also foolhardy, considering the power of the charm Paytim held. When the prism ship had traveled a safe distance from the fire witch's demesne, skimming above an endless canopy of blue-green spruce and fir, Saloona politely cleared her throat.

"I am curious as to what use a musical charm might be to one as learned in the incendiary arts as yourself."

Paytim stared at the rod in her lap. She frowned, then flicked her fingers as though they were wet. A thread of flame appeared in the air, darkened to smoke that, as it dispersed, left a fluttering fold of purple velvet that fell onto Paytim's knee. Quickly, she draped it around the silver rod. Both rod and cloth disappeared.

"There," she said, and Saloona noted the relief in her tone. "For a day and a night, we can mention it with impunity." She sighed, staring down at the foothills of Cobalt Mountain. "I have been summoned to the Paeolinas' court to attend the coronation after-ball."

"I was unaware the Queen was ill."

"The Queen was not aware of it either," replied Paytim. "Her brother poisoned her and seized control of the Crimson Messuage. He has impertinently invited me to attend his coronation as Paeolina the Twenty-Ninth."

"An occasion for celebration. The charm is then a gift for him?"

"Only insofar as death is that benefaction offered by envious gods to humankind. My intent is to destroy the entire lineage of Paeolina, so that I will never again be subjected to their abhorrent notions of festivity."

"It seems excessive," suggested Saloona.

"You have never eaten with them."

For several minutes, they sat without talking. The prism ship hummed high above the trees, arrowing homeward. A red-dimmed fog enveloped the sky as the dying sun edged toward the horizon, and the first mal-de-mutes began to keen far below.

Finally, Saloona turned to the fire witch, her gray eyes guileless. "And you feel that this—spell—will be more provident than your own fire charms?"

"I *feel* nothing. I *know* that this is a charm of great power that relies upon some subtle manipulation of harmonics, rather than pyro-techny. In the unlikely event that there are survivors besides ourselves, or an inquest, I will not be an obvious suspect."

"And *my* innocence?"

A flurry of sparks as Paytim made a dismissive gesture and point-edly looked away from Saloona. "You are a humble fungalist, awed by the very mention of the Crimson Messuage and its repugnant dynasty. Your innocence is irrefutable."

The mal-de-mutes' wails rose to a fervid pitch as the prism ship began its long descent to Saloona's farmstead, and the humble fungal-ist gazed thoughtfully into the enveloping darkness.

Paytim was understandably disgruntled over the destruction of her home, and, to Saloona's chagrin, showed little interest in preparing breakfast the next morning, or even assisting her hostess as Saloona banged about the tiny kitchen, looking for clean or cleanish skillets and the bottle of vitrina oil she'd last used three years before.

"Your cooking skills seem to have atrophied," Paytim observed. She sat at the small twig table, surrounded by baskets of dried fungus and a shining array of alembics, pipettes, crucibles, and the like, along with discarded circuits and motherboards for the prism ship, and a mummified mouse. Luminous letters scrolled across a panel beside the table, details and deadlines related to various charms and receipts, several of which were due to be completed the next morning. "I miss my basilisk."

"My skills never approached your own. It seems a waste of time to improve them." Saloona located the bottle of vitrina oil, poured a small amount into a rusty saucepan, and adjusted the heating coil. When the oil spattered, she tossed in several large handfuls of dove-like tricholomas and some fresh ramps, then poked them with a spoon. "You have yet to advise me as to how I will address the customer whose charm you ruined."

Paytim scowled. The divining rod sat upon the table beside her, still wrapped in its Velvet Bolt of Invisibility. She waved her hand above it tentatively, waited until the resulting flurry of silver sparks disappeared before replying. "That flaccid oaf? I have seen to him."

"How?"

"An ustulating spell directed at his paramour's bathing chamber. The squireen has been reduced to ash. The optimate's need to retain his affection has therefore diminished."

Saloona's nostrils flared. "That was cruel and unwarranted," she said, and tossed another bunch of ramps into the skillet.

"Pah. The optimate has already taken another lover. You are being uncharacteristically sentimental."

Saloona inhaled sharply, then turned back to the stove. Paytim was correct: this was more emotion than Saloona had displayed, or felt, in decades.

The realization unnerved her. And her dismay was not assuaged by the thought that this unaccustomed flicker of sensation had manifested itself after Paytim had uttered aloud the names of the harmonic spell that was, for the moment, contained by the Velvet Bolt.

Saloona shook the saucepan with more vigor than necessary. Since that moment in the tower, she continued to hear a low, tuneless humming in her ears, so soft she might have mistaken it for the song of bees, or the night wind stirring the firs outside her bedroom window.

But it was only late afternoon. There was no wind. There were no bees, which were unnecessary to propagate mushrooms and other fungi.

Yet the noise persisted. Saloona almost imagined that the humming grew more urgent, almost minatory.

"Do you hear that?" she asked Paytim. "A sound like hornets in the eaves?"

The fire witch cast her a look of such disdain that Saloona turned back to her stove.

Too late: the ramps were scorched. Hastily she dumped everything onto a single pewter dish and set it on the twig table.

"This—charm." Saloona pulled a stool alongside Paytim and began to eat. "Its potency seems great. I don't understand why you have need of my feeble powers to implement it at the Crimson Messuage."

Paytim regarded the mushrooms with distaste. "Your false modesty is unbecoming, Saloona. Also, I need your ship." She glanced out the window to where a maroon glow marked the onset of dawn. "The Crimson Messuage is gravely suspicious of me, as you well know, but that's never stopped them from wanting me to join their retinue as Court Incendiary. In addition, I have a torturous history with this particular Paeolina. He made disagreeable suggestions to me many years ago, and, when rebuffed, grew surly and resentful. I am certain that his invitation will lead me into a trap."

"Why didn't you refuse it, then?"

"It would merely have been tendered at another time. Or else he might have attempted to take me by force. I tire of their game, Saloona. I would like to end it now, and devote myself to more pleasurable activities. My basilisk." She dabbed at a sizzling tear. "And my cooking…"

A sideways glance at Saloona became a more meaningful look directed at the blackened saucepan. Saloona swallowed a mouthful of tricholomas.

"I still don't—"

Paytim banged her fist against the table. "You will be my Velvet Bolt! I need you to sow clouds of unknowing, of rapture, forgetfulness, desire, what-have-you—whatever you wish, whatever distractions you can conjure from this—"

She stormed across the cottage to the window, and pointed at the ranks of neatly tended mushroom beds, flushed with the first rays of morning. "Disarm the Paeolinas and their subordinates, so that we enter the court unaccosted, and with the Black Peal intact. During the evening's entertainment, I will enact the spell: their corrupt dynasty will fall at last!"

Saloona looked doubtful. "What is to keep us from succumbing as well?"

"That too will be your doing." The fire witch cast a sly glance at the pharmacopoeia bag hanging at Saloona's waist. "You possess the Ubiquitous Antidote, do you not?"

Saloona ran her fingers across the leather pouch, and felt the familiar outline of the crystal vial inside it. "I do. But very little remains of last year's tincture, and I must wait another month before I can harvest the spores to infuse more."

Paytim sniffed.

Saloona finished the last of the mushrooms and pushed aside her platter. The faint pricklings of emotion had not subsided when her stomach was filled. If anything, she now felt even more distressed, and ever more reluctant to commit to this hapless venture. Paytim's must be a very powerful spell, to so quickly undo decades of restraint and self-containment. It would be dangerous if the fire witch were aware of Saloona's sudden lability.

"You require the use of my prism ship and my fungal electuaries. I remain uncertain of the benefits to myself."

"Ungrateful slut! I saved your life!"

"After you attempted to wrest it from me!"

Paytim tapped distractedly at the windowpane. The glass grew molten beneath her fingertips, then congealed again, so that the view outside blurred. "The robust holdings of the Crimson Messuage will be ours."

"I am content here."

"The Crimson Court has a legendary kitchen. Too long have you languished here among your toadstools and toxic chanterells, Saloona Morn! At great danger to myself, I have secured you an invitation so that you may sample the Paeolinas' nettlefish froth and their fine baked viands, also a cellar known throughout the Metarin Mountains for vintages as rare as they are temulent. Still you remain skeptical of my motivations."

Saloona rose and went to stand beside the fire witch. Small flaws now flecked the window, like tiny craters or starbursts. The scents of sauteed mushrooms and burnt ramps faded into those of ozone and hot sand. Her hair rose slightly, tingling as with electricity. If she were to refuse the fire witch, Paytim was likely to exact a disagreeable vindication.

"I will do what I can." Saloona pressed a palm against the glass. "I have heard that the Paeolinas' kitchen is extensive and the chef's repertoire noteworthy if idiosyncratic. But if I fail…"

"If you fail, you will die knowing that you have tasted nettlefish froth, a liqueur more captivating than locust jelly. And you will have heard the Seventeenth Iteration of Blase's 'Azoic *Notturno*.' Some have claimed that death is a small price to pay for such a serenade."

"I have never been a music lover."

"Nor I," said Paytim. She laid her hand upon Saloona's shoulder. "Come now. Time for a proper breakfast."

By the morning of the after-ball, Saloona had devised a half-dozen charms and nostrums of varying power. The fire witch wanted nothing to interfere with her deployment of the Black Peal: her plan, therefore, was to sow the air with sores and spells that would discourage or retard any effort to restrain her once inside the court. The most severe was a spell of Impulsive Corrosion, caused by spores of panther caps, pink mycenas, and fragile elf cups infused with azalea honey and caladium. The rest made ample use of fungi that caused convulsions, temporary paralysis, hallucinations, reverse metamorphosis, spasms, twitches, and mental confusions.

Saloona refused to create any charm that might induce fatality. Still, for many years a favored entertainment had been researching the means by which her crop could depopulate large areas of the surrounding mountains. She grew poisonous mushrooms alongside their benign and sometimes all-but-indistinguishable relatives, and took pride in recognizing the subtle differences between, say, the devil's bolete and its honey-scented cousin, the summer bolete. Her longtime sangfroid had made this a macabre but innocent pleasure. It had never crossed her mind that she might someday harvest spores and stems and caps from this toxic wonderland.

She took no delight now in concocting her poisons. More alarmingly, she *did* feel guilt. This too she associated with the long echo of the Black Peal. It must be a most powerful charm, to overcome the emotional inoculation she had experienced from handling so many psychotropic substances for so long.

"It seems inappropriate to sow such tumult among innocent guests," she observed to the fire witch.

"I assure you, no one within the Crimson Messuage is innocent."

"*I* am innocent!"

Paytim held up a deadly gaelerina, a fatal mushroom which Saloona claimed tasted exquisite. "A dubious statement. Innocent? You use that word too often and inappropriately. 'Naive' would be more accurate. Or 'hypocritical.'"

"Hypocritical or not, we will be fully reliant upon your Ubiquitous Antidote," said Saloona, whose efforts to create a spell to cause temporary deafness had been ineffectual. "If this spell is as powerful as it seems…"

"So few spells are not reversed by your marvelous restorative," replied Paytim in silky tones. "You are certain there is sufficient to protect us both?"

Saloon removed the crystal vial from her pouch. A small amount of glaucous liquid remained, which the fire witch regarded dubiously. "There is enough to preserve us, if the Black Peal does not prove resistant. Its potency is such that a very small amount is effective. Yes, there is enough—but no more than that. We'll be cutting it fine, and not a drop can be wasted."

"If necessary, we can stop our ears with beeswax."

"If that succeeds, this is a far more feeble charm than previously suggested," said Saloona, and replaced the vial. Paytim Noringal said nothing; only stood before a deeply recessed window and stared mournfully at the dark line of spruce and cat-fir that marked the horizon.

She was looking for her basilisk. Saloona considered a sharp retort about the unlikelihood of its return.

But pity stayed her tongue, and apprehension at the thought of annoying the fire witch, whose temper was formidable. Saloona had never seen her neighbor exhibit much fondness for other humans. Paytim's treatment of her former lover, the Court lutist, was not anomalous.

Yet she displayed great, even excessive, affection for the basilisks she bred. They were lovely creatures, otter-sized and liquid in their movements, with glossy, sharply defined scales in vibrant shades of coral, cinnabar, chocolate-brown, and orange; their tails whiplike and their claws sharp enough to slice quince-apple rinds. They had beautiful, faceted eyes, a clear topaz yellow. Unlike their mythological counterparts, their gaze was not lethal. Their breath, however, was fiery as an athanor, and could turn sand to glass at a distance of three paces.

They were almost impossible to tame. To Saloona's knowledge, only the fire witch had ever succeeded in doing so. Her affection was returned by her charges, who consumed whatever was offered to them, living creatures or inert matter, but showed a marked preference for well-seasoned hardwood. Saloona imagined that was why Paytim's gaze returned to the nearby forest, despite the inferior quality of the evergreens.

"Perhaps it will find its way here." Saloona wiped fungal detritus from her fingertips. "You have always claimed that they have a well-developed homing instinct."

"Perhaps." Paytim sighed. "But this is not its home. And in a few hours, we depart."

Saloona touched her hand. She hoped the gesture was reassuring—she was out of practice with such things. She very much needed the fire witch's assistance during this final stage of assembling each spell. Since breakfast, they had worked side by side in the small, steel-and-glass-clad laboratory that stood in the darkest corner of Saloona's farmstead, deep within a grove of towering black spruce.

There, beneath glowing tubes of luminar and neon, Saloona utilized an ancient ion atomizer that reduced spores and toxic residues to a nearly invisible dust. The fire witch then used Saloona's telescoping syringes to inject the toxins into a series of jewel-toned vesicles. Paytim strung these gemlike beads onto a chain of finest platinum, which would adorn Saloona when she entered the after-ball. Saloona and Paytim had taken mithradatic doses of each poison.

When the last vesicle had been strung, they returned to Saloona's cottage. There she decanted half of what remained of the Ubiquitous Antidote into a vial and gave it to the fire witch. Paytim then organized lunch. Saloona continued to express reservations regarding the night to come.

"I received no personal invitation to this celebration. Surely they will not be expecting me."

Paytim stood beside the stove, preparing two perfect omelets laced with sauteed ramps and oryx bacon. "My response to the court was clear: you will be my guest."

"I haven't left this place for nine years."

"You are well overdue for a journey." Paytim slid an omelet onto a copper plate and set it in front of Saloona, alongside a thimble-sized lymon tartlet and a glass of fresh pepper jelly. "There. Eat it while it's hot."

"I have nothing to wear."

A wisp of white smoke emerged from the fire witch's left nostril. "It would be a grievous day indeed when a Cobalt Mountain witch could not conjure attire suitable for paying court to a ruler of such legendary incompetence as Paeolina the Twenty-Ninth."

"And if my incompetence outshines his?" Saloona stabbed irritably at her omelet. "What then?"

"It will be for such a brief moment, only you will be aware of it. Unless, of course, your spells of confusion fail, and the Ubiquitous Antidote is deficient against the Black Peal. In which case..."

Paytim's voice faded into an uncomfortable silence. The two witches looked at each other, contemplating this unsavory prospect. A spasm assailed Saloona, and she clapped her hands to her ears.

"Do you hear that?" she cried.

The fire witch paled. "I hear nothing," she said, then added, "but I suspect the Velvet Bolt has expired. We must not speak of the musical charm again. Or even think of it."

Saloona bit her lip. She prodded her omelet with her fork, and reflected unhappily on how little joy she had taken from Paytim's cooking in the last day and a half.

This too is due to that malign spell, she thought.

Before another fit of trembling could overtake her, she began to eat, with far less avidity than had been her wont.

Sky and shadows mingled in an amaranth mist as twilight fell that evening. At the edge of the forest, the prism ship had for some hours kept up a high-pitched litany of admonition, interspersed with heart-rending cries. Since Saloona now seemed to possess a heart, the ship's lament frayed her nerves to the snapping point, and drove the fire witch wild with anger. Twice Saloona had to physically restrain her from reducing the ship to smoking metal and charred wire.

"Then silence it yourself!" demanded Paytim.

"I cannot. The neural fibers that give it sentience also propel it and govern its navigation."

Paytim's eyes narrowed dangerously. "Then we will walk."

"And arrive tomorrow," said Saloona with impatience. "Perhaps this is an opportune moment to test your beeswax plugs."

The fire witch exhaled with such force that the hem of a nearby curtain curled into gray ash. Saloona ignored this and returned to her bedroom.

Clothes were strewn everywhere. Stained lab tunics; an ugly crinoline diapered with paper-thin sheets of tellurium that whistled a jaunty air as she tossed it aside; an ancient silk kimono, never worn, embroidered with useless sigils; rubber booties and garden frocks; a pelisse she had made herself from a Deodand's skin, which still gave off a whiff of spoiled meat and blewits.

Saloona stuffed these back into the armoire from which they'd emerged, then sat brooding for some minutes on the edge of her little carven bed. She had lived here alone, had taken no lover for many years now, and had virtually no interest in fashion. Still, a sartorial cantrap was well within her powers.

But if one lacked an affinity for fashion, or even a mild interest, what use was such a spell? Might not the attire it procured turn out be inelegant, even fatally offensive? Certainly it would be unsuitable for an affair of such magnificence as the after-ball.

Saloona was, in fact, naive. She shared the province's general disdain for the ruling dynasty, but she had never visited court, or entertained the notion that she someday might. Her anxiety at the prospect was therefore extreme. She once more flung open the door of her armoire, inspected the garments she had just rejected, and continued to find them wanting.

After a fraught quarter-hour, she still wore her faded lab tunic. "Are you ready?" Paytim's voice echoed shrilly down the hall.

"Another minute." Saloona bit her lower lip. She undressed hastily, retaining only her linen chemise and crimson latex stockings—the color, she thought, might be viewed as a sign of admiration. She pulled on a pair of loose sateen trousers, a deep mauve, and then an airy silk blouson, white but filigreed with tiny eyes that opened to reveal scarlet irises whenever bright light shone upon the fabric.

"Saloona!" The fire witch sounded almost frantic. "*Now.*"

Saloona gave a wordless cry, swept her marigold hair into an untidy chignon that she secured with a pair of golden mantids whose claws tugged painfully at her roots. A final glance into a mirror indicated that she looked even more louche than she'd feared. The subtly glowing necklace of toxic vesicles around her throat seemed particularly out of place, its false bijoux glowing like Viasyan adamant. The entire effect was not mitigated by her worn leather slippers, which had long curling toes that ended in orange tassels.

But she had no time to change her shoes. As Paytim's footsteps boomed down the corridor, Saloona grabbed the silk kimono and rushed from her room.

"I'm ready," she said breathlessly, wrapping herself in the kimono's folds.

The fire witch scarcely glanced at her; merely dug her fingers into Saloona's elbow and steered her out the front door and toward the paddock. "Your ship knows the way?"

An answering retort, midway between a turbine explosion and the shriek of a woman in childbirth, indicated that the prism ship was aware of the destination.

Saloona nodded, then glanced at her companion, her eyes widening.

The fire witch rewarded her with a compressed smile. "It's been such ages since I've worn this. I'm surprised it still fits."

From her white shoulders to her narrow ankles, Paytim was encased in a gown of pliant eeft-skin, in shades of beryl, seafoam, moonlit jade. Where twilight touched the cleft between her breasts, opalescent sparks shimmered and spun. Wristlets of fiery gold wound her arms, wrought like adders and fileels. A comb of hammered copper, shaped like a basilisk's head, restrained her shining hair so that only a few golden tendrils fell saucily against her cheeks.

"Your attire becomes you," said Saloona.

"Yes." The fire witch smiled mirthlessly, displaying the placebit carved from her lover's finger-bone; then raised her hand. The wand that had confounded even Resta Gestille glowed as though it were an ingot just hauled from the flames. It was so bright that Paytim blinked and looked aside.

More discomfiting to Saloona Morn were the sounds that emanated from the wand. A subtle, refined yet cunning cascade of notes, at once bell-like yet ominously profound, as though played upon an instrument whose tympanum was the earth's very skin, its sounding rods the nearby crags and stony spires. The notes rang inside Saloona's skull, and she gasped.

But before she drew her next breath, the sound faded. The ensuing silence, fraught with malign portent, Saloona found more disturbing than the uncanny music.

She had no time to ponder her unease. With a soft command, Paytim urged her toward the paddock. As they approached, the air grew increasingly turbulent. The evergreens' heavy branches thrashed. Dead fir needles and bracken rose and whirled in miniature wind-funnels.

Fenceposts buckled, then exploded into splinters. A flock of mal-de-mutes rose from the topmost branches of the tallest spruce and fled screaming into the darkening sky.

"Can't you control it?" Paytim shouted.

Saloona shielded her eyes against a bolt of violet plasma. "I don't think it wants to go."

As she spoke, the air thickened until the ship's outlines grew visible, coruscant with lightning.

"BETRAYAL DEPRAVITY DISSOLUTION DESPAIR," the ship thundered. "INIQUITY CATASTROPHE DOOM DOOM DOOM."

"I'll speak to it." Saloona hurried past the fire witch, beckoning the ship open. Translucent petals emerged from the air and she slipped onboard.

"You must bear us to the Crimson Messuage without delay." Saloona pressed her palm against the navigational membrane. "We are, I am, a guest of his Majesty Paeolina the Twenty-Eighth."

"TWENTY-NINTH," boomed the ship, but, as Saloona exerted more pressure upon the porous membrane, its violence abated and its voice dropped to a rasp. "A chaotic and incestuous heterarchy, their lineage is damned!"

"*I must go.*" Saloona glanced through the rippling plasma haze to where the fire witch stood, her mouth tight and her eyes fixed upon the blood-tinged western sky. "Paytim Noringal wields a terrifying spell. I fear to cross her."

"What is the spell?"

Saloona lowered her face until her lips brushed the ship's warm plasmatic membrane, and breathed her reply.

"Paytim Noringal claims it is the Black Peal; the Seventeenth Iteration of Blase's 'Azoic *Notturno*,' which Gesta Restille committed heinous crimes to employ. In vain," she added, and directed a cogent look toward the fire witch.

"A harmonic charm of indisputable force," the ship remarked after brief reflection. "Best I kill you now, painlessly."

"No!" Saloona snatched her hand from the navigational membrane. "It may be the spell can be averted. If not, I will certainly escape and you will bear me back home."

Her tone implied that she felt otherwise, but the ship's power field relaxed, from vivid purple to a more subdued shade of puce.

"Does it know the way?" Paytim Noringal demanded as the petals opened once more so that she could alight.

"Yes, of course," Saloona said. "Please, recline there upon the couch. I must offer my ship guidance for the first portion of the journey, then I will join you."

Without speaking further, they took their places in the cabin. Saloona closed her eyes and once again placed her hand upon the tensile membrane.

"Bear us to the Crimson Messuage," she commanded in a low voice.

The prism ship shuddered, but, after a momentary hesitation, rose smoothly into the air, and banked so that its prow pointed northeast. Lightning streamed from the thickening clouds as the ship sped above the mountains, its passage marked by violent bursts of blue-white flame and pulses of phosphorescence like St. Elmo's Fire. Those few persons who saw it from the ground took shelter, fearing one of the vicious tempests which shook the mountains from time to time.

Yet as they cowered in silos and subterranean closets, their skin prickled as a faint invidious music seeped into their consciousness, a sound at once aching and desperate. To those who heard it, sleep did not arrive that night, nor for some nights to come. When it did, the sleepers cried aloud, begging for release from the visions that overtook them. Even *en passant*, such was the power of the "Azoic *Notturno*."

The Crimson Messuage first appeared as a twinkling of fallen stars, scarlet and gold and vermilion, scattered within a narrow cleft within the sharp-teethed Metarin Mountains. Once the prism ship began its descent, Saloona discerned the outlines of conch-shaped towers and minarets, outer gates with crenelated battlements built of crumbling soft cinnabar, and the extensive mazed gardens where great tusked maskelons prowled, and, it was said, fed upon bastard Paeolina infants.

"Is that it?" she wondered aloud.

"It is," said Paytim Noringal. She had been silent until now, her energies devoted to creating and maintaining a masking spell that would disguise the rod until they had gained entry to the after-ball. "Once, this was a great peak of friable red stone. An ambitious ancestor of the present King began its construction an eon ago. Twelve hundred slaves spent fifteen years clearing forest and rubble from the mountaintop. It was another half-century before the present structure was carved from the vermilion rock, and it took the endeavors of a giant tunneling wang-beetle to create the innermost donjons and chambers of state within the edifice."

"A great many slaves must have died in the process."

"True, though their bones are not interred here or anywhere else. Wang beetles are prodigious and indiscriminate eaters, though I was told that this one expired from gluttony and its carapace remains wedged within a forgotten corridor some hundreds of ells below us."

"You possess a great deal of lore pertaining to this fortress," observed Saloona.

"Hayland made a hobby of learning all he could of this accursed place. Better he had found entertainment elsewhere."

The fire witch's tone suggested that she had forgotten who initiated her lover into the rigors of the Red Dip. Saloona was too despondent to point this out.

"I could remain within the ship and await your return when the festivities are over," she said as the prism ship hovered above a grassy hollow near a drive clotted with other conveyances. "That might expedite our safe return to my farmstead."

"Our safe return is neither assured nor necessarily desirable," the fire witch retorted. "Far nobler it is to bring down a despot's throne! What cost thus are our petty lives, expended to further such a worthy enterprise?"

The ship grounded itself with a bump.

"What cost?" Saloona turned, furious. "I do not share your suicidal impulses, and my presence is certainly unnecessary for you to achieve them. Why did you engage me in this improvident venture?"

Paytim recoiled. She clutched the Black Peal, now disguised as a mottled nosegay, to her breast.

"Why not?" she replied. "You yourself admitted that you needed to get out more. Come, this seat is uncomfortable to the extreme, my leg is badly cramped."

The ship's petals expanded and the fire witch disembarked, hobbling. Saloona followed. The ship trembled beneath her footsteps, and she patted it.

"There, there, don't fret, I will be back. Wait here. I won't be late."

The ship gave a final disconsolate shudder. Its violet plasma-field faded to a metallic gleam. Then the entire vessel retracted into the grass, evident only by a cloudy glister as of a circle of snail-slime.

"Leave your mercurial vessel," commanded the fire witch. "We will have our choice of all these conveyances, if we survive." She gestured at the waiting cabriolets and winged caravans, parked alongside the bridled destriers and sleeping gorgosaurs that lined the long curving drive.

Saloona cast a last, woeful look at her ship, then continued after Paytim.

Her heart felt leaden. She could no longer pretend that her decades-long emotional abeyance had not been undone, perhaps irrevocably, by a few days' exposure to the rod that contained the Black Peal. For the first time in her life, she found herself recalling earlier, more clement times, experiences she had not realized were avatars of happiness. A green sward dappled with hundreds of tiny, milk-white umbrellas, first spore-rich fruits of warm summer rain; the song of thrushes and rosy-breasted hawfinches; a magenta cloud peeling from the surface of the dying sun and disintegrating into violet shreds, harbinger of Earth's final days. All these things Saloona had glimpsed, and thousands more; yet never had she shared a single one with another person.

This is regret, a voice whispered inside her skull. *This is what it means to have lived alone.*

"Quickly now, Saloona Morn—we're late as it is." The fire witch grabbed Saloona's arm. "Here—"

The fire witch thrust a packet into her hand, turned, and hastened toward an immense carven arch that opened onto a hallway larger than any manse Saloona had ever seen. Liveried janissaries leaned against the fortress walls, and several guests milled outside the entry. A bearded wench; an obese man with wattles like the dewlaps of a lichened sloth; glass-skinned gaeants from Thrill whose faces were swathed in a white haze that obscured their features while still suggesting an enigmatic beauty.

In dismay, Saloona examined her own attire—trousers hopelessly rumpled, the absurd curling-toed slippers soaked with dew; shapeless kimono drooping from her shoulders. Only the toxic necklace seemed remotely suitable for an enterance into the Crimson Messuage. She turned to stare resentfully at the fire witch.

Paytim shrugged. "You're with me," she said, and approached the gate.

Saloona clenched her fist, crushing the packet Paytim had given her. Its contents were not damaged, as she discerned when she opened it and found that it contained two yellowish blobs, the beeswax earplugs Paytim had provided against the Black Peal. In her fury, Saloona considered grinding them into the dirt, but was reluctant to further despoil her slippers.

"Your invitation?"

Saloona looked up to see the fire witch confronting a young man costumed as a harlequin.

Paytim raised her hand. "My invitation?"

One serpentine wristlet raised itself as if to strike, then opened its mouth. Out spat a glowing ruby bead that hung in the air as a ghostly, high-pitched voice began to recite.

Paytim Noringal, Incendiary and Recusant! You exile has been revoked, following the abrupt and unfortunate death of Her Majesty Paeolina the Twenty-Eighth. His

Majesty Paeolina the Twenty-Ninth hereby requests your attendance at the after-ball following his coronation.

The fire witch dropped her hand. The serpent retracted, the apparition disappeared in a sparkle of gold flame.

The harlequin inclined his head. "Paytim Noringal. Forgive me."

"My guest, Saloona Morn, a renowned Cobalt Mountain witch," said Paytim, and brandished her false nosegay. "Now bid us enter."

They walked down a narrow corridor carved from the soft red stone. Antic music beckoned them, and the scents of burning hyssop, sweet clistre, tangerine peel. A short distance away, within the atrium, Saloona glimpsed revelers in sumptuous dress, garlanded with salya-blossom and ropes of garnet. As they drew near the entry, the fire witch abruptly stopped and grasped Saloona's arm.

"I find your garb increasingly inadequate for a celebration of this magnificence—I fear your presence will draw undue attention to the both of us and prevent the implementation of our implacable charm."

Saloona nodded, and, with precipitate steps, turned to depart. "I could not agree more, I will await you outside."

"There is no need of that. A simple cantrap will ensure your modishness. Shut your eyes lest a disarming glitter blind you."

Saloona paused, disappointed, but agreed. Behind closed eyelids, she detected a subtle evocation of fireworks, then felt her clothes ruffled into slight disarray before arranging themselves into a pleasing texture.

"There," said Paytim with satisfaction.

Saloona opened her eyes to find her inadequate garments replaced by folds of ice-colored silk and her hair enclosed by a stiff taffeta net in the shape of a chambered nautilus. Instead of the absurd tasseled slippers, her feet were shod in silver-toed mules trimmed with living gleamants—equally ridiculous, but far more modish. The toxic necklace, at last, seemed well-partnered with the rest of her wardrobe. Instinctively, her hand reached for her waist. She was reassured by the touch of her pharmacopoeia pouch, now disguised as an eeftskin reticule, and her fingers traced the familiar outline of the crystal vial within that contained the Ubiquitous Antidote.

"Come now," said Paytim. "Perhaps the King himself will desire you as a partner in the gavot."

Saloona paled at this suggestion, but her companion had already swept into the atrium. As Saloona followed, she was assailed by additional fragrant odors and a raunchier, underlying smell of sweat, along with strains of laughter and genial music. Overhead, a heaven's-worth of lumieres shone in crepuscular eddies of violet and firefly green. Dancers engaged in the complex turns of Spur-Your-Master, or coupled recklessly in recessed alcoves where they were observed by crapulous onlookers sipping canisters of nettlefish liqueur and crimson lager.

"Is the King in evidence?" inquired Saloona.

Paytim gestured diffidently at a gilded platform. "He disports himself there, clad in the Punctilious Trousers that are his mark of office. As Earth has declined into senescence and valetudinarian decay, so too have the Paeolinas. Last of a debauched line: none will mourn his death."

Saloona observed an urceolate figure who held a jeroboam of frothing liquor. Bedraggled yellow feathers clung to his distended torso. The remnants of a lacy filibeg clung to the twisted circlets of the Crimson crown, its garnets glinting dully, and the Punctilious Trousers bore unpleasant stains.

Still the King capered and shrieked with laughter. He staggered between equally bibulous guests who shoved him back and forth as though he were a dandle-ball.

"It is not an impressive sight," Saloona concurred. "Yet surely not all of these assembled are without virtue, and deserving of destruction?"

"You think not? See there! Lalula Lindinii, as debased as she is lovely behind that wimple—she skewered her entire family as they slept, then fed their corpses to the grues. And there, milky-faced Wanfredo della Ruiz, who shares his bed with a gloth. And there, the conjoined twins Dil and Dorla Klaxen-Haw, whose erotic contortions involve mewling infants and a plasmatic whipsaw. There is not a one here whom Zandoggith the Just would not condemn to ceaseless torment, if She were among us now."

"How then will we escape punishment?" asked Saloona. "You have yet to reveal your stratagem for our escape."

"Fortunate indeed are we that Zandoggith is not in evidence." The fire witch ran her fingers across the false bijoux at Saloona's throat, glancing at the malign nosegay in her other hand. She then gave Saloona a crafty look, and pointed across the crowded room. "I believe you will find refreshment at that banquette. Fortify yourself with nettlefish froth, then sow your fungal confusions amongst this swaggering crowd. I will perform an appraisal of this space and its egress; after that, the Black Peal will ring, and you and I can manage a hasty departure."

Before Saloona could protest, Paytim darted into the crowd and disappeared from sight. Saloona wasted several minutes searching for her in vain, before deciding to avail herself of the Paeolinas' noted gastronomy.

This she found to be disappointing. The black-backed porpoise infused with essence of quince-apple and juniper was cloying, the matalusk-hooves insipid, and a locust blancmange grossly inferior to Paytim Noringal's jelly.

Only the nettlefish froth exceeded her expectations, a pinkish liqueur of wonderful clarity and astringent flavor. Three glasses eased her anxiety to the extent that Saloona momentarily forgot the reason for her presence at the celebration: she wandered listlessly among the throng, enjoying glimpses of her own silk-clad form in the highly polished walls, and the occasional admiring glance she received from an inebriated courtier or dame.

It was after one such had made excessively libidinous suggestions to her that Saloona, aggrieved, unclasped the necklace, muttered an activating charm, and crushed the first of the toxic vesicles beneath his nostrils.

"A sumptuous odor," the courtier leered. Immediately, he loosed a disarming squeal and fell onto his back, wriggling arms and legs agitatedly before expiring into a sudden, deep slumber.

Saloona regarded her handiwork, then began to make her way across the crowded atrium. Every few steps, she would remove another vesicle, invoke the appropriate incantation, and crush the gemlike receptable between her fingertips. She did not pause to look back until she had made a circuit of the room and deployed every fungal poison. Only then did she turn and, with a self-satisfied smile, note the startling perturbation in the crowd.

First one and then another merrymaker leapt into the air, thrashing and whirling as with St. Vitus Dance, and as quickly dropped to the floor, insensible. Others froze in place like costumed statuary. Still others began to laugh with rash hilarity, then, with maddened eyes, tore off their garments and raced through the atrium, crowing like cockerels and gargle-doves.

"Sweet Bentha's hips, the King's lunacy has contaged them!" a courtier exclaimed.

Saloona stood on tiptoe, and observed a tall figure racing toward the royal dais. The fire witch dashed onto the platform, flinging aside dancers and musicians and janissaries until she stood before the King, who screamed with laughter when he saw her.

"Here's a cormorant to be caught by tickling!" he cried, and attempted to grasp her by the waist. "Long have I awaited your return to our jolly company! Come, dance with me, sweet sot!"

"*Cymbolus Paeolina!*"

The fire witch's voice rang through the atrium. Gasps could be heard at the sound of the King's given name, and a few improvident guffaws. But the King only swayed back and forth, laughter burbling from his flaccid lips as the fire witch raised her arm.

"Witness now the destruction of your witless lineage!" she cried. "Let bones and sinews be the harmonium upon which your last gavot is played!"

Dreadful light candled Paytim Noringal's eyes. Her wristlets melted into strands of hissing gold; the basilisk comb bared its teeth. She lifted her hand, displaying a wand of glaring adamant, aflicker with abstruse numerals and unknown symbols. A fiery line traversed its length, and the rod split in two parts, each ablaze with clefs and breves and mediants, forking clews and fabrudans; every one an eidolon of some arcane note or tongue or hymn.

Saloona blinked, too stunned to flee or even move, as with a piercing cry the fire witch raised the wands above her head and struck one against the other. Silence, save for the ragged breathing of the King.

It is a fraud, thought Saloona, and from within the crowd heard similar sighs and expressions of relief.

Quickly, she turned to go, deeming this an expeditious time to return to her ship, when from somewhere high above sounded a single note of penetrating sweetness.

Saloona froze, enraptured. Such a note might Estragal have blown upon his yellow reed when he first played morning to the Earth, and roused dawn from deep within the dreaming sea. She began to weep, recalling a girlhood afternoon when she fell asleep among a field of coral fungus and fairy clubs, and woke to a sky painted with shooting stars.

Never had she heard such music! The lingering note suffused her with benevolence, a taste as of hydromel upon her tongue; and every face she saw reflected her own, mingling rapture and regret, desire and satiation; transport and pensive yearning.

All save Paytim Noringal's. With acrobatic intensity, she dismounted from the dais, paused to imbibe the contents of a small vial, and fled toward the door.

Saloona frowned. Her rapture faded into a dim memory of something less pleasant, a more astringent flavor upon her tongue...

The Ubiquitous Antidote.

Frantically, she sought within the folds of her silken gown for the reticule containing her pharmacopoeia. Her fingers tore at its ribands, dug inside to retrieve the crystal vial. Saloona unstoppered it and brought it to her mouth.

Only a droplet touched her tongue. In disbelief, she tapped it against her lips, then inspected it more closely.

The vial had been emptied.

Perfidious fire witch!

Too late, Paytim's betrayal grew plain: she had insisted that Saloona come along solely to make use of her prism ship and steal her share of the Antidote, doubling her own protection. At this moment, she would be stealing another conveyance outside, while her naive neighbor perished from Paytim's treachery. Desperately, Saloona sucked at the crystal tube, attempting to absorb some particle of resistance before she succumbed to the Black Peal.

But even now a new and haunting tune replaced the melancholy note. Fairy horns and tambours, flutes and sonorous oblelloes joined a bolero that swelled and quickened then died away, only to resume in a frenzied, even brutal, cadence. Saloona stumbled toward the room's perimeter, as around her dazed revelers batted fretfully at the air and stumbled past each other, like children playing Find Your Lady.

"Variana! Oh fair Variana, what betrayal is this?"

"Never shall I part from you, Capiloso, you have my heart."

"Essik Longstar, oh my poor sweet child…"

The air rang with wrenching cries: all mistook the living for those long dead. The music dissolved, only to return, with renewed and clamorous vigor. Mothers lamented slain children; betrayed lovers gouged their own cheeks and breasts. Janissaries rent their livery and grappled, mistaking colleagues for adulterous sweethearts, and Saloona paused in her ill-timed departure.

She knew this wild lullaby—surely it had been sung to her in her cradle? She hesitated, and her feet began to pick out a series of complex steps upon the tiled floor.

Yet some speck of the Ubiquitous Antidote still moved within her. She kicked the unwieldy silver-toed mules from her feet and fought her way to the wall. There she paused for breath, and gazed about the atrium for sign of Paytim Noringal.

The fire witch had disappeared. On the royal dais, groping masquers surrounded the King, who stood with mouth agape as though to catch the cascading notes upon his tongue. Trills and subtle drumbeats, a twanging volley of zithers and bandores, sweet mandols and violones—all swelled to a deafening roar, as the savage rhapsody employed the bewitched guests as its orchestra.

The King's gaping mouth unhinged. Strands of pliant flesh unfurled from his sallow face to form a crimson lyre. Ribs sprang from his chest like tines and commenced to play a mesmerizing glissando. With an echo of kettle-drums, his skull toppled from its gory spindle and cracked, and the garnet-studded Crimson Crown rolled across the tiles.

So it was that every guest in that company became an instrument upon which Blase's notturno played—all save Saloona Morn. Sanguine piccolos shrilled, accompanied by lyres strung with sinew and hair, the clatter of skull castanets and sternum manichords tapped by fleshless fingers. An audience of one heard this macabre symphony, sustained by the power of even the small amount of the Ubiquitous Antidote she had been able to consume; though gladly would she have missed the performance.

The infernal symphony swelled to a crescendo. With each note, a fragment of the fortress toppled, a rain of crimson stone and painted tiles crashing around Saloona's motionless form. Overwrought as she was, she could not move; only watch as the fortress was reduced to a vast ruin of cinnabar and garnet, slick with blood, where the gleamants fed. So ended the rancorous line of Paeolina, which had begun with a gavot.

The Black Peal ebbed. The sanguine orchestra fell silent. Saloona Morn started, her ears throbbing, and with alarm noted what remained of the edifice crumbling behind her. The wall fell away, to reveal a violet turbulence.

"RUINATION CATACLYSM DOOM DOOM DOOM."

With a cry, Saloona recognized her prism ship, petals unfolding as it hovered in the dust-choked air. She lunged into it with a gasp.

"Thank you!"

The ship's plasma field surrounded her. Saloona pressed her hand upon its membrane to impart the proper coordinates.

But the ship had already banked. Silently, Saloona stared down at the wreckage of the Crimson Messuage. Cabrielots and destriers lay buried beneath smoking heaps of stone. Of the fortress, nothing remained save a glowering wreck of vermilion rock wreathed in somber flame. Despite the fire witch's perfidy, Saloona sighed in remorse.

"I told you so," said the prism ship, vexed, and bore her home.

The ship returned just as magenta dawn stained the sky above the foothills, and the last mal-de-mutes roosted, whispering and fluttering, among the topmost branches of the evergreens.

"You may sleep now." Saloona touched the ship's membrane. It whirred softly, then settled into a quiescent state.

Saloona hopped out. The mossy ground felt deliciously cool beneath her bare feet. She lifted the hem of her silken gown, hastening toward her cottage, then wrinkled her nose.

A short distance from the front door, the ground was charred. Moss and lichen had been burned away in a circle an ell in diameter. Saloona looked around, confused, until she spotted a small sinuous form crouching behind a blackened rock. She winced.

The basilisk.

Saloona bit her lip, then held out her hand and made reassuring chuffing sounds. The basilisk hissed weakly, tail erect with distrust, turned and slunk toward the forest, a trail of singed bracken in its wake.

In the days that followed, Saloona attempted to lure it with tidbits she thought might be enticing—spruce planks, knots of hardwood, the rails of a broken chair. The basilisk only stared at her reproachfully from the edge of the trees, and sometimes scorched her spore nets for spite.

I'm surprised it hasn't starved by now, she thought one chilly afternoon, and began to assemble another desultory meal for herself. Moments later, a commotion rose from the prism ship's paddock.

"HALLOO! BEWARE! EN GARDE!"

Saloona peered out the window. A tall, black-clad figure strode through the mossy field, the basilisk in its arms.

Saloona met her at the door. "Mother's sister's favored child," she said, and watched in trepidation as Paytim stooped to let the basilisk run free inside the cottage. "Your arrival comes as a surprise."

Paytim ignored her. She straightened to gaze with disapproval at the usual farrago of unwashed dishes and dried fungus scattered around the kitchen. Her clothing was disheveled, her black robes smirched with ash and rust-colored stains. There were several unhealed scars upon her arms and face. After a moment, she turned to Saloona.

"You have a wholesome look," she observed coolly. A second, garnet placebit now winked beside the one formed of the lutist's fingerbone. "Your antidote is indeed more powerful than I imagined."

Saloona said nothing. The basilisk nosed at a basket of dried tree-ears, sending up a plume of smoke. When Saloona tried to shoo it off, it yawped at her. Yellow flames emerged from its mouth and she quickly retreated.

Paytim shot Saloona an imperious look, then marched across the kitchen to the hearth.

"Well then." With a flick of her hand the fire witch ignited the cookstove, then grabbed a saucepan. "Who's ready for lunch?"

Uncle Lou

Nina's Uncle Lou lived in Hampstead, on a narrow, leafy side road that overlooked the Heath—from this vantage, a seemingly endless sweep of green, studded with ancient oaks where ravens clacked and acorns rained down to be gathered by small children and, sometimes, over-eager dogs loosed for a run. Nina could remember collecting acorns with her parents when she was that age, not much bigger than a small dog herself, and carefully piling them where squirrels could find them.

Back then, she'd found this part of London vaguely sinister. The trees, probably, so gnarled and immense and reminiscent of a disturbing illustration in one of her picture books. Now of course she knew it was an impossibly posh area, late-model hybrids and Lotuses and Volvos parked in the drives, Irish and Polish nannies pushing Silver Cross prams, women slender as herons walking terriers that could fit in the palm of Nina's hand. Hampstead had been posh when she was a girl, too, but then the burnished brick houses and wrought-iron fences had possessed a louche air, as though the Kray twins might be up to something in the carriage house.

Nina was fourteen when she realized that rakish edge emanated not from Hampstead but from Uncle Lou himself, with his long hair, bespoke suits from Dougie Millings, and gold-tasseled Moroccan slippers that curled up at the toes like a genie's. He was her favorite uncle—her only uncle, and her only relation except for a centenarian great-great-aunt supposedly entrenched in a retirement community on the Costa del Sol. Nina was an only child, with no first cousins and grandparents long dead. Her divorced parents were dead too, years ago when Nina was still at university.

Since then, she had been in the habit of visiting Uncle Lou once a month or so, when his travels brought him home. He would disappear for months at a time and, when he returned, always answered her questions as to his whereabouts by placing a finger to his lips.

His peripatetic lifestyle had slowed in the last decade, so she now saw him more often. He was a travel writer, creator of the popular *World by Night* series. *Budapest by Night* had been his first, unexpected bestseller, quickly spawning *Paris by Night, London by Night, Marseilles by Night, Vienna by Night* and so on ad infinitum. This was in the 1960s and early 1970s, when the world was much larger and far more exotic. Bohemian tourism was just gaining a toehold in the travel industry, fueled by rumors of Bryon Gysin's pilgrimage to Jakarta with Brian Jones to observe whirling dervishes, and the legions of hippies decamping to Katmandu to eat yak butter whilst negotiating a drug deal.

Yet no matter how obscure or remote a place, Uncle Lou had been there before you, and already returned to his flat in Pallis Mews to bash out an account of where to find the best all-night noodle shop in Bangkok; or a black-market mushroom stall beneath the catacombs in Rome; or a Stockholm voyeurs' club masquerading as a film society devoted to works that featured the forgotten silent movie star Sigrid Blau.

"Doesn't he ever feel guilty?" Nina's mother had once asked her. Lou was her husband's much-older brother; he had been in the War, and afterward spent several years in Eastern Europe, where his activities were unknown but remained the object of much speculation by Nina's parents. He had returned to London sporting a beard and a newly-fashionable mane of long hair. The beard was not a permanent affectation—Uncle Lou had been clean-shaven before the War, yet afterward was remarkably hirsute, shaving at least once and sometimes twice a day. But he kept the flowing black hair, which became a trademark of his author photos.

Nina's mother had always found him "showy," her code word for homosexual, though Uncle Lou in fact was a notorious ladies man.

Nina had frowned at her mother's question. "Guilty about what?"

"About promoting criminal activities?"

"He's not promoting anything," said Nina. "The things he writes about help the local economy."

"I suppose that's what you call it," her mother sniffed, and returned to her delphiniums.

This afternoon, early October sunlight washed across the cobblestone walk leading to Pallis Mews. Uncle Lou's vintage Aston Martin DB4 was parked out front beneath a green tarpaulin, with an impasto of bird droppings that suggested it had not been driven in some time. Pale yellow leaves had banked up against the front door to the flat, and Nina plucked a torn plastic bag from the ivy and clematis vines that covered the brick wall.

She had never visited Uncle Lou without an invitation by telephone or, these days, email. The summons was always precise, for late afternoon or early evening; this one had read *Drop by 5:15 Thursday 19th*. In his kitchen, Uncle Lou had a large wall calendar, a sort of scroll, with the phases of the moon marked on it and myriad jottings in his fine, minuscule penmanship, indicating the exact hour and minute in which various meetings had been scheduled. At home he never met with more than one visitor at a time; the nature of his work was solitary as well as nocturnal.

When she was still in her teens, Nina had once arrived ten minutes early. She could hear Uncle Lou inside, washing dishes as he listened to Radio 2, and even glimpsed him strolling past the front window to turn the music down. But the door did not open until the appointed time.

Today it opened even before she could knock.

"Nina, dear." Her uncle smiled and beckoned her inside. "You look lovely. Watch that pile there, I haven't got them out to the bin yet."

Nina sidestepped a heap of newspapers as he closed the door. Uncle Lou had always been meticulous, even fussy. He'd employed a cleaning woman who came once a week to keep the white Floti rugs spotless and arrange the kilim pillows neatly on the white leather sofa and matching chairs; to straighten the Hockney painting and make sure the Dansk dishes were in their cupboards.

But several years ago, the cleaning woman had moved to Brighton to be closer to her grandchildren. Uncle Lou hadn't bothered to find someone new, and the flat had developed the defiantly unkempt air of a clubgoer who knows she is too old to wear transparent vinyl blouses, even with a camisole beneath, but continues to do so anyway.

"I know, it's a bit of a mess." Uncle Lou sighed and bent to pick up a stray newspaper that was attempting escape, and set it back atop the stack with a hand that trembled slightly. His Moroccan slippers flapped around his bony feet, gold tassels gone and curled toes sadly flattened. "But it's so expensive now to find anyone. Come on in, dear, do you want a drink?"

"No thanks. Or yes, well, if you're going to have something."

Uncle Lou leaned over to graze her cheek with a kiss. He hadn't shaved, and she noted an alarming turquoise blister—actually, a blob of toothpaste—on his neck.

"That's my girl," he said, and shuffled into the kitchen.

While he got drinks, Nina wandered into his office, a brick-walled space covered with bookshelves that held copies of the *By Night* books in dozens, perhaps hundreds, of various translations. There were more untidy stacks here, of unopened mail that had not yet made its way onto Uncle Lou's desk.

She glanced at one of the envelopes. Its postal date was a month previous. She looked over her shoulder, and hastily flipped through more envelopes, finding some dated back to the spring. At the sound of Uncle Lou's footsteps in the hall she turned quickly and went to meet him.

"Thanks." She took the martini glass he offered her—it was clean, at least—and raised it to *ting* against his.

"Chin chin," said Uncle Lou.

She walked with him to the dining room, which overlooked a good-sized courtyard. Years ago Uncle Lou had let the outside space revert to a tangle of mulberry bushes, etiolated plane trees, and ground ivy. It would have made a nice dog run, but Uncle Lou had never kept a dog. There were signs of some kind of animals rooting around—foxes, probably, which were common in Hampstead, though Nina had never caught a whiff of their distinctive musky scent.

They settled at the dining table. Uncle Lou set out a plate of olives and some slightly stale biscuits. They drank and chatted about a travel piece in last week's *Guardian*, a noisy dog in Nina's neighborhood, people they knew in common.

"Have you heard from Valerie Minton ?" asked Nina. She finished her drink and nibbled at an olive. "You haven't mentioned her for a while."

Uncle Lou sighed. "Oh dear, very sad. I guess I forgot to tell you. She died in March. A heart thing—a blessing, really. She had that early-onset Alzheimer's." He downed the rest of his martini and set the empty glass beside hers. "Here's a piece of good advice: don't get old."

"Oh, Uncle Lou." Nina hugged him. "You're not old."

But that of course was a lie. She could feel how thin he'd gotten, and frail. And the flat was all too clearly becoming a burden in terms of upkeep.

She grasped his hand and stared at him. His long hair was white, thinner than it had been. His face was lined, but a lifetime of keeping late hours had saved him from skin-damaging ultraviolet rays and preserved a certain youthful suppleness. With his high cheekbones, stark blade of a nose and cleft chin, he might have been an aging actor, with eyes a disconcerting shade of amber, so pale they appeared almost colorless in strong light. The theatrical effect was heightened by his wardrobe, which this afternoon consisted of an embroidered India-print shirt over wide-wale corduroy trousers that had once been canary yellow but had faded to the near-white of lemon pith, and the heavy silver ring he always wore on his right pointer finger.

The ring wobbled now as that finger shook, scolding her. "I am older than old, Nina. Older than God, who has never forgiven me for it."

Nina laughed, and he turned to gaze wistfully out into the court-yard. How old *was* Uncle Lou? In his eighties, at least. Many of his old friends were dead; others had moved to live with their children, or into retirement communities. Nina's own flat was too small for another person; she could move in with him, she supposed, but she knew Uncle Lou wouldn't hear of it. A few years earlier, he had sold the By Night trademark and backlist to a web entrepreneur for an impressive sum. Perhaps he could be encouraged to look into one of those posh facilities where elderly people of means lived?

She wouldn't bring it up this afternoon, but made a mental note to do some research herself into what was available near Hampstead.

Uncle Lou squeezed her hand. "Do you feel up to a walk on the Heath?"

Nina nodded. "Great idea."

They strolled along a path that meandered over a gentle rise crowned by an ancient oak. There were always families with young children here, and lots of dogs off leash.

"Uh-oh," said Nina, as a silken-furred red setter came bounding toward them. She moved protectively to his side. "Incoming…"

Dogs behaved in a peculiar fashion around Uncle Lou. Those that had previously encountered him acted as the setter did now: as it drew near, it dropped to its belly and inched toward him, whining softly, tail wagging madly.

Strange dogs, however, barked or snarled, ears pressed tight against their skulls and tails held low, and often fled before Uncle Lou could hold out his hand and make reassuring *cht cht* sounds that Nina could barely hear.

"Hello there." Uncle Lou stopped and gazed down at the setter, smiling. His knees bent slightly and he winced as he reached to touch the dog's forehead. "Conor, isn't it? Good dog."

At the old man's touch the setter scrambled to its feet and danced around him, ears flapping.

"Sorry, sorry!" A man rushed up and grasped the dog's collar, clipping a leash onto it. "Don't want him to knock you over!"

Uncle Lou shook his head. "Oh, he wouldn't do that. Would you, Conor?"

He stooped to take the dog's head between his hands and gazed into its eyes. The setter grew absolutely still, as though it sensed a game bird nearby; then dropped to its belly, head cocked as it stared up at Uncle Lou.

"Well, he likes you, doesn't he?" The man patted the setter's head, smiling. "Come on then, Conor. Let's go."

Nina waved as the man strode off, the setter straining at the leash. Uncle Lou stood beside her, watching until the two figures disappeared into the trees. He turned to his niece, nodding as though all this had occurred according to some plan.

"I'd like you to accompany me to an event." He gestured at the path, indicating they should begin to head back home. "If you're not too busy."

"Of course," said Nina. "Where is it?"

"At the zoo."

"The zoo?" Nina looked over in surprise. Uncle Lou had always been far more likely to invite his niece to attend a clandestine midnight gathering of political dissidents or artists, than to suggest a visit to the zoo.

"Yes. The Whipsnade Zoo, not Regents Park, so we'll have to drive up to Dunstable. A fundraiser for a new building, a home for endangered fruit bats I think, or maybe it's kiwis? Something nocturnal, anyway. There'll be press around, the local gentry, maybe a few minor celebrities. You know the sort of thing. Someone in the PR department obviously thought it would be amusing if I was in attendance. You can be my date."

He slipped his arm into hers, and Nina laughed. "Sure. Sounds like fun. When is it? Do I need to dress up?"

"Next Wednesday. I believe the invitation says to wear black. Not very imaginative. But you always look lovely, dear."

They'd reached the Pallis Mews flat. Uncle Lou paused to pluck a clematis blossom from the ivy-covered wall, and turned to poke its stem through a buttonhole in Nina's jacket. "There. Purple is your color, isn't it? Thank you for dropping by."

He kissed her cheek and Nina embraced him, hugging him tightly. "I'll see you next week."

Uncle Lou nodded, long white hair stirring in the evening breeze, and walked unsteadily back inside.

The following week Nina showed up at the appointed quarter-hour, 4:45. A bit earlier than customary for Uncle Lou, but they wanted to allow plenty of time for rush hour traffic on the MI. Out front, the tarp had been removed from the Aston Martin, which gleamed like quicksilver in the twilight.

"Hello, darling, don't you look marvelous!" exclaimed Uncle Lou as she stepped into the flat. "I haven't seen that dress before, have I? Lovely."

He kissed her cheek, and she noticed his own cheeks were flushed and his tawny eyes bright.

"You look lovely, too," she said, laughing. "Is there some ulterior motive for this event? Am I the beard for an assignation?"

For an instant Uncle Lou appeared alarmed, but then he shook his head.

"No." He made a show of straightening his velvet jacket, a somewhat frayed black paisley with silver embroidery. "It's been a while since I was out and about, that's all. And I need to be worthy of *you*, of course."

She waited as he moved about the flat, collecting keys, the large black envelope containing the invitation, a plastic carrier bag from Sainsburys, an umbrella.

"I think it's supposed to be nice," said Nina, eyeing the umbrella.

"You're probably right." Uncle Lou set the umbrella back atop a hall table and paused, catching his breath. After a moment he slid a hand into his pocket, withdrew it to hold out a set of car keys.

"Here." He put the keys into Nina's palm and closed her fingers around them. "I'd like you to drive."

"What?" Nina's eyes widened. "The—your car?"

Uncle Lou nodded. "Yes. I don't trust myself anymore. It used to be I saw better at night than daytime, but now..." He grimaced. "Last time I took it out I drove onto the curb near Tesco. You can drive a standard, right?"

"Yes—of course. But—"

"I'm giving it to you." He turned and picked up a large manila envelope on the side table. "Everything's in here, I've done all the paperwork already. Title and deed. It's yours. There are some other papers in there as well. You might look at them when you have some spare time."

Nina stared at the keys in her hand. "But—are you sure, Uncle Lou?"

"Absolutely. Impress that boyfriend of yours at the law firm. I can always borrow it back if I need to. Now, we'd better go—I don't want to be late."

He tucked the manila envelope beneath his arm. Once inside the car, he slid it into the glovebox. "Let's remember it's there," he said, and sank into the leather seat.

They ran into heavy traffic heading north, but this eased as they approached Dunstable. The zoo was in the countryside a few miles outside town, within a greenbelt that was in stark contrast to the depressing sprawl behind them. Uncle Lou rolled down his window, letting in the smell of autumn leaves and smoke. On a distant green hillside, the immense chalk figure of a lion had been carved. Above the hill, a full moon had just begun to rise, tarnished silver against the periwinkle sky.

"Look at that," said Nina. "Isn't that beautiful?"

"Isn't it," said Uncle Lou, and squeezed her hand upon the gear-shift.

They arrived at the zoo entrance shortly after the reception's opening time.

"Don't park there," Uncle Lou said when Nina put on her turn signal for the main carpark. "Keep going—there, on the left. Much less crowded, and you'll be able to leave quickly later."

Nina angled the Aston Martin through a narrow gate that opened into a much smaller lot. It held only a handful of vehicles, most of them zoo vans and trucks.

"Are we allowed to park here?" she asked, after following Uncle Lou's directions to ease the Aston Martin beneath a large oak.

"Oh, yes. It never really fills up. Bit of a secret." With an effort, he extricated himself from the car, steadying himself against the hood and sighing. "I swear, that car gets smaller every time I get inside it." He pointed at a gap between an overgrown hedge. "That way."

"How do you know about this?" asked Nina, stepping gingerly through the gap.

"I have friends here I visit sometimes. Ah, that must be where we're supposed to be…"

This zoo was much more parklike than the London Zoo; more like the grounds of a stately home, only minus the home, and with elephants and oryx and other large wildlife. Dusk had deepened into early evening, the moon poised above them in a lapis sky where a few faint stars shimmered. Unearthly noises echoed through the night: high-pitched chitters; a loud snuffling that became a bellow; an odd hollow pumping sound.

"Least bittern," said Uncle Lou, cocking his head in the direction of the sound.

Nina squinted in the fading light. "How do you know that?"

"I'm a font of useless knowledge. I've built my career on it."

A path led them toward a large field where a crowd milled around an open-sided white marquee tent. A few security guards and several men and women in staff uniforms that marked them as animal keepers mingled with people wearing loose interpretations of fancy dress. At a small booth beside the tent, a middle-aged woman in a black faux-fur capelet examined Uncle Lou's invitation.

"I know who you are," she said, beaming up at him. "I met my husband because of *Athens by Night*. Is this your daughter?"

"My niece." Uncle Lou tucked Nina's arm into his.

The woman checked their names off a list and gestured toward the tent. "Go get some champagne. Enjoy!"

The reception was to raise funds for a new, state-of-the art Owl House, which would provide habitat for the endangered Eurasian Eagle-Owl and Pygmy Owl, along with more common species. Beneath the marquee, tables draped in black and silver held trays of canapes and elaborate hors d'oeuvre made to resemble owls, full moons, and bats. In one corner, a large owl with a slender chain attached to its leg perched upon a leather gauntlet covering the arm of a tall, blonde young man in zoo staff livery. A number of guests had gathered here, and the owl regarded them with baleful hauteur, now and then ruffling its feathers and clacking its beak noisily.

After making a beeline for the bar, Nina and Uncle Lou wandered around the tent, drinking their champagne and admiring a large display with three-dimensional models of the proposed Owl House. A few people walked over to clasp Uncle Lou's hand and greet him by name, including Miranda Eccles, an ancient woman writer of some renown. Nina had often heard the rumor that the two had been lovers. While they spoke, Nina slipped away to get two more glasses of champagne. By the time she returned, the elderly woman was gone.

"Let's go say hello to that owl," said Uncle Lou.

He handed his empty glass to a passing waiter and took a full one from Nina. They edged their way to the front of the group, being careful not to spill their champagne. The owl had turned its back on the onlookers.

"It looks rather like Miranda, doesn't it?" observed Uncle Lou.

The owl's head abruptly swiveled in a disconcerting two-hundred-and-sixty-degree arc. Its yellow eyes fixed on Uncle Lou, the pupils large as pound coins. Without warning it raised its wings and flapped them menacingly, beak parting to emit an ear-splitting screech.

Nina gasped. A few people cried out, then laughed nervously as the owl-keeper swiftly produced a canvas hood that he quickly dropped over the bird.

"He's getting restless," he explained, adjusting the hood. "Full moon, he wants to hunt. And he's not used to so many people."

"I feel the same way." Uncle Lou took Nina's elbow and steered her toward an exit. "Let's take a walk outside."

They handed off their empty glasses and stepped back into the night. Uncle Lou seemed invigorated by the champagne: he threw his head back, gazing at the moon; laughed then pointed to a black tracery of trees some distance away.

"There," he said.

He began walking so quickly that Nina had to run to catch up. When she reached his side, he took her hand, slowing his pace.

"You've been a very good niece." He glanced down at her. For the first time Nina noticed he had neglected to shave, perhaps for several days: gray stubble covered his jaw and chin. "I don't know how my brother and your mother managed to produce such a wonderful daughter, but I'm very glad they did."

"Oh, Uncle Lou." Nina's eyes filled with tears. "I feel the same way."

"I know you do. Here." He stopped, with some effort twisted the heavy silver ring from his hand. He grasped Nina's wrist and slid the ring onto her right pointer finger. "I want you to have this."

She looked at him in surprise. "It fits! It always looked so big."

Moonlight glinted on the silver band as Uncle Lou drew it to his lips and kissed her knuckle, the gray hairs on his chin soft where they brushed her fingertips.

"Of course it fits. You have my hands," he said, and let hers drop. "Come on."

They passed artfully landscaped habitats with placards that indicated that antelopes or Bactrian camels lived there, behind hidden moats or fences cunningly designed to resemble vines or reeds or waist-high grass. A gated road permitted cars and zoo buses to drive through a mock savanna where lions and cheetahs prowled.

Nina saw no sign of any animals, though she occasionally caught the ripe scents of dung or musk, the muddy green smell of a man-made pond or marsh. The snorts and hoots had diminished as night deepened and creatures either settled to sleep or, in the case of predators, grew silent and watchful.

But then a single wavering cry rang out from the direction of the trees, ending as abruptly as it began. Nina's entire body flashed cold.

"What was that?" she whispered. But Uncle Lou didn't reply.

They reached the stand of trees, where the gravel walkway forked. Without hesitation Uncle Lou bore to the left.

Here, more trees loomed alongside the path, their branches entwining above unruly thickets of thorny brush. Acorns and beech mast crunchds underfoot, so that it seemed as though they had entered a forest. There was a spicy smell of bracken, and another scent, unfamiliar but unmistakably an animal's.

After a few minutes Uncle Lou stopped. He glanced behind them, and for a moment remained still, listening.

"This way," he said, and ducked beneath the trees.

"Are we allowed here?" Nina called after him in a low urgent voice.

Uncle Lou's words echoed back to her. "At night, everything is allowed. Shhh!"

She hesitated, trying to peer though the heavy greenery; finally ducked and began to push her way through, shielding her face with one hand. Brambles plucked at her dress, and she flinched as a thorn scraped against one leg.

But then the underbrush receded. She stepped into a small clearing thick with dead leaves. Several large trees loomed against the moonlit sky. Uncle Lou stood beneath one of these, breathing heavily as he stared at a small hill several yards away. More trees grew on its slope, between boulders and creeping vines.

"Uncle Lou?"

She took a step toward him, froze as a dark shape flowed between the boulders then disappeared. Before she could cry out she heard Uncle Lou's soft voice.

"There's a fence."

She swallowed, blinking, looked where he pointed and saw a faint latticework of twisted chainlink. She waited for her heart to slow, then darted to his side.

And yes, now she could discern that behind the chainlink fence was a deep cement moat, maybe twenty feet wide and extending into the darkness in either direction. Vines straggled down its sides, and overhanging mats of moss and dead leaves.

They were at the back of one of the enclosures, a place where visitors were absolutely *not* allowed.

"*Uncle Lou,*" Nina whispered, her voice rising anxiously.

As she spoke, the shadowy form rematerialized, still on the far side of the moat, and directly across from them. It lowered its head between massive shoulders, moonlight flaring in its eyes so that they momentarily glowed red, then stretched out its front legs until its belly grazed the ground. A wolf.

Nina stared at it, torn between amazement and an atavistic fear unassuaged by the presence of the moat. When a second form slipped beside the first, she jumped.

"They won't hurt you," murmured Uncle Lou.

A third wolf trotted from the trees, and another, and another, until at last seven were ranged at the foot of the hill. They gazed at the old man, tongues lolling from their long jaws, and then each lay down in turn upon the grass in a watchful pose.

"What are they doing?" breathed Nina.

"The same thing we are," replied Uncle Lou. "Excuse me for a moment—nature calls…"

He patted her shoulder and walked briskly toward another tree.

Nina politely turned away—he sometimes had to do this when they were embarked upon a long stroll on the Heath, always returning to shake his head and mutter, "Old man's bladder."

She looked back at the wolves, who now appeared somewhat restive. The largest one's head snapped up. It stared at something over-head, then scrambled to its feet. At the same moment, Nina heard a rustling in the treetops, followed by a creaking sound.

"Uncle Lou?" She glanced at the tree where he'd gone to relieve himself. "Everything all right?"

The rustling grew louder. Nina looked up, and saw one of the upper boughs of the tree bending down at an alarming angle, so that its tip hung over the moat. A large whitish animal was clambering down its length, sending dead leaves and bits of debris to the ground beneath. Nina clapped a hand to her mouth as a shaft of moonlight struck the bough, revealing Uncle Lou, naked and slowing to a crawl as the branch bowed under him.

The wolves had all leapt up and stood in a row at the enclosure's edge, eyes fixed on the white figure above them. With a loud *crack*, the bough snapped. At the same instant, Uncle Lou sprang from it, his pale form mottled with shadow as he landed upon the grass and rolled between the creatures there.

With a cry Nina ran forward, stopped and fought to see her uncle in the blur of dust and leaves and fur on the other side of the hidden moat. The wolves danced around it, tails held low, heads high, then drew back as another wolf struggled to its feet.

It was nearly the same size as the largest wolf, its muzzle white, and iron-gray fur tipped with silver. It shook its head, sending off a flurry of leaves and twigs, stood very still as the other big male approached to sniff its hindquarters, then its throat. Finally it touched the newcomer's white muzzle, growling playfully as the two engaged in mock battle and the other wolves darted forward, tails wagging as they joined in.

Nina watched, too stunned to move. Not until the wolves turned and began to stream back into the shadows did she call out.

"Wait!"

The biggest wolf paused to glance back at her, then disappeared into the underbrush with the others. Only the grizzled wolf slowed, and looked over its shoulder at Nina. For a long moment it held her gaze, its tawny eyes and pale muzzle gilded by the moonlight. Then it too turned and trotted into the darkness.

Nina shook her head, trying to catch her breath. Astonishment curdled into terror as she thought of the reception not far away. She raced to the tree Uncle Lou had climbed, and beneath it found the plastic Sainsbury's bag. Stuffed inside were his clothes, velvet jacket and corduroy trousers, socks and underwear, and at the very bottom the worn Moroccan slippers.

At sight of them she began to cry, but quickly wiped her eyes. Clutching the bag to her chest, she pushed her way back through the trees and overgrown brush until she reached the path again.

Somehow she found her way back to the carpark where she'd left the Aston Martin. She passed no one, walking as fast as she dared before breaking into a run as she neared the hedge that bounded the lot. The moon had dipped below the trees. The sounds of the reception had long since dwindled to the distant drone of departing cars.

She started the Aston Martin, heart pounding as she eased it onto the access road and headed toward the main highway, sobbing openly now, always careful not to exceed the speed limit.

At last she reached her apartment. She parked the car in the underground garage, leaving a note on the windscreen for the security guard so it would not be towed; retrieved the manila envelope from the glovebox, grabbed the bag containing Uncle Lou's clothes, and went upstairs. She poured herself a stiff drink—a martini—downed it and with shaking hands opened the envelope.

Inside was a long, affectionate letter from her uncle, along with the title to the Aston Martin, and precisely detailed instructions as to how to dispose of his clothing and answer the awkward and inevitable questions that would soon arise regarding his disappearance. There was also contact information for his longtime accountant and solicitor, as well as for an old friend who lived in central Romania—and, of course, a copy of his will.

In addition to the car, he left the Pallis Mews flat and all it contained to Nina, along with his shares in the By Night enterprise. And there was an extremely generous bequest to the Whipsnade Zoo, with a provision that a sizable portion of it be used for the continued upkeep and improvement of the gray wolves' habitat.

Nina sold the Aston Martin. Upkeep was costly, and she worried about it being vandalized or stolen. After six months she moved into the Pallis Mews flat, refurbishing it slightly and donating the unworn clothing to Oxfam, though she kept the Moroccan slippers. She continues to visit Uncle Lou every week, taking the train to Luton and then the bus to the zoo. The gray wolf exhibit is seldom crowded, even on Sundays, and Nina often has it to herself. Sometimes, the grizzled old wolf sits at the edge of the enclosure and gazes at her with his tawny eyes, and occasionally raises his white muzzle in a yodeling cry.

But more often than not, she finds him outstretched upon one of the moss-covered boulders, eyes closed, breathing gently: the very picture of lupine bliss as he sleeps in the afternoon sun.

Errantry

I was hanging out in Angus's apartment above the print shop, scoring some of his ADHD medication, when Tommy Devaraux ran upstairs to tell us he'd just seen the Folding Man over at the Old Court Grill. This was some years after the new century had cracked open and left me and my friends scrambled, even more feckless than we'd been thirty years earlier when we met as teenagers in Kamensic Village. The three of us had been romantically involved off and on during high school and for a few years afterward, held together by the wobbly gravitational pull exerted by adolescence and the strange, malign beauty of Kamensic, a once-rural town that had since been ravaged by gentrification and whose name had recently been trademarked by a domestic housewares tycoon.

Angus had never left Kamensic; he'd spent the last three decades nurturing a musical career that never quite took off, despite a minor 1977 hit that continued to generate residuals and a ringtone that now echoed eerily across the floor of the New York Stock Exchange. His most recent job had been with a brokerage firm absorbed by MortNet. The three kids from his first marriage were grown, but the younger ones, twins, had just started school, and child support and legal bills from the second divorce had stripped him of almost everything.

His ex-wife Sheila and the twins remained in the McMansion out by Kamensic Meadows, but Angus lived in a third-floor flat he rented from another old friend who owned the struggling printing company below. The entire rickety wood-frame building smelled of dust and ink, the faintly resinous odor of paper mingled with acrid chemical pigments and the reek of melted plastic. In bed at night in Angus's room, with the old presses rumbling on the floor below, it felt as though we were on board a train. Walls and floors vibrated around us, and a sallow streetlamp coated the window with a syrupy greenish light. A few yards away, real trains racketed between the city and the outer exurbs.

I lived sixty miles north of Kamensic, in the next county, but spent more time in my old stomping grounds than reason or propriety allowed. Angus was my half-brother, the result of what Shakespearean scholars term a bed-trick. We didn't know of our complicated parentage when we first slept together, but once we learned about it we figured it was too late and what the hell. Few people besides us ever knew, and most of them are now dead. My own career, as assistant professor of Arthurian studies at a small college upstate, had flamed out due to accusations of sexual harassment (dropped when a student recanted his story) and drug and alcohol abuse (upheld). Despite my dismissal, I found work as a private tutor, coaching rich kids on their college admissions essays.

"Vivian," Tommy said breathlessly when I opened the door. "Angus here?"

I brushed my cheek against Tommy's as he swept inside and crossed to where Angus sat hunched over his computer. Tommy peered at the monitor and frowned. "Where's Estelle?"

Tommy had a little obsessive thing that dovetailed neatly with Angus's frenetic energy, as in their latest collaboration, a thirty-seven-song cycle Angus was writing about Estelle, an imaginary woman based on a real woman, a stockbroker Tommy had dated once. She eventually hit him with a restraining order and moved to Vermont.

Angus scowled. "I'm taking a break from freaking Estelle."

"Well, sacrifice that Voidwalker and log off," said Tommy. "I just saw the Folding Man."

"At the Old Court?" Angus ground out his cigarette and lit another. "He's there now? Why didn't you just call us?"

Tommy glanced at me imploringly. He was tall but sparely built, softer than he'd been but still boyish, with round tortoiseshell glasses on a snub nose, his long dark hair gone to gray; slightly louche in a frayed Brooks Brothers jacket and shiny black engineer's boots. He was a Special Ed teacher at a private school and dealt with autistic teenagers, many of them violent. He'd been attacked so often by kids bigger and stronger than he was that he'd started to have panic attacks, and now took so much Xanax just to get through the working day that his customary expression was a rictus of mournful, slightly hostile chagrin—he looked like the Mock Turtle after a lost weekend.

"Well, he left," he said. "Plus my cell phone died. But he gave me this—"

He sank into a swivel chair beside Angus, hands cupped on his knees as though he held a butterfly. The illusion held for an instant when he opened his hands to display a tiny diadem of russet and yellow petals that fluttered when he breathed upon it.

"Nice," said Angus grudgingly. "He'll be gone by now."

I crouched beside Tommy. "Can I see?"

"Sure.

I picked it up and weighed it tentatively in my palm. Angus's Focalin was starting to have its way with me, a diffuse, sunny-day buzz that meshed nicely with the day outside: mid-afternoon, early May, lilac in bloom, kids riding bikes along the village sidewalks. I drew my hand to my face and caught a whiff of the Old Court's distinctive odor, hamburgers and Pine-Sol; but also, inexplicably, a smell of the sea, salt and hot glass.

I blew on the bit of folded paper. It fell onto the floor. Angus grabbed it before I could pick it up again.

"He gave it to me," Tommy said in an aggrieved tone.

But Angus was already opening it. Tommy and I stood beside him as he carefully unfolded wings, triangles, unveiling creases in once-glossy paper, swatches of azure and silver, topaz, pine-green. The yellow and fawn-colored petals must have sprung from the other side of the page, torn from a magazine or brochure.

"Someone's been to the beach." Angus held up a finger dusted with glittering specks, spilled sugar or sand; licked it and smoothed out the paper on his desk.

"What does it say?" asked Tommy.

"'YOU ARE HERE.'"

I edged between them to get a better look. The paper was four or five inches square, crosshatched with grayish lines indicating where it had been folded countless times. It was almost impossible to imagine it had ever had a shape other than this one, and impossible to remember just what that shape had been—an insect? Tiger lilies?

"Beach roses," said Tommy. "That's what it's a picture of."

"How the hell can you know that?" demanded Angus.

"It's a map," I said.

Angus's cellphone buzzed. He glanced at it, muttered "Sheila" and turned it off. "Let's see."

I adjusted my glasses and frowned. "It's hard to see, but there—those lines? It says Route 22."

"That's the Old Court there," Tommy agreed, squinting at a blotch on a smudge of shoreline. "Those dotted lines, that's the old road that runs parallel to it, out towards that apple farm where they want to put the development."

Ashes dropped from Angus's cigarette onto the ersatz map. When he blew them away, a tiny spark glowed in one corner.

"There." Tommy stubbed out the ember with his finger. "It ends there."

"Like I said." Angus finished his cigarette. "X marks the spot. Let's go check it out. Who wants to get stoned?"

Angus had retained a company car, I never understood how. The back was filled with his stuff, sheet music, CDs, manila envelopes, Happy Meals toys, a guitar case. I sat in the front with Angus's hand on my knee. Tommy shoved stuff aside and slumped in the back, his face pressed against the window. He looked like a kid on a long drive, at once resigned and expectant. I thought, not for the first time, how little had changed since we really were kids: still bombing around on a Saturday afternoon, drunk or stoned or generally messed up, still screwing each other when no one else would have us, still singing along with the radio.

"Is there a channel just for your songs?" asked Tommy as we drove over the railroad tracks and headed north to old Route 22. Angus tapped the radio screen until he found something he liked. "Like is there a satellite that just beams 'Do It All Day'?"

Angus nodded. "That would be the Burnout Channel."

"This is the Cowsills," I said. "That song about the park and other things."

"*And then I knew,*" chanted Tommy, "*that she had made me happy.*"

"Happy, happy," echoed Angus. He began to sing his own words.

> "*I love the Folding Man*
> *He may be just a drunk*
> *And I'm a worn-out skunk…*"

Outside the remnants of old Kamensic slid past, stone churches, the sprawling Victorian where Angus had grown up, now a B&B; the ancient cemetery with its strange stone animals; Deer Park Inn, a former dive that had been cleaned up and christened the Deer Park Tavern, its shattered blacktop newly paved and full of SUVs and Priuses. It was easy to blame these changes on Marian Lavecque, the domestic maven whose reign had redrawn the town's aesthetic and cultural boundaries.

But I knew the decline stretched back longer than that, to the years when Angus and I had first become entangled. So it was hard sometimes—for me anyway, since my academic background had trained me to see patterns everywhere, a subtle tapestry woven into the grungiest Missoni knockoff—not to feel that our *folie a deux* had broken something in the place we loved most.

One upshot was that we had to go farther afield now to find a bar that suited us. I'd never heard of the Folding Man being anywhere but the Old Court.

I reached to touch Tommy's knee. "You okay back there?"

"Sure," he said. "We're on a quest." He smiled as Angus's voice filled the car.

"I love the Folding Man
He may be just a geek
And I'm a burned-out freak…"

Tommy was the one who'd always believed in things. Even though he could never really explain to you exactly what those things were; only trace circles in the air when he was drunk, or go into long rambling exegeses of conspiracies between real estate developers and the Zen Buddhists who'd built a retreat house on what had once been old-growth forest, or the purported sexual relationship, based on a mutual desire to make artisanal cheese, that existed between Estelle, the woman he'd been obsessed with, and a dotcom millionaire who also lived in Vermont. I felt protective of Tommy, although when drunk he could become bellicose, even violent. Asleep he resembled a high school athlete fallen on hard times, his T-shirt riding up to show a slack torso, gray hair, an appendectomy scar like a wincing mouth, a bad tattoo of a five-pointed star.

Whereas Angus retained the body he'd had as a teenager, his skin smooth and unblemished, pale as barley; he slept curled on his side and breathed softly, like a child, occasionally sighing as in some deep regret he couldn't acknowledge in waking life. Then the lines on his face seemed to fade, and his eyes, closed, held no hint of what burned there when he stared at you.

"Let's stop for a minute," I said as we crested the hill overlooking the Old Court.

"He won't be there." Angus glanced into the rearview mirror. "You said he left."

"Yeah, he left." Tommy opened his window. A green smell filled the car, young ferns and the leaves of crushed meadowsweet. "But stop anyway."

Inside, the Old Court was sunlit, its curved oak bar glossy as caramel and warm to the touch. A few elderly bikers sat drinking beer or coffee and watching the Golf Channel. We sat at the far end, where it was quieter, in front of the brass bowl that held the Folding Man's handiwork.

"Back already?" Nance, the bartender, smiled at Tommy, then glanced out the window to see whose car was parked there: not Tommy's, so she could serve him. "You want the same?"

Tommy and I had red wine, Angus a rum and Coke. Tommy drank fast—he always did—and ordered another. I drank mine almost as quickly, then shut my eyes, reached into the brass bowl and withdrew a piece of folded paper.

The Folding Man's work isn't exactly origami. Tommy has showed some of it to a woman he knows who does origami, and she said it was like nothing she'd ever seen before. The Folding Man doesn't talk about it, either, which is probably why Tommy became obsessed with him. Nothing gets Tommy as revved up as being ignored—Angus says he's seen Tommy get a hard-on when a woman rejects him.

Not that Tommy had ever actually met the Folding Man, until now. None of us had, even though he'd been a fixture at the Old Court for as long as we'd been drinking there. We first began to notice his work in the early 1980s when, before or after a wild night, we'd find these little folded figures left on the floor near where we'd been sitting.

"This is like that guy in *Blade Runner*," said Tommy once. He'd picked up something that resembled a winged scorpion. "See?"

I looked at it closely and saw it had the face of Angelica Huston and, instead of pincers, a pair of spoons for claws.

But then Tommy carefully unfolded it, smoothing it on the bar.

"Don't get it wet," warned Angus.

"I won't." Tommy looked puzzled. He slid the crumpled paper to me. "It's gone."

"What's gone?"

I looked at the paper, and saw it was a square taken from an ad for Yves St. Laurent Opium perfume—the word OPIUM was there, and part of the bottle, and I could even smell a musky trace of the fragrance.

But there was no woman anywhere in the ad. I turned the paper over: nada. No spoons, either.

"Edward James Olmos."

Tommy and I turned to stare blankly at Angus.

"That's who played that character. " He took the paper and scrutinized it, then flicked his cigarette lighter and set it on fire and dropped it in his ashtray. "In *Blade Runner*. Edward James Olmos. Great actor."

The Folding Man's stuff was always like that. Things that were never quite what they seemed to be. Sea anemones with eyes and wheels, body parts—vulvas were a popular theme—that sprouted fingers, exotic birds with too many heads and hooves instead of feathers, a lunar lander printed with a map of the Sea of Tranquility, the extravagant effects produced by some infernal combination of paper-folding and whatever was actually printed on the paper. None of them was any larger than the area I could circumscribe with my thumb and forefinger, and some were much smaller.

But if you unfolded them, they were never what they *didn't* seem to be, either—you ended up with nothing but a page from a magazine or travel brochure, or a paper menu from McDonald's or the Kamensic Diner, or (in the case of the lunar lander) a fragment of the Playbill for *Via Galactica*. They were like origami figures from the Burgess Shale, beautiful but also slightly nightmarish.

And what made it even stranger was that no one except for me and Tommy and, to a lesser degree, Angus, ever seemed to think they were weird at all. No one paid much attention to them; no one thought they were mysterious. When Tommy started asking about who made them, Nance just shrugged.

"This guy, comes in sometimes to watch the game. I think maybe he used to smoke or something, like he wants to do something with his hands. So he does those."

"What's his name?" said Tommy.

Nance shook her head. "I don't know. We just call him the folding man."

"You don't know his name?" Angus stared at her, his tone slightly belligerent, as it often was. "What, he never puts down a credit card? You know everyone's name."

Elizabeth Hand

"He drinks rail whiskey, and he pays cash. Ask him yourself if you really want to know."

But before now we'd never seen him, not ever, not once, though over the years Tommy had chased down customers and bartenders to receive detailed descriptions of what he looked like: older, paunchy, gray hair; weathered face; unshaven, eyes that were usually described as blue or gray; glasses, faded corduroys and a stained brown windbreaker.

"He looks like a fucking wino, Tommy," Angus exploded once, when the hundredth customer had been quizzed after a thumbnail-sized frog with match-head eyes and the faces of the original Jackson 5 had materialized beneath Tommy's barstool. "Give it a fucking break, okay?"

But Tommy couldn't give it a break, any more than he could keep from getting fixated on women he hardly knew. Neither could I, and, after a while, neither could Angus. Though Angus was the one who made the ground rule about never taking any of the folded paper figures out of the Old Court.

"There's enough crap in my apartment. Yours, too, Tommy."

Nance didn't like customers taking them from the brass bowl, either.

"Leave them!" she'd yell if someone tried to pocket one at the end of the night. "They're part of the decor!"

I knew Tommy had nicked some. I found one under his pillow once, a lovely, delicate thing shaped like a swan, or a borzoi, or maybe it was a meerschaum pipe, with rows of teeth and a tiny pagoda on what I thought was its head (or bowl). I was going to make a joke about it, but Tommy was in the bathroom; and the longer I lay there with that weird, nearly weightless filigree in the palm of my hand, the harder it was to look at anything else, or think of anything except the way it seemed to glow, a pearlescent, rubeous color, like the inside of a child's ear when you shine a flashlight behind it.

When I heard Tommy come out of the bathroom I slipped it back, carefully, beneath the pillow. Later, when I searched for it again,

I found nothing but a crumpled sale flyer from the old Kamensic Hardware Store.

Now I set my wineglass onto the bar, opened my eyes and looked at what I had picked from the brass bowl. A fern, gold rather than green, its fiddlehead resembling the beaked prow of a Viking ship.

"Let's go." Tommy stuck some bills under his empty glass and stood.

"We just got here," said Angus.

"I don't want to lose him."

Angus looked at me, annoyed, then finished his drink. "Yeah, whatever. Come on, Vivian."

I replaced the fern and gulped the rest of my wine, and we returned to the car. I sat in the back so Tommy could ride up with Angus and navigate.

I said, "You didn't tell us what he looked like."

Tommy spread the piece of paper on his knee. "He looked like a wino."

"Did you talk to him? Did he say anything?"

"Yeah." Tommy turned to look at me. He grinned, that manic School's Out grin that still made everything seem possible. "I asked him how he did it, how he made everything. And he said, 'Everything fits. You'll figure it out.'"

"'Everything fits, you'll figure it out?'" repeated Angus. "Who is this guy, Mr. Rogers?"

Tommy only smiled. I leaned forward to kiss him, while Angus shook his head and we drove on.

We headed north on the old Brandywine Turnpike, a barely maintained road that runs roughly parallel to Route 22, and connects Kamensic via various gravel roads and shortcuts to the outlying towns and deeper woodlands that, for the moment, had escaped development metastasizing from the megalopolis. The boulder-strewn, glacier-carved terrain was inhospitable to builders, steeply sloped and falling away suddenly into ravines overgrown with mountain ash and rock juniper that gave off a sharp tang of gin.

There were patches of genuine old-growth forest here, ancient towering hemlocks, white oaks and hornbeams. Occasionally we'd pass an abandoned gas station or roadhouse, or the remains of tiny settlements long fallen into ruin beside spur roads that retained the names of their founders: Tintertown Road, Smithtown Road, Fancher's Corner. It was like driving back in time into the old Kamensic, the real Kamensic, the place we'd mapped through all our various lovers and drug dealers and music gigs over the last thirty years.

Only of course we were really driving *away* from Kamensic, slipping in and out of the town's borders, until we reached its outermost edge, the place where even the tax maps got sketchy.

This was where Muscanth Mountain and Sugar Mountain converged on Lake Muscanth. The mountains weren't mountains really, just big hills, but the lake was a real lake. In the 1920s a group of socialists had established a short-lived utopian community there, a summer encampment called The Fallows. Most of the cabins and the main lodge had rotted away fifty years ago.

But some remained, in varying states of decay—Angus and I first had sex together in one of these, in 1973—and two or three had even been renovated as second homes. Zoning covenants designed to protect the wetland had kept the McMansions away, and some of the same old hippies who had taken over the cottages in the 1960s and '70s still lived there, or were rumored to—I hadn't been out to the lake in at least a dozen years.

"You know, this is going to totally fuck up my alignment." Angus swore as the car scraped across the rutted track. To the right, you could glimpse Lake Muscanth in flashes of silvery-blue through dense stands of evergreen, like fish darting through murky water. "Damn it! Tom, I'm sorry, but if we don't find this place soon I'm—"

"Turn there." Tommy pointed to where the road divided a few yards ahead of us. "It should be just past where it curves."

Angus peered through the windshield. "I dunno, man. Those branches, they look like they're going to come down right on top of us."

"That's where the place is, dude," said Tommy, as I stuck my head between the two of them to get a better view.

Angus was right. The narrow road, barely more than a path here, was flanked by thick stands of tamarack and cedar. They were so overgrown that in spots above the road their branches met and became tangled in a dense, low overhanging mat of black and green. Angus tossed his cigarette out the window and veered cautiously to the right.

The effect wasn't of diving through a tunnel; more like being under the canopy of a bazaar or souk. Branches scraped the car in place of importuning shopkeepers grabbing at us.

Angus swore as tiny pinecones hailed down onto the roof. "I'm going back."

Tommy looked stricken. "Hey, we're almost there."

"It's a company car, Tommy!"

"I'll pay to have it painted, okay? Look, see? There it is, that house there—"

Angus glanced to the side then nodded. "Yeah, well, okay."

There was no driveway, just a flattish bit of ground where broken glass and scrap metal glinted through patchy moss and teaberry. Angus pulled onto this and turned the ignition off.

"So did this guy give you a phone number or something?" Angus asked after a moment. "Are we expected?"

Tommy sat with his fingers on the door handle and stared outside. The place was small, not a house at all but a cabin made of split logs painted brown. It wasn't much bigger than a motel cottage, with pine-green shutters and trim, a battered screen door that looked as though it had been flung open by someone who'd left in a big hurry and a bad mood. A sagging screened-in porch overlooked the lake. Stones had come loose from the fieldstone chimney and were scattered forlornly beneath the pine trees, like misshapen soccer balls. A rusted holding tank bulged beneath a broken window that had been repaired with a square of cardboard.

"Nice," said Angus.

No one got out of the car. Angus shot Tommy a bitter look, then took a roach from his pocket, lit it and smoked in silence. When he held it out to me and Tommy, we demurred. I'd become adept at fine-tuning the cocktail of drugs I needed to filter out the world, and Tommy's school job mandated random drug testing.

"So Tom." Angus replaced the roach. The hand he'd kept on the steering wheel relaxed somewhat. "Where's your man?"

Tommy stared at the cabin. His face had that expression I loved, unabashed wonder struggling with suspicion and a long-entrenched fear of ridicule. It was a slightly crazed look, and I knew from long experience what could follow. Weird accusations, smashed guitars, broken fingers. But the alcohol and Xanax had done their job.

"I don't even care if he's here or not," said Tommy lightly, and stepped outside. "Remember when we used to come out to the lake all the time?"

"I do."

I hopped out and stood beside him. A warm wind blew off the water, bringing the smells of mud and cedar bark. A red-winged blackbird sang, and a lone peeper near the water's edge. Tommy put his arm across my shoulder, the Folding Man's map still in his hand. A moment later I felt Angus on my other side. His fingers touched mine and his mouth tightened as he gazed at the cabin, but after a moment he sighed.

"Yeah, this was a good idea." He looked at me and smiled, then knocked Tommy's arm from my shoulder. "No hogging the girl, dude. Let's check this place out."

Tommy headed towards the front door. Angus walked to the side to check out the broken window.

"Hey." He grabbed the cardboard by one corner and tried to wrest it from the window frame.

I came up alongside him. "What is it?"

"It's an album. Well, an album cover. Watch it—"

The cardboard buckled then abruptly popped out from the window. Angus examined it cursorily, slid his hand inside the sleeve and shook his head—no vinyl—then held it up for me to see: a black square with an inset color photo of two guys in full hippie regalia and psychedelic wording beneath.

TYRANNOSAURUS REX
PROPHETS SEERS AND SAGES
THE ANGELS OF THE AGES

"Is that T. Rex?"

He grinned. "I always, *always* wanted this album. I could never find it."

"You could probably find it now on eBay."

"I never wanted it that much." He laughed. "Actually, I totally forgot I wanted it, till now."

I took the cardboard sleeve. It was damp and smelled of mildew; black mold covered Marc Bolan's face and cape. When I tried to look inside, the soft cardboard tore.

I handed it back to Angus. "Is it worth anything?"

"Not anymore." He glanced at it then shrugged. "Nah, it's toast. It doesn't even have the record inside."

"I bet it's been rereleased. You should get it, it might give you and Tommy some ideas for Estelle."

Angus grimaced. "Trust me, Tommy doesn't need any more ideas about goddamn Estelle."

The song cycle had been my idea. "You're like a troubadour, Tommy," I had told him back when his obsession with the broker had spun completely out of control. "Their whole thing revolved around idealized unrequited love. You would have fit right in."

"Did their whole thing revolve around stalking women at Best Buy?" I remember Angus asked.

"That was an accident," said Tommy. "A total coincidence, she even admitted it."

"Did the troubadors ever get laid?" said Angus. "Because that would clinch the deal for me."

"I think you should channel all this into something constructive," I suggested. "Music, you guys haven't written anything together for a while."

The first songs Tommy wrote all used the woman's real name.

"I don't think that's a good idea, Tommy," I'd said when he played me the CD he'd burned from his computer. "Considering the restraining order and all."

"But I love her name." He had appeared genuinely distressed. "It's part of her, it's an extension of her, of everything she is—"

"You don't have a clue as to who she fucking is!" Angus grabbed the CD. "You went out with her once before she dumped you. It was like you dated a blow-up doll."

"She didn't dump me!"

"You're right—you were never involved enough to *be* dumped. You were downsized, Tommy. Admit it and get over it. Lot of fish in the sea, Tom."

Tommy got over it, sort of. In the song, he changed the woman's name to Estelle, at any rate.

It remained a sore point with Angus. He turned and skimmed the album cover towards the lake. I walked to join Tommy on the cabin's front steps.

I asked, "What're you doing?

"Mail tampering."

A stoved-in mailbox dangled beside the door. I watched as Tommy prised it open, fished around inside and withdrew a wad of moldering letters, junk mail, mostly. He peeled oversized envelopes away from sales flyers, releasing a fetid smell, finally held up an envelope with the familiar ConEd logo.

"It's a cut-off notice," he said in triumph. Angus had wandered back and looked at him dubiously. "It's got his name on it. Orson Shemeltoss."

"Orson Shemeltoss? What the hell kind of name is that?"

Tommy ignored him. The wind sent the screen door swinging; he pushed it away, then knocked loudly on the front door. "Mr. Shemeltoss? Hello? Mr. Shemeltoss?"

Silence. Angus looked at me. We both started to laugh.

"Hey, shut up," said Tommy.

Angus pushed him aside, cracked the door open and yelled.

"Yo, Orson! Tommy's here."

Tommy swore, but Angus had already stepped inside.

"It's okay." I patted Tommy's shoulder. "You're sure this is his place, right? So he's expecting you."

"I guess," said Tommy.

He pushed the door open and went after Angus. I followed, almost immediately drew up short. "Holy shit."

The room—and what was it, anyway? Living room? hallway? foyer?—I couldn't tell, but it was so crammed with junk that walking was nearly impossible. It was like wading across a sandbar at high tide, through stacks of newspaper and magazines and books that once had towered above my head but had now collapsed to form a waist-high reef of paper. Things shifted underfoot as I moved, and when I tried to clamber on top of a stack it wobbled then flew apart in a storm of white and gray.

"Vivian, over here!"

I pushed myself up, coughing as I breathed in paper dust and mold. A dog barked, close enough that I looked around anxiously.

But I saw no sign of a dog, or Tommy; only Angus standing a few feet away, surrounded by overflowing bookshelves.

"It's better over here." He reached across a mound of magazines to grab my hand, and pulled me towards him. "C'mon, thatta girl—"

"It's like the print shop exploded," I said, still coughing. The smell of mold was so strong it burned my nostrils.

"It's a lot worse than that." Angus stared in disbelief. "This guy has some issues about letting go."

Everywhere around us was—stuff. Junk mail and books and magazines, mostly, also a lot of photos—snapshots, old Polaroids—but other things, too. Board games, Bratz dolls, stuffed animals; oddments of clothing, stiletto heels and lingerie and studded collars; eight-track tapes and a battered saxophone, all protruding from the morass of paper like the detritus left by a receding flood. Vinyl record albums filled a wall of buckled metal shelving. Here and there I could discern bits of furniture—the uppermost rungs of a ladderback chair, a headboard.

And, scattered everywhere, the eerie paper figures that were the Folding Man's handiwork. I dropped Angus's hand and picked up one of them, a horned creature made of aluminum foil. Inexplicably, and despite the pervasive smell of mildew, my mouth began to water. It was only after I unfolded the little form that I saw the Arby's logo printed on it.

"Where's Tommy?" I asked.

"I dunno."

Angus turned and began to push his way to the far side of the room. I tossed the bit of foil and grabbed another figure—there were hundreds of them, thousands maybe, so many it was impossible not to think of them as somehow alive, burrowing up through those countless layers of junk.

I wondered if it was like an archeological dig, or geological strata: was there a Golden Age buried under there, before *People* magazine ruled the earth? If I reached the very bottom, would I find Little Nemo and the Katzenjammer Kids?

I doubted it. I could see nothing but junk. All the magazines seemed to be well-worn, and many were torn or missing their covers. The other stuff seemed to be ruined as well, toys cracked or broken or missing parts, clothes soiled or unraveling. The photos were ripped or water damaged, and a lot appeared to be charred or otherwise damaged by smoke or fire.

It was like the town dump, only worse—you could scavenge things from the dump. But it was difficult to imagine there was anything here worth saving, except for the thousands of origami-like figures. I picked one up. It was larger than most, big enough to cover my palm, plain white paper. It resembled a bird of some sort, a heron maybe, with tiny six-fingered hands instead of wings and a broad flattened bill like a shovel. Its eyes were wide and staring: an owl's eyes, not a heron's. I unfolded it and smoothed it out atop a heap of *National*

Geographics. A missing flyer, the kind you see in post offices or police stations, with a black-and-white image of a teenage girl's face photocopied from a high school portrait. Dark curly hair, freckles, dark eyes. Last seen May 14, 1982, Osceola, Wisconsin.

"Oh," said Angus in a low voice.

I glanced at him, but he wasn't looking at me. He was leaning against a small bare patch of wall, turning the pages of a small red-bound book.

I picked my way carefully to his side. "What is it?"

"I used to read this to Corey when he was little." He didn't look up, just continued to turn the pages, stopping to pull them gently apart where they were stuck together. "Every night, it was the only thing he ever wanted to hear. He knew it by heart. I never knew what happened to it."

I stood beside him and stared at a picture of a rabbit in a rocking chair, cats playing on a rug, a wall of bookshelves.

"It's even missing the same page," Angus said softly. His face twisted. He turned from me, reaching for his pocket. Tommy's alarmed voice came from somwhere across the room.

"I wouldn't light up in here!"

Angus frowned, then reluctantly nodded. "Yeah, right. Bad idea."

I said nothing, and after a moment began to make my way unsteadily towards where Tommy's voice had come from. A few times I almost fell, and tried to catch myself by instinctively grabbing at whatever was closest to me—handfuls of newspapers, an oversized Sears family photo in a shattered frame, the tip of an artificial Christmas tree.

But this only made it more difficult to move, as the stacks invariably tottered and fell, so that I found myself half-buried in the Folding Man's junk. I thought of the advice given to hikers trapped in an avalanche—to surf through the snow or, if buried, to swim upwards, to the surface—and pushed back an unpleasant image of what else might be under these layers of mildewed paper and chewed-up toys.

The dog barked again, closer this time.

"Tommy? You see a dog somewhere?" I yelled, but got no reply.

I straightened and looked back. Angus had slumped to sit precariously on a sagging mound of papers, head bowed as he turned the pages of the little book back and forth, back and forth. I shut my eyes and ran my hand across piles of paper till I felt a paper figure, picked it up and opened my eyes. The squarish head of an animal, catlike, with a small snout and large eyes that, as I unfolded it and flattened it, faded into a ripped piece of paper with dark washes of green and brown and blue and red words beneath.

GOOD NIGHT BEARS
GOOD NIGHT CHAIRS

I dropped it and took a few painstaking steps in the direction of a door. I could hear faint scrabbling, and then Tommy exclaiming softly. I wondered if he'd found the dog. I stopped, listening.

I heard nothing. I glanced down and saw a white cylinder poking up between a copy of *Oui* magazine and what looked like the keyboard from an old typewriter. I pushed aside the typewriter, grabbed the cylinder and pulled it free: not a folded figure but a small poster rolled into a tube.

The edges were stuck together, and tore as I unrolled it. The once-glossy paper had been nibbled at by insects or mice, and was dusted with dull green spores that powdered the air when I held it up.

But towards the center the image was still clearly visible, vibrant even; and as recognizable to me as my own face.

It was a print of Uccello's "The Hunt in the Forest." The original hung in the Ashmolean Museum at Oxford. I had never seen it, but when I was nine I'd come across the picture in a children's book about King Arthur and the Middle Ages. The painting actually dated to the Renaissance—the late 1460s—and it had nothing to do with Arthur, or England.

But for me it was inextricably tied up with everything I had ever dreamed or imagined about that world. A sense of immanence and urgency, of simple things—horses, dogs, people, grass—charged with an expectant, slightly sinister meaning I couldn't grasp but still felt, even as a kid. The hunters in their crimson tunics astride their mounts and the horses rearing from turf whorled with white flowers, pale arabesques in a green carpet; the greyhounds springing joyously, heads thrown back and paws upraised as though partaking in some wild dance; the beaters—boys in tunics colored like Easter eggs, creamy yellow and pink and periwinkle blue—chased after the dogs. To the left of the painting, a single black-clad man—knight? lord? cleric?— rode a horse richly caparisoned as the rest. Dogs and horses and men and boys all ran in the same direction, towards the center of the painting where a half-dozen stags leapt, poised and improbable as the flattened targets in a shooting range.

And above everything, mysterious, columnar trees that opened into leafy parasols, like the carven pillars in a vast and endless cathedral, trees and hunters and animals finally receding into darkness as black and undifferentiated as the inside of a lacquered box.

I had not seen the image, or thought of it, in years. But it all came back to me now in a confused, almost fretful rush, like the memory of the sort of dream you have when sick.

"Vivian." I started at the sound of Tommy's voice, calling from inside the next room. "Viv—"

I dropped the poster and pushed my way to the open door. A narrow path led into the room, wide enough that I could pass without knocking anything over.

"Tommy?" I strained to see him over a mound of old clothes. "You okay?"

It must have been a bedroom once, though I saw no furniture, nothing but old clothes and shoes, wads of rolled-up belts like nested snakes.

But I could see the wall, close enough that I could almost touch it, with a closet door that hung loosely where one of its hinges had twisted from the sheetrock. Tommy was crouched beside the door. One hand was extended towards something on the floor inside the closet; the other was pressed against his cheek as he shook his head and murmured wordlessly.

I thought it was the dog. I swore under my breath and felt sick, looked over my shoulder as I called for Angus. I stumbled the last few steps through tangled clothing until I reached Tommy's side, and knelt beside him.

It wasn't a dog. It was a woman, nineteen or twenty, lying on one side with her knees drawn up and her clenched fists against her chin. I gasped and grabbed at the wall to steady myself.

"Shh," whispered Tommy. He reached to touch her forehead, then drew his hand gently down her face, tracing freckled cheekbones, her chapped lower lip. "She's sleeping."

Angus staggered into the room behind me. "Holy shit. Is she dead? What are—"

"*Shh.*" Tommy turned to look at us. His eyes were wide, not with amazement but something more like barely suppressed rage, or terror, or even pain.

Then he blinked, and for the first time seemed to notice me. "Hey, Vivian. Angus. Look. Look—"

I turned to stare at Angus, too stunned even to be afraid. He stared back, speechless. We both looked at Tommy again.

His hand cradled the girl's cheek as he crooned to her beneath his breath. Without warning, her eyelids fluttered. I jumped. Angus gasped then grabbed my arm.

"Fucking hell," he whispered. "Fucking hell, fucking—"

"Shut *up.*" Tommy's face was fierce; but then the girl stirred, moaning. He turned from us and set his hands lightly on her shoulders.

"It's okay," he said. "You're okay, I'm here, someone's here…"

She tried to sit up, then gave a small cry. Her head drooped; she retched and Tommy held her as she spat up a trickle of liquid.

"That's a girl," he murmured. "That's my girl…"

I could see her clearly now, her hair dark and matted, thick, a few curls springing loose to frame her pale face. She wore a man's white button-down shirt, seamed with dirt and rust stains, blue jeans, white tennis socks with filthy pom-poms at the ankles.

"Is she okay?" said Angus.

"Sure she's okay," said Tommy in that same low, reassuring voice. "Sure she's okay, she's going to be just fine…"

I stumbled forward to help him carry her. Angus tried to clear a way for us, kicking at old clothes and magazines as we lurched from room to room, staggering between the piles of trash, until finally we all stood by the front door. The girl's head lolled against Tommy's shoulder. Angus looked at her in concern, but I also saw how his gaze flickered to her soiled shirt with its missing buttons, the frayed cloth gaping open so you could see her breasts, the spray of freckles across her clavicle and throat.

"What's your name?" he asked.

She looked up. Not at us: at Tommy, who stared down at her with lips compressed, smiling slightly.

"Stella." Her voice rose tremulously on the second syllable, as though it were a question. "Stella."

The dog barked again, not inside the house this time but somewhere nearby, just out of sight among the evergreens. Angus ran to the car as Tommy and I helped the girl across the mossy ground.

"There's so much crap in there, I don't even know if there's room." Angus clambered into the backseat and started shoving stuff onto the floor. "Shit!"

"It's okay," said Tommy. He'd removed his jacket and was helping the girl pull her arms through its sleeves. "We'll make room."

"Yeah, but what about this!" Angus shook his guitar case. "What about her? We need to call the police, or—"

"Just get in," said Tommy. He eased the girl into the backseat. Angus hurried to the trunk and shoved in the guitar case. "We'll make it fit, we'll figure it out."

I leaned inside and pulled the seat belt across the girl's chest. "Thank you," she whispered. Her eyes were almost black, with irises so dark they seemed to have no pupil. Her breath smelled of leaf mould and cloves.

My heart thumped so hard it hurt. I smiled, then backed away so that Tommy could slide in beside her.

"Let's go," he said.

I got into the front with Angus. "Now what?"

He shrugged and tossed something into my lap: the ruined picture book he'd read inside. "I have no fucking clue," he said, and started the engine. "But I guess we'll figure out something."

I rolled my window down and leaned out. A flurry of wings, a keening cry as a pair of wood ducks rose from the lake and flew agitatedly towards the trees. The wind had shifted; it carried now the smell of rain, of lilacs. I glanced into the backseat and saw the girl sitting with her face upturned to Tommy's. His hand was on her knee, his own face stared straight ahead, to where the road stretched before us, darker now, the dirt and gravel rain-spattered and the ferns at road's-edge unfurling, pale green and misty white. I heard another bark, and then a second, echoing yelp; the distant sound of voices, laughter. As the car rounded a curve I looked back and saw several small lean forms, white and gray, too blurred for me to discern clearly, racing through the underbrush before they broke free momentarily into a bright clearing, muzzles gleaming in a sudden shaft of sun before they disappeared once more into the trees.

Acknowledgments

My thanks to all of my editors for their guidance and support in bringing these stories to light: Jack Dann, Gardner Dozois, Neil Gaiman, Steve Jones, John Klima, Eric Marin, George R. R. Martin, Al Sarrantonio, and Gordon Van Gelder.

Most of all, my gratitude to Bradford Morrow, editor of *Conjunctions,* who over the years has provided a home for my own work and that of so many other writers, and whose encouragement and vision are a continuing inspiration for me.

Publication History

About the Author

Elizabeth Hand, a *New York Times* and *Washington Post* notable author, has written eleven novels, including *Mortal Love*, and four collections of short fiction. Her most recent novels are *Radiant Days* and *Available Dark*. Her thriller *Generation Loss* received the inaugural Shirley Jackson Award. She has also received the James Tiptree Award, the Nebula Award (twice), the World Fantasy Award (four times), and many others. Her novella, "The Maiden Flight of McCauley's *Bellerophon*" was a Hugo finalist. Hand is a longtime contributor to numerous publications, including the *Washington Post, Salon, L.A. Times, Fantasy & Science Fiction,* and *DownEast Magazine.* She divides her time between the coast of Maine and North London, where she is working on the third Cass Neary thriller, *Flash Burn,* and a neo-gothic YA novel, *Wylding Hall.*

Shirley Jackson Award winner · *Publishers Weekly* Top 10 Best Books of the Year · io9 Best SF&F Books of the Year · Story Prize Notable Book · Tiptree Award Honor List · Philip K. Dick Award finalist

"Each tale is a beautifully written character study. . . . McHugh's great talent is in reminding us that the future could never be weirder — or sadder — than what lurks in the human psyche. This is definitely one of the best works of science fiction you'll read this year, or any thereafter."—Annalee Newitz, NPR

paper · $16 · 9781931520294 | ebook · $9.95 · 9781931520355

"I can't think of any other writer whose stories terrify me the way Johnson's do."—Lev Grossman

AT THE MOUTH OF THE RIVER OF BEES

~ stories ~

Kij Johnson

★ "Strange, beautiful, and occasionally disturbing territory without ever missing a beat. . . . Johnson's language is beautiful, her descriptions of setting visceral, and her characters compellingly drawn. . . . [S]ometimes off-putting, sometimes funny, and always thought provoking."—*Publishers Weekly* (starred review)

Includes the Hugo and Nebula Award winner "The Man Who Bridged the Mist."

paper · $16 · 9781931520805 | ebook · $9.95 · 9781931520812

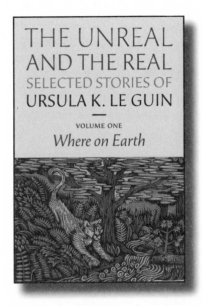

Ursula K. Le Guin's stories have shaped the way many readers see the world. By giving voice to the voiceless, hope to the outsider, and speaking truth to power—all the time maintaining her independence and sense of humor—she has proven herself a truly great writer.

This two-volume selection—as selected and organized by the author—contains almost forty stories and both volumes include new introductions by Le Guin.

"She is the reigning queen of . . . but immediately we come to a difficulty, for what is the fitting name of her kingdom? Or, in view of her abiding concern with the ambiguities of gender, her queendom, or perhaps—considering how she likes to mix and match—her quinkdom? Or may she more properly be said to have not one such realm, but two?"—Margaret Atwood, *New York Review of Books*

The Unreal and the Real: Selected Stories Volume One: Where on Earth
cloth · $24 · 9781618730343 | ebook · $14.95 · 9781618730367

The Unreal and the Real: Selected Stories Volume Two: Outer Space, Inner Lands
cloth · $24 · 9781618730350 | ebook · $14.95 · 9781618730374